More than CONQUERORS

MORE THAN CONQUERORS

A PLANTING FAITH NOVEL

CAROLE TOWRISS

To those facing life's trials:
Know that we are never alone.
The Lord will fight for us;
we have only to be still.

When Paul and his companions had passed through Amphipolis and Apollonia, they came to Thessalonica, where there was a Jewish synagogue. As was his custom, Paul went into the synagogue, and on three Sabbath days he reasoned with them from the Scriptures, explaining and proving that the Messiah had to suffer and rise from the dead. "This Jesus I am proclaiming to you is the Messiah," he said. Some of the Jews were persuaded and joined Paul and Silas, as did a large number of God-fearing Greeks and quite a few prominent women. But other Jews were jealous; so they rounded up some bad characters from the marketplace, formed a mob and started a riot in the city. They rushed to Jason's house in search of Paul and Silas in order to bring them out to the crowd. But when they did not find them, they dragged Jason and some other believers before the city officials, shouting: "These men who have caused trouble all over the world have now come here, and Jason has welcomed them into his house. They are all defying Caesar's decrees, saying that there is another king, one called Jesus." When they heard this, the crowd and the city officials were thrown into turmoil. Then they made Jason and the others post bond and let them go. As soon as it was night, the believers sent Paul and Silas away to Berea. On arriving there, they went to the Jewish synagogue.

Acts 17.1-10

CHARACTERS

BIBLICAL/HISTORICAL

Paulos • apostle of Yeshua
Silas • Jewish companion of Paulos
Timotheos / Timos • the youngest of Paulos's companions
Jason • Jewish man in Thessalonike, glassblower
Gamaliel • a leading Pharisee and respected teacher in Jerusalem
Aristarchos / Ari • a young Greek man, Jason's closet friend
Gaius / Gai • a boy of Thessalonike
Secundus • the chief ruler of Thessalonike
Claudius (Tiberius Claudius Caesar Augustus Germanicus) • a Roman emperor of the Julio-Claudian dynasty, ruling from AD 41 to 54

FICTIONAL

<u>Kassi's family</u>
Kassandra / Kassi • daughter of Secundus
Kadmos, Eirene, Penelope • brother, sister-in-law, niece
Abydos, Larissa, Helene, Sophia • brother, sister-in-law, nieces
Lida • slave
Mannus • slave

<u>Jason's family</u>
Yoel • Jason's uncle, leader of the synagogue
Leah • Jason's aunt, Yoel's wife

<u>In the bakery</u>
Isadora / Isa • former slave of Kassi's father
Thalia • widow, Isa's niece
Gaius, Melas, Pheres • Thalia's sons
Asteria • young girl, divorced, Publius's niece
Maera • Publius's niece, divorced
Phaedra • a woman of Thessalonike
Hector, Orion • Phaedra's sons

In Thessalonike

Damianos • son of the governor's aide
Julia • Ari's mother
Zelia • Kassi's friend
Belos • potter in the village
Glaukos • son of Belos
Publius • sells prepared food in the agora
Hesiod • forum advocate
Solon • unofficial advocate, agoraios

GLOSSARY

Ancient Greek
agora • an outdoor market
agoraios (pl. agoraioi) • a lawyer who frequents the agora to find clients
agoranomos • ah-gor-AH-no-mos • the market overseer responsible for ensuring
    fair trade
archisynagogos • synagogue leader
amphora (pl. amphorae) • a tall pottery jar with two handles and a narrow neck
andron • room specifically for men in a Greek house
chairé • KAI-ray • greeting (literally: Be glad! Or Rejoice!)
chiton • a tunic for men or women, that fastens at the shoulders
ekklesia • eh-clay-SEE-uh • a gathering of citizens, *later* a church
eucharisto • thank you
kyria • mistress
kyrie • KEER-ee-ay • master, lord (when addressing the man)
mamma • mom
meli • honey, a term of endearment
meter • mother
nai • yes
obeliskos • skewered meat, grilled over a fire
pappa • dad, daddy
pappos • grandfather
pastelli • a bar made of honey and sesame seeds
pater • father
politarch • POL-ee-tark • member of the ruling council in a Greek city
popina • a cook-shop selling hot foods, mainly used by the less wealthy
s'agapo • I love you
theia • aunt

Latin
atrium • an open-air space in the front of a house designed to greet visitors
cardo • the principal north-south street in Roman cities
christos • lit: the anointed one, messiah
codex (pl. codices) • sheets of vellum, papyrus, or parchment bound on one side and
    given a protective cover
culina • kitchen
domus • a family residence occupied by the upper classes

forum • an open area mainly used for political or religious purposes

insula (pl. insulae) • a high-rise apartment block, typically poorly built

modius • Roman unit for dry measures roughly equivalent to two gallons

pater • father

peristyle • an open-air space in a house surrounded a columned, roofed walkway

pistrinum • bakery

stoa • a covered walkway surrounding a forum or agora

tablinum • home office in a Greek or Roman house

triclinium • a formal dining room containing a low table with couches on three sides

via • road, street

vivat imperator • long live the emperor!

<u>Ancient Hebrew</u>

abba • father

ahuva/ahuvati • beloved (to a male/female)

Adonai • lit: my Lord

imma • mother

mashiach • lit: the anointed one, christos

mikveh • a bath used for of ritual immersion

Shabbat • Sabbath

shalom • lit: peace. A common greeting among Jews

Shema • a declaration of faith in one God; the first line of Deuteronomy 6.4

dodh • uncle

dodah • aunt

todah (rabah) • thank you (very much)

<u>Money</u>

denarius (pl. denarii) • silver Roman coin worth approximately a day's pay and approximately equal to a drachma

drachma (pl. drachmae) • silver Greek coins worth approximately a day's pay

sestertius • brass Roman coin worth one-fourth of a denarius

<u>Time</u>

Both the Roman day and the night were divided into twelve equal hours, divided by sunrise and sunset. The length of the hours changed with the seasons. The sixth hour would be noon or midnight.

INTRODUCTION

After spending a few months in Philippi and establishing a church there, in approximately 50 AD the apostle Paul journeyed southwest to the city of Thessalonike, accompanied by Silas and Timothy.

Thessalonike was, in many important ways, quite different from Philippi. While Philippi was a Roman colony, Thessalonike was declared a free city by Augustus and Mark Antony. This was a supreme and rare honor, and offered freedom from taxation, unhindered self-governance, freedom to hold public assemblies, the right to mint money, and the privilege of having no Roman troops based within the city.

With a population of 200,000, Thessalonike was one of the biggest cities in the empire. It was the chief seaport of Makedonia and the seat of administration of the province. By the time of Paul, it was a thriving walled city, with the Egnatian Way running through it from southeast to northwest. Near the middle of the city was the agora, or forum.

Thessalonike was large enough to host a vibrant Jewish community and a synagogue. The Jewish leaders guarded their faith zealously and fought against anyone or anything that threatened it.

When Paul appeared and preached Christ crucified, the leaders geared up for a battle.

The church in Thessalonike began—and thrived—in the throes of persecution, where men and women learned well the message of the prophet Isaiah:

> *When you pass through the waters, I will be with you;*
> *and when you pass through the rivers,*
> *they will not sweep over you.*
> *When you walk through the fire,*
> *you will not be burned;*
> *the flames will not set you ablaze.*
> *You are Mine.*

1

"For I know the plans I have for you," declares the Lord, "plans to prosper you and not to harm you, plans to give you hope and a future."

— JEREMIAH 29.11

THESSALONIKE, LATE FALL, 50 A.D.

THE TRANQUILITY OF KASSANDRA'S EARLY MORNING WALK TO THE SEA was shattered when a pottery jar slammed into her shoulder. She stumbled sideways, losing her footing, but was caught by Mannus, one of Pappa's slaves.

Older than Pappa but still powerfully built, Mannus set her on her feet and marched to the edge of the *cardo*, the city's primary road, seeking the source of the projectile.

Rubbing her shoulder, Kassi followed him. At the edge, she peered around his broad shoulders. On a narrow, roughly paved street, an old woman knelt, hands clasped at her chest. A brute of a man glared down at her from the rickety steps of the corner *insula*, one of the hundreds of dilapidated apartment buildings in that area.

"Please," she begged. "I won't be long. I need my things."

"It's too late. Now go away!" The man turned his back on her and disappeared inside, slamming the door behind him.

The woman fell forward, forearms hitting the ground. Her head drooped, nearly touching the rough stones. Long, gray hair fell around her face like a curtain.

Anger and indignation crawled up Kassi's throat, leaving a sour taste. "Poor woman." She started to move toward her, but Mannus held out a well-muscled arm to block her path. "We should go, *kyria.*"

Kassi cringed. Although the slaves had called her *mistress* since she could walk, she'd never become used to it. She looked from the woman to Mannus, and back again. "She needs our help."

"I beg you not to get involved. These people ... They are not your problem." His fierce gray eyes and the jagged scar on his left cheek made him appear angry even when he wasn't.

Kassi bristled. "How can you say that?"

"It is my job to say it, kyria."

She watched the frail figure on her knees a moment longer. Stains covered her clothing. Even her body was soiled. The soles of her sandals were worn through. The sleeves of her tattered *chiton* revealed arms as thin as sticks.

Kassi studied the woman. Beneath the dirt, a pair of parallel lines had been etched into her skin from shoulder to elbow. Between them lay a wavy line, punctuated with small dots.

She stepped off the walkway, holding the hem of her chiton above her ankles, and hurried toward the sobbing woman. Tucking her tunic between her thighs and calves, she knelt beside her. "Is there anything I can do? Can I help you get home?"

The old woman raised her head but still faced the building. "I have no home.

"But where do you live?"

"I have no place to live!" She flung a gnarled hand at the closed door. "The owner made all of us leave. He wants to build a new insula, adding more floors with smaller rooms so he can charge his exorbitant rents to more people." She spit on the ground.

Kassi grimaced. "And your belongings?"

Her chin sank to her chest. "He won't let me get them. Not that there's much. A spare chiton, my cooking pots…"

How could she live with so little? Kassi owned more chitons than she could wear. Their *culina* was filled with pots and jars and food. She slept on a wool-stuffed mattress.

Finally, the woman lifted her head to face Kassi. Soft brown eyes filled with tears. A tiny scar above her left eye seemed somehow familiar.

Kassi helped her to her feet, and Mannus moved to stand behind her, his eyes never leaving Kassi.

"What's your name?" asked Kassi.

"I am called Isa, kyria."

"Why don't we help you collect your things?" She turned to Mannus, his disapproving stare covering his face. "Will you go with her? He won't argue with you."

More than once, Mannus had been mistaken for a rich man instead of a slave. Pappa dressed his slaves well, and Mannus had a naturally regal bearing. It was rare that anyone questioned him.

A frown flitted across his face, but he dipped his head. He turned to the woman and extended a hand toward the narrow stairway, inviting her to precede him.

Kassi touched Isa's arm. "It's all right. Show him to your belongings."

Isa furrowed her thinning brows. "That man will never let me in, no matter who I'm with."

Kassi brought her mouth to the woman's ear. "As a young man, Mannus was a soldier in Germania," she whispered. "Trust me, even if the owner tries to stop him, he will not succeed."

Mannus followed the old woman as she clambered up the wobbly steps.

Kassi held her breath as he took the first step but released it when it withstood the big man's weight. They soon returned safely, a ragged cloth bag dangling from his hand.

Did that bag hold all her belongings? "Any trouble?"

"He wasn't happy." Mannus allowed a fleeting grin.

"Are you hungry?"

The woman didn't answer, but she had to be starving. She couldn't weigh more than a bag of grain. Her collarbones poked against her tunic, her elbows were bony, and skin seemed to drip from her cheekbones.

"Let's go to the *agora* to get you something to eat." Kassi wrapped an arm around the woman's tiny waist and led her a few streets down to the market, then steered her to a *popina* on the nearest corner. Hot shops abounded in the city, but this one offered the best prices as well as the tastiest food. The shop faced the street and the market, a counter on each side topped with marble, allowing twice as much room to serve hungry shoppers. Tables and stools occupied the area in front, while an enormous, dyed linen sail offered shade not only to the owner but to those who lingered to eat and drink.

"This is my friend. Come." She beckoned, grabbing Isa by the hand. "*Chairé*, Publius!"

"Hello to you!" The vendor's round face boasted bright eyes and a brighter smile.

"May I have two, no three?"—She glanced at Mannus, who frowned and shook his head—"two servings of your delicious *obeliskos*?"

"For you, anything." The vendor let out a hearty laugh as he reached for one of ten or more long skewers which rested between two small ceramic stands. Each was lined with tiny indentations to keep the wooden pieces in place as they straddled one of the small fire pits built into the counter. Publius selected a stick full of cubes of sizzling meat and grilled onions, then lay it across a round of flat bread. He pulled out the skewer, added soft goat cheese, and handed it to Kassi before making another.

Kassi offered it to Isa. A moment later she accepted one for herself. "*Eucharisto*, Publius."

"You're quite welcome. Come again." His smile lightened the otherwise dark mood.

"You know we will." Kassi bit into a juicy slice of cooked goat, a finger wiping away the liquid running down her chin, then moved back as Mannus stepped forward, reaching into a cloth pouch full of coins. She turned to see Isa gobble half the stuffed bread. When had she last eaten?

Isa's cheeks pinked. She drew the back of her hand across her mouth.

"What will you do now? Where will you stay?"

"Even if I had a place, I have nothing to pay for it with."

Kassi stopped mid-bite. "Then where will you go tonight?"

The woman cleared her throat, jutting out her chin. "I have friends."

"And they'll let you stay with them? Feed you?"

Isa refused to meet Kassi's eyes.

"You're sure you'll be all right?"

Isa's face was set as stone. "Don't worry about me, kyria. I'll be fine."

Kassi studied her face. Was she telling the truth? It was hard to tell. "I'll have Publius make another for you, yes?"

Isa shrugged.

"May we please go now, kyria?" Mannus gave another coin to the vendor.

Kassi nodded and dutifully followed him to the other end of the market. Several steps away, she looked back over her shoulder.

The woman was gone.

But who was she? And did it matter? There wasn't much more Kassi could do to help her.

Or was there?

ALONE IN THE family's glass shop, Jason blew steadily into a thin iron tube, turning a blob of translucent melted glass into a bubble. As it grew, bands of transparent glass distorted among the green, forming a vaguely striped but delightful pattern.

Sucking in air, he gripped the middle of the pipe and turned it to inspect his work.

Perfect. It would make a beautiful vase.

He cherished these rare, quiet days when he could experiment with glass. Their business was built on selling everyday glassware—cups, bowls, platters. Most were simple enough that even the poor could afford them, buying ten or fifteen cups for a day's wage or half that many plates.

But unlike *Abba*, Jason loved creating the intricate vessels that required time, thought, patience, and imagination.

"Jason!" A booming voice interrupted his thoughts. A young man about his age leaned against the open door of the shop, grinning, one ankle crossed over the other.

Jason chuckled. With his short, blond hair and muscular frame, Ari resembled one of the countless statues of Greek gods brought to life.

Ari had never lifted anything weighing more than a plate of food, but his parents had managed to keep him from developing the odious personality of most of the city's wealthy elite, who considered themselves better than all others. He was kind, compassionate, and brutally honest, and they'd been best friends for as long as Jason could remember.

"Give me a moment." Jason attached a shorter rod to the bottom of the vase with a dab of molten glass, then rapped on the larger rod to dislodge it from the vase. He placed the vessel into an opening in the front of a large, hive-shaped brick furnace to reheat for a moment to become malleable again. After withdrawing it, he let the

"What are you doing here? Shouldn't you be at the agora, making new friends who will vote for you?"

Ari laughed. "Thought I'd bring you along. Ease my worry a bit."

Jason withdrew the vase and sat on a stool before inserting a pair of narrow metal tongs into the neck. He rolled the rod back and forth on his knees to shape it. "I'm sure you'll be elected this time. Laertes has retired, has he not?"

"He has, but that doesn't mean much. Secundus has been promoting Kosmos quite heavily."

Jason dislodged the short rod and rubbed the bottom of the vase with a smooth brick to flatten it.

"I love watching you do that," Ari said.

Jason laughed. "Thanks. Let me get someone to watch the furnace." He gently set the glass on the shelf of a smaller furnace, then stepped next door to the potter's shop. "Belos, can Glaukos keep an eye on my fire while I go to the agora?"

The wiry, older man looked up from his wheel. "Of course. He should be back in a moment. Going to vote?"

Jason nodded. "I won't be long."

The autumn air cooled Jason's skin. They strolled along a crude, rough stone path from the craftsmen's village northeast of town to the massive arched gate in the eastern wall. They continued along the *Via Olympos*, the unofficial dividing line between the older, wealthier upper city and the rest of Thessalonike. On either side of the wide road paved with perfectly fitted stones, columns soared, supporting a covered walkway. In moments, they reached the bustling upper agora that occupied the corner of the Via Olympos and the cardo.

Crowds had transformed the usually dignified *forum*, populated only by the city's elite, into a noisy, crowded space smelling of sweat. The sun had passed its highest point, and the election was nearing its end. In the center of the tiled, open space stood a table with ten enormous, tall, pottery containers. Slaves hovered in pairs, one holding a basket of sea-polished stones, the other counting out five to those who approached in return for a token that proved their citizenship and, therefore, their right to vote. Jason surrendered his token and held out his hand to receive the pebbles.

Before each *amphora* lay a wax tablet with the name of one candidate. Jason found Ari's name first and dropped his stone down the neck of the tall pottery jar. It thudded against what must be less than twenty others. Jason's heart sank. There was no way Ari would win with so few votes. He dropped the four remaining tokens in other vessels.

Ari trudged near, his face dark. "Doesn't look good."

Jason studied the complex design of the marble floor beneath his sandals. What could he say?

"Maybe it's time to give up."

Jason clapped a hand on Ari's shoulder. "How about something to eat?"

Ari nodded, but as they set foot on the via once more, Glaukos raced toward them from the direction of the shop.

Jason hurried to meet him. "What are you doing here? Who's watching the furnace?" One stray ember could bring down the whole of the village.

They boy spoke between deep breaths. "Pappa is watching it. Two men have arrived, and they insist on seeing you immediately."

"Who are they?"

Glaukos shrugged. "I don't know. They only talked to Pappa, and he sent me to find you." He turned and bolted back down the street.

Jason sprinted to the gate and then toward the village, Ari close on his heels.

Two men waited at the door. The younger focused on anything other than Jason, while the taller one tapped his foot. He took a step forward as Jason approached. "You are Jason, son of Simon the glassmaker?"

"I am." The muscles in his chest and back tensed. "Who are you?" And why are they asking about Abba?

"We're from Amphipolis. We have a message."

The tension eased—a bit. His parents must have stayed in Amphipolis and sent word.

"My parents are delayed?" His eyes moved from one to the other, wordlessly begging for confirmation.

The older one swallowed. "I'm sorry, but we've come to tell you your parents were attacked outside our city walls."

The words hit him like a club. Still, it could be worse. "Then I must go to them. Take me there." He tried to force his way between them into his shop. What would he need?

The visitor placed his palm on Jason's chest, holding him in place. "They will be brought home to you."

Brought home? The pain in his chest sharpened, shooting throughout his body. "Then ... are ..." His words refused to form sentences, to make any sense at all.

The visitor shook his head. "I'm sorry. They didn't survive."

Breath left his lungs, and he could draw in no more. His body ached as if in a vise, tightening, crushing. He wrapped his arms around his chest, as if he could constrain the ache.

"Can we get someone for you?" The younger messenger's voice was soft.

Get someone? He heard the words, but understanding failed him. His legs began to shudder.

Ari moved to his side and wrapped an arm around Jason's waist. "I'll stay with him. Go get the *archisynagogos*."

"The synagogue leader?" The older visitor shook his head. "We don't handle—"

"He's his father's brother, Jason's *dodh*. His uncle." Ari snapped at the men. "His name is Yoel. Bring him here. Please." He beckoned to the potter's son. "Take them to the synagogue."

"Of course." Glaukos nodded and scurried off, the men hurrying to keep up.

"Give him some wine." Belos offered a small amphora and glass cup.

Ari poured a cup of wine and held it out. "Here, drink this."

Jason stared at him. "They're dead."

"I know," Ari whispered. "Drink this."

He downed the liquid in one gulp. "They're *dead*."

He'd known people who'd died before. Death was a part of life. But *Imma*, Abba ...

Agony pounded him like a wave against the city's sea wall. He clutched his tunic at his chest as if he could stop the unrelenting anguish, fill the sudden void in his heart.

How would he survive this?

2

"*For as the heavens are higher than the earth, so are my ways higher than your ways and my thoughts than your thoughts.*"

— ISAIAH 55.9

EVEN AFTER SEVEN DAYS OF MOURNING, JASON COULDN'T FORCE himself to believe Imma and Abba were gone. The biggest—and best—part of his life had been ripped from him, leaving a gaping hole.

Yoel had taken care of the funeral. Jason remembered little of it, other than the size of the crowd. Yoel had insisted Jason spend the week at their house, and the time was surprisingly comforting. Visitors came and went, bringing food, reliving memories, or sitting silently with them. Several Greeks who'd had business dealings with his parents came to the door as well.

Yoel refused to let them enter his house.

But the week was nearly over. Though he felt neither ready nor competent, it was time to return home—and to the business Abba had worked so hard to build.

Yoel's wife embraced him. "Are you sure you want to go back to an empty house? You know you're welcome to stay here as long as you like."

"I know, *Dodah*."

She placed a hand on his chest. "He means well. And he does love you."

Her face radiated love. She'd been like a second imma to him, and he'd always called her *aunt*, while Yoel had been distant for as long as Jason could remember, as if he wanted to hide his connection to Abba and his family. He even insisted Jason call him Yoel, not *uncle*. Abba had laughed it off, but the insult still skewered Jason's heart.

"I know. But nothing I do pleases him. Nothing Abba did was ever acceptable either."

"He just doesn't want you to forget your heritage."

Jason hugged her and trudged across the courtyard, then down the alley beside the synagogue. Abba's house was only a few streets from Yoel's, but it seemed worlds away. As Hebrew as Yoel was, Abba had fully assimilated into Greek society.

And Yoel had never forgiven him.

He reached the Via Regia, the via that marked the southern boundary of the residential section. South of this via lived those with the least status. The cheapest *insulae* took up entire blocks. Artisan shops occupied the lowest floors, and apartments were jammed together on the others. The higher the floor, the cheaper the rent. Jason's house fronted the Via on the eastern end.

Key in hand, he sucked in a long, slow breath. He unlocked the front door and shoved it open, then stepped inside the house that was not quite Greek and not quite Jewish. It was once familiar and comforting, full of joy and laughter. Now it felt strange and awkward. Empty.

In typical Greek style, a pair of bed chambers sat on each side of the *atrium*. He wandered toward his parents' chamber. Abba's cloak lay on the floor, while the bleached white tunic Imma wore to synagogue each week was neatly folded on top of the clothes chest at the foot of the bed. He heard her scold Abba as she did every day.

He stepped back into the atrium and walked the short hall to the columned *peristyle* that occupied most of the indoor space. Small trees planted along the edges stretched their limbs toward the open sky. Passing stone benches arranged in a perfect square, he crossed the tiled floor to Imma's culina. The feature Imma had loved most about Greek houses was the large kitchen. She loved to cook, and she loved doing it by herself, not in groups as in the Jewish community. As he surveyed the empty room, he could hear her reciting the psalms of David as she stirred the pot simmering over a low fire. He smelled chopped onions and minced garlic sizzling in olive oil while she sang praises to Yahweh. He saw her lips move in silent prayer as she kneaded the bread for their *Shabbat* meal.

He felt her kiss on his cheek as she passed him, carrying food to the table.

He returned to the peristyle and dropped onto a stone bench, elbows on his knees, staring at the mosaic below his feet.

What do I do now?

He would need to attend to the shop. Imma had kept all the records, handled the contracts and money. They should be here somewhere, but would he be able to make sense of any of them? It had taken both him and Abba to keep up with the orders. Now he would need someone else to help him keep the records.

And who would take care of the house? The cleaning? The cooking? He couldn't do it all. Should he hire someone for that as well? Would he have enough money?

He chuckled dryly. Perhaps he should have listened to Imma and married before now. He should have known she was always right.

"Jason?" Ari appeared at the edge of the peristyle.

"Ari?" Jason stood and beckoned. "Come in, come in."

Aristarchos approached, a cloth-wrapped parcel in one hand. He wrapped his arms around Jason, hugging him fiercely. "I'm so sorry, Jase."

Such simple words, yet they meant a great deal. More than all the platitudes he'd heard all week from strangers and disapproving relatives. He squeezed his eyes to keep back the tears.

Ari let go and sat facing Jason.

"I thought I'd see you earlier this week."

Ari's mouth fell open. "Didn't Yoel tell you?"

"Tell me what?"

"I came by several times, but he wouldn't let me in. I asked him to tell you I'd come. I didn't want you to think I didn't even try."

Oh, Yoel. Jason knew he'd had sent away the Greek visitors, but Ari? "I'm so sorry."

"No need for *you* to apologize."

"Yoel believes Jewish traditions are for Jews only."

"And death is a Jewish tradition?"

Jason shook his head. Ari knew better than most how Jason felt. He'd lost his own *pater* several years ago. "Only the week of mourning."

"My *meter* sent these." Ari folded back the cloth to reveal a silver platter. "She said they're your favorite." He leaned forward and set a silver dish of sesame and honey bars beside Jason.

"*Pastelli.*" Jason smiled. Her kindness was like balm to his aching soul. "She's right. They are. Please thank your mother for me."

"I will. She'd love to see you. Come to dinner."

Jason winced. "Not yet." He needed time alone.

Ari nodded. "Is there anything I can do for you?"

An idea sparked. "There is, actually." He rose. "Come into the *tablinum.*" Jason led him back down the hall to the family office. "There are records in here. I'm not sure what I'm looking for, though. Imma—" He swallowed as his voice cracked. "Imma managed the financial part of the business. I just worked the glass."

Ari scanned the scrolls and tablets scattered on the desk. "How can I help?"

"If you don't mind, can you look them over? Tell me what you learn?"

"Are you sure you want me in your family's business like that?"

Ari couldn't know how his words stung. "I'm all that's left of my family. And I covet your help."

Ari grasped his upper arm. "Jase, I'm so sorry. I didn't mean—"

He nodded. "I know you didn't."

"When did you last sleep?"

"I haven't much, all week."

"Why don't you get some rest and I'll see what I can figure out? Maybe tomorrow we'll go check out the shop."

"Thank you. Take them to your house if it helps." He shrugged. "I can't do much here anyway." He lumbered to his chamber at the front of the house, flopped onto the wool-stuffed mattress, and prayed for sleep's sweet oblivion.

KASSI LAY AWAKE on her wool-stuffed mattress in the dark, staring at the painted ceiling of her chamber. How long had she been awake?

Most of the night, as the old woman's haggard face refused to leave her alone. The tattoo, the scar, her eyes... But could it be? Was this gaunt, disheveled, dirty beggar the beautiful, graceful, healthy woman who had lovingly cared for Mamma for so many years? Kassi had heard about the poor her entire life, had seen them occasionally, although only when she ventured to the agora accompanied by Mannus. What else had been hidden from her?

Pappa always said the poor didn't work hard enough. But was that true of this woman?

If this was Dora, the slave who cared for Mamma—and for Kassi—for so many years, it was unquestionably false. She'd never stopped moving when she was at the house. Her rough hands showed a lifetime of arduous work. Clearly, she was the victim of circumstances beyond her control.

The first weak tinges of morning light would not make their appearance for a few hours. Kassi rose and put a cloak over her sleeping tunic. After grabbing the oil lamp from the niche by her door, she crept from her chamber down the hall to the culina. The remnants of a fire still burned in the stone oven, so she took a slim twig from a nearby container and poked at the embers to coax them to life.

A young slave, no more than a child, entered and halted just inside in the doorway. "Kyria, are you well? May I do something for you?"

She flashed a tired smile. "No, I just can't sleep. But thank you for asking."

The night slave frowned and padded off.

She measured salt and flour onto the table in a mound, then stuck two fingers in the center and swirled them in a small circle, making the well half as large as the mound of flour. She reached for a container on the table and poured out a bubbly liquid. Digging her hands into the mixture, she slowly mixed the mother dough into the flour and salt, careful to slowly mix in all the flour. She moved to the shelves and ran her fingers over the glass containers. Walnuts, pine nuts, almonds, honey, sliced olives ... she pulled the jar of figs from the shelf.

Dora's ...or rather, *Isa's* face came to her mind. As a child, she'd once found Isa and Lida in the kitchen making the evening meal together and watched until Pappa scolded her. But she'd stayed long enough to see the women laughing and joking as they cooked. Isa had looked so different then—a full, round face framed by long dark hair pulled into a knot at the back of her head.

What she must have suffered these last five years. But what could Kassi do to help her now?

Giving her money was not the answer. Though her meter had left her a large inheritance, Kassi hadn't enough money to provide for Isa's needs for the rest of her life. And how many more were there like her? She thought about the line of women in the market who had resorted to begging ... or worse. They needed some way to earn money, to support themselves and their children.

She dumped the dried fruit onto the table and chopped them into small cubes.

All these women could bake, wash, clean, cook. Care for children. Spin wool and make clothes. But even one day begging in the market would earn them a soiled reputation that would follow them for the rest of their lives. The residents of the upper city safeguarded their status as much as their wealth, and no one in the *ano poli* would hire them now.

There were popinas and other businesses who could likely use a cleaner all over Thessalonike, but even if she found them, it was doubtful many of them would hire a woman without the endorsement of a former owner.

In synagogue, she'd heard teachings about helping those who had little. Caring for the poor was commanded by the Jewish God. She was not Jewish, but she'd come to know that *Adonai* was the only God. Shouldn't she then obey him?

Popping a piece of chopped fig into her mouth with one hand, she added the rest of the dried fruit to her dough with the other. The thought of a beautiful five-strand braided bread flavored with fig, olive oil, and sea salt made her mouth water, but after rising and baking, it would be hours before she tasted it. She kneaded the dough, cut it into five equal pieces, and began braiding it. Outside to the middle, outside to the middle ...

Most of the people she knew didn't hire workers, they bought slaves. It was more cost efficient in the long run and the more slaves one owned, the more respect one gained.

An idea began to form. But was it workable?

If no one else would hire, them, maybe she could. But how? She had no business, but she had the money Mamma had left to her.

Should she start one? What kind? Where?

The questions overwhelmed the answers, and her head began to hurt.

The sun had begun its climb as she worked, and the room had brightened. If she could get a little sleep, perhaps she could think more clearly. She squeezed the ends of the strands together and tucked the knot under the loaf then moved the unbaked bread to a baking stone and set it aside to rise.

She padded down the hall back toward her chamber. A soft murmur halted her, and she peered around the corner.

Pappa stood before the niche in the wall of the atrium, hands spread, palms and face to heaven, whispering meaningless words to a lifeless god. The scent of frankincense lingered in the room. As much as she relished the scent, she detested the silver Pappa wasted on it. Why did he bother with such nonsense? He claimed that he ascribed no power to the countless Greek—or Roman—deities. Not once had those deities granted even the smallest petition. But success in the Roman Empire demanded proper sacrifices, public devotion, and attendance at the almost weekly feasts, and Pappa adhered to those demands without fail.

3

The fear of the LORD is the beginning of wisdom;
  all who follow his precepts have good understanding.
  To him belongs eternal praise.

— PSALM 111.10

JASON STOOD AT THE DOOR TO YOEL'S HOME, WILLING HIMSELF TO knock but dreading an answer. Why had he agreed to return to Yoel's house for the Shabbat evening meal?

Because Dodah Leah had asked him to, and he hated disappointing her.

He knocked on the door and was instantly pulled into an embrace, her head reaching only his chest. She'd never failed to greet him with a hug.

She pulled back and looked up at him. "Jason, I missed you. I became used to having you around."

"You got used to me in a week?" He frowned.

She laughed, a gentle sound his weary heart drank in. "In only one week." She let him step inside and closed the door.

A hallway divided the small home in two, with sleeping chambers toward the back on either side. The small culina was on his left, and the dining area—the most Greek area in the house—was on his right.

"Have you eaten yet today?"

He shook his head.

"Then eat. Some food will make you feel better." She led him to the *triclinium,* where a low table waited, surrounded on three sides by wide couches. Two had their feet pointed away from the table, while the third was parallel to it. A pair of oil lamps sat close to each other in the center, flames dancing brightly.

"You always say that, Dodah. You always have. But a hearty meal can't fix everything." He dropped onto a couch and reclined.

She chuckled lightly as she disappeared into the culina, as if his statement couldn't be more ridiculous.

Yoel entered the room, a glass in hand. Short but stocky, he somehow managed to always seem to be the biggest man in the room. He wore his long gray beard as a badge of holiness and constantly remarked on Abba and Jason's smooth faces.

Let him work with fire all day and see how he likes a face covered with hair.

"What about your life is so bad, Jason? What is there that cannot be fixed by food and family?" As host, he reclined on the couch in the middle as Dodah entered with a pitcher and then filled the cups.

"Nothing. I didn't mean my life is bad. I meant ... sometimes things don't get fixed." Jason reclined on his left side.

"You need to come to synagogue."

"*Nai,* Yoel." Just agree with him.

"And give thanks to Adonai for all that you have."

Saying thanks to a silent God doesn't fix everything either. But better to keep that thought to himself.

"Adonai is powerful. As Moses wrote, 'Your right hand, Adonai, glorious in power, Your right hand, Adonai, shatters the enemy.'" He pointed a finger at Jason. "If you paid attention in synagogue, you would know that."

"Nai." Jason selected a slice of fresh pear. Perhaps if his mouth was full of fruit, he wouldn't say anything disrespectful.

Doubtful, as Yoel wouldn't stop until he'd pushed Jason to his breaking point, as usual.

Dodah perched on the edge of the remaining couch. She caught his eye and offered a sympathetic grin. How had she put up with such a man all these years?

A young woman entered the room carrying a plate heaped with roast fish and root vegetables.

"That looks delicious, Hannah. Thank you." Dodah smiled at the servant.

Jason waited until she had left the room, jerking a thumb in her direction. "She's new."

"Yes," Dodah replied. "Elisheba got married. To Ezekiel. You must know him. He's part of the synagogue."

Jason thought a moment. "I think so."

"He observes *all* the commandments." Yoel's comment was less a compliment to Ezekiel than a jab at Jason.

He stifled a groan.

"Let's eat, shall we?" Dodah was the only one who ever dared to make Yoel change the subject.

Yoel cast a look her way but sat up and then stood. "Blessed are You, Adonai our God, King of the universe, who brings forth bread from the earth."

"Amen."

Dodah pulled the platter closer. With a sharp knife, she cut the fish into bite-sized pieces.

"I don't see how Hannah will ever marry. She forgets about half of whatever Leah tells her." Yoel grunted.

"So did Elisheba. And now she will make a wonderful wife to Ezekiel," she said.

"How many girls have gone through this house?" Jason asked.

She shrugged. "Oh, I've lost count."

At least one a year. Without children of her own, Dodah had become a mother-figure to many of the Jewish girls in Thessalonike, especially those who had lost their own immas. She taught them whatever it was they hadn't been able to learn at home—cooking, cleaning, sewing, lighting the Shabbat lamps. After, most of them found proper Jewish husbands and had their own children. It was an odd Shabbat when at least one of them didn't give her a grateful hug. Many of their happy husbands had thanked her as well.

Jason ripped off a chunk of warm bread and placed it on his tongue. He was hungrier than he'd realized, which wasn't surprising since he'd not really eaten since he'd left two days ago. An apple, some honeyed wine. The pastelli Ari had brought. He took a bite of the roasted fish and savored the flavors of garlic, vinegar, and olive oil.

"Delicious, as always, Dodah."

"*Todah*, Jason."

"You're welcome."

"Have you had any offers?" Yoel stuffed a piece of fish in his mouth.

"Offers?" Jason frowned. What was he talking about? "Offers of what?"

"To buy the shop, of course."

"Why would someone offer to buy the shop?"

Yoel set his cup on the table. "Because you're selling it." He tilted his head. "Aren't you?"

"No! Why would you think that?" Jason shoved down the anger swelling in his belly.

"I ... I just assumed. You can't possibly handle it alone."

How could he say that when he had never been to the work-shop? "I've been doing most of the actual production of the glass for about two years. Abba did make the deals, and Imma took care of the money, but I can get help with that."

"You think you're good enough to do that?"

"Yoel!" Dodah reached across the table for Jason's hand while glaring at her husband.

Yoel shrugged. "What?" He returned his gaze to Jason. "Promise me you'll think about it, yes?"

No. He met Yoel's gaze and shoved his plate away. "I'm not hungry. I think it's time I go home."

"It's time for you to *come* home." Yoel's eyes drilled into his.

"Come home?"

He spread his hands. "To the community. To your family. Sell the shop and that horrible house and come back. Live among your own people."

Jason stalked from the dining area.

Dodah hurried after him, reaching him as he placed his hand on the door latch. She lightly grasped his arm, turning him to face her.

"Jason, he's only trying to help."

"He's trying to control me. He's *not* my abba."

She shook her head. "That's how he loves. I've grown used to it."

"I haven't. And I won't. Did you notice he didn't mention Abba? Not once." He winced at the almost physical pain stabbing his chest. "The only time he said his name the whole week I was here was during prayer. It's like he never existed."

"He grieves deeply, I promise you. Deeply, but privately. He's suffered a great loss."

Jason stiffened. "Not as great as I have."

"Of course not." She laid a hand on his cheek. "I've been praying for you since we heard. I will never stop."

"Todah." His voice dropped to a whisper, and he opened the door.

"You'll come back? Next Shabbat, at least?"

Come back? Not likely. Right now, he wished he hadn't come at all.

KASSI GRABBED her cloak before leaving her chamber. The morning sun had only begun to warm the air, and the stone synagogue hoarded the overnight chill.

Mannus close behind her, Kassi followed the familiar route to the south end of Thessalonike. Her eyes scanned the insulae on either side of the cardo for any sign of Isa. Had she found some place safe?

At the last paved road, she turned left and entered the Jewish section of the city, tucked up against the sea wall.

The synagogue sat in the middle of a long row of modest houses. She rounded the building to the large double doors that stood open to welcome the community. Four steps led down to a long, narrow room with stone benches, three rows high, lining all four sides. In the center, a small table held a stack of scrolls. A lone stool faced it. Six columns lined each long side, with three on each narrow end, supporting wooden beams which held the roof.

Kassi found a seat next to her closest friend, Zelia, who had invited her to a synagogue service three summers ago.

"Does your pater know you're here?" Compassion lighted Zelia's soft brown eyes.

"He knows." Kassi nodded. "He's not happy about it, but he knows. He hasn't forbidden me yet, so I'm here. For now."

"You need to get married, so he won't be in charge of you anymore." Zelia chuckled.

"Right. I'll have a different man telling me what to do. Where to go. What to believe."

"At least he'll be younger than your pater."

"Hopefully." Not from what she'd seen of many marriages, though.

The crowd silenced as the short, old man who led them in the prayers each week rose and approached the table. Hands held high, head tipped back as though addressing the sky, his voice was always much louder than necessary to fill the small building. "O *Adonai*, open my lips, and my mouth shall declare Your praise."

Kassi repeated the words in her mind as the man spoke aloud.

"Blessed are You, Adonai our God and the God of our ancestors, God of Abraham, Isaac, and Jacob, great, mighty, and awesome God; supreme God, Who bestows lovingkindness by creating everything in the universe. You remember the kindness of our ancestors and lovingly bring redemption to their descendants for the sake of Your Name."

"Amen," the worshippers responded. Most were Jewish families, but a fair number of Greeks, mostly women from the ano poli, completed the crowd.

Kassi thought back to the first time she had attended the Shabbat service. That one visit divided her life into two parts—before and after she came to know of the Living God.

The man continued with the benedictions, then he led them all in the *Shema*.

"Hear, O Israel, the Lord our God, the Lord is one, and you shall love the Lord your God with all your heart, all your being, and all your might."

The Lord is one. Such a comforting thought. That single concept was what drew her to the faith of the Jews. She'd never understood the idea of hundreds of competing gods—jealous, spiteful, vindictive beings who enjoyed toying with their human creations. Even as a little girl, she'd known that couldn't be right.

She leaned toward Zelia. "Have I ever thanked you for inviting me to synagogue?"

Zelia fought a laugh. "Many times. Now hush."

When the prayer concluded, the leader took his seat two rows in front of Kassi and Zelia.

A tall, wiry man approached the table, and the messenger handed him a scroll.

The reader paused, scroll in hand. "Before I begin the reading of the Law, I wish to offer my condolences to our archisynagogos, Yoel, for the passing of his brother." He nodded in the old man's direction, and Yoel dipped his head in acknowledgement.

In front of her, and behind the leader, a young man lowered his head almost to his knees, clenched fists covering his ears. She'd seen him in the synagogue many times with a couple who must be his parents, but she had no idea who he was. Today he was alone.

Why did this statement infuriate him so? Or sadden him? It was hard to tell. And who was the leader's brother who had died? Were his wife and family here?

As the end of the service neared, Kassi studied the man seated in front of her. Throughout the morning, he'd moved not a muscle except to rest his forearms on his knees. His head had remained lowered.

Should she try to comfort him? Perhaps not in the synagogue. Most had accepted the Greeks who came to learn about their God, but many resented the number of women whom they assumed should be following the gods of their husbands. Maybe later, outside.

God of Israel, heal this man's heart.

The old man again stood to lead the assembly in a last prayer, and Kassi bowed her head. When she opened her eyes, the seat before her was empty.

Kassi and Zelia followed the crowd out of the building.

As always, Mannus waited for her across the street with several other escorts. Zelia waved goodbye and headed north.

Mannus crossed to meet her. "Home, kyria?"

"I'd like to stop at the popina first. I'm craving an obeliskos."

He raised a brow for only a moment, but silently followed her toward the cardo.

The late autumn sun warmed her shoulders as she turned into the market. "Publius, one obeliskos, if you will."

"For you, anything." He filled a flatbread to overflowing with meat and handed it to her.

"Eucharisto." How did he get such flavor in his meat? She glanced around as she chewed.

On the south side of the agora, beggars stood with hands outstretched. Some were bolder than others, accosting shoppers who looked the other way, ignoring the plaintive cries.

Isa stood behind the others, her hand out but her voice silent.

Leaving her food behind, Kassi raced across the market.

Mannus's feet pounded heavily behind her.

"Isa! What are you doing here?"

The woman glared. "What does it look like? I'm hungry. They don't give the food away."

Kassi pulled her aside. "You told me you had a place to stay. Food to eat."

"I didn't say that."

Kassi thought back to the woman's words. "You allowed me to think that."

"I *allowed* you to feel good about helping the poor. Isn't that what you people want?"

Shame crept into her heart, and her face heated. "I do want to help."

"You can't." Isa raised a brow, her scar cutting the eyebrow in two. "Go back to your *domus*, Kassandra."

"You're Dora, aren't you?" How did she go from slave in the house of one of the richest men in the city to a woman without home, family, or food?

"I am no longer that woman. Call me Isa."

"What happened to you?"

"When your meter died, your pater had no use for me, and he sold me. A year ago, my new master freed me and left the city. Now I have nothing. No place to live, no money to buy food."

"A year ago? Where have you been sleeping? How did you survive all this time?"

She gestured to the row of women near them. "Like this."

An invisible fist crushed Kassi's heart. "Where do you sleep?"

"Wherever I can find shelter. I've often slept in the mausoleum outside the gates. Sometimes behind the temples. Summer wasn't too bad."

Kassi reached into her sash and pulled out every coin she had. She grabbed Isa's hand and pressed the coins into her palm. "Here. This should last you for several days. I *will* be back, and I will find a way to care for you."

She shrugged and looked away. "If you say so."

Kassi moved to catch her gaze. "You have no reason to believe me, I know. But I will be back before the week is done." She pointed toward the popina on the corner. "Go see Publius. Tell him I sent you. I'll tell him to take good care of you."

Isa walked away without comment.

Kassi stared after her. Pappa wouldn't agree, but Isa had once been a part of their family. And although their responsibility for her legally ended when Pappa sold her, something had gone drastically awry.

Kassi aimed to find out what had happened and make it right.

4

...but those who hope in the Lord will renew their strength.
    They will soar on wings like eagles;
    they will run and not grow weary,
    they will walk and not be faint.

— ISAIAH 40.31

"WHICH ONE DID YOU LIKE THE BEST?" KASSI TOSSED A SIDELONG glance at Mannus as they strolled up the cardo toward the ano poli.

"I couldn't say, kyria. I have not been made aware of the reason you suddenly wish to purchase an abandoned building."

She stopped suddenly. "I'm sorry. I've been so caught up in this new idea, I forgot to share it with you."

He halted and turned to face her. "There is no reason you should have shared with me. I simply do what I am asked."

She stepped closer. "Oh, but your opinion would mean so much to me."

His stern face softened. "Why?"

"Because I consider you to be an intelligent and thoughtful man."

The softness disappeared. "I am only a slave."

"Not my slave."

"Nevertheless." He turned and set off again, his strides longer than usual, and she hurried to catch up.

"My plan is to open a *pistrinum*. Nearly every woman knows how to bake bread. I'll hire Isa and other women like her, and they will all share the profit. They'll be able to support themselves without resorting to"—her cheeks heated at the thought—"hanging around the agora."

He nodded.

"Which building do you think would be best for that? We saw so many, it'll be hard to choose."

"I cannot say. I know nothing of bakeries or business."

He obviously was not going to share his thoughts with her. Might as well change the subject. "Do you think he's back yet?"

"It's a bit early, but you never know with him."

As they turned toward home, she glanced down the Via Olympos. The agora wasn't empty, but it wasn't busy, either. Pappa could still be at the council house, or he could be home wondering where she was. Her stomach churned. How would she explain where she'd been?

They reached the domus, and she hurried inside. At least he wasn't pacing the atrium waiting for her.

She opened the door of her chamber and tossed her cloak on the bed before heading for the kitchen. She peeked inside the tablinum as she passed. It was empty. Tension drained from her body.

In the culina, she grabbed for a jar of flour from the shelves and poured it onto the worktable, then added water and began mixing dough.

The late afternoon sun shined through the windows near the top of the southern wall, adding to the heat from the cooking fire. Kassi dragged her forearm across her brow and pulled it away damp with sweat.

Lida, one of Pappa's slaves, breezed into the room from the slaves' entrance, her gaze fixed on the contents of a basket. "Kassi, I found pomegranates at the agora. I didn't know they'd ripened yet." She held out a basket of the deep red fruit. "Aren't they beautiful?" She raised her head. "I thought—"

Lida stopped in mid-word, and Kassi glanced up to see the smile drain from Lida's face. She looked over her shoulder toward the entrance.

Pappa stood in the doorway. One cold look from him as he strolled near sent Lida scurrying away from the worktable to the storage room on the other side of the kitchen. He placed a hand on Kassi's shoulder and a quick kiss on her cheek.

"Chairé, Pappa. How was your day?"

He rounded the table and stood on the other side. "I've spoken to you about your relationship with your slaves."

"They're your slaves, not mine." Kassi barely kept her irritation from showing in her voice. Lida had raised Kassi ever since Mamma had died. She was far more a meter than a slave.

"You have flour on your face."

She reached for a clean towel and wiped her cheeks and chin.

He motioned to his forehead.

"Sorry." She dragged the towel across her brow.

Pappa scowled as he waved a hand at the table. "This is beneath you. Why do you think I have slaves? So you can relax and enjoy your life."

"I find baking bread relaxing, and I have no one to talk to other than Lida. I enjoy baking bread and I like trying new recipes. At the end of it, I have something to show for it— something I created. When the family enjoys what I have made, it gives me joy."

Pappa pursed his lips but let the remark go. "I'm going to the temple of Apollo in five days. I wish for you to accompany me."

Her hands, buried in bread dough, closed into fists, and the mixture squeezed between her fingers. "Pappa, please don't make me do this."

He reached for a shelled walnut and popped it in his mouth. After a long moment, he swallowed and fixed his dark eyes on her. "I'm not *making* you do anything. I'm *asking* you to come with me to the temple to make an offering."

"It is not required of women."

He nodded. "You're right, it's not. But I've been far too lenient with you and your ... unconventional behaviors. You should have married a year ago at the latest. And there is always the issue of your attendance at the synagogue."

She extricated her hands from the dough and rubbed them together, sending pieces of dough flying. "Many women attend the synagogue. Some of the city's most prominent wives and daughters. Who do you think invited me?"

He brushed a crumb of dough from his immaculate linen chiton. "Yes, I know. Zelia. But her pater is not a *politarch*. You, as the daughter of the chief ruler of this city, carry more responsibility."

She leaned forward, her hands flat on the table, and met his steely gaze. How could he say such things to her? "I am aware of the scrutiny your position as politarch draws. I have never once embarrassed you."

"Until today."

She froze. "Today?"

"Do you honestly think I don't know everything that happens in my city? You were seen all over town, in empty buildings."

Her mind raced as she tried to decide how to answer. But what was there to say?

"I'm sorry, Pappa. But I was perfectly safe. Mannus accompanied me."

"I'm pleased you had sense enough to do that. But people are beginning to talk."

Her hand flew to her chest. "About me?"

"Worse. About me. Your meter is no longer here to attend with me, to help gain respect for me..." He reached for another nut. "It's been said I cannot control my own family. Your appearance at a temple will make it clear you are a proper daughter."

Her heart ached. There was no way she would win this fight. "Five days from now is Shabbat. Must it be then?" Her voice cracked.

He scoffed. "Then pick a day. There's a temple on almost every corner and a feast every other week." He stalked toward the door but halted at the end of the table. "And soon."

She waited until his heavy footfalls ceased before she let out a breath. How could he make her choose between her God and her pater?

To be fair, he likely had no idea what she now thought of the God of the Jews. She'd never talked to him about it, but in her time at the synagogue, she had come to know that the God of the Jews was the only true deity. And He allowed no competition.

Pappa did not believe the Roman gods had any power, yet he continued to reverence them—at least publicly.

What would she do?

Kassi placed the dough on a wooden ladle and shoved it in the oven, then hurried down the hall to her chamber.

She ducked inside and moved toward the corner of her room and sat before a table covered with unopened bottles of cosmetics and perfumes. Staring at the polished bronze mirror on the wall, she studied her image. She'd been told her entire life how much she looked like her meter, but she couldn't see it. Mamma had been beautiful. Kassi was plain.

She dragged a brush through her long, dark hair, so different from Mamma's. Her hair had been full of beautiful walnut-colored waves, while Kassi's was stick straight and boring.

She reached for a bottle that stood above the others and drew her fingers over the glass that contained the perfumed oil Mamma had worn every day. After the funeral, Kassi had slipped into her parents' chamber and snatched the exquisite bottle from the assortment of lotions, oils, and other beauty products. Made of glass the color of an angry sea, it was shaped like a flat-bottomed ball. Wispy threads of white glass wound their way around the bottom and swirled around the neck, while a colorless glass stopper rested atop the long, thin neck.

It had been ridiculously expensive when Pappa bought it for his wife over a decade ago. A work of such quality was still not cheap, but glass was now so inexpensive, even the poor could afford basic pieces.

She removed the stopper and inhaled deeply. The fragrance of lavender oil both calmed and saddened her. How was it that the faintest whiff still made her heart ache? A vague memory of Mamma holding her, leaving the flowery scent on her skin, enveloped her. She stopped up the bottle, shutting off the scent and the memory.

There could be only one reason he had mentioned her meter. Mamma had been the perfect politarch's wife. She was always impeccably dressed, never spoke an angry word, and supported Pappa unconditionally. She lit up every room she entered but never overshadowed him.

Kassi would never live up to her example. And even if she could, did she want to?

There had to be more to life than silk chitons and polite smiles, and Kassi intended to find it.

As the sun set over the sea, Jason knocked on the door of a wide, two-story domus on the Via Olympos. Half columns attached to the wall stood on either side of the door, supporting a three-sided lintel. The rest of the facade was unadorned.

The woman who answered smiled brightly, dark eyes crinkling at the edges.

She enveloped Jason into a hug before he crossed the threshold. "I'm so glad you decided to come. I was sorry to hear about your parents. They were delightful people. I'll miss them."

Julia had to be one of the only residents of the ano poli who would admit to even knowing them. Glassblowers were considered better than most tradesmen and could make a great deal of money due to the demand for colorless glass objects of all kinds. But they were still only artisans, and the wealthy didn't like to be seen being friendly with them.

She led him to the room reserved for the men of the house then disappeared. Moments later, she returned to the *andron* with a platter of sliced apples and pears, dried figs, cheese, and olives in one hand and an amphora in the other.

With all their slaves, she still served him herself more often than not.

"Ari said you'd rather eat in here, just you two?"

He nodded as she set the platter on a low table surrounded by backless couches and sat across from him.

"Not ready for our noisy family yet?" She smiled softly.

He shook his head as he sat. "Not yet."

"I understand. I wouldn't be either." She shook her head, long brown hair bouncing against her shoulders.

Sandaled footsteps called their attention to the door, and a moment later Ari strolled in. He dropped onto a long Roman-style couch, elbow on the single arm, feet hanging over the other end.

"How was the meeting?" Julia asked.

"Boring, but necessary, I suppose."

Guilt and shame crashed onto Jason's shoulders. The election! He'd forgotten to ask Ari about it. The results would have been announced while he was in seclusion at Yoel's.

"Ari, I'm so sorry. I forgot all about it." He winced, trying to decide how to ask. If Ari had won, he'd have told Jason by now. "Did you hear?"

He nodded, his face grim. "I did. I was told only a week ago."

Not again. Ari had been suggested as a politarch for the last two years. His father and his grandfather had each served Thessalonike for many years as one of its five politarchs. His grandfather was so beloved, he was called Aristarchos, best ruler, and the name was passed down. But Secundus, the acknowledged leader of the group, had managed to spread so much gossip about Ari that he couldn't get elected.

Jason rose and crossed to Ari, who swung his feet around and sat up to make a place for Jason to sit.

"Ari, I'm so sorry."

"Thank you." He released a sigh closer to a groan than a breath. "It'll be hard, but I guess I'll have to do all I can to live up to the legacy of my pater and his pater. Of course, I'll be much busier now, and I won't be able to see you as often—"

"What?" Jason hopped to his feet. "You mean ..."

Ari rose up, chest puffed out. "I am the newest politarch of Makedonia's finest city!"

Jason punched his arm. "You're terrible!"

"He certainly is." Julia laughed.

Ari grinned, rubbing his arm. "I know."

Jason grabbed the pitcher and poured three glasses of wine, handing one to Ari and one to Julia. "I'm so happy for you, Ari. You deserve it."

Julia took one sip. "I'll leave you now. Your food will be delivered soon. You'll let me know if you need anything else?"

"Of course."

She kissed her son on the cheek and left the room.

"Why didn't you say anything?" asked Jason.

"Your parents ..." He shrugged. "It didn't seem so important anymore. I figured it could wait."

"Well, I'm thrilled for you. I'm certain you'll be a great leader."

Ari shook his head. "Secundus is not pleased."

Jason drank the wine, the salty seawater highlighting its sweetness. "Not much he can do about it now."

"He can make life miserable for me. He and the other two have been rulers for years. Even Laertes is much older. I'm younger, inexperienced. If he ever lets me speak, he'll ridicule whatever I suggest."

"Maybe. But Secundus is a man who lives for rules. He's also quite concerned for his reputation as a wise leader. He may have tried to move mountains to keep you off the council, but now that you're on, I doubt he'll do much that will make him look too bad."

"I hope not." Ari sat and reached for a bunch of grapes before reclining on his side once again.

A servant entered with a platter of roasted goat, root vegetables, and fresh bread. Another followed with two stone plates. All were placed on the small table between them.

"Have you found anything in the books?" Jason leaned forward and selected a piece of turnip.

"I'm sorry. The council has kept me busier than I expected, but I'm almost done. Your imma kept excellent records. Everything is there, it's just not well organized."

"Sounds like her. The shop and the tablinum were always a mess, but she always knew exactly where everything was. My abba would ask her for a tablet, or some piece of information, and if she couldn't recite it without looking, she could put her hands on it instantly."

"Give me a few more days. The council is meeting every day, all day for the next week, but I can work on this during the evenings."

"Can you tell if I can afford to keep an apprentice?"

"Will you teach him the craft? If not, you may owe his family some compensation."

Jason nodded. "I can teach him. Abba taught me, so ..."

"Then you should be able to. You wouldn't be paying wages, only for his food."

"Good. I'm going to need him if I'm to keep the business going."

There really was no *if*. He simply had to keep the shop. Abba had worked hard to make it successful. He delighted in working with his son and talked often of Jason one day owning it. His family had been known for their work in glass for generations.

He didn't plan to be the one to bring it crashing to an end.

5

THE SCENTS OF SALTWATER AND SEA AIR SURROUNDED JASON AS HE stood at the edge of the harbor by the seawall.

He tapped a foot as he scanned the ocean. Abba always placed an order for raw glass to arrive on the last ship of the season. The ship should have arrived two days ago. If it didn't arrive soon, it might mean the vessel had taken refuge in any one of a hundred ports between here and Alexandria, unable to complete the journey before the sea was "closed" for the winter.

And if that happened, his glass business wouldn't survive until spring.

The harbormaster approached and stood beside Jason for a

while, facing the sea. "I'm so sorry, Jason. Your abba was a good man."

"Thank you." The gentle condolence eased the ache a bit but not by much. How many hours had he stood on this spot with Abba waiting for a ship to deliver glass?

"It'll come. I'd have heard if a ship bound for here had been forced to winter elsewhere. And the weather's been quite mild this year." He kept his eyes on the water.

"I know. Thank you."

"I think you have a couple more days before you need worry."

"It's just that our—*my* business could die without that glass. It would put me in serious trouble."

"I don't think it'll come to that." He glanced at the long building that served as a warehouse on the other side of the coast pathway, then jerked a thumb toward it. "I think someone needs me." He strolled to a trio of men hovering near the doorway, spoke with them, and returned to Jason.

"Those men are looking for the synagogue. I said you would direct them."

"Of course. If the ship arrives—"

"Don't worry. I'll watch for it. You don't need to spend all day here."

"Thank you." He'd only wanted to ask the man to hold it for him, but as usual, he'd offered more than necessary.

Jason approached the visitors and waited for a pause in their conversation. "Welcome to Thessalonike. I understand you're seeking the synagogue?"

"Yes, we are." An older man with a full white beard answered, a bright smile on his face.

"May I ask what it is you're hoping to find? Lodging, teaching, meals ...?"

The speaker pointed to his left at the man in the middle, about his own age. "You should talk to him. He's in charge."

Jason turned to the apparent leader. There was nothing in his appearance that would distinguish him as a leader. He was short, with a well-trimmed dark beard and thinning hair circling the sides of his head. His clothes were made of common wool, but they looked new and exceptionally well made, as did the tunics and cloaks of the other two. They must have had money, at least recently.

The third was a young man, about Jason's age or perhaps a year or two younger. He peered out from under a mass of curly dark hair.

The leader took one step forward. "I'm Paulos."

A Greek name? Why would a Greek want the synagogue?

"My Hebrew name is Shaul, if that helps."

"Ah." It did.

"This is Silas." He pointed first to his right, then to his left. "And Timotheos. We call him Timos."

"*Shalom*. My dodh is the archisynagogos. I'll take you to him if you wish."

"*Todah rabah*. We'd appreciate that very much."

Jason extended an arm toward the arched gate that led into the city. "Where have you come from?"

"We were in Philippi for a few months," Paulos answered.

"I hear it's a beautiful city. A Roman colony, yes?"

Paulos remained silent.

"Yes, it's quite Roman. The city itself is lovely." Timotheos filled the silence left by his friends. Yet the sentence felt unfinished, as if something else was not quite so lovely.

"The synagogue can offer you beds, meals, whatever you may need. Were you hoping to study there?"

Silas chuckled.

"Paulos studied under Gamaliel," Timos said.

Jason halted for a moment. "Gamaliel?" Gamaliel was royalty in strict Jewish circles. Yoel would be beyond thrilled. "The archisynagogos will be delighted to meet you. There are few learned Jews here in Thessalonike."

Paulos kept in step with Jason, and the other two followed behind.

They crossed under the gate, then turned onto the narrow road closest to the city's southern wall. Small houses, remarkably similar, lined that side.

Jason stopped in front of a plain building, narrow windows lining the top of the wall. "This is the synagogue. The entrance is on the other side." He led them down a quiet alley that spilled out onto a large, grassy courtyard stretching the length of the community. Houses backing up against the wall lined the far side as well. Women and older girls gathered at one end, each kneeling before a stone quern, hands wrapped around a smaller stone shaped like a loaf of bread. Back and forth, they crushed golden kernels of barley into flour.

At the other end, six men huddled, deep in conversation. In between, children chased each other, squealing with glee.

Jason gestured to the men. "That's the leader. His name is Yoel." He led the three men toward the group, stopping a stone's throw away, waiting for recognition.

Yoel approached.

"These visitors are seeking the synagogue. This is Timotheos, and Silas, and this"—Jason put his hand on Paulos's shoulder—"is Paulos. He studied under Gamaliel."

Yoel's eyes widened for a long moment before he placed himself between Jason and the scholar and steered Paulos away.

Typical. Jason turned to go.

Timotheos touched his arm. "Todah rabah for your help."

"You're welcome."

"I'm sure Paulos would like to thank you as well."

Jason chuckled dryly. "He won't get away that easily."

As if he sensed Jason watching him, Paulos looked back toward him, a soft smile conveying his appreciation.

"Will we see you at synagogue? And your family?" asked Timotheos.

I have no family. Except Yoel. He forced a smile. "I'll be there."

Timotheos was only trying to be friendly. Still, the hurt was no less. He'd never been to synagogue without Abba and Imma before the last two Shabbats.

He'd better get used to it. He'd be doing everything alone now.

"AND WHO PLANNED the murder of Julius Caesar in the Senate?" Kassi studied the three young girls in front of her, seated on a pair of backless couches in the peristyle of her father's house, a tablet in each lap. A cool breeze scattered the scent of the many-colored flowers planted along its edges.

"Brutus—" Penelope began.

"Not you, Pen." Kassi patted the fair-haired girl's knee. "I know you know. Let one of your cousins answer."

Penelope pouted and folded her arms over her chest.

Kassi looked to the other two. With their dark wavy hair and round faces, the sisters favored their pater, her oldest brother Argos, although they had also inherited their mother's light eyes.

"Brutus, Cassius, Decimus, and ..." Sophia, the oldest, bit her lip.

Kassi switched her gaze to the other cousin. "Helene?"

Helene shrugged. "Gaius?"

Kassi shook her head. "All right, Penelope."

Penelope puffed her chest and raised her stylus in the air in triumph. "Trebonius!"

"Very good."

Sophia rolled her eyes.

"And what happened after that?" Kassi asked.

Penelope opened her mouth, but Kassi stilled her with a look.

"I know! Octavius became the ruler," Helene answered.

"Yes! And..." Kassi raised one brow. When Helene wavered, she nodded. "You know this."

Helene frowned, pursing her lips. "Brutus and Cassius didn't like it?"

"Right again! You've learned more than you realize."

Helene beamed at Kassi's praise.

"They fought against Octavius and Marcus Antonius," Penelope added.

"And who won?" asked Kassi.

"Octavius!" Sophia sat up straight, excited to finally know an answer.

"Exccllent, Sophia! And now, the most important question: *Where* did this epic battle take place?"

"The fields of Philippi!" The girls shouted in unison.

Kassi laughed. "Yes! A little north of here. Perhaps one day we should visit the field on which they fought." Kassi leaned near, as if to share a secret with her nieces. "Rome thinks it is the most important city in the Empire, but Makedonia is where all the most important events take place."

"Quite true." Pappa strolled through the room, pausing near the girls. "We were an empire long before the Romans ever thought of ruling the world." He leaned toward the cousins. "But we won't remind them of that," he said, his voice dropping to a whisper.

The girls giggled, craning their necks to meet his gaze. "Hello, Pappos!"

"Hello, my girls." He grinned at Kassi. "*All* my girls."

"Hello, Pappa." She smiled.

"Everyone hungry?" he asked.

"Yes!" They cried in unison.

"I'll see you later then. I'm sure Lida will have something delicious prepared."

Kassi continued the lessons. When the scents of roasting fish and root vegetables began to distract them, Kassi sent her nieces to wash and change into cleaner chitons before the meal, and she made her way into the triclinium.

The couches were rearranged so that two sides had a couch

parallel to the table twice a week, when Pappa encouraged—his word for required—his three children and their families to join him for the evening meal, a habit he'd begun after Mamma died.

Kassi sat next to her sisters-in-law. Her nieces occupied the other bench, Argos and her other brother Kadmos reclined on one couch, and Pappa occupied the remaining one.

Lida entered the room followed by two other slaves, each carrying a large stone platter piled high with food—fish covered with goat cheese, turnips, carrots, artichokes, and stacks of bread made of soft wheat flour. They set the steaming platters at each end of the table.

Kadmos's wife Eirene put her hand around Penelope's as the girl reached for a chunk of fish. "It's not a contest. There's plenty for everyone."

Penelope scowled but relented.

Kassi helped the girls put several pieces of fish and vegetables on the small glass plates before them before taking some for herself.

Argos washed down several bites with wine. "Still going to that Jewish thing?" He stared at Kassi as he reached for more.

She squashed her immediate reaction and instead smiled sweetly. "I go to the synagogue on the last day of the week. I find it … uplifting."

"Uplifting? In what sense?" asked Eirene.

"In the sense that there is one wise and benevolent Deity and not dozens who have little control over themselves, let alone what happens in this world. A God who loves and cares for His creation and—"

"Don't be ridiculous." Argos scoffed and stuffed a huge piece of turnip in his mouth. "There can't be only one. How could one god be in control of everything?" He spoke around a mouthful of food.

"The Greeks are the wisest people on earth," Kadmos spoke before she could answer. "Wiser than the Jews who can't even govern themselves. Why in the world would we do anything they do?"

Kassi sipped honeyed wine, deciding how best to answer. "We've been conquered by Rome just as they have."

"And does this benevolent deity hold himself above the emperor?" Disdain dripped from Pappa's voice as he spoke to her from the far end of the table.

"The emperor is only a man." Although she'd steeled herself against the coming onslaught, she flinched as Pappa slammed the table with his fist.

"Silence!" He glared at each of them in turn. "This talk is treasonous. I'll not hear any more!"

She should have known the conversation would end like this. It always did when the subject of the synagogue arose.

And Argos delighted in bringing it up.

6

Commit to the Lord whatever you do,
and he will establish your plans.

— PROVERBS 16.3

IF SHE WENT THROUGH WITH THIS—IT WOULD CHANGE EVERYTHING. How everybody—especially Pappa and her brothers—saw her, thought about her. And she wasn't sure it would even work.

Kassandra studied the massive warehouse that occupied the corner of the cardo and the Via Regia. Her heart raced as she crossed the threshold into a dreary, cut-stone building, leaving Mannus waiting at the entrance. One sandaled foot hit the floor, sending clouds of dust billowing around her ankles. Sunlight poured through a row of windows set above, painting shimmering rectangles on marble tiles. She drew fingers along walls that rose to the height of her shoulders, dividing each half of the building into eight equal stalls, with a wide center aisle.

"It's perfect." She'd tried to keep her joy from showing on her face, but had she succeeded?

The man beside her grimaced, lines appearing over his thick brows. His hollow cheeks and pale skin might lead her to think he was starving, though she knew he was quite wealthy.

"Perfect? It's filthy. It's been abandoned for years." He slid his sandal along the floor. "There's still chaff all over. I'd given up trying to sell it. What do you intend to do in an abandoned granary?"

"Do you need to know the answer to that question in order to complete the sale?"

"No, but—"

She raised her head, her chin jutted out. "Then let us proceed."

He pulled out an abacus, sending colorful beads scurrying up and down metal rods with stick-thin fingers. Click-click-click. "Four thousand *drachmae*."

Had her extensive research let her down? She doubted it. "That's more than twice what it's worth."

"No, I don't think so." He shook his head but refused to meet her eyes.

She would not let him ruin her plan. "Yes, it is."

He shrugged. "That is my price." He tucked the abacus under his arm and folded his hands in front of his body, standing as tall as he could, which wasn't much taller than she was.

Her obvious satisfaction with the building must have led him to believe he could ask for more than his first offer. She could try to convince him that since no one else wanted it, he should be happy to sell it to her at his original price.

Or she could take the fast and easy way.

She glanced at Mannus, keeping vigil at the door. She groaned silently, but she hadn't the patience to do otherwise.

Kassi placed one finger over pursed lips. "Perhaps I should have brought Pappa with me."

He nodded sagely. "Indeed. Women simply do not have the head for business."

She released an exaggerated sigh, gesturing loosely toward the north. "Very well then, let us go to him. He's at the council house."

"The coun…" He frowned. "Why would we go there?"

"Oh, didn't I mention? My pater is Secundus."

All color drained from his face. "Secundus?"

She feigned surprise. "Yes. Do you know him?" Of course he did. Everyone knew the chief politarch.

He waved a hand. "No, no. We needn't bother him." His hands shaking, he worked the abacus once again. "Is one thousand nine hundred acceptable?"

"Excellent." She retrieved a roll piece of parchment that had been tucked in her sash. "Here is your bill of exchange. It's already made out for the proper amount."

He accepted the document, turning it over and squinting at it. "How did you know …?"

"I've talked to many, many dealers in the last few days, and I have visited every empty building within the city's walls. That is what this building is worth and all I was willing to pay."

"And how do I know this will be honored?"

She raised her brows. "Do I need to remind you of my pater?"

"But this draft is in your name, not his."

"Because it's my money, and I will be the owner, not him."

He grimaced, shaking his head.

"Do you think he would let his name be sullied by a *daughter*? The draft will be honored, I assure you."

"Very well." He left the warehouse.

Kassi hurried out behind him, only glancing at Mannus. "I'll be right back."

He loped behind her as she hurried up the cardo and turned onto a narrow, unpaved street. She'd learned there were empty apartments in this insula from Publius and had given Isa enough coin for a few weeks.

She picked her way around puddles of human waste to the

fourth building on the left, holding her tunic above her ankles to avoid soiling the hem.

She paused at the bottom of the stairs. How did people live like this? The smells wafting from this building and those nearby were nauseating. Her stomach was empty, or what food she had in it would be coming back up.

She climbed to the third floor, then knocked on the door at the end of a long, dark hall.

"Isa?" She called through the door.

"One moment." A voice called from inside, and the older woman toddled out. "What do you want?" She frowned, glancing over Kassi's shoulder at Mannus.

"I have something to show you."

"What?"

"Please come."

"I'm tired."

"Please. It's not far." Kassi slipped her arm through Isa's and headed for the warehouse.

Isa grumbled the entire way.

Kassi opened the double doors.

"This entire building is mine now. I plan to start a pistrinum, and you can work for me baking bread. You'll be paid well, and you will also share the profits."

Isa clapped a hand to her chest, her eyes tearing up. "Are you serious?"

Kassi nodded. "I am."

"But why?"

"I wanted a way for you and other women who have been left alone to feed yourselves and your children without begging or ... whatever else you may be forced to do."

Isa launched herself at Kassi, who stumbled back as she was smothered in a ferocious embrace. Hot tears slithered under the neck of Kassi's tunic as sobs shook the woman's frail body. "You are more like your mamma than I thought." At last, she pulled away and stepped back. "Thank you. I don't know what I would have done. I was so close to ..." She fidgeted with the sash around her waist. "You have saved me."

"Nonsense, Isa. You will save yourself. I'm only giving you an opportunity."

"I'm so sorry for the way I've spoken to you." She swiped away tears from her cheek. "I will pay back every last coin."

"As a woman, I can't legally loan you money," Kassi said. "You owe me nothing. First, we'll get the shop up and running, and then we'll help other women."

"Kyria—"

"I am not your kyria. I never was. I am a friend." She pointed to the scar on Isa's brow. "Maybe not when I did this, though."

Isa smiled softly. "It was an accident. You were so small."

"Big enough to smash a vase when I didn't get my way." She shook her head and chuckled. "I had no idea pottery shards could fly so far."

"It was long ago."

"I have a few legal issues to attend to. It needs a thorough cleaning, but it's soundly built, has lots of light, and is already divided into workspaces. We can start as soon as we get it cleaned up. Do you think you can see to that? Hire a couple others to help you if you need." She reached into her sash once again and retrieved a silver coin. "Buy whatever you need."

"Cleaning is one thing I am particularly good at." Isa grinned and accepted the *denarius*. "This will be shining like the full moon sooner than you can imagine." She hurried away.

Kassi scanned the building once more and sucked in a long, slow breath.

Mannus appeared at her side. "Are you sure you want to do this, kyria?"

"I am. Why? Do you not approve?" She knew what his answer would be before he spoke.

He pursed his lips. "Actually, I do."

Kassi opened her mouth, but no words came out. "You- you do?"

He nodded. "It's nice—shocking, but nice—to see anyone from the ano poli care about someone who needs a little help. Let alone do anything about it."

She'd had no idea he felt that way. Then again, why would she? They'd never spoken about anything other than her plans and his orders to accompany her.

His face paled and he stepped back. "Kyria, I beg your forgiveness. I have taken a liberty not mine to take." He bowed his head and stared at the floor.

She laid a hand on his shoulder. "No, Mannus. I'm the one who should ask your forgiveness. I've been as selfish as the rest of us."

He raised his head. "Not quite, kyria." A grin flitted across his face. "You've always had a kind heart."

"I'm glad you think so, because I'm going to need your help to make this work."

As JASON STUDIED the wax tablets spread on several couches that Ari had dragged into the tablinum, despair settled on him like a cloak. The financial records were far more disorganized than he'd realized. "How did you make any sense of this?"

Ari laughed. "It's actually not as bad as it looks."

Hope poked through Jason's distress.

Ari gestured to the shelf with *codices* lined up neatly. "It seems she started a new book each year. They go back to when they first started. Look here." He pulled a *codex* from a shelf, wrapping his fingers around the stack of parchments sewn together on one edge. "It seems that once each order was fulfilled, she copied all the relevant details from a tablet into here and had the buyer sign for it." He pulled back the thin wooden cover and pointed to a line in the middle of a page. "Twelve glass platters, one cubit long by one-half cubit wide, colorless. For Titos the teacher. Nine drachmae."

A scrawled name occupied the margin.

Jason studied the page. "This entry is from three months ago. I remember the order."

Ari replaced the codex and then bent to touch a stack of tablets. "These are all completed orders. They aren't for large amounts, and they're all from the last few months. They've all been recorded and signed for, and I think you can erase them."

Jason nodded.

He tapped a small stack of parchments on the desk. "I also found a few contracts. These are for unusually large or expensive orders, or for products they wouldn't be able to sell if the customer never collected and paid. It seems some of these were even recorded by the *agoranomos*."

"Really?" A surprising revelation. Abba always seemed so trusting. Perhaps he'd been cheated. Or perhaps Imma insisted he involve the market overseer.

Ari pointed to the bottom of the page. "See the stamp next to this signature? Only a few were recorded."

"But no surprises."

Ari winced. "There *is* one."

Oh, no. Jason held his breath. "What?"

Ari pulled a piece of parchment from the stack. "There is one order that hasn't been completed, and it's quite large. And a copy was deposited with the agoranomos, so you'll have to be careful to follow every detail."

"How large? Can I fill it in time?"

"You tell me. This is for Damianos."

"The son of the aide to the governor?"

Ari nodded. "He wants two thousand drinking cups to celebrate the feast of Dionysos. Not to mention the opening of his new bathhouse which, I am sure not coincidentally, is the first day of the feast."

Jason's heart sank. "Two thousand?" His parents had either

forgotten or didn't have time to tell him of this order. "For how much?"

"Three hundred drachmae."

Twice as much as the price of simple, unadorned cups. "By when?"

"The festival starts on winter solstice, the seventh day of Poseidon. He wants them two days before, but that day is Shabbat—I checked—so you'll need to have them finished three days before—the fourth."

Jason paced. He'd already lost over a week due to his parents' deaths and another week for Ari to review the books. Not counting tomorrow or the next day—Shabbat—he had thirty-two days.

"What is the date on this contract?"

Ari glanced at the top of the parchment. "Two weeks ago."

Two weeks. Why had they said nothing? Of course, with two experienced artisans as well as Imma, there would have been no problem. No reason to worry. They evidently had wanted to finish the Amphipolis order before starting on this one.

"Can you do it?" Ari asked.

Jason ran through the calculations in his head. "I can produce about seventy in a day this time of year, maybe eighty. If I push, and nothing goes wrong, I can do it, but only with the help of an apprentice." He dropped onto a bench next to the parchments. "Or perhaps I should do as Yoel suggests and sell the shop."

"Oh, Jase, no. You can't."

He shrugged. "I'd rather not, but can I keep it?" He sat. "Tell me more about what's in the contract."

Ari picked up the parchment. "What do you want to know?"

"Any details that will let me know if I can do this."

"All right, two thousand drinking cups, at least two days before the first day of the festival..." His voice trailed off as he skimmed the document. "I don't see any other specifics."

"Any mention of color?"

Ari searched the page. "I don't see that either."

"Does it say anything about how they are to be made?"

"What do you mean?"

"Does it mention a mold, either that I can use one or I can't?"

"Ummm ... no. It states two thousand cups, all the same size, all with 'Dionysos god of wine' on them."

"Doesn't say free blown?'

Ari shook his head.

"Does it say what size?"

Ari pursed his lips as he poured over the text once more. "I don't see size mentioned."

"Good. Very good. With a mold, it goes much faster. If we have one already. But I absolutely must have an apprentice." He rubbed the back of his neck. "Anything about the delivery, other than the date?"

"All must be delivered at the same time two days before the festival, at the bathhouse."

"I have to find some space to store them?" He groaned. "I'll figure that out later."

"Good." Had Abba discussed size and color with Damianos? At any rate, none of those details were in the contract. "I need to see if he created a mold already. If not, that could add several days to the process."

"There is one more thing." Ari grimaced.

Jason knew that face. It could only be bad. He didn't even want to ask. "What?"

"Damianos has written a *very* substantial penalty into the contract if you don't fulfill the order in every detail or if it is delivered late."

He swallowed. "How much?"

"Twice the amount of the contract."

All the air left his lungs.

What should he do? He could try to sell the shop with the contract in hand, but he was the only glassblower in Thessalonike, and it was doubtful he could find anyone in a nearby city willing to take on such an obligation. Could he sell and pay the penalty from the proceeds? Would he make enough to pay the penalty, let alone have anything left?

Who knew?

All he did know was that he couldn't fail.

7

*As was his custom, Paul went into the synagogue, and on three
Sabbath days he reasoned with them from the Scriptures ...*

— ACTS 17.2

AS THE SUN BEGAN ITS DAILY UPWARD JOURNEY, YOEL STRODE ACROSS
the courtyard and kicked off his sandals before entering the simple
structure that roofed the *mikveh*. Cold had saturated the marble tiles
of the ritual pool during the long night, and he jerked his bare foot
back for a moment. Stepping again, more carefully, onto the hard
floor, he moved to the edge and paused at the top of the stairs. He
slipped the cloak from his shoulders, and the early morning breeze
kissed his skin. Bones creaking, he descended the narrow stairs,
slowly immersing himself in the chilled water. He bent his knees,
allowing the water to cover his head before straightening.

He slid his hand down his face, wiping water from his eyes.
"Blessed are you, Eternal God, King of the universe, who has sancti-

fied us with Your commandments and has commanded us concerning immersion."

He dipped under the water twice more and then spoke the second blessing. "Blessed is the Eternal, the God of all creation, who has blessed me with life, sustained me, and enabled me to reach this moment." He turned and climbed to the top, then reached for the clean towel he'd brought with him.

After he dried and donned a fresh tunic, he stepped into his sandals and headed toward his house.

His chest swelled as he sucked in the frigid air. It couldn't be from pride, as pride was a sin against Adonai. No, it had to be joy. Yoel lived for Shabbat. The whole community coming together in the synagogue, the teachings of the elders, and most of all, the reading of the sacred texts. He relished hearing the stories of the patriarchs and their wives—Abraham and Sarah, Isaac and Rebekah, Jacob and Rachel. He loved watching the faces of children hearing the stories for the first time, excited to hear a bit more each week.

He closed the door quietly behind him as he entered his home. The only thing that made other days a bit more enjoyable than Shabbat was the smell of fresh bread. Forbidden to cook, Leah could only offer yesterday's bread, hard cheese, and fruit—fresh when in season and dried when not.

He entered the triclinium behind his wife, who carried a plate of the last of the season's fresh pears and dried cherries.

"Shalom, *ahuva*." She placed a quick kiss on his cheek.

Yoel recoiled and glanced around, making sure Paulos had not seen. "I love you too, beloved." He dropped onto the center couch and reclined on his left arm.

Leah shook her head. "No one is in here. I've learned that lesson well. I would never embarrass you."

"Yoel, I thought I heard you come in." Paulos entered and sat on the couch to the right of Yoel's while Silas and Timotheos took the couch to his left.

Yoel studied the visitors, their hair dry.

Silas and Timotheos he could perhaps excuse, but had the Pharisee not immersed yet? Yoel had pointed the mikveh out to Paulos the night he arrived, but perhaps the man had forgotten. "The mikveh is across the courtyard should you need to use it." Yoel gestured in the bath's general direction.

Paulos smiled and nodded. "Todah."

Yoel closed his eyes and recited the blessing over the simple meal.

"Amen." Paulos reclined and reached for a round of flat bread. "Thank you, Leah. This looks delicious, even the day after." He ripped the bread in two, making no move to leave.

Yoel smiled to hide his confusion. "If you eat quickly, you'll still have time to immerse before we need to leave."

Again, Paulos nodded. "That won't be necessary, but todah."

Strictly speaking, it wasn't. It was only *required* before the holy feasts, but most of the men in the synagogue immersed at least once a month. Why would a Pharisee decide it was not important? Did he know something the Jews of Makedonia didn't?

"What is your reading this morning?" asked Timotheos.

"Today we will be hearing the story of Jacob," answered Yoel.

"One of my favorites." Paulos said. "But they're all my favorites."

"The reading of the prophet should be ..." His mind blanked. How could he forget such a thing?

"Isaiah, no?" Paulos said.

"Yes, Isaiah." Yoel cleared his throat. "Would you like to read to us from the writings of the prophet and give us a lesson? I am the synagogue leader, after all. It is my decision."

Paulos nodded. "I would be honored, my friend. Now if you'll excuse me, I'll ready myself for the synagogue." He rose. "Leah, thank you once again for the meal."

Paulos disappeared into the guest chamber while his words echoed in Yoel's ears. *My friend.* If only the elders had heard this exalted and learned man address him this way.

Moments later, Paulos emerged dressed in the clothes of a Pharisee. The fringed prayer shawl was quite thin, and the prayer boxes strapped to his arm and forehead were rather small. Yoel's were at least twice that size, maybe larger, but traveling with a heavy shawl and cumbersome boxes might be difficult for a man Paulos's age.

Yoel led the visitors across the courtyard to the synagogue. The walk was short but was still in full view of everyone in the community. He'd timed their entrance to be a little later than usual, although still well before service started, so all the faithful would notice him escorting the Pharisee.

Yoel's heart pounded in his ears as he made his way to the building. He struggled to keep from breaking out in a huge grin. Thank Adonai He had sent Paulos to him!

This could only increase his standing in the synagogue and solidify his position as archisynagogos.

JASON NEARED THE SYNAGOGUE, the dull gray sky a perfect reflection of his mood.

Around the entrance, men surrounded Yoel and the Pharisee, studying and judging.

Yoel stood next to Paulos, shoulders back, basking in reflected praise. He wore a smug smile, as if he himself had tracked down Paulos and brought him to Thessalonike.

No matter. Jason didn't need—or want—any praise for bringing them here. They would likely only cause trouble. He eyed Paulos for a long moment. He'd heard about Pharisees all his life, but this man seemed less awe-inspiring than Yoel had described them.

Probably used to being overlooked, Timotheos and Silas hovered to the side. How tiring must it get? Why did they put up with it?

Dodah joined Jason, her presence cooling his anger. "He knows the scriptures like his own name. I think you'll like him."

He shrugged. "We'll see."

Watching the two of them, Jason tried to separate Paulos from his dodh in his mind, but it was difficult. He slipped inside and waited, longing to be anywhere else.

Yoel led his guests inside and seated them beside him, in a place of honor on the front row. The elders claimed their seats on the other side of the room.

When the prayers and the readings from the books of Moses and the Law were completed, Paulos rose, walked to the center of the room, and stood before the holy scrolls lying on the table. He picked one up and found the proper section.

"But you, Israel, my servant, Jacob, whom I have chosen,

you descendants of Abraham my friend,

I took you from the ends of the earth, from its farthest corners I called you.

I said, 'You are my servant;' I have chosen you and have not rejected you.

So do not fear, for I am with you; do not be dismayed, for I am your God.

I will strengthen you and help you; I will uphold you with my righteous right hand."

Paulos replaced the scroll on the table. "My brothers, my fellow Israelites." He turned as he scanned the room, pausing at the section where the Greek God-fearers sat. He smiled, spreading his hands toward them as if embracing them. "And you who fear the only true God along with us, welcome, and listen."

Jason sat straighter. *Welcome?* That cannot be what Yoel expected. The leadership tolerated the Greeks only because it earned them favor with the city officials.

And filled the treasury.

Following custom, Paulos sat to begin his lesson. "Long ago, the living God chose, from all the peoples and nations on the earth, our ancestors, Abraham, Isaac, and Jacob, and redeemed them."

That sounded more like the usual lessons. The elders were

forever reminding the Greeks they were not part of the chosen.

"He led us to Egypt to avoid the famine, and while we were there, he made a single family into a strong nation. Centuries later, Egypt feared that very strength and made us slaves. But Adonai remained faithful. He kept His promises, and in a great show of His power, He led us out of Egypt laden with gifts. He parted the sea so we could walk on dry land. He defeated the Amalekites and brought water from a rock.

"But after all that, when we stood on the border of the promised land, instead of trusting Him, we feared the enemy, even when Adonai vowed to go before us into battle. We refused to obey, and for forty years He endured our grumbling in the wilderness. But again, He remained faithful, and He gave us the land He had vowed to give to Abraham and his descendants as an inheritance."

Jason looked at the faces of his fellow Jews, expectant and proud as they listened to the promises Jason had heard since he took his first steps. One day, perhaps soon, Adonai would send the long-awaited *Mashiach* who would again free them from oppression and return them to their homeland, where Israel would finally be the great nation it should be.

"Four hundred and fifty years later, again we rebelled," Paulos continued. "We refused to accept Adonai as our ruler and demanded a human leader, so He gave us judges. We then demanded a king to be like the other nations, and God gave us Shaul son of Kish, who was like me, a man of the tribe of Benjamin, and who reigned for forty years."

Yoel sat up a bit straighter at the mention of their shared heritage. He never let anyone forget he was a Benjamite, and doubtless he reasoned this would solidify his connection to Paulos.

"When Adonai removed Shaul, he chose not a warrior but an unknown shepherd boy to be the next king. Adonai said of him, 'I have found David to be a man after My heart, who will carry out all My wishes.' But David, too, strayed from God's plan, and the kingdom ruptured. Because we, as humans, will always fail."

Paulos locked eyes with Jason. "The good news is, Adonai will never fail. He is always faithful; he always keeps His promises. He will *never* leave us."

Pretty big promise. But why did Paulos act like he was speaking personally to Jason? Could he count on Adonai always being there?

He'd led the Israelites out of Egypt only after over four hundred years of slavery. And then He sentenced them to forty years in the wilderness. How could He allow the Assyrians and the Babylonians —let alone the hated Romans—and whoever else to conquer His chosen people and invade His holy city?

Where had He been when Abba and Imma were killed?

His mouth soured. How could Jason ever depend on One so fickle? And if he couldn't count on Him, why waste his time hearing His words?

Jason bolted upright and slipped out, ignoring the questioning stares of everyone in the room, including his dodh and dodah.

He could not stay one moment longer.

———

KASSI HADN'T SEEN her building since putting Isa in charge of cleaning it and arranging for it to be painted. Since it was on the way home from synagogue, she may as well check on it. She pressed a hand over her mouth to stifle the small gasp as she approached. The wall facing the street had been painted a bright yellow, and the double wooden doors had been oiled and polished to a shine.

She pulled open a door and stepped inside. Isa had done a marvelous job. The tile floors sparkled in the morning sun. The cobwebs in the corners and the dust on the half-walls had disappeared without a trace. The walls were now a bright blue.

"Oooohh."

Kassi spun to face the door where Isa stood with her hands over cheeks, then hurried to the entrance. "Are you all right?"

She took one step inside. "It's so beautiful! It's like a palace." She continued down the aisle, spinning as she walked.

Kassi followed. It was hardly a palace, but perhaps in Isa's view

...

"And what's this?" Isa neared a large object in the center of the far wall. Shaped like an enormous beehive, a bread oven sat on a platform of bricks, bringing the opening to about waist high. The hollow platform was filled with firewood.

Isa brought one finger near the edge, not quite touching it. "Th-this wasn't here before."

"Oh, they finished already." Kassi ran her hand over the top, the rough bricks scraping her skin. "I had it built. It should be big enough to bake twelve loaves at once."

"Why?"

"I hope to have more women working here." She put her arm around Isa's shoulders and steered her to the center of the aisle, gesturing to the different stalls. "Since you're the first one here, you get first choice of your working space."

Isa eyed each of the twelve stalls. "The one closest to the oven."

"Good choice." Kassi laughed. "How about we start tomorrow?"

She nodded.

"I'm going to give you a key."

"You trust me with a key?"

"Pappa trusted you with my meter. I can trust you with a building."

Isa blinked away tears.

"I have to take care of a few more things, so I'll see you tomorrow, around the first hour?"

Isa nodded.

Kassi needed to make sure the bakery could run without her continual presence, and she had a lot to do to make that happen. Finding a steady source of flour was at the top of her list. She moved outside. "Mannus, we need to find the mill."

"Yes, kyria. It is on the east wall. I'll lead you."

She followed him toward the wall. The only information she

had about its location was that it needed the water from the aqueduct and that the aqueduct crossed over the wall north of the Via Olympos.

It must be a sizable building, big enough to hold a waterwheel. She searched the buildings ahead of her as she quickened her steps to keep up with Mannus.

The mill came into view and the sound of falling water ahead grew louder. An enormous pipe dumped its liquid cargo into a channel, which turned a winged wheel wider than she was tall, which then spun a couple gears that rotated a pair of horizontal millstones, one atop the other. The bottom remained stationary while the upper mill turned, grinding barley grains into flour.

"Watch it too long, and it'll lull you to sleep."

Beside her, a man gazed at the flour that spilled from a small opening under the bottom stone.

"Are you the miller?"

"I am."

"I need flour. I'm going to need a lot of flour, every day."

"How much?"

"I'm not sure yet. How about a *modius*?"

"Every week?"

"Every day."

"Wha...?" He laughed. "What are you going to do with a modius a day?"

"Bake bread."

He scoffed. "Twenty loaves? You can't bake twenty loaves a day."

His attitude was becoming annoying. "I can if I have several people working. I own a pistrinum."

"I don't know of any bakery around here."

"I just bought it. We open tomorrow."

"But twenty?" He let out a low whistle. "You must have a lot of slaves."

"Not slaves."

He stared at her, uncomprehending.

She remained silent. She didn't need to explain anything to him.

He shrugged. "If you say so."

"I need it every day, and I need it delivered."

He crossed his arms and smiled. "I don't deliver."

His condescending attitude irritated her. "Then I'll find another miller." She chuckled. "You're giving up a lot of profit for a short walk."

"I'll need to be working all day if you want that much. I might even need to add another set of millstones. I don't have time to deliver."

There were other millers, but this one was said to sell the best flour. "Within the week, I will have someone come pick it up each morning. But for the next several days, I need it delivered."

"All right. You'll have your first bag in two days."

"Tomorrow."

He shook his head. "I have many other orders…"

"I'll take half a modius every day this week. From then on, I need it all, and I need it first thing in the morning. And soon, I will likely need much more."

"I'm not sure I can do that. I am only one man. And I can't afford to hire a helper."

She could easily hire someone to pick it up, or … "What if I found you someone to help? If I can find you a boy who needs a job, you can pay him a *sestertius* a day—a quarter of the daily wage—for the first half year. Then see what he's worth to you."

"You'll send someone?"

"I'll send him until I find someone else." She pointed a thumb at Mannus.

The miller thought a moment before he nodded. "I'll have tomorrow's ready in the morning."

"At the second hour, please. It's the bright yellow building on the Via Regia."

One task completed, but another added. Where would she find a boy to work for the miller?

8

All hard work brings a profit, but mere talk leads only to poverty.

— PROVERBS 14.23

KASSI OPENED THE DOOR TO HER CHAMBER TO SEE MANNUS WAITING patiently.

She ran through the task that faced her as they made their way down the cardo to the pistrinum. Worktables for each stall were being delivered within the hour. She still needed at least oil and salt to begin. Maybe olives. Nuts and fruit and seeds could come later.

As they neared the Via Regia, she gestured down the wide road. "Mannus, why don't you go get the flour?"

"You will be alone."

She laughed and pointed to Publius's popina on her right. "I'm going to the agora. The bakery is right across the street." She pointed to the bright yellow building on her left.

She reached the agora and approached the cardo side of the hot shop.

"Kassi, what are you doing here at this hour?" He glanced over her shoulder. "And where is your guard?"

She chuckled. "It's a long story. And he's not a guard."

He grinned. "If you say so. What can I get for you?"

"I need an amphora of olive oil and olives, and a bag of salt."

He moved to the stall beside the popina. "Don't you have a slave buy what you need?"

"It's not for the house. See that building? Two doors down?"

"The yellow one? It's hard to miss." He laughed.

"It's mine."

His smile disappeared and a wince took its place. "Oh, Kassi, I'm sorry—"

"Don't worry about it. It is a little ..." How should she describe it?

"Bright?"

She laughed. "Yes. I wasn't planning on it being quite this yellow, but maybe it will help bring customers, out of curiosity if nothing else."

"Customers?"

"I'm opening a pistrinum. Today. Can you deliver what I need? Quickly?"

"Of course. I'll have it to you in moments."

"Perfect." She hurried across the cardo. The double doors weren't open yet, but since they had no bread, it didn't matter.

She pulled one heavy door ajar and peered inside but saw no one. Where was Isa? She strode to the back of the building near the oven. In the stall, Isa comforted a woman, brushing tears from her cheeks. Three boys hovered nearby. All four—and their tunics—were desperately in need of washing. She was perhaps ten years older than Kassi, at least judging by the ages of her children. She looked far older, however. How hard had her life been?

"Isa, who's this?"

"This is my sister's daughter, Thalia. She is freeborn."

They shared the same eyes, but otherwise they looked nothing alike. Perhaps she took after her pater.

"Her husband died, and my sister is also gone," Isa said. "Thalia has nowhere to live, and no way to feed herself and her children."

Kassi rested a hand on the woman's back. "Thalia, I'm so sorry." This was the plan all along—to help as many women as she could —but Kassi hadn't expected it to start before she'd even opened. "I can't offer you a place to live, but you can work here with Isa."

Isa wrapped her arm around Thalia's waist. "She's staying with me."

"Will the landlord charge you more rent?"

"I don't think so," said Isa.

"Good." Kassi's eyes moved to the boys. "And these are your children?"

The woman froze, eyes full of fear. "I- I didn't know where else to take them."

The youngest grabbed his imma's legs and buried his face in her tunic.

"No, it's fine. They're welcome here."

"My oldest boy, Melas, is twelve, and Gaius is ten." She placed her head on the youngest. "Pheres is five. They'll be no trouble. I promise you."

The boys appeared to be younger than the woman claimed but may have only been small for their age. "I'm sure they won't. Have you eaten lately?"

She shook her head.

"When did you eat last?"

"Two days ago."

Kassi suppressed a gasp, and her throat constricted. Two days? What to do first? Baths, clothes, food? *Think, Kassi.*

Although they were undoubtedly hungry, a bath and some clean clothes would allow then to relax and enjoy a meal. "Let's see ... Isa, why don't you take them to the agora and get them new tunics?

They can take them to the baths while you get some food." Kassi offered each woman some coins.

Thalia's cheeks turned as red as Lida's pomegranates. "Oh, no, kyria. I would never ask you to do that." She backed away, shaking her head.

"You didn't ask." She gave the coins to Isa instead. "Oil and salt here will be soon, and Mannus is bringing flour. I'll stay here and get the fire going, so as soon as we have everything we can start. All right?"

"We won't be long." Isa steered Thalia toward the double doors.

After only a few steps, Thalia turned and rushed back. She grabbed Kassi's hands and kissed them. "Eucharisto." She repeated the word over and over before hurrying to catch up with Isa.

Kassi's throat burned and she blinked to avoid crying. Thalia had lost her husband, her home, her only means of support.

And now she was depending on Kassi.

Could she live up to the woman's expectations?

JASON'S STOMACH CHURNED. Entering Abba's shop would be no easier than returning home for the first time.

He hadn't wanted to return to an empty house either, but within a few days it felt like home again. Perhaps it would be the same with the shop.

He closed the door behind him and locked it, then stepped onto the via. Columns still lined the stone-paved Via Regia. Though not as opulent as the Via Olympos, it was wide, paved, and clean. At the corner he turned onto the road that paralleled the eastern wall.

The houses grew larger and more lavish the farther north he traveled, and within a few moments he passed under the arch of the gate and stepped onto a rough dirt path.

He soon found himself at the entrance to the craftsman's village that was home to all the artisans that used flame—potters, glassworkers, metalworkers. A river bounded the forest to the north, giving them easy access to water and plenty of wood.

Adonai, give me strength.

At the door to the shop, he hesitated and recited the psalm he'd heard Abba say every morning of his life. "This is the day Adonai has made; we will rejoice and be glad in it."

A heavy sigh escaped him. There was little to rejoice over.

He opened the door. The shop was at once familiar and strange, the stillness stifling.

Oh, to hear Abba's gentle voice and the roar of the fire. To once more watch perspiration drip down Abba's face and to taste the salt of his own sweat on his lips. His throat tightened at the thought that he'd never again stand across from Abba as they inflated bubbles of glass, occasionally dissolving into laughter as a competition ensued over who could create the largest bubble. Invariably both fragile globes shattered, and Jason was left to crawl on his hands and knees gathering all the shards so they could be melted again. Abba hated waste.

It was always worth it.

He balled his hands into fists, pushed his shoulders back, and entered. The shop was twice as long as it was wide, and only the perimeter was roofed to allow heat and smoke to escape.

On the far wall, the master furnace, used to melt the raw glass chunks, stood abandoned, cold, and silent. A smaller furnace, used to slowly cool the hot glass, sat to the left. Shelves ran down both long walls toward the door.

He checked the belly of the oven. Still plenty of wood. He grabbed a fistful of dried grass and pine needles and laid them on top of the partially burned wood, then showered it with sparks from a striker. When one caught, he blew on it until a bright orange flame nestled comfortably among the logs.

He surveyed the room. Abba had been no better organized than Imma, though the disorganized state of the workshop had never bothered Jason before. As with Imma, Abba knew where everything was. If Jason couldn't find it, he had only to ask.

But now he needed to know himself what they... no, what *he* had, where it was, and what was lacking. And since it would take hours for the furnace to grow hot enough to melt glass, he may as well get things organized.

An open crate sat near the door. The harbormaster must have had it delivered the day the visitors arrived. He'd need to thank him later. He knelt and scooped a handful of the unshaped chunks from the basket inside. The familiar clunk-clunk as they filtered through his fingers brought up bittersweet memories of his childhood. He shook off the memories and stood.

Imma had been Abba's first assistant, before he could afford to hire an apprentice. As hot and sweaty as Abba, she would crouch before a low table at his feet, holding molds together while Abba inflated a bubble of glass inside them. She would then pull them apart and inspect them for flaws.

As their business grew, Abba engaged an apprentice, and Imma handled the money and orders. When the apprentice moved on to Apollonia to start his own shop, Jason had taken over.

Jason had completed the formal training, but would he ever be as good as Abba? Would he be able to continue without them?

He would have to—he had no choice. He trudged around the shop, gathering the tools scattered in various places. Blocks, blow-pipes, knives, crimps—he added each to its own kind in baskets on the shelves.

He put away the last tool, a knife, and stepped back. With every tool in its place, the shop looked less lived in.

Less familiar.

It was now his, though, and he preferred order.

The day's remaining sunlight filtered through the trees beyond the village. He had just enough time to sort through the molds before the light failed.

On the shelves along the other wall, clay molds sat scattered among other glass objects—vases, platters, pitchers, some of them quite intricate, of every color and size. Why had Abba never made more of them? They would be worth far more than simple plates and cups. He inspected a platter the color of the sky, ran his fingers over a deep amethyst perfume bottle, then moved the finished objects to one side and molds to the other.

The outsides revealed little of the design. He twisted and turned each mold, reading backwards. If there was a completed glass object made from that mold, he placed them together. Had Abba already made one for Damianos?

After examining twenty or more, he was about to give up. Then he spied one more on the top shelf, pushed to the back. He retrieved the sample. Bunches of grapes with intertwined grapevines—one of Dionysos's most recognizable symbols—covered the body. The words DIONYSOS GOD OF WINE circled the rim. Weight lifted from his shoulders.

There was only one, but he could easily make another in moments.

An answer to a prayer he'd never prayed.

Perhaps this wouldn't be as hard as he'd feared.

———

YOEL LOWERED himself to the backless couch outside his house. He leaned against the wall and surveyed the women and older girls grinding flour, the older boys studying with the community's teachers, and the children chasing butterflies.

He popped an olive in his mouth, rolling it on his tongue and savoring the briny flavor before biting it in half. He couldn't keep the grin on his face from exploding. Except for Jason's hasty departure, yesterday could not have gone better. Paulos was now everyone's favorite, and Yoel had been the one to introduce him.

What other community in Makedonia had a genuine Pharisee as their speaker? None that he knew of.

Now to figure out how to keep him there.

"Shalom, Yoel." Paulos's deep voice as he stepped out of the house drew Yoel's attention.

"And a blessed morning to you, Paulos." He looked behind the visitor. "And the others?"

"They've gone to explore the city. Timos will visit every shop until he wears out Silas, who will find rest in a shaded spot." Paulos chuckled as he sat next to Yoel.

Leah approached with a platter of hot bread in her hands. "Shalom, Paulos. I hope you're hungry." She set the platter between them.

"Todah, Leah."

Yoel reached for a piece but pulled his hand back and blew on his fingers. "I do that every time. Don't know when I'll learn." He grinned. "Leah always saves some flour from the day before Shabbat so she can make me fresh bread early." He gestured to the women grinding grain and laughing. "They won't have any until tonight. I married a wise woman."

"Indeed." Paulos ripped a piece in two and blew on half. "The elders seem to be pleased with your leadership."

"I believe so. They have not told me otherwise."

"Tell me about your community here." Paulos bit into the steaming bread.

Yoel swallowed. "The Jewish community is strong. All—or almost all—the Jews in Thessalonike live here, close to the synagogue." He pointed to the activity before them. "Unlike the Greeks, with their atriums and indoor gardens, we share a single courtyard, as we share our lives. When one is in need, all are in need, so we help each other. We rejoice together. We mourn together."

"That sounds wonderful. I'm pleased you've been able to forge such solid ties among the people."

"I'd like to take the credit, but we have no choice. The Greeks are welcoming enough, but they do not understand the way Adonai commands us to live. We have no choice but to act as one."

"Tell me more about your elders. The chief among them is Micah?"

"Yes, Micah. He is a wise man, a good leader, but his son can be hot-headed."

"That's Lior?"

Yoel raised a brow. "You can tell?"

"Well, for one, he looks exactly like his abba. Two, he seemed protective of Micah while trying hard to please him at the same time."

"Very observant."

Paulos leaned against the wall and crossed one ankle over the other. "I noticed your nephew left early yesterday."

Perhaps too observant.

Burning shame started at the back of Yoel's neck and crawled to his cheeks. He shifted his weight. "I beg your forgiveness. I have no idea why he did that." This was not what he needed. If Paulos lost confidence in the community's leaders, he would never stay.

"It was less than two weeks ago his abba died, yes?"

"What does that have to do with this?" Yoel folded his arms. "It was his abba's lax teaching that led Jason to be so irreverent."

"Jason has suffered a tremendous loss. You must allow him time to grieve."

"I know, but—"

"I haven't heard you mention his abba once since I arrived."

Yoel huffed. How dare he? "Simon was not faithful. He embraced many of the ways of our neighbors."

"And that means you cannot mourn him?"

Yoel bristled. Paulos may be a Pharisee and the most learned man he had ever met, but he knew nothing about Yoel's life or his family.

Paulos moved the platter to the ground beside him. He twisted toward Yoel, tucking one foot behind his other knee and leaning his shoulder against the wall. "I met Timos in Lystra. His abba had been dead for several years, and he too was angry, even after so long. It's a troublesome thing for a boy to grow up without his abba. It's also hard for a young man to lose his abba just as he becomes a man himself. Jason's doing the best he can, I think."

If Paulos had seen him at dinner last week, he might not think so. "What do you suggest I do?"

"Jason needs to know you mourn Simon. He's only heard you criticize your brother. Let him know you hurt with him and that you'll try to help him however you can."

"I don't know what I can do. I can't help him in his business, and I can't help him at home. He doesn't live in the community."

"Let him know Simon was important to you, that *he's* important to you." He rose. "I think I'll go meet those boys and see how their studies are progressing."

Yoel pushed down a rising sense of fear. He needed to make sure Paulos wasn't displeased with him, but he couldn't let Jason think he approved of his abominable behavior.

He'd have to think of something before Shabbat dinner came around again, because there was no way he was going to let Jason's faithlessness reflect badly on him.

9

Whatever your hand finds to do, do it with all your might...

— ECCLESIASTES 9.10A

MIDDAY SUNSHINE JOINED WITH THE HEAT FROM THE OVEN, WARMING the pistrinum to an uncomfortable temperature—something Kassi had not planned for. Perhaps they needed to remove the glass from the long, narrow windows that sat below the roofline.

The center table was piled high with loaves of all kinds—flat, leavened, braided, round—and the scents of burning wood and baking bread filled the building. Kassi inspected a few of the loaves, breaking off a chunk of one to taste it. Delicious. They were off to a promising start.

One of the wooden doors had swung closed. She searched the ground for a rock or something else heavy enough to prop it open but was interrupted by Thalia's son, a heavy bag of flour balanced on his shoulder. Both he and his meter were thrilled he was to work for the miller. Thalia could use the extra money, and Melas was just happy to be away from so many women.

Bending to shove a rock under the door, she pointed toward the back. "Thank you, Melas. You can put it against the wall by the oven."

"I know. You already told me." He scowled over his shoulder.

"Melas." Thalia marched toward her son. "You will apologize. Now."

"Yes, Mamma." He looked over his shoulder. "I'm sorry." His voice was strident, but his eyes showed pain.

"Thank you," Kassi said.

"Can I go?"

"Of course."

Thalia neared her. "I'm so sorry. He's just upset at … at everything."

"Don't worry. I understand." Kassi patted her hand.

But how could she understand? She'd lost her meter, but he'd lost everything—his father, his home, his education, his friends … and he was handling it better than she would have at his age. "It's all right. We're all learning some—"

The women quickly moved to one side as the miller stormed into the bakery, the collar of Thalia's middle son clamped in his meaty fist. He shoved Gaius so hard that his knees slammed to the floor.

"No!" Thalia dropped to the floor beside him.

Hands on hips, she faced the miller. "What are you doing?"

The miller glared at her. "I've told him several times already to stay away from the mill. He keeps hanging around, scaring away my customers."

"Scaring them away? How? He's a child!"

"He skulks around, staring, not talking … and now he's spilled an amphora of flour. A whole amphora! It's not free. And *you* will pay for it."

"You still can't hurt him."

"I can do as I please. Who will stop me? You?" He jabbed a pudgy finger into her shoulder.

Breath coming faster, Kassi pushed his hand away and pointed to the door. "Get out of my building. Now."

He drew closer, his sandals a hand's breadth from hers. "*Your* building? Don't you mean your husband's, or your pater's? Perhaps I should tell him how well you take care of his business." He sneered.

She pulled her shoulders up, hoping to appear a bit taller. "It's *my* building. Bought with my money. But you're welcome to talk to my pater if you feel it necessary. He's the chief politarch."

The vendor's face blanched. His plan of attack stymied, he sputtered and fumed. "Keep him away from my mill. Or the brother loses his job, and you lose your flour." He stomped out of the bakery.

Kassi knelt. "Gaius, are you all right? Let me see your knee."

He shoved her hand away. "It's fine. I'm not hurt."

Thalia wrapped her arms around him.

He rested his head against her chest. "I'm sorry, Mamma."

"What were you doing at the mill?" Kassi asked.

He drew the back of his hand under his nose. "Just watching. I like watching the grain pour in the hole, get crushed between the stones, and come out as flour."

Thalia frowned. "That sounds boring. Why do you want to watch that?"

Gaius shrugged. "I don't know. I just do."

Kassi sat, tucking her feet beneath her. "What do you like about it?"

He paused, his brows knitting together. "I like watching him make something. He starts with barley kernels and ends up with flour. And ... never mind."

She touched his other knee. "No. Tell me."

"It's stupid."

"Thoughts can't be stupid. Only actions," Thalia said.

"I want to help. Mamma works so hard. Melas works—even

Pheres helps by sweeping up, and they're both younger than I am." He pouted. "I should be working for the miller. Not Melas."

"You tried, remember? You couldn't lift the bag. He's younger but stronger. But you're right. We need to find something you can do to help. Is it only making flour you're interested in? Because I don't think he'll let you help him." Kassi grinned.

"Probably not." He returned her smile. "There's a lot I find interesting on the agora. Especially where they make things."

"You like that? Making things?"

He nodded eagerly. "I like seeing one thing turn into another."

"All right. Tomorrow I'll try to find you something to do. Will that make you happy?"

"Happier. Eucharisto, kyria."

"Not kyria. Just Kassi." She rose and peaked outside to be sure the miller had gone.

She'd promised to help, but most vendors taught their own sons, not someone else's. Where would she find something for him?

God of Israel, would You ever help someone like me? Would you help me to help others?

YOEL'S FOOTFALLS bounced off the stone walls as he paced in the empty synagogue. The thoughts that had plagued him for the last two days refused to give him any peace.

How could Jason do this to him? Such a wonderful Shabbat with a visiting Pharisee—that *Yoel* had brought to teach—who delivered a stirring lesson.

Then his own nephew had stormed out in the middle.

And if Paulos brought it up, the elders would have something to say about it.

He ran his fingers down one of the columns. This ancient synagogue, built almost two hundred years ago by Jews who had left Alexandria, had been his life, his family's life. It had been enlarged and renovated several times, but the gathering room remained essentially the same. Men in his family had been synagogue leaders for generations, and now it was his turn, his privilege, to keep it safe, clean, and holy, to ensure the people were taught well, and to watch over the community.

To do that, he needed to make sure his own family was in order. True, Simon lived apart from the community, but he'd supported the synagogue with his presence and his offerings. Yoel had no son of his own, and he'd once hoped Jason would take the position after him. That hope vanished like morning mist when Simon left. Now Yoel would be the last in the line.

He retrieved the oil lamp from its niche nearest the door and blew out the dying flame. Continuing around the perimeter of the room, he extinguished the others one by one.

"Yoel, what are you doing here? I've been looking for you."

Yoel turned at his wife's gentle voice. "Where else would I be?" He returned to his task.

Leah neared him. "What's kept you today? It doesn't take this long to close the synagogue after morning prayers."

"I'm almost done. Are Paulos and his friends at the house?"

"No, but I expect them back for the evening meal." She paused, eyeing him. "I don't suppose you've talked to Jason."

He shook his head. "I can't believe he did that to me."

Her delicate brows furrowed. "Did what to you?"

He threw his arms in the air. "He left. Everyone saw him."

"To you? How was this done *to you*?"

Yoel widened his eyes. "Of course, it was done to me. Who else? He's embarrassed me terribly."

He cringed as Leah put on her scolding face and stalked closer. "Synagogue is about worshiping Adonai, not making you look good."

"I know. I know. But the day we have a Pharisee visit? A student of Gamaliel, no less? Of all days."

"Maybe he had a good reason not to be here. Have you talked to him?"

He dug the toe of his sandal into the floor.

"You haven't, have you?"

"He seemed fine."

"He was not *fine*."

He looked up. "So, he was a little upset."

"Yoel ben Samuel, you know very well he was more than a *little* upset."

Yoel closed his eyes, willing her to finish.

"And you also know he had good reason to be." She waited until he returned her gaze.

Go talk to him, please?" Her voice softened.

"I will."

"Soon?"

"Yes, *ahuvati*. As soon as I finish here." He kissed her cheek before she left him.

Yoel made sure no flame remained burning, then shut the door behind him.

Although he'd never actually visited Simon's shop, he knew vaguely where it was. The walk to the city's eastern gate was shorter than he'd imagined, and he reached the doorway faster than he expected.

What should he say?

"Yoel." Jason's voice caught him off guard. "What are you doing here?"

The second time today he'd been asked that question.

"I came to see you."

Jason leaned a broom against a nearby shelf and folded his arms. "You've never come to see me here. You never came to see Abba either."

He tried to smile. "I'm here now." Yoel glanced around at a wooden crate in the center of the room, shelves filled with tools and glass objects, iron rods leaning in a corner, and furnaces. "What are you working on?"

Jason's shoulders relaxed. "When I was sorting out everything in Abba's office, I found an enormous order. Two thousand drinking cups in three weeks. It's going to be next to impossible to get them all done."

Sounded like something Simon would do. "Why in the world would your abba accept such an order?"

The vein in Jason's jaw bulged for an instant. "Well, at the time, there were two of us. I've also lost almost two weeks. I assume he meant to start when they returned from Amphipolis."

"I would not consider time mourning your abba time 'lost.'" He cringed at Jason's glare. Perhaps not the kindest remark. "I'm sorry. I know what you meant. But you don't need to work *every* day, do you?"

"It's important I finish this order on time."

"The Shabbat is more important, don't you think?"

"I was at service."

"You left early. Did you come here, or did you keep the Shabbat holy, as required?"

Jason closed the distance between them.

Yoel had never noticed how much his eyes were like Simon's—gold specks that flashed when he was angry. "I've never missed service. And I will do my best to attend every Shabbat. But if I do not deliver two thousand cups to Damianos by the fourth of Poseidon, I will have to pay a penalty of twice the amount of the order. I cannot afford that. I would lose the shop and possibly Abba's house."

"I'm sorry about that." But this was Simon's doing, not Yoel's.

Jason raised an eyebrow. "Perhaps you can help."

"How?"

"I need an assistant. Do you know of any boys interested in learning a skill?"

"I could never approve of—let alone encourage—someone else leaving the community."

Jason clenched his teeth. "I'm not taking them to pagan temples. They can still live at home, and I'll teach them a trade they can feed a family with one day."

"Like you can now?"

"How was I or anyone else to know Abba and Imma would both be *murdered?*"

If only Jason had listened two weeks ago. "This is why I told you to sell the shop."

Jason held up one finger. "First, had I sold the shop the day Abba died, we would still owe the penalty." He added another. "Second, you have no say in how I run this shop."

"Your abba is not here, and obviously you need supervision. And there's quite a lot your abba taught you that needs to be undone."

Jason's mouth fell open. "Like what?"

"Like how important it is to keep Shabbat holy."

Jason threw his arms in the air. "What? How can you say that?"

"Your abba never embraced his Jewish heritage. He wanted to be Greek."

"That's not true!" He stormed several paces away.

"He gave you a Greek name, moved out of the community, shaved his beard, and taught you to do the same."

Fire blazed in his eyes as Jason strode to within a hand's breadth of Yoel. "He *never* missed the Shabbat service, and neither have I. *Yet.* He also taught me the Shema and the psalms of David. He recited the three prayers a day and taught them to me. He kept every commandment, and every morning we said the prayers before we picked up a single tool."

Yoel's heart sank to his sandals. "I didn't know that. I apologize."

"There's a lot you don't know." His voice dripped with bitterness.

Yoel was losing control of this conversation. He needed to be able to talk to Jason without the distraction of the shop. "Come to dinner this Shabbat. Your dodah misses seeing you."

"And you don't?"

"Of course I do." He reached to grasp Jason's arm, but he backed away. "Promise you'll come."

"No promises. *If* I have time, *maybe* I'll be there."

Yoel smiled weakly and backed out of the shop.

Had he made things worse?

JASON WAS EXHAUSTED. Yesterday he'd organized the tools and supplies, and now everything was in its place. He'd found a mold, though he still needed to make a copy, and he'd spent today cleaning every corner, every shelf, every tool.

He had everything necessary to begin but help.

What he needed most was to find an assistant he could afford. Making objects from molds required two people. Someone had to hold the mold together while he inflated the glass. There was no way around that.

Yoel had refused to help him find a Jewish boy, and Jason had few contacts in the Greek community. Ari would be in council for the next week or more, but it was doubtful anyone he knew would allow his son to work for a Jewish glassblower.

He closed the shop behind him. His stomach growled, but he had little to eat at home. Perhaps one or two of the vendors in the lower agora would still be open. Twinkling stars dotted the night sky as he crossed under the arch, but instead of taking the road closest to the wall that led home, he walked along the Via Olympos before turning onto the cardo. The scents of roasting fish and meat only made him hungrier.

Those scents disappeared as he walked south, replaced by the smell of lentil or vegetable soup. As he neared the corner of the Via

Regia and the cardo, the smell of fresh bread filled his nose. Someone was up late baking. Thank Adonai.

A few more steps brought the darkened agora into view. He stopped by the hot shop and placed his hand on the counter. Still warm. It hadn't been closed for long. He scanned the market. Not a single lamp burned. The scent of bread must have come from a nearby house.

His stomach would have to wait until morning.

Across the cardo sat a brightly lit, not to mention brightly painted, building. He crossed the road and approached the yellow structure, studying it. Wasn't this the abandoned granary?

His mouth watered as the scent of warm honey wafted from the doors.

Was there food inside? More importantly, would they sell him some?

He crept closer and peered inside. A trio of women, two younger and one much older, laughed around a worktable. Three boys munched on flatbread filled with meat. A wide table occupied the center aisle with a few lonely loaves atop it.

A bakery? He didn't remember a bakery in the artisan district.

A woman strode toward him. She cocked her head and looked him over from head to toe.

He couldn't quite decipher the look on her face—annoyance, disapproval, disbelief?

Finally, her beautiful brown eyes met his gaze. "May I help you?"

"I wanted something to eat."

She glanced toward the agora. "Are the shops all closed?"

He nodded. He'd never known a vendor who hesitated to make a sale. Most of them fought to steal customers from each other.

She was silent for a moment. "Come in. I make a handful of loaves to have first thing in the morning, but we don't have much left this time of day."

"I'm not picky, just hungry."

She handed him a loaf bursting with olives. "Will this do?" Her voice had softened, but she still seemed uneasy at his presence.

The loaf was still warm. He ripped off a bite and ate it. Soft and salty with a crusty outside. "This is delicious. How much?" He held out a handful of coins.

She tucked a wayward lock of hair the color of walnuts behind her ear as she picked out two of the smallest.

"May I have another?" He glanced at the empty stalls as he handed her two more. "Do you work here?"

"I'm the owner." She stepped to the table and grabbed another loaf.

"I'm sorry. I wasn't expecting ... ummm ..." How did he get out of this?

"A woman?" She aimed a glare his way.

He gave her a crooked grin, hoping to deflect her disdain.

She returned to him, her eyes hard. "I am doing nothing illegal. I purchased this building with my own money. It's in my name. And I paid more of my money to have it cleaned and painted and to have an oven built."

He held his free hand up in surrender. "You want to open a bakery? It's fine with me."

"It's not a bakery."

"Oh. I thought ..." He gestured to the back wall. "I mean there's an oven, amphorae of what I assume is grain—"

Her face softened. "I'm sorry. I meant it's not just a bakery. Each of the women here"—she gestured to Isa and Thalia—"or that soon *will* be here has been widowed or abandoned, with no way to support themselves or their children. Women aren't safe in the agora—they are mistaken for prostitutes, or at the very least they are ignored, treated like they're..." She raised her hands at her sides, palms up. "Like they're invisible. So, I decided to create a place where women could be safe and where other women could support them by buying from them."

He swallowed a mouthful of bread and olives. "That's a great idea."

"It is?" Her dark eyes widened.

"Of course. Why not?" He shrugged. A thought struck him as he counted the empty stalls. "My name is Jason. I own the glass shop outside the eastern wall, and I'm in a bit of trouble. I'm wondering if you can help me."

She frowned. "What kind of trouble?"

"I need to make two thousand glass cups before the festival of Dionysos."

The frown melted into an amused smile. "I'm afraid I don't know how to make glass cups."

"No, I know. I meant I need space."

"Space?"

"To store them. I can't deliver them until the order is complete. I don't have that much room in my workshop. But I notice most of your stalls are empty."

"I don't know. I intend to have them all filled as soon as possible."

"I can keep a day's worth but not much more. I'll bring them here each night. And it would only be until the festival."

She hesitated, chewing on a full, pink lip.

"I'll pay double the rent they pay."

"They don't pay rent."

"Then you need my rent." He hoped.

"I don't need it, but I could use it to help them."

"Thank you very much." He spoke before she could change her mind. "I'll be back in a few days."

One problem solved.

His heart was lighter, and his stomach began to quiet.

Tomorrow he would worry about an apprentice.

10

The Lord makes firm the steps of the one who delights in him;
though he may stumble, he will not fall,
for the Lord upholds him with his hand.

— PSALM 37.23-24

WHEN KASSI ARRIVED AT THE PISTRINUM, THE FIRE BLAZED, AND several loaves were already baking. Still more were on the counter, and Thalia was helping a customer complete a purchase. All before the second hour of the day.

"Thank you, Mannus."

"I'll return before sunset." He turned and left.

"Isa, this is wonderful, you've done so much work. I wasn't expecting us to be doing so much in four days."

"Most of your sales will be early."

"*Our* sales. But I didn't expect you to do it all."

Isa grinned. "We're used to rising before dawn. Besides, I figured it would be much harder for you to leave your house this early."

"You're right. It is. I'm not sure how long I can keep it up before Pappa ... Who knows what he'll do? But the bakery is mine, and he can't take it away. Don't worry about that."

Thalia neared them but stopped several strides away.

"Thalia, did you want something?" Kassi asked.

"It's ... I—I have a friend." She winced. "Her husband divorced her because he thought she had been unfaithful. She wasn't, but of course his word was believed over hers, and he needed no proof."

"What can I do?"

"Can she come here? With me? I mean ... she can share my space."

"Of course she can. There's plenty of room." She pointed to the stalls, most of them still empty. "That's why I bought this place."

Thalia's shoulders relaxed. "Good. Because she's here. But if we're too busy, she can come back later." She motioned to a beautiful young girl waiting beside the door. "This is Asteria."

Kassi strode down the aisle to the door. "Hello, Asteria. I'm glad you're here."

"Eucharisto." She shook her head. "But as I told Thalia, I don't know how to make bread. My pappa had slaves, and then my husband had slaves ... I never learned how."

Kassi smiled, hoping to alleviate Asteria's anxiety. "I'll teach you. Come with me." She wrapped an arm around her waist and led her toward the oven. "We have two amphorae here. If they both have flour, use flour from the emptiest one. We'll start with an easy recipe first."

She grabbed a bowl from the shelf placed waist-high and reached deep into the wide-mouthed pottery container. She filled it three times, dumping each cupful into the bowl, followed by two cups of water.

"Now we add a little salt and mix it." She added a generous pinch, then carried the bowl to an empty stall and set it on the table. "Now knead it."

Asteria's eyes widened as she put a finger to her chest. "Me?"

Kassi nodded. "Stick your hands in there."

Asteria grimaced but slid the fingers of first one hand and then the other into the bowl and began turning the mixture into dough.

Isa tapped Kassi's shoulder. "There's someone at the door."

The sun highlighted a man standing in the doorway, his face hard to make out.

"Thank you. Can you help Asteria while I see what he wants?"

Kassi strolled to the visitor, taking her time, assessing him. He didn't appear threatening. Dark curls fell over his forehead nearly to his eyes. A smile lit up his vaguely familiar face. How old was he? Not yet twenty.

"May I help you?"

"I heard you sell bread here."

"Bread is sold in the agora."

He didn't appear to take her hint. "We heard you help women who have no other recourse. Is this the right place?"

Her stomach tensed. What did he want? "It is, but usually it's women who buy from us."

He grinned. "You don't want our money?" He extended a hand holding several bronze coins.

He was more persistent than she'd have expected.

"Why come here?"

"We need bread, and if I can help someone at the same time, why not?"

She relaxed. "What's your name?"

"Call me Timos."

"Come in, Timos."

She led him to the table. From their worktables, they studied him as he followed her inside and selected a loaf. Apparently reassured, they went back to kneading.

"Still warm." He brought it to his nose and inhaled. "Smells delicious. I can't wait to eat it."

"Take a bite."

"Now?"

"Sure."

He complied, pulling off a small piece and placing it on his tongue. "It *is* good."

Recognition dawned. "Didn't I see you at the synagogue yesterday?"

He swallowed a mouthful of bread. "You were there?" He pulled off a bigger chunk.

She nodded. "I go every week. I loved listening to your friend. What's his name? Petros?"

"Paulos. He studied under the greatest Jewish teacher. He knows the sacred texts better than anyone I've ever known."

"It shows. I'd love to hear more. Will he be there next Shabbat?"

"Nai. He's at the harbor looking for work repairing sails on the ships wintering here."

"He's a *skenopoios*?"

"His abba was a leatherworker as well. He does excellent work. Quite beautiful."

She rounded the corner to stand beside him. "My pater is the chief politarch. He talked about having the shade sails over the agoras repaired now that the air is cooling. He can do that, right? It's not leather, but it seems similar."

His eyes lit up. "That would be perfect. It requires the same skills and the same tools."

"I'll talk to him tonight, then."

"Thank you very much. That would be incredibly helpful."

"It would take many weeks. Are you planning to be here that long?"

"We are. And steady work would help immensely." He ripped off another bite of bread. "One more, please?"

She traded an olive loaf for a coin.

"I should get this to Silas. He's probably wondering where I am." He turned to go but paused. "Who has the best popina in the agora?"

She grinned. "Go to Publius. He has the best obeliskos. And tell him you're my friend."

"Eucharisto."

"Come back in a few days. I'll let you know what my pappa says."

"I'll be back tomorrow for more bread."

"I'll see you then."

Men buying bread from women so they could help women. That was something she'd never expected. Maybe this would turn out better than she'd hoped.

Jason sat legs crossed at the low table in the center of the shop and unwrapped the lump of clay he'd bought from the potter. The last of the day's light streamed in through the open roof, illuminating the workspace. A low fire burned in the furnace, keeping the glass from hardening again.

It shouldn't take too long to make a copy of the mold. Once it was made, he'd worry about finding help, but from where? It was hot, uncomfortable, grueling work, even for someone as skilled and strong as Jason.

He squeezed the clay in one fist and then the other to soften it, then twisted and stretched it to give it some pliability. He set the tawny blob down and reached for the completed glass he'd found on the shelf.

Pinching off small bits, he pressed clay into each indentation and over every grape, each twisted tendril, and every crawling vine. He continued adding a bit at a time, then did the same along the top where the name "DIONYSOS GOD OF WINE" was inscribed. He added more until the entire glass was covered in a thick layer.

He added the last two globs, one to each side, then used two fingers and his thumb to form crude handles. Each jutted out about three finger widths and ended in a rough knob. They didn't need to be pretty, just long enough to hold without touching the hotter clay and strong enough to not break when pushed to hold the pieces together as the glass bubble expanded within.

The handles formed, he smoothed his thumbs over the remaining surface, exerting enough force to ensure there were no bubbles or blank spaces below the surface. Holding it up to the fading light, he inspected the mold from the inside, searching for any defects that would mar his creations.

He drew the blade of his dagger down one side from rim to base, and then the other, making sure the new cuts lined up with the marks on the inside. Finally, he carefully slid the knife around the base to delineate the third piece of the mold.

He'd almost completed the circle when the blade slipped, slicing a deep cut in the first finger of his left hand. Blood spurted, spilling onto the mold and staining it red. He dropped the clay-encased glass, then jumped up and hurried to the shelves as crimson rivulets snaked down his hand. He grabbed a cloth and wrapped the fabric tightly around his bloody finger, hoping to stop the blood. His finger throbbed, but he kept the pressure on.

Would he be able to use his hand tomorrow?

After a long, painful moment, he dared peel back the cloth. The cut still gaped, but the bleeding had stopped. He rewrapped it, tucking one end under the folds to secure it enough to finish.

He returned to the table. The clay was dented where it had hit the table but thank Adonai the glass wasn't cracked. He smoothed over the cut left by the errant knife as well as the dent.

At least the mold was finished. He set it on the shelf of the smaller furnace to dry. Tomorrow, he'd take it to the potter to fire.

He couldn't accomplish anymore until the next day, so he might as well get a good night's sleep. It could be his last for a long time. He shut the door and headed home, long, dusky shadows stretching out before him.

Damianos's order weighed heavy on his mind. Two thousand

cups. Every day he didn't start on the order, the number he had to complete each day climbed higher.

But without an apprentice ... Yoel had made it clear no Jew would be allowed to work for him. That left the Greeks, and he had no way of finding a Greek boy who needed work.

A thought struck. Maybe the baker would know someone who needed a job. She was helping women find work. He shifted his path to lead him to the pistrinum.

He knocked on the door. No answer. Perhaps he was too late. Most bakeries operated from before dawn to early afternoon, closing around the time most men headed for the baths. As he turned to go, the door opened enough for him to see her lovely face.

"Jason. This is a surprise."

"I'm hoping you can do me a favor."

"Another one?" Her smile was beautiful. And unnerving.

"I shouldn't have bothered you." He glanced over her shoulder at the women kneading dough at the tables. "I thought you might have finished for the day."

"Almost. Right now, some of the women are still learning to make the more complicated breads." She opened the door and allowed him to enter.

She bent over the long table, hair falling forward over her shoulders as she perused the bread. "These are our last loaves for today. Fresh from the oven. Would you like one? Or two?" Finally, she selected an onion loaf and a braided loaf dotted with sesame seeds.

He held out both hands, and she gasped. "What happened to your hand?"

"It's just a cut."

"Does it hurt?"

It did, quite a lot, but should he let her know that?

He grimaced. "A bit."

She set the loaves back on the table. "How did you get it?" One hand under his, she tugged at the end of the cloth, her touch sending shivers up his arm.

"Making a mold."

"Does this happen often?"

"We rarely need to make molds. Only for special orders."

She freed the loose end and pulled it, slowly unwrapping the rest, then hovered her fingers over his finger. "It looks terrible. Are you sure it doesn't hurt more than a bit?" She narrowed one eye at him. "I have two brothers. I know 'not at all' means 'a little,' and 'a little' means 'a lot.'"

He laughed. "It does hurt more than a bit."

"Let me put some honey on it for you. Come here." She grabbed his wrist and led him toward the back of the store. He tried to ignore the stares and whispers of the other women, but it was no use. At least they didn't seem afraid of him.

And it felt good to have a woman fuss over him again. As Imma would have … were she still alive.

———

KASSI LED Jason to an empty worktable and pulled up a tall stool. "Sit. Have you eaten today?"

He hesitated as he sat, which likely meant no.

She retrieved one of the loaves she'd selected for him, then broke off several pieces and set them on the table. She took a box from the top shelf next to the oven and searched for clean cloth strips. After dipping one in fresh water, she grabbed a small pot of honey and returned to him.

He flinched when she dabbed at the blood. From his hand, really. It must have bled fiercely. Once clean, she picked up a new cloth and dipped it in the amphora of honey.

"So, what favor do you need today?" She applied the sticky, golden liquid to the wound.

"I need an apprentice. Or at least an assistant."

She wrapped his finger. "For your glass shop?"

He nodded as he swallowed a chunk of bread. He winced and sucked in air, blowing it back out.

"Hot?" She laughed.

"Very."

"What's the difference? Between an apprentice and an assistant?"

"An apprentice would work for me for several years while I teach him everything I know. The first year, I pay his family for his food, and he gets no pay. He gets some the second year and more each year after that as he learns the craft. At the end of his time, he would know everything he'd need to set up his own shop."

"And an assistant?"

"An assistant would be temporary, and I wouldn't be teaching him. He would help with whatever I need."

"Any skills required?"

He shook his head as he reached for another piece. "Just willing to learn. And work."

Could the God of the Israelites be answering her prayer already?

"Thalia's oldest boy is twelve. Is that too young?"

"Is he strong?"

"Strong enough. He'll be stronger once he's eaten well for a few weeks."

"Is he not eating now?"

Her heart ached. She hadn't meant to disclose quite so much. "He hadn't been eating much at all. His mother was widowed and lost her apartment as well as her husband's income."

"How does such a thing happen?"

She stiffened. "What do you mean?"

"That would never happen in the Jewish community. The entire group would come to her aid. She'd have to marry again a year or so later, but never would any of them go hungry." He paused. "Did she have no one to help her?"

Perhaps he had a point. It would be lovely to be part of such a community. "I guess not."

"Is the boy here?"

She moved to the last stall and explained Jason's offer to Thalia while she cast frequent and furtive glances his way.

Finally, Kassi put her arm around her shoulder and led her to Jason. "This is Thalia. And this is Jason."

"You would hire my boy?" A frown creased her forehead.

He frowned. "Is there any reason I shouldn't?"

She shook her head. "No! He's a good boy. He learns quickly and works hard."

"I'm glad to hear it."

"Every day?"

"I'm not supposed to work the last day of the week, but I might have to for the next few weeks."

"But he lives with me?"

"Nai." He smiled, revealing a dimple in his right cheek Kassi hadn't yet noticed. "He lives with you. I pay for his food. He'd be required to stay overnight occasionally, perhaps every ten days, to keep the fire stoked."

"Why?" Kassi asked.

"The furnace has to be lit at all times to keep the glass melted. Otherwise, it takes hours to get hot enough again to remelt the glass."

"Then why only every tenth day?" Thalia asked.

"My shop is in the craftsmen's village outside the gate. I'm the only glass worker, but there are many potters there, and their kilns need to be kept hot as well. We take turns watching the fires. One man can check on them all, but we use two. Less chance of his falling asleep and letting the ovens cool."

Thalia paused for a long moment, then smiled shyly. "Nai." She glanced back at her son. "He'll be so glad. He's been aching for something to do."

Kassi beckoned to Gaius. He neared, eyes wide, but his fear dissipated when Jason smiled.

"What's your name?"

"Gaius," said Thalia.

"Gaius, hello. Would you like to learn how to blow glass?"

His head bobbed. "Yes, please. That sounds exciting."

"Exciting, no. But interesting. And you'll learn everything you need to know to be a glassblower when we're done. If you want."

"How long would that take?"

"It depends on how fast you learn, but about three or four years."

Kassi resisted chuckling when the boy's face fell. Four years was a lifetime to someone his age.

"Don't worry about that yet. Help me for a few weeks, and you don't have to keep going if you don't like it."

The boy gave a solemn nod. "All right. I'll do it."

"I'll pick you up here at dawn. All right?"

"I'll be here."

She chucked softly. Only yesterday she'd told Gai she would try to find him a position. She'd asked the God of Israel to help her, and He had.

She wouldn't have believed it herself if it hadn't happened to her.

THE SCENTS OF GARLIC, onions, and cooked fish tantalized Kassi as she followed Mannus into the villa. She entered her chamber, letting her cloak fall from her shoulders. She tossed it on the bed and moved to the table where Lida had left a pitcher of clean water and a towel. She washed her face, then kicked off her dusty sandals, washed her feet, and slipped on the shoes she kept to wear in the house.

She entered the triclinium as Pappa looked up from his couch. "Why are you late?"

"I had a slight problem at the bakery. A new woman—"

He held out a hand, stopping her words. "I don't need to know any more."

"I'm sorry, Pappa."

"The meal begins at dusk. You need to plan your time better."

The sun barely touched the sea, but with Pappa, there was no room for error. She took a seat between her nieces. "I had planned it well, but I can't control the actions of others."

Argos cast a glare her way. "This is why women should not be allowed to own a business."

She reached for a piece of fish. "The politarchs—not to mention the empire—have not forbidden it."

Argos kept his glare on her. "Perhaps the politarchs should consider doing so."

She met his gaze. "Then I thank God *you* are not a politarch."

"Which god?" He smirked.

Kassi let his question remain unanswered.

"Enough, Argos." Pappa's voice was low but hard.

Her brother at least knew not to argue with him. "Nai, Pappa."

Kassi returned her brother's smug smile.

"Kassandra." Pappa shut her down as well.

"Nai, Pappa." She concentrated on her food.

"We eat as a family twice a week. The boys refuse invitations from other families and city officials to be here. I don't want you to let your little venture keep you from us."

His words stung. Little venture? "Pappa, this is not something I do merely to occupy my time. This is important."

"Important or not, from now on you will do it without the aid of Mannus."

"How important can it be if it can be done by women?" Kadmos asked.

Kadmos had never accomplished anything that Pappa had not planned out for him, but anything he or Argos did was met with copious praise. Yet even the most significant thing she did was at best ignored and at worst disparaged, not only by her brothers but by Pappa as well.

"I think what she's doing is wonderful," Larissa said.

"Why would you think that?" Argos asked his wife.

"I've known several women from north of the Via who, for whatever reason, found themselves alone with no one to support them. It's almost impossible for a woman to survive without a man."

"Perhaps they should have tried harder to please their men, then," Kadmos said.

"Can a woman keep a man from dying?" Larissa's voice held a tinge of anger.

Kassi cringed. Pappa did not respond well to angry women.

"One of the women in the bakery has been widowed, but there are other ways to end up alone," Kassi said. "One of the women was accused of infidelity by her husband—"

"He must have had a reason. It was obviously true," Kadmos said.

It was no use. They would never understand how hard it was for women, how unfair the world could be, or how important helping them was to her.

She would never be more than another useless woman.

...explaining and proving that
the Messiah had to suffer and rise from the dead.

— *ACTS* 17.3A

ANOTHER HOUR OF LIGHT REMAINED, AND JASON NEEDED TO MAKE USE of it, but he'd promised Yoel he'd try to come for the Shabbat meal. Yoel would have told Dodah, and Jason couldn't bear to disappoint her.

But she would scold him if he showed up smelling like a wet sheep. If he wanted to get out of the baths in time, he needed to leave now.

He rose and set the last glass of the day on the ledge of the cooling furnace as his new apprentice entered with a fistful of honey sesame bars. "Gai, I have to visit my dodh. You can clean up here and then keep watch on the fire. When the vigil checks in, you can go home."

"Yes, *kyrie*." He set aside his sweets and grabbed the broom propped in the corner.

"Eat your pastelli first."

Gai grinned and plopped onto the stool in front of the furnace, stuffing almost a whole bar in his mouth.

"Want to go in my place?"

The boy's face lost all expression. "I-I don't understand, kyrie."

Jason chuckled. "Never mind." He pulled the fresh tunic he'd brought from the shelf and hurried toward the baths. At this time of day, most people would have completed their baths and headed for home, leaving the baths almost empty. He hoped.

He handed the door attendant a brass coin as he stepped into the first room. He removed his sweaty tunic and placed it on a hook, leaving the clean one on the bench below it. Although the chance of theft was unlikely at this hour, he tipped the bath slave another coin to make sure his clothes didn't disappear. His sandals stayed on his feet to protect them from the heated floor.

He wrapped a cloth around his waist and stepped into the next room. After smearing his body with oil, he scraped his skin with a curved metal instrument, taking the offending sweat with it. He plunged into the hot water pool and finished in the chilled waters of the final pool. No time today to relax.

Once dried and dressed, he hurried down the cardo toward the Jewish community. Shabbat would begin in moments, but he was close enough to reach Yoel's house without breaking the Shabbat laws.

Dodah greeted him at the door with her usual forceful embrace. "Welcome. Yoel told me you were coming, but I wasn't sure, after ..."

"I'm here." He returned her hug. "But only because he said *you* asked for me," he whispered.

"I know he's difficult. But Paulos and his friends are here. It should be an interesting night." She led him into the triclinium where the others reclined around the low table. He claimed a spot next to Timos as Yoel rose to recite the blessing, his deep voice loud enough to carry across to the synagogue. Was he blessing the meals of the entire community?

Jason watched the visitors while Yoel prayed. Their faces were serene, as if they had not a care in the world.

Yoel sat, and Dodah poured the watered wine. A platter of roast fish occupied the center of the table, surrounded by fresh bread, dill-covered carrots, and boiled cabbage flavored with sage. Perfectly sliced light green pears alternated with slices of bright red apples on a round glass platter, a bowl of pistachios in the middle.

His stomach growled.

Maybe he should make peace with Yoel just to enjoy Dodah's cooking. He reached for an apple slice and bit into it, the sweet fresh flavor delighting his tongue.

"This looks delicious, Leah. Todah rabah," Timotheos said.

"Yes, thank you, Dodah," added Jason.

"Jason, your dodh tells me you are a glassblower, as was your abba." Paulos reclined across from Jason, ignoring the food, his attention fully on Jason.

He swallowed. "I am. Our shop ... my shop is outside the gate along with the potters and smiths."

"And are you kept busy?"

He nodded. "We ... I'm the only glassblower in Thessalonike, so I'm working almost every day."

"Shabbat included," mumbled Yoel.

Jason bristled, but Paulos ignored the insult. "I'd love to watch you sometime. It's fascinating to me to think that something like this platter"—he touched the serving dish "was once a shapeless, hard blob of raw glass."

"How do you make the glass?" Timos asked.

"I don't make the raw glass. That's made in Alexandria or Judea. They mix sand with a couple other ingredients and melt it. Then it's cooled, broken into pieces about the size of my fist, and shipped all over the empire."

Silas reached for a piece of fish. "Why only in those two places?"

"It takes a certain kind of sand. Nowhere else has enough of it."

"Judea, you say?" Paulos rubbed his chin. "I don't remember seeing any glass shops while I was there."

"They produce raw glass on a much greater scale than glass pieces. You might not even recognize it as glass at that stage. And it's only been the last twenty-five years or so that glassblowing's been a growing industry. Many glassworkers are Jewish. Our family, in fact, came from Alexandria. We've been glassmakers going back generations, producing the raw glass. One of them left Egypt to settle elsewhere and landed here. Then it became possible to add color, and when blowing was perfected, quite recently, the possibilities became endless."

"I'm sure Paulos isn't interested in our family history." Yoel held up the amphora. "More wine?" He filled his own glass then handed the amphora to Dodah, who rose and refilled the others.

"Have I told you about the new mosaic we're putting in the floor of the synagogue? We've only begun talking about it ..."

Jason shut out Yoel's voice. His would be the only one heard for the rest of the evening.

KASSI PULLED a horsehair brush through her unruly locks. She opened the precious blue bottle and breathed in Mamma's perfume, and for once her heart didn't ache quite so much.

Grabbing a deep yellow cloak from the chest at the end of her bed, she slipped out of the house and headed toward the synagogue. The week had been long and hard. Pappa, her siblings ... It seemed no one approved of her or her actions.

Except for the glassblower.

Why did he keep popping into her mind?

She was excited to hear the visitor Paulos speak again, to learn more about Adonai. The sacred texts had taught her much, but Paulos talked like he *knew* Adonai personally. She ached to know

Him like that. If she were part of His chosen people, perhaps she could. Since that could never happen, she'd have to settle for learning as much as she could.

But she needed to stop at Isa's first.

Isa answered her knock quickly. "Kassi, please come in."

Kassi entered. The rooms—what she could see of them—were smaller than she'd imagined but tidy. Glassless windows allowed faint light as well as chilled air. The first room held a small table with a loaf of bread, three apples, a small amphora, five pottery plates, and five cups. Two rolled mats sat near the door. In the small room behind, she could see the ends of three mats, each with a small bag lying at its foot. Thalia and Isa must let the boys share the sleeping chamber while they slept in the bigger room.

Her throat tightened. Her chamber alone was bigger than these two rooms. And what had she done to deserve that?

Probably about as much as these women had done to earn this.

Thalia emerged from the back room, her arm around Gaius's shoulder.

"Thank you for letting him come to synagogue with me this morning," Kassi said.

"Of course," Thalia said. "He's been waiting for you all morning."

Gaius grabbed his cloak. "Shall we go?"

Kassi opened the door for him, but Thalia grabbed the neck of his chiton. "Kiss, please."

Gaius's cheeks flamed bright red, and Kassi left the room, hoping to relieve his embarrassment a bit. He came out a moment later, and they hurried to the stairs.

"So, Gai, why did you want to come with me?"

"Some people in the insula were talking about the new speaker. Isa told me you went each week, and I wanted to see what they were talking about."

Dust swirled around their feet as they stepped off the last stair onto the street. "Why so interested?"

"There are too many gods. I can't keep them all straight. It isn't right that gods only want to make people miserable. And then if you don't sacrifice the right thing, although no one seems to know what that is, they punish you." His face darkened. "I made a sacrifice when Pappa was ill. I asked Zeus to make him better. It didn't work. So, when I heard about a god who doesn't require sacrifices, I wanted to learn more."

"I'm sorry about your pappa. But I agree. That's why I started going to synagogue."

"Do you believe this god is real?" His eyes begged her to say yes.

"I do. Very much. In fact, I think He is the only real God there is."

"But he's the god of the Jews, right?"

"You know, I think He is the God of everyone. He created everyone, so I believe He cares for all people. I don't explain it well. I think Paulos will do a better job."

They turned right onto the paved, immaculate cardo. She let her tunic fall to her ankles and breathed deeply. "The synagogue is just inside the city gate."

Moments later, they arrived at the nondescript building.

"This is it?" Gaius twisted his face as if he'd eaten a sour grape.

"Yes." She chuckled. True, it wasn't impressive compared to Greek temples— magnificent, imposing, and always massive. Though the synagogue was small and plain on the outside, mosaics covered the walls and floor. Unlike those in Greek homes, none of them featured any faces at all. She'd learned Jews considered idolatry to be the worst sin, so to stay far away from it, they rejected any art with depictions of people or animals—mosaics, sculptures, or paintings, and instead favored brilliant geometric designs in bold colors.

"Come on. We sit in the top row."

"Why?"

"We're Greek," she whispered. "They let us come to hear the reading of the texts, but they get the first two rows. It's a small room though, and we're still close enough to hear everything." She led him down the row and sat next to Zelia.

She peered around Kassi at the boy, frowning. "Who's this?"

"This is Gaius. His meter's one of the bakers. Gai, this is Zelia, a friend of mine since childhood."

Zelia nodded politely but did not speak to Gaius, instead returning her attention to the table holding the scrolls.

The service began as every other Shabbat, with the leader taking his place at the center of the room and reciting the blessings. "Adonai, open my lips, and my mouth will speak Your praises."

Open my lips. The words struck her today as they never had. Could she not speak His praises without His first opening her mouth? Could she not seek Him without Him first opening her eyes, her heart?

But would He, if she wasn't one of His people?

JASON SLIPPED into the synagogue as Yoel prayed. Instead of taking his usual seat in the second row behind Yoel, he sat close to the door. He shouldn't even be here. He should be busy in his shop since he was already behind. But his arm had begun to ache from holding an iron rod dipped in melted glass all day, and he knew Gaius could use a few hours extra sleep.

Come to think of it, so could he. If he wasn't in his shop, staying in bed would have been the next best thing.

But no matter how angry he was at Yoel, no matter what he thought of the usefulness—or uselessness—of synagogue, he couldn't bring himself to miss Shabbat service.

The sweet aroma of burning, scented olive oil filled the room, giving light to every corner. The rustle of robes and hushed conversations gave an austere holiness to the room.

None of it made Jason feel any closer to Adonai.

If the benches were cushioned instead of hard stone, the room would be more inviting. As it was, he couldn't wait to leave. He could still get in more than half a day's work if Yoel would stop delaying, making sure everyone knew he was responsible for bringing the Pharisee.

The messenger circled the room, delivering the reading assignments, and sat beside Yoel. Jason looked to see who had taken his place behind him. Ezekiel and Hannah.

And was that Gai behind them? With the baker? How had he never noticed her attending before? He'd have to remember to ask her the next time he took the glass to the bakery.

When the final portion of the law had been read, Yoel held the scroll out to Paulos. "Learned friend, please come read to us from the prophet Isaiah and then share with us once again your teaching."

Jason hadn't heard much of Paulos's teaching last week. Now he would see if the Pharisee was as wonderful as Yoel reported.

The teacher took the scroll but instead of opening it, he set it on the table along with the others. Every eye was focused on him, each face bright with expectation.

"My brothers, my fellow Israelites, and you who fear the only true God along with us, welcome, and listen to the words of the prophet Isaiah. 'For to us a child is born, to us a son is given, and the government will be on his shoulders. And he will be called Wonderful Counselor, Mighty God, Everlasting Father, Prince of Peace.'"

Paulos spoke the prophet's words as easily as if he were reciting what he ate yesterday. How did he do that? Yoel had once told Jason that Pharisees memorized all the sacred texts. It appeared to be true.

YOEL SAT TALLER as the Pharisee allowed the words of Isaiah to roll off his tongue. A genuine Pharisee, here in Yoel's tiny synagogue, teaching his people the lessons of Israel's greatest prophet.

"'Of the greatness of his government and peace there will be no end,'" Paulos continued. "'He will reign on David's throne and over his kingdom, establishing and upholding it with justice and right-eousness, from that time on and forever. The zeal of the Lord Almighty will accomplish this.' These are the words of Isaiah."

Paulos scanned the room as he spoke, his eyes resting on each person for a moment. "In this section of the prophet's words, we see he is speaking of a time yet to come, a time of untold peace and plenty, a time of wisdom for everyone. And yet we know no such time has come. Want and war still abound, not only in Israel but in all the world.

"Through Isaiah, Adonai promised us a Son who would reign on David's throne, a just and righteous king. I am here to tell you today that this Son, this promised Mashiach, has come. His name is Yeshua ben Yosef."

Across from Yoel, the elders glared. Murmurs flew around the room as the Jewish worshippers tried to figure out to whom Paulos might be referring.

"And how do we know this Child is the promised King? Isaiah also said the Lord would give us a sign. A virgin will conceive and give birth to a Son, and she will call Him Immanuel. And I tell you today, an angel of the Lord appeared to a virgin in Nazareth—as you will recall, Isaiah also foretold He would be called a Nazarene—and gave her this message: 'You are to call Him Yeshua. He will be great and will be called the Son of the Most High. And Adonai will give Him the throne of His father David, and He will reign over Jacob's descendants forever."

Around Yoel, the room began to spin. His neck grew hot.

"The Child grew to be a man," continued Paulos. "But neither the people of Jerusalem nor their leaders recognized Him as Mashiach. In condemning Him, they too fulfilled prophecy, as

Zechariah said, 'They will look on Me, the One they have pierced.' God has kept his promise to send a king from the house of David. Yeshua is this King."

The murmuring ceased, and silence filled the room like a dark cloud. "God was pleased to dwell fully in His Son, and through Yeshua the Mashiach, Adonai reconciled all people to Himself. For although we once were alienated from God, Yeshua's physical death presents us holy in His sight, without blemish and free from all accusation."

Please, please stop talking about this. For the first time in his life, Yoel wished he could be anywhere other than synagogue. His head hurt; his stomached ached. He scanned the crowd. Most of the Jews frowned, whispered, scoffed. Their disbelief might be the only thing that saved him.

"I am here to tell you the good news: The Mashiach which Adonai promised, He has delivered to us in the Man Yeshua. Through Yeshua alone, the forgiveness of sins is proclaimed to you. Through Him, *everyone* who believes is set free from every sin, a justification we were never able to obtain under the law of Moses."

Yoel's world closed in on him. The elders would avoid making a spectacle by chastising him here and now, but they wouldn't be happy, and they would make their disapproval known. He glanced across the room at Micah. His face was, as always, impossible to read.

Had Yoel committed an error from which he could never recover?

12

Anxiety weighs down the heart,
but a kind word cheers it up.

— PROVERBS 12.25

KASSI LAY SEVERAL STRANDS OF DOUGH, BURSTING WITH CHOPPED olives, next to one another. "Now, to do one with five braids, we start like the others, and squeeze them together at the top."

Isa pinched the dough. "Now what?"

"Separate them into a group of three and one of two." Kassi did it as she spoke. "Then move the outermost of the three to the inside."

Isa picked up the outside strand and placed it beside the other two.

"Now you've got a new group of three, so repeat. Keep the strands as close to the top as you can. We don't want any big spaces."

With one finger, Isa nudged the relocated strand as close to the pinched end as possible.

"Perfect. Now you keep doing that until they're all too short to keep going, then close it up at the bottom and smooth out the ends."

Isa picked up the outside strand and continued, often glancing up at Kassi. As she reached for the last one, her hands stilled.

"Isa?"

The older woman pointed at the door.

Kassi looked over her shoulder. A tall, broad-shouldered man stood in the doorway, arms crossed, studying the room. One corner of his lip curled, eyes narrowed, as if surveying a pile of refuse.

His bearing and dress marked him as one of the city's elites. He looked vaguely familiar. Had she seen him at one of Pappa's dinner parties? She searched her memory.

But what would someone of his status be doing here, south of not only the Via Olympos, but the Via Regia as well?

Of course, she was here, south of both, but he didn't look eager to help anyone but himself.

"I'll be right back." Kassi moved to the door. "May I help you?"

His gaze moved slowly from her sandals to her head.

She shivered under his stare.

"You're Kassandra?"

Why did he sound disappointed? "I am. And you are ...?"

He jutted out his chin. "I'm Damianos. Son of Leandros, advisor to the governor."

Was she in trouble? Had she forgotten to complete some legal requirement before opening the pistrinum?

"Your pater said I'd find you here. I wasn't sure I should believe him, but he was right."

"He usually is. Now how can I help you?"

He laughed. "He also said you were stubborn. But I can fix that."

She furrowed her brow. "What do you mean? I don't need to be fixed. My pater would never say such a thing."

He stretched his neck and puffed out his chest. "Your pater visited mine this morning. He offered you in marriage. To me."

Her blood ran cold, but she refused to show fear. She wouldn't give him the satisfaction.

He glanced around the shop, examining each woman. She stepped in front of him to pull his attention back to her. "Please don't stare. It makes them uncomfortable."

He laughed again, a sound that held derision rather than joy.

"If you're not here to buy bread, you can leave."

"Then I'll buy something."

"What would you like?"

He shrugged. "Pick something for me."

She moved to the table. "Most of our bread is gone, as it's almost time for the evening meal. I have a few braided loaves left."

He followed. "Who made those?"

"I did." She offered two loaves, one with three strands and another with six.

He ran his hand over the second loaf. "Good work."

How would he know? He couldn't have any idea what it took to make the dough, let alone form it into a loaf such as that one.

"How much?"

"A sestertius. Each."

His jaw dropped. "That's twice as much as what I pay in the agora!"

"Buy bread there often?"

He flinched. "No, but I do know how much it costs."

From sending slaves to buy it for you. "The loaves in the agora are plain. We have loaves like that in the mornings, but they disappear quickly." She held the pair up. "These are complicated. They require more dough, twice the work, and twice the time. So twice the price."

He reached into his belt and pulled out two large brass coins.

She reached for them. "Why is a man such as you buying bread at all, let alone here?"

"I wanted to see this place before I have it torn down."

She gasped. "You can't tear it down. It's mine!"

"And once we're married, what's yours becomes mine, to do with as I please."

"A married woman is allowed to own property. It is not yours to 'do with as you please.'"

"In theory. But do you think anyone will deal with you once I tell them not to? Where will you get your flour? And these women..." He chuckled. "They are easily dealt with."

Dealt with? She clenched her hands into fists, as if that could control the rage building inside her. What would happen to them if she weren't here? So many horrible situations flashed through her mind. She may end up married to a brute of a man, but they would suffer far worse.

An evil smile crossed his face. "Actually, they could all live here. Once I demolish this building, I could build some cheap apartments. I can put fifty in a space this size." He smirked. "I'll even give them first choice."

That made no sense. "This building is made of stone. Why tear it down to put up one made of wood?"

"I'll use it elsewhere. I need to expand my villa. I'll not waste dressed stone on people such as these."

Could he be any more arrogant? And selfish? She didn't have time to waste on him. "Goodbye, Damianos."

"You can call me Damianos. For now."

Her face must have reflected her confusion.

"For now. Because later you'll address me as *kyrie*." He laughed once again as he sauntered away.

She hated the sound of his voice. How could she ever spend a lifetime listening to it?

YOEL CHEWED his fingernails as he paced in the courtyard.

Three days had passed since Shabbat. Three days since Paulos had mentioned that disgraced and convicted rebel from Jerusalem.

The day was drawing to a close, and Yoel had heard nothing from the elders.

He hadn't seen any of them, either, which meant they were huddled somewhere together, plotting what to do.

Talking about *him*.

The door to his house opened, and Leah approached him with a glass in hand.

"I brought you some fresh pomegranate juice. I know how much you look forward to it every year."

He reached for the glass. "Pomegranates are ready?"

"I found these today in the agora."

He sipped the dark purple juice. The sweetly sour taste coated his tongue and throat. She must have been juicing them all morning. It was a true labor of love. One of many she performed every day.

And how often did he thank her? Not often enough.

He reached for her hand. "Todah rabah, ahuvati."

She narrowed one eye. "Are you well?"

He sighed. "I've been waiting for the elders to come and tell me they are replacing me."

"Why would they do that?"

"You heard Paulos. Such nonsense. How could he hold up that ... that *criminal* as the Mashiach?"

"They can't hold you responsible for his words."

"He is my guest." He thumped his fist on his chest. "*I* invited him to speak. *I* told the elders he was a learned man, a Pharisee, no less, and that he would teach our people well." Breathing through his nose to calm himself, he dropped to the bench.

She sat beside him. "It's not your fault he spoke of this Yeshua."

"I am the archisynagogos. They will make it my fault." He drained his glass.

Leah glanced toward the courtyard. "Here they come." She tipped her head in their direction and took the empty glass from his hand. "You are a good leader. Don't let them make you forget it." She rose and headed inside.

"Leah?"

She looked over her shoulder.

"Todah. For the juice, and for everything else you do for me."

"You're welcome, ahuva." She smiled sweetly at him. She meant it to encourage him, but it didn't.

Yoel stood and faced the men approaching. Micah led the way, his face stoic, as were the weathered faces of the others. Most of them, anyway. Lior's held a slight smirk. He'd been spreading rumors about Yoel ever since he took over as leader. No doubt Lior wanted the position for himself.

Yoel dipped his head in greeting. "Micah, how good to see you."

"Yoel. I trust your day has been a blessed one."

Not really. "To what do I owe the honor of this visit?"

The others formed a semicircle around Micah.

"You can't figure it out?" Lior's voice was filled with disdain.

Micah shot a glare at his son. "Do I need to remind you of what we discussed earlier?"

Lior frowned, never taking his dagger-like glare from Yoel.

Micah returned his attention to Yoel. "We have come today to express our grave concerns about our visitor."

"I understand."

"Did he tell you what he planned to speak about?"

"Of course not." Yoel let out a harsh breath. "Do you think I would have allowed him to speak had I known he would bring up this man from Jerusalem?"

Micah nodded soberly. "I thought as much."

"I believed he would speak about the reading, about Isaiah. I still have no idea how he jumped from the prophet to this Yeshua." Yoel threw his hands up. "He's such a learned man. I truly don't understand how he can believe, let alone encourage others to believe, such a preposterous idea."

"Can we leave it to you to inform him this will not be tolerated?"

"Absolutely. I will make it abundantly clear that this line of thought will not be allowed in the synagogue again."

Micah cleared his throat. "There are some among us who believe you cannot be trusted to control this man."

Yoel's gaze shot to Lior.

"I disagree with them," Micah said. "I convinced them to give you—and Paulos—one more week."

Yoel returned his attention to the old man. "Todah rabah, Micah."

"However, if he again mentions Yeshua, or teaches any other unapproved lesson, both he and you will be dealt with. Severely."

"I understand perfectly."

Micah bowed his head, spun on his heels, and left.

The others followed suit—except for Lior.

"May the remainder of your day be blessed." His phony smile did nothing to conceal his hostility.

Yoel breathed a long sigh of relief. He had one more chance. One lone opportunity to keep his position, both in the synagogue and in the community. His entire life would depend on the words of another.

He needed to convince Paulos not to destroy his life.

***

JASON NESTLED the last cup of the day into a shallow, straw-filled crate and counted again ... forty cups in each crate. He stacked one atop the other, then curled his fingers between the slats of the bottom crate and hoisted them onto his shoulder. One more day's work completed. Now to drop it off at the bakery and head home. He should eat something first, but his body cried for sleep. His muscles ached, and a painful heat rash had appeared on his right arm.

"All right, Gai. Time to go home."

Gaius flashed him a smile and leaned the broom in the corner. He bounded out the door ahead of him.

Jason pulled on a cloak not only to ward off the cold but to cover the ugly rash. The beautiful baker didn't need to see it. He pulled the thatch door closed behind him and proceeded to the bakery, trudging the increasingly familiar path. The scents of roasted fish and occasionally meat disappeared the further he got from the ano poli, replaced by that of boiling vegetables and barley stew.

Gaius turned into his street but stopped a few steps away and faced Jason again. "Tomorrow?"

Jason smiled and nodded. "Of course."

Why did Gaius ask him every day if he should come back the next? The uncertainty he'd experienced in his short life must be overwhelming. Jason would do whatever it took to give him what security he could.

Most of the shops in the south had been closed for some time. Roman owners closed in time for late afternoon baths, and their Roman customers did the same. Wealthy Greeks did as the Romans did, and poorer Greeks could afford little from the shops.

The bakery occupied an entire insula, dwarfing the small workshops nearby. Its door was closed. He lifted one knee and rested the crate on it, then shook the handle. The door rattled. It had to be making noise inside, but no one came to open it.

He turned to go, but something crashed inside. What was that? Was the baker all right?

"Kassi? Are you in there?"

He yanked on the ring. The door gave way, and he peeked inside. "Kassi?"

"Jason?" Her voice wavered a bit.

"Kassi, are you all right? Are you hurt?" He pounded on the door.

She cleared her throat. "You can bring the glasses in."

He couldn't see her, so he made his way to the back, scanning the stalls. They were filled with clean tables stocked with bowls and small bottles, but Kassi was not to be seen.

He turned into the last stall and grunted as he lifted the crates from his shoulder and stacked them on top of the others.

He turned to go, but a sniffle stopped him. "Kassi?" He crossed to where she stood next to a bread table, facing the wall. Her shoulders were hunched, arms wrapped around her middle.

"Are you all right?"

She said nothing.

He rounded the table. With her head bowed, he couldn't see her face, but the tears on her cheek told him she was not well.

"Kassi, what happened? Are you hurt?" he repeated.

She shook her head. "No. I'm fine." Her voice cracked.

He bent, dipping his head lower than hers to catch her gaze.

Her red eyes, runny nose, and wet cheeks belied her denial.

He laid a hand softly on her upper arm. "What happened? Can I help?"

She sniffled and brushed the tears from her cheeks with both hands, then fixed him with a stare. "Not unless you can change the way the world works."

"What do you mean?"

"A couple of weeks ago, my pappa told me he was tired of my 'foolishness,' as he called it."

"What foolishness?" She'd never seemed foolish or frivolous to him, far from it.

She waved a hand around. "This."

He chuckled. "Owning a bakery?"

"I think he could handle that. It's associating with 'those kinds' of people." She winced.

"Those kinds?"

"Those not of the ano poli." She chuckled dryly. "That, he cannot abide."

"Forgive me if this is a stupid question, but if that was weeks ago, why are you crying now?"

"My *betrothed* sauntered in here this afternoon, as if the bakery belonged to him."

A twinge of jealousy reared up. But why? He barely knew her. "Who is he?"

"Do you know Damianos? He owns the bathhouse."

"Damianos?" His stomach somersaulted. "I know Damianos well."

"You do?"

"Actually, I've never met him." He gestured to the growing stack of glassware. "But all of these are for him, for the opening of his bathhouse and the festival of Dionysos." His problems with Damianos revolved around money. Worst case, he lost the business, and probably his home. But for Kassi ... he couldn't imagine living with that man. He'd never let her out of the house.

"He said this would all belong to him. He plans to tear it down and build a shabby insula. He even said he'd give the women first choice of an apartment. And if I cause him trouble and try to keep it going, he'll tell all the vendors not to sell to me. Without flour, or at least the grain, we can't do anything. The women will be worse off than before."

Her compassion for others amazed him. Her entire life was being threatened, and she was worried about the women in her care.

"Is there anything I can do? I have some money saved. I could buy it from you. It would legally be mine so he couldn't take it, but it would really be yours. I'm sure I don't have enough, but perhaps I could pay you a little at a time."

Her dark eyes grew widened. "You would do that?"

"If it helps."

The tears flowed again. "I can't let you do that."

"I'd be happy to, if that kept away your tears." He hovered a hand over her check and brushed away a tear with his thumb.

She studied his face. "Why couldn't Pappa have promised me to someone like you?"

His heart skipped a beat and he jerked his hand away.

Her cheeks reddened, and her hand flew to her mouth. "I'm so sorry. Pappa always says I speak before I think. Please, forgive me."

He swallowed. His heart had restarted with a vengeance. "No forgiveness necessary." He looked toward the door. "I should go."

He hurried out and onto the street, the door slamming behind him.

Had he stayed, he'd have told her he'd marry her tomorrow.

13

What a person desires is unfailing love;
better to be poor than a liar.

— PROVERBS 19.22

JASON STUFFED A PIECE OF YESTERDAY'S BREAD IN HIS MOUTH AS HE hurried out the door. The sun had not yet risen over the mountain tops, and the air still had a biting chill to it.

When he arrived at the shop, Gaius was waiting for him with a blazing furnace and a fresh apple. The boy offered up the crimson fruit. "From Mamma."

"Todah. And thank her for me, too." Jason bit off a huge chunk and savored it. "Nice and sweet. Just the way I like them."

Gaius dropped his gaze and dug the toe of his sandal into the dirt floor.

Jason swallowed. "Is something wrong?"

"Can I ask you something?"

"Of course."

"Will you teach me to do what you do?"

"Of course. That's part of your apprenticeship."

"But when?" His bright eyes begged for an opportunity.

Jason rubbed his free hand on the back of his head. "It's only been a week."

But what would it hurt to teach him now? Jason could use a break now and then. After only a week, his shoulder and arm already ached from holding the iron rod covered in molten glass. With a mold, the only thing Gaius could do wrong was not blow hard enough to get the molten glass into every crevice and depression. That would only cost him time, as the glass could be remelted and used later.

But time was precious.

Still, if Jason became so sore he couldn't keep up the pace, he'd be no worse off.

"All right. Let's try it."

Gai's face lit like a child tasting honey for the first time.

"Get the molds out. I'll do one and explain everything I'm doing. Then I'll let you try."

"Yes, kyrie." He rushed to the shelf to get the molds, then hurried back and set both on the floor, one on either end.

Jason grabbed a blowpipe. "All right, come here."

Gaius came to the furnace.

"We stick the tip of the pipe into the pool of molten glass and slowly turn it to coat all sides with a thick layer of glass. You'll need to keep your hands up high where it's cooler. Now, this part you know. I pull the pipe out and blow a small bubble to get it started, then I place that into the open mold. You close it, and I blow. The important thing to remember, as you blow, is to do it as forcefully as you can, so the melted glass fills the mold completely before it starts to cool and harden. Remember the ones I did that first day?"

By sunset that day, Jason had been too tired to blow hard enough and had produced several glasses that did not fill the mold.

The grapes looked like a blob of purple dung, all the tiny orbs melding into one misshapen mass.

Gaius chuckled. "They were pretty strange."

Jason laughed with him as he pulled the pipe from the furnace. "Yes, they were. And useless. So, you need to blow like you're trying to push back an advancing gladiator with your breath."

Gaius knelt and spread open a mold, and Jason placed the end of the rod inside. Gaius brought the pieces together and held tight as Jason blew, his eyes on Jason's mouth. When Jason finished, Gaius opened the mold and inspected one side. Jason jiggled the pipe a bit to free the object from the other half.

"Perfect," Gaius said. "As always." He grinned. "Well, maybe not always."

Jason lowered himself to the stool, resting the pipe across his knees.

"Get the pontil."

Gaius grabbed a smaller rod, gathered a bit of hot glass on the end, and attached it to the bottom of the cup. Jason reached for the pinchers and freed the top of the vessel from the blowpipe, then handed the pontil to Gai. "Heat it up."

Gaius's eyes widened. "Me?"

"Sure. Might as well." Jason placed the rod on the floor and reached for the wooden tongs in a basket beside him, while Gaius carried the pontil to the smaller furnace and inserted the cup into the flame.

"That should be long enough. Bring it here."

Gaius did as he was told and handed the pontil to Jason, who laid it across his legs and then placed the tongs into the small opening at the object's neck. "Now you roll the pontil back and forth over your legs, slowly making this opening as wide as the rest of the cup."

A rim slowly formed as the opening spread.

Jason held the cup up by the pontil and studied it, turning it first one way and then the other. "Looks good. Now what do we do?"

"Remove the rod."

"Yes." He banged on the small rod, and it snapped off, then he pressed the warm tongs to the bottom to smooth it out.

"All done."

Gaius took the cup from Jason's outstretched palm and placed it on the shelf in the cooling furnace.

"Now you try." Jason handed him the blowpipe.

A bit of fear diluted the expectant joy in Gaius's face.

"You'll do fine. You can't hurt anything. Unless you drop hot glass on me."

Gaius grinned and gathered glass on the pipe, blew a small bubble, then brought it to the molding bench where Jason knelt, his hands around a mold.

Hot glass pressing against the fired clay mold warmed Jason's hands as Gaius blew. It certainly felt like he had blown hard enough. Jason freed the object and checked it. He twisted his wrist to check all sides. Only one small imperfection. "The S in Dionysos isn't readable."

Gaius's face fell. "I'm so sorry, kyrie." He offered up the pipe. "I won't do any more."

"No! You did great. Better than I did my first time. Let's try again. Get a little more glass this time to make sure there's enough to fill all the depressions."

"Yes, kyrie."

"Get another pipe."

The boy loaded up another pipe, and this time his efforts produced a perfect cup. Jason attached the pontil and watched as Gaius formed the mouth and rim.

Gaius held it up as if it were an offering to the pagan gods.

Jason checked all sides again. "It's excellent."

"It is?"

"Yes." Jason patted his shoulder. "But we have seventy-eight more to do today, so let's keep going."

KASSI PONDERED the amphorae once overflowing with dried fruit, olives, goat cheese, and sesame seeds but now containing only broken bits. How could they run out of so many ingredients so fast?

"Isa, I'm going to the agora." Kassi called to the back of the bakery. "Can you keep everything running here?"

"Of course. And don't forget the olive oil."

"I'll have that delivered." Kassi left for the agora. After arranging with the fruit vendor to deliver dried figs and grapes, she purchased cheese then headed to the far end of the agora to find nuts and seeds. The seed vendor was often surly but had the best prices and excellent products.

"What do you need today?" He spoke without looking up.

"Poppy seeds and an amphora of walnuts." She noticed an open bag of sesame seeds. If she bought honey, they could make sesame-honey bars. "And I'll take some of those sesame seeds as well, for pastelli."

"You'll need more sesame seeds than that small package then."

"You're right. Can you send a whole amphora to the pistrinum along with the walnuts?" She reached into the leather bag tied to her belt and retrieved two bronze coins. "Here you go."

He grunted.

She gathered the poppy seeds and headed toward Publius's stall. His bright smile was the perfect antidote to the seed vendor's perpetually bad mood.

"Chairé, Kassi. How are you this sunny day?" It was a wonder his jovial, booming voice didn't cheer up the entire agora.

She laughed. "It is a beautiful day, isn't it?"

"What can I sell you?"

"Olives. Oil. And I need honey. A lot of it. I'm making sesame-honey cakes."

"You're in luck then. I have some fresh honey today, straight from the farm. Want a taste?"

"Please."

Publius dipped a piece of bread into the sweet golden liquid and held it out for her.

"Mmm. That's different. What's that flavor?" She licked her lips. "Thyme?"

"Yes! The farmer added fields of thyme to the clover."

"It's delicious. I'll take an amphora."

"I'll send it right away."

"You know what? Send two. And one of olives, and two of your best oil."

His ample belly bounced as he laughed. "You always get my best." He turned to his nephew. "Two honey, one olive, and two oil. To the bakery." The boy began loading the amphorae on a small cart. "And bring back the empty ones."

The scent of his roasting lamb reached her nose. "I'll take an obeliskos, too. A small one."

He shifted to the popina next to his stall. "How is the bakery doing? It's been how long now?"

"Two weeks. But we're doing better than I could have imagined. I have three women so far."

"Can you supply me?" He held up a round of flatbread and lay the meat inside it.

"Are you serious?"

"I am. The baker I've used for years keeps raising his prices, though his quality has suffered."

"I don't know if we could keep up yet." She grimaced. "If I had one more person, I could."

He cleared his throat, and for the first time in her memory, his face clouded. "I may know of someone."

"You do?"

"Come with me." He set the half-filled bread on the table and clapped his nephew on the back. "Wait until I'm back to deliver those. And don't give anything away to your friends this time." He led her down the narrow alley that ran along the agora. On the far side of the market sat a cluster of small but expensive-looking houses. "My niece showed up at my house last night. She ..." His voice broke. "Her husband sent her away. Her parents won't take her back."

"Not that it matters, but do you know why?"

"He drinks far too much wine, often undiluted. He gets drunk and does foolish things. Apparently, he's been sleeping with one of the slaves, and she now carries his child. When Maera complained ... well, you'll see."

They exited onto a narrow, paved road. He stopped with his hand on a door. "I should warn you. She looks terrible. Her eye is black, and her lip is split. She won't talk to me, and she hasn't left her room since she arrived. You know my wife died last year, and I don't know what to do." He shrugged. "I tried to hug her when she arrived, but she cried out ... there must be more bruising beneath her clothing."

He opened the door and motioned for her to enter before him. She waited in the atrium while he went down a hall and reappeared with a girl no older than Kassi.

Kassi suppressed a gasp. The woman's face and arms were covered in purple bruises. Her head was bowed, her feet bare. Her dress was torn and her hair matted. The cut on her lip was held together with dried blood.

Kassi handed Publius her basket. "Can you send these to the shop along with the oil and honey? Oh, and tell Isa to close up if I'm not back in time."

"Of course." He blinked several times. "You know we never had children," he whispered. "She's as close to a daughter as I have. She's of course welcome to stay here, but I know that won't be enough. Her heart is broken, and I don't know how to help her."

"I'll talk to her."

"Her name is Maera. Whatever you need should be in the culina. I borrowed some clothes, but she hasn't changed yet." He offered a weak smile and left.

Kassi took one step nearer. "My name is Kassi."

Silence.

"May I help get you into a fresh tunic?"

After a long moment, the girl bobbed her head one time.

Kassi neared her but did not touch her. "Let's go into the culina, all right?"

Maera followed her to the back of the house, and Kassi found some cloth, water, honey, and the clean clothes. Publius had gathered everything Maera would need to clean up, but she hadn't done so yet.

Kassi would need to move slowly. She dipped a cloth into the bowl of water and scanned the room. There were no benches, chairs, or stools.

"Why don't we go to the triclinium?" Kassi grabbed the clothes and led her to the room next door.

Maera sat, and Kassi knelt before her. "May I have your arm?" She reached for her hand. "I'm going to try to be as gentle as I can. Let me know if I hurt you, all right?"

Maera nodded.

Kassi washed her arms and neck, then drew the cloth over her forehead, and cheeks. Maera winced and sucked in a breath when Kassi touched her eye but didn't pull away.

"Should we change your chiton?"

Maera stood and allowed Kassi to unpin the sleeves. The chiton, made of the finest linen, fell to the floor, revealing silk undergarments. Her husband had taken care of her material needs at least.

Her torso was dotted with splotches of varying colors. It wasn't the first time she'd been beaten.

Kassi washed her, keeping the pressure light and avoiding the worst of the bruises. "I'm going to let you dress while I get some more water. Then we can wash your hair." After emptying the bowl of water and refilling it, she rummaged through the culina's shelves for vinegar. She returned to the dining area and found Maera looking much better. She even held her head up.

While Maera bent over a bowl on the table, Kassi poured water onto her hair. It wasn't as bad as it had looked. A little dried blood, likely from her lip, but no horrible knots. Kassi poured vinegar over it, using her fingers to separate the locks, then followed with one last rinse of water. She dried her hair as much as possible with a cloth before dabbing honey on her split lip. "There. You must feel much better now."

Maera allowed a slight smile and winced.

A soft knock sounded on the front door. Kassi hurried to the front and opened it.

Publius held a basket full of fresh bread, soft cheese, and olives, along with a small amphora. "I brought you both some food." He searched her face. "How is she?"

"Much better."

He let out a quick breath. "I hope she can eat something now. She's so thin."

"I'll see what I can do. She's clean and safe, so she might be ready to eat."

"The bread's from your shop. Isa sent it." He handed her the basket and left.

Kassi carried the basket to the dining room. "Maera, your uncle sent us some lovely food. Are you hungry?"

Maera eyed the warm bread.

"Would you like some? It's from my bakery."

Maera took a small bite. "It's good." The first words Kassi had heard her speak.

Kassi poured wine, and they shared the bread and cheese.

Maera yawned.

"I'll leave you to rest now, but I can return tomorrow. Would you like that?"

She nodded. "Eucharisto."

"Your uncle can tell you about the pistrinum. You're welcome to join us if you like."

Kassi's heart soared as she returned to the bakery. She could not give up helping these women.

No matter what.

Pappa would just have to understand.

YOEL DROPPED onto the couch outside his house facing the courtyard. The days were so short this time of year, and the shortest was not quite three weeks away. That day should be a joyous one, as afterward the sun remained in the sky longer each day, but as usual, the Greeks and Romans had turned it into a day of drunkenness, promiscuity, and the celebration of false gods.

He put such thoughts away and breathed in the scents of Leah's Shabbat bread. What did she put in it today? Dried figs? Olives? Nuts? He sniffed again but couldn't tell.

No matter. He loved them all.

Across the yard, Micah sat outside his house, a child on his lap. The boy laughed and tried to grab an apple held by the elder, who managed to yank it out of the way each time, sending the child into fits of giggles.

The one regret of Yoel's life was that Adonai had not blessed them with children. When he was younger, he could block out the silence, the empty rooms, the large table with only two plates. Leah had managed to fill her loneliness by teaching young girls, who now often brought their own children to visit, but Yoel had chosen to remain as busy as possible at the synagogue.

Now that the years had ravaged his body, he was less active, quieter, slower, and the discomforting thoughts could not as easily be kept away. Other men his age spent hours in the courtyard playing with grandchildren, while Yoel could only watch.

"Yoel, shalom." Paulos took a seat beside him. "Another Shabbat is almost upon us."

"Yes. That's good, because I'm very hungry." He laughed. "Paulos, may I ask, are you married? Do you have children?"

Paulos was silent for a long moment. "I was married once. She died before we had children."

Micah's laughter reached them as his grandson finally wrenched the apple from his hand and bolted across the garden.

Yoel looked away. "I'm sorry. It's an empty life without children."

"It can be. I was empty and angry for many years before I met Yeshua."

"He didn't give you descendants, so how did that help?" Yoel couldn't stop the misery from coating his words.

"No, He gave me no children, but He gave me so much more. He gave me hope and forgiveness and a purpose."

This was not a conversation Yoel wanted to begin moments before dinner. But he might as well deliver the elders' warning since Leah's summons would stop any hint of conflict.

Yoel shifted in his seat. "Paulos, I have been warned by the elders, and I must now warn you."

"What about?"

"About this Yeshua. You can't mention him again."

Paulos leaned forward, forearms on his knees. "I must deliver the message Adonai gives me."

Yoel whipped his head toward the visitor. "You claim Adonai instructed you to deliver such a message?"

"I would not speak it otherwise."

"Setting aside the notion that Adonai talks to you, why would He have you speak such nonsense?"

Paulos sat up straight and twisted to face Yoel. "It is not nonsense. It is the fulfillment of centuries of prophecy. From the very beginning Adonai has promised a Redeemer."

"Of course, He has. But why do you think the promised one is a criminal and a rebel?"

Paulos smiled. "Why do you think He cannot be the Promised One?"

This was exactly the conversation Yoel had hoped to avoid. "Moses says, 'Adonai is not mortal.' He is eternal, above time, beyond space. He has always been and will always be. He cannot be born and cannot die." He threw his hands in the air. "To say He assumes human form at all, let alone comes to us as a helpless baby and then is crucified, makes Him small. It denies His divinity!"

"He came to us as a man so that we would have a High Priest who suffered as we suffer, and who overcame death."

"All right. The prophet Micah said His greatness will reach to the ends of the earth. *We've* barely heard of Him, let alone the ends of the earth. And Isaiah said the Mashiach would establish peace on earth, that He would reign on the throne of David. There is no peace, and the man on the throne is no descendant of David. Your Yeshua accomplished none of the things that have been prophesied."

"Ah, but that is only if you assume the Mashiach was supposed to bring peace among nations, peace between *men*." Paulos spread his arms wide. "He brought peace between men and Himself— forgiveness, freedom from sin."

"But he was a nobody. How could he bring peace of any kind?"

Paulos leaned a shoulder against the wall. "Isaiah also said of Him, 'He had no beauty or majesty to attract us to Him. He was despised, rejected, familiar with pain. On the cross, He was pierced for our transgressions and crushed for our iniquities. The punishment that brought us peace was borne by Him, and by His wounds we are healed.'"

Leah appeared at the door. "The meal is ready."

"This is accomplishing nothing. I have delivered the warning." He rose and faced Paulos. "Do *not* speak of Yeshua tomorrow." He followed Leah into the house.

Whether Paulos would heed the warning remained to be seen.

14

"This Jesus I am proclaiming to you is the Messiah," he said.

— ACTS 17.3B

YOEL CHEWED HIS THUMBNAIL AS PAULOS MADE HIS WAY TO THE center of the synagogue.

"Listen now to the words of the Lord as told to us by the prophet Isaiah." Paulos found the proper place in the scroll, but again, spoke without reading.

"'This is what God the Lord says—

the Creator of the heavens, who stretches them out,

who spreads out the earth with all that springs from it,

who gives breath to its people, and life to those who walk on it:

"I, the Lord, have called you in righteousness; I will take hold of your hand.

I will keep you and will make you to be a covenant for the people

and a light for the Gentiles,

to open eyes that are blind, to free captives from prison

and to release from the dungeon those who sit in darkness.'"''

Paulos set the scroll down. "In the past, Adonai spoke to us through prophets, but now He has spoken to us by His Son, Yeshua. Through Him, the forgiveness of sins is proclaimed to us all, and *everyone* who believes is set free from all sin. This is a justification we were not able to obtain under the law of Moses, and which the Gentiles have been unable to attain at all. Until now."

Every muscle in Yoel's body tightened. What could Paulos mean by *until now*?

"The prophet Isaiah said, 'My house shall be called a house of prayer for *all* nations.' And Adonai, who gathers the outcasts of Israel, says He will bring others to Himself as well. He told Abraham, 'I will bless those who bless you and curse those who curse you, and all peoples on earth will be blessed through you.' Through Isaiah he says, 'It is too small a thing for you to be My servant to restore the tribes of Jacob and bring back those of Israel I have kept. I will also make you a light for the Gentiles, that My salvation may reach to the ends of the earth.'"

Yoel groaned silently. He'd always known the Greeks would bring trouble, but he'd been overruled when he expressed his opposition to their attendance. Could this possibly get any worse?

"This is a good and honorable thing for Israel," the Pharisee continued, his face as bright as a groom's. "Indeed, Adonai commands us to rejoice at this news. Zechariah tells us to 'Shout and be glad because Adonai is coming and will live among us. Many nations will be joined with Adonai in that day and will become His people.'"

Dark murmuring among the faithful grew louder, but the Pharisee did not stop.

"And Hosea tells us Adonai will call those who were not my people My people.' Paulos raised his voice a bit. "And He will call those who were not His beloved His beloved.'"

Yoel squirmed in his seat. Micah said hearing Adonai's holy words, even if they were meant for His chosen people and not for them, could only help the Greeks, perhaps introduce them to a holier way of living. And while they could never be one of His family, perhaps embracing the Jewish way of life would bring the Jewish community more favor in the city.

But now the Pharisee had offered salvation to the Greeks!

Yoel couldn't stand to even think the words. And though he'd been opposed to Greeks in the synagogue all along, he would be the one held responsible for this ... this *abomination*.

He'd be removed from his position, shamed before the community.

He might have to leave Thessalonike.

His deepest fears had come to pass. Paulos had ruined his life.

If only Jason had never bought him to the house ...

***

WITH GAIUS at his feet holding tightly to the mold, Jason blew steadily into the pipe. The bubble of melted glass slowly rose above the top to form the neck, and Jason pulled his mouth from the pipe.

Gai pulled the sides of the mold apart, revealing a perfect glass cup.

"Now the pontil."

"I know. We've done this eighty times a day for weeks." Gaius inserted the shorter rod into the furnace and gathered a tiny blob of glass, then held it out.

Jason laughed as he brought the cup near, touching the base of it to the hot glass on the rod. "It's only been twelve days. And we'll do it eighty times a day for thirteen more." The first Shabbat, after service, they'd completed only forty-five. Skipping today's service had kept them from falling even farther behind, but he had no idea when they would have time to catch up. Eighty a day was almost too much as it was.

A rap on the door frame drew their attention.

Jason turned his gaze to the man in the entrance. His spotless linen chiton draped his body perfectly. A deep blue cloak hung from his shoulders, attached with gold fibulae. Even his sandals were free of dust as if he'd entered the village on a cloud.

"Yes?"

"I came to check on my order."

The man offered no other explanation, as if everyone would intuitively know who he was and what he might want. The only order Jason was working on was for ... "Damianos?"

He smiled as he stepped inside. "I ordered two thousand glass cups for the festival of Dionysos."

"I'm working on them right now." He took the glass from a stunned Gaius and led Damianos toward the straw-filled crate in the corner.

Damianos knelt and selected one. He turned it over and over, studying the bottom, the sides, the inside. He ran his finger along the rim, allowing a small nod of approval before frowning. "Where are the handles?"

"Handles?" A shard of panic pierced Jason's chest. His mind raced through everything the contract specified, but Ari had never mentioned handles.

"Yes. It should have a handle."

"The contract didn't mention that."

"I told the other man. The older one. I assumed he was the owner. Where is he?" He pivoted on one foot and scanned the room, searching. "I want to talk to *him*, not some ... subordinate."

Jason harnessed the angry grief that begged to escape. "*That man* was my abba. He—" He paused to clear his throat. "He's not here."

He replaced the cup and stood. "Where is he? I only deal with those who are in charge."

"He's dead." Enough with being subtle. "This is my shop now, and you can deal with me or with no one."

Damianos ran remorseless eyes over Jason. "All right. I told him

I wanted handles." He scoffed. "I knew I should have gone to the shop in Apollonia."

"You mean the one owned by the man my abba trained?"

"And I didn't want blue. I wanted purple. You know, the color of *grapes*."

"None of that was in the contract."

Damianos tilted his head. "I think it was."

"We can go to the office of the agoranomos if you like." Jason moved toward the door.

"No. I'll check my copy later." He pointed to the crate. "If this is all you've completed, I don't see how you'll finish on time."

"This is only today's work."

Damianos raised a brow. "Where are all the others?"

"I'm storing them elsewhere." He wouldn't risk telling Damianos where. Who knows what he might do? If he didn't want them until two days before the festival, he wouldn't get them one day earlier. "You wanted them all delivered at the same time."

"How many have you made?"

Jason quickly calculated. Twelve days, eighty per day. Almost ... "Not quite one thousand."

Damianos scoffed. "We signed a contract over five weeks ago. You have less than two weeks left, and you're not even halfway to the total required."

"I know exactly how many days I have. I lost a week after ..." He paused, trying to ignore the sharp stab of pain. "I have counted the days, and I'll finish on time. I promise you."

"Promises are worthless. Only actions count."

"You will have them on the fourth day of Poseidon."

Damianos crossed his arms. "I need them earlier. I have to get them—"

"The contract specifies two days before. I plan to finish three days earlier as it is." Although if he didn't catch up, he might need that extra day.

Damianos glared. "We'll see about that. I'll read the contract over again. If I discover you haven't met every requirement..." He headed out but stopped at the door and turned around. "One thing I'm certain is in there—the penalty."

"I am fully aware of the penalty." *Achingly, agonizingly aware.*

"Then you'd better be prepared to pay it." The man stormed from the shop.

Gaius rose. "Is that ...?"

"Yes. That's who we're making the glasses for."

"Why is he so rude? It's like he wants us to fail."

"It is, isn't it?" Anger, jealousy, and compassion vied for prominence in his head at the thought of Kassi spending her life with that arrogant man.

"But don't worry, Gai. You and I will complete this order on time, and then we won't have to deal with him ever again." Jason wasn't quite lying, but he wasn't at all sure they would finish. One mistake —a fire gone cold, a broken mold, even just a miscount—could ruin everything.

And Damianos wasn't someone to have as an enemy.

KASSI COULD NOT GET the words out of her head.

"Through him *everyone* who believes is set free from every sin, a justification no one could obtain under the law of Moses," the man had said the day before.

Did that really mean everyone? Or only the Jewish people who had the law of Moses in the first place?

Kassi leaned into the dough she kneaded, shoving part of it forward with the heel of her hand. She folded the dough back on itself and leaned into it again.

But that wouldn't include the Greeks. It couldn't. The Jews were fiercely jealous of their God and His relationship with them. They allowed the Greeks to come hear the readings of the sacred texts each week, but they were never part of the community.

"Kassi!"

Isa's strident voice shook her from her thoughts.

"What?"

"I called your name three times." Isa smiled, but her worry showed through.

"I'm so sorry. Did you need me?"

"No, but I think you need to stop working that before it becomes rock hard."

Kassi looked at the flattened ball of dough before her. She pulled at it, and it stretched. A little.

"Guess I stopped just in time." She chuckled. "I *hate* waste."

"I know you do." Isa frowned. "You seem very distracted."

"I am a bit, I guess. I heard something yesterday I'm trying to understand."

"Why don't you let me finish that, and you can go to the agora or something? Clear your head."

Kassi rubbed her hands together, dislodging bits of dough. "I should before I ruin it all." She stuck a finger in the dough. "I was going to add olives, but I think it's too late for that. We'll probably have to eat this ourselves. I don't think we can sell it." She wiped her hands on a towel. "Thank you, Isa."

Isa nodded.

"I'll be back soon." Kassi crossed the cardo and strolled toward the agora. Pastelli would be tasty. They hadn't made any at the bakery yet, since she hadn't obtained the long, shallow pans they'd need.

Maybe the glassblower could make them.

Memories of his kind eyes and gentle touch from the other night flooded her with warmth. If only she hadn't blurted out that reckless wish that Pappa had promised her to someone like Jason instead of Damianos.

She shuddered and banished that repulsive man from her thoughts.

She found the stall with the bars and purchased two, then

continued walking under the portico toward the far end of the market. She bit into a bar, the sweet honey and crunchy sesame seeds coating her tongue.

What did Paulos call the promised redeemer? All she could remember was "Prince of Peace." What was the rest? Counselor ... Mighty ... something ...

It was no use. She couldn't recall. Maybe he would say it again next time.

Ahead of her, Timos, the friend of Paulos who had come to the bakery to buy bread, was at the fish shop. He would know. She quickened her steps to catch him. His transaction would be completed soon, and she might never find him again in the busy agora.

Timos reached for the cooked fish as he handed the vendor his coins. She angled toward the center of the market to intercept him as he left but realized how foolish she must appear. Cheeks burning, she turned and headed back to the covered walkway.

Halfway there, she peeked over her shoulder to be sure he hadn't seen her, but he was gone.

She breathed a sigh of relief and faced forward again, but Timos, along with Silas and Paulos, strolled toward her. They must have stepped onto the walkway when she expected them to leave the agora altogether.

"Good morning, Kassi." Timos's bright smile calmed her fears. Apparently, he didn't think she was crazy. "I'd like you to meet Paulos and Silas."

It took a moment to force words from her dry mouth. "I ... I heard you yesterday in the synagogue."

Paulos smiled, his eyes soft. "I saw you."

His voice washed over her like water, soothing her soul. She'd never heard Pappa speak so gently.

Timos jerked a thumb over his shoulder. "Would you like to join us? We were about to share our midday meal."

Would he allow her to ask about yesterday? Even if he didn't, she longed to be around people so serene, so confidently at peace with themselves and the world—something she'd never experienced.

"Yes, I would. Thank you."

"Silas loves to watch the waves, so we like to sit by the sea. Is that all right with you?"

She nodded.

Timos led them beyond the southern gate. A knee-high wall bordered the road to the harbor.

Silas brushed some dirt from a spot on the wall and sat. Paulos sat on one side of him, and she took the other. Timos wandered closer to the sea.

Silas grinned. "He says I am the one who likes to watch the waves, but I think it's him." He took a bite of his fish.

Paulos turned to her. "So, Kassandra, what did you think of my message yesterday?"

Silas laughed. "The synagogue leaders weren't happy with him."

"They weren't?" Kassi frowned. "Why?"

"The Jewish leaders—everywhere, not only here—do not believe Yeshua is the Promised One." He bit into his flatbread.

"Why not?" she asked.

"Many reasons. Mainly because it takes away their power." Silas answered since Paulos had a mouth full of bread. "And their wealth."

"I must admit," Paulos said, "that Yoel does not seem like the synagogue leaders we've met in other places. He doesn't claim a large portion of the tithes for himself."

"They do that?"

"In some places." Paulos nodded. "But to my original question. You, Kassandra—what did *you* think?"

"Well, it isn't for me, is it?"

"What's not for you?" Paulos twisted to face her more squarely.

"The message." She swallowed. "The redeemer. The forgiveness. Any of it. It's for the Jews."

Paulos's face lit like the sun had come from behind a cloud. "Oh, but it *is* for you. It's for *everyone*."

"You said that yesterday, but I assumed you meant all Jews."

With his food in his lap, Paulos spread his arms as if to embrace the whole town. "When Yeshua was born, angels announced His birth, and they said they had joyful news for *all* people."

She'd never heard that. "They did?"

"Yes. And Yeshua himself said, 'If *anyone* hears My words, and does not obey them, I don't judge him, because I didn't come to judge the world. I came to *save* the world.' The world, Kassandra. That means everyone—Jews, Greeks, Romans, *anyone*."

"But how can that be?" That didn't make sense.

A young man hurried toward them. His short tunic identified him as a city slave. He stopped before them and dipped his head. "Paulos?"

Paulos raised a finger. "That's me."

"The agoranomos wishes to speak to you about the shade sails. He awaits you in the warehouse."

Paulos nodded before turning to Kassi. "I'm so sorry, Kassandra. We'll be sure to finish this conversation later."

"Of course."

The men gathered the remains of their meal and followed the slave, with Timos rushing to catch up.

Kassi sighed. Any answers she might get would have to wait.

JASON WAS BEHIND, having created only seventy-one glasses. Not hugely short of the quota for the day, but nine a day would easily add up to a number that could not be overcome.

"One more. Then we're done for today. Your turn."

Gaius blew into the pipe, and Jason held the mold against the pressure. As Gaius forced the last bit of air from his lungs, the mold cracked. Glass protruded through the cracks, ruining the cup and the mold.

Gaius let go of the pipe and backed away. "I'm so sorry, kyrie. I-I don't know what happened. I don't think I did anything differently." He dropped to his knees, hands clasped at his chest. "Please do not beat me. I will pay for it. Somehow."

Beat him? Why would he think that?

"I'm not going to hit you, Gaius."

"Oh. Then I'll clean up before I go." His voice wavered. "Thank you for all you've taught me. I have learned much." He stood.

"Why does this sound like you're leaving me?"

He stared at the dirt under his feet. "I assumed you wouldn't want me around anymore."

Jason stood before the boy and placed his hands on his upper arms. "Gaius, look at me."

He dragged his gaze to Jason, his eyes moist.

"This was not your fault. I've broken molds before. So did my abba. They're made of clay, and they wear out. We have another left, and I can make more."

His eyes widened. "You're not sending me away?"

"Of course not. But why don't you go home? I'll need you back at first light, so eat a good meal, and get some rest. I'll bring you some pastelli in the morning."

A bright smile covered Gaius's face. "Yes, kyrie. Eucharisto!" He loped off.

It was only a mistake, and he couldn't blame Gaius. But it was a costly error. He needed time to make another mold. He couldn't risk breaking the one remaining and being caught with none.

And time was one thing he didn't have.

15

Those who repay my good with evil
    lodge accusations against me,
    though I seek only to do what is good.

— PSALM 38.20

JASON GROWLED WHEN BANGING ON HIS DOOR INTERRUPTED HIS SLEEP. His shuttered window defied the dusky light trying to enter. Between the long hours and the stabbing pain in his shoulder and arm every time he moved, he wasn't resting well, and rising long before dawn wasn't helping.

He rose and padded to the front door, his bare feet flinching on the cold tile.

The pounding continued.

"I'm coming!" He opened the door to his uncle, face red, hands clenched.

As much as he didn't get along with Yoel, he hated to see him in such distress.

"Dodh? What's wrong? Is Dodah all right?"

"No, she's not. And neither am I." He jabbed a finger toward Jason. "And it's your fault." Yoel's face grew redder by the moment.

He stepped back. "My fault? What did I do?"

"You brought them here!" He could hardly sputter the words through his rage.

"Who? What are you taking about?"

"That Pharisee and his friends."

"Dodh, please come inside." Jason extended an arm. "Tell me what happened."

Yoel glared for a long moment but made his way through the atrium. to the garden.

Jason followed and sat facing him. "You brought them to my home, and now he preaches falsehoods and lies. And *I* will be held responsible."

Jason listened to Yoel's list of fears and complaints, saying nothing. Perhaps he should apologize, though what he had to apologize for, he couldn't guess. Still, if it would help mend the fractured relationship Jason had with his only living relatives, he had to figure it out.

"I have to go." Yoel rose. "I expect the elders will be at my home at any moment."

"What do they want from you? You can't be responsible for what another man says."

"It's *all* my responsibility. At least for now." He chuckled mirthlessly and slouched toward the door, a tired, old man replacing the livid uncle of moments ago.

Why would a Pharisee do something like this to his uncle? Why say such wild things, knowing it would cause chaos and confusion? Besides, from everything Jason had been taught since he was a babe, his words couldn't be true.

He glanced skyward. The sun was now fully risen, and he needed to get to the shop. What he wanted to do was find Paulos and get some answers. He returned to his chamber and dressed, then slipped out of his house to make a quick trip to the market for the pastelli he'd promised Gai.

He was halfway across the cardo when he noticed Paulos and his followers entering the agora.

This was all their fault. How could they do this to Yoel, to the people who'd given him food and shelter for almost three weeks? Paulos needed to explain himself.

"Paulos." Jason neared him, his anger probably showing more than he'd intended.

"Shalom, Jason."

Paulos's innocent smile hid the guilt he must be feeling. The man had to know what his actions would mean for Yoel. "What did you expect to accomplish yesterday?"

Paulos frowned. "What do you mean?"

"You know what I mean. All that talk about Adonai accepting the Gentiles. You must have known what kind of reaction that would provoke. Yoel warned you, and you did it anyway. You'll leave this town, sooner or later, but my dodh and dodah have to live here and bear the shame of your actions." He spread his hands. "They're old and could lose everything. How could you? You don't care about anyone but yourself, do you?"

Paulos opened his mouth but said nothing.

Jason let his hands fall against his thighs. "I don't know what I thought talking to you would accomplish." He turned to go.

"Jason, please. Let me explain." Paulos called after him.

He halted and spun back around. "Why?"

"Please?"

What could it hurt?

"My friend, I had no choice. I could obey either Yoel and your elders, or I could obey Adonai. What would you have done in my place?"

A ridiculous excuse. "Adonai wanted you to destroy my family?"

"No. Adonai wants to offer salvation to your family ... and to everyone else. We are all His creation, and He wants all to be forgiven."

"How can they be forgiven without a sacrifice? I'm no Pharisee, but I know the text says, 'There is no forgiveness without the shedding of blood.'"

A smile brightened the old man's face. "Yes. That's right. But there is now no need to shed the blood of a lamb every morning and evening. Yeshua spilled *His own* blood for us. He loved us so much He gave Himself up for us as a fragrant offering—a final sacrifice, sufficient for all."

"That's a nice thought, but it seems you care more about the Gentiles than your own people."

Pain clouded his eyes. "Oh, Jason." His voice was low, raspy. "How far that is from the truth." He stared at some point in the distance—or in the past—it was hard to tell. "I would cut myself off from the Mashiach if it meant that you, your uncle, *all* my people would believe in Him."

What an outrageous sentiment. "You would? Why?"

"Because *we* are God's chosen people! To *us* He gave His glorious presence, the covenant, the temple, His very words! Through *our* bloodline is the genealogy of the Mashiach."

"So why include the Gentiles?"

"Because it is not merely the natural offspring of Abraham who are considered the children of God—rather, all children born because of God's promise are counted as descendants."

"I don't follow."

"God says in Hosea, 'I will call them "My people" who are not My people.'"

"How can those who are not His people become His people? It's nonsense."

"Because all you need do to become His child is accept His sacrifice as payment for your sin."

"That's it? Just accept it, and all our sins vanish?" Jason tried not to scoff.

"Exactly."

"After centuries of sacrificing and priests and ... That cannot be all there is to it."

That infuriating smile returned. "And yet it is."

The day was getting away from him. Jason needed to get away from such babble, from these ridiculous words that destroyed Yoel's life.

"I have to go."

Paulos's sincerity—and his love for his people—was unquestionable. But no matter what he said, it couldn't be that simple.

———

YOEL WHISPERED a prayer as the group filed into his home.

The room closed in on him as he faced the elders standing before him like a tribunal. He clasped his hands as demands were listed. His heart pounded in his ears, thoughts chased each other, and fears multiplied.

"Please don't make me do this. Think of the reputation of the community, of the synagogue."

"That *is* what we're thinking of." Lior stepped nearer, his pudgy face uncomfortably close to Yoel's. "Think of our reputation if we let this error stand without correcting it." His nostrils flared, hot breath reaching Yoel's face.

Micah's bony hand landed on Lior's shoulder, and the younger man's breathing calmed. Slightly.

"Last week was bad enough, bringing up that criminal and claiming he was the Mashiach. But this ..." Micah shrugged and shook his head. "To suggest that what Adonai meant for the chosen people of Adonai can be offered to anyone ... to people who have never learned—let alone obeyed—the law given to us by Moses ... It's unfathomable. Unforgivable."

"We cannot abide this," another said. "The damage has already been done. I don't know if it can be fixed. The teaching that will be required to undo his lies will take weeks, maybe months."

Lior looked down his nose at Yoel. "This is all your doing. You brought him here. You make him go."

Micah moved between his son and Yoel. "Lior, you are the one who needs to go."

Lior stumbled back a step, eyes wide, mouth open. "What?" His voice rose. "I'm not the one who brought this on our people. He is!" He pointed at Yoel.

"You are not helping matters." Micah remained calm. "In fact, I want all of you to go. I will speak to Yoel alone. Perhaps without all the emotion and interruptions, we can solve this problem."

The others disappeared.

"The only way to solve this is for the visitors to go," Lior said. "And perhaps Yoel should go with them."

"Lior! Leave us, now!"

Yoel recoiled. He had never heard Micah raise his voice to anyone, let alone his own son. And if he raised his voice to Lior ... This did not bode well for him.

Lior stalked out, muttering.

Micah sat on the center couch. "Yoel, join me."

Leave it to Micah to take the place of honor. In Yoel's own home.

Yoel chose another seat. "You come into my home uninvited, berate me, insult me, threaten me ... what more do you want from me?"

Micah leaned forward, his forearms on his knees. "Yoel, I know you're angry, and part of me understands. But we gave you a chance to stop this."

Yoel forced his breathing to calm. "I cannot help it if he lied to me. He assured me he wouldn't repeat the lies of last Shabbat."

"But he did. And now we must deal with it." Micah straightened and folded his hands in his lap. "Paulos needs to be stopped. He needs to be told he is no longer welcome in the synagogue."

"But he is a Pharisee." Yoel jumped up. "How do we keep him

from speaking in the synagogue?" He raised his hands to his sides, palms up. "He will never accept this. It is unthinkable. He won't accept something so ... so humiliating."

Micah studied Yoel. "Why are you defending him?"

"I'm not defending him. Far from it. I'm saying this will not work as you think. A man in his position is not used to being told what to do. Or not do."

"It's not his humiliation we are concerned about. It's ours. How much more embarrassing would it be if it becomes known across the world the Jews of Thessalonike are freely giving away Adonai's greatest gift—salvation—to Gentiles?"

Yoel took his seat again. "Just because someone says it, does not mean we're doing it."

"Those outside our city may not see the difference."

"This is your decision. I think *you* should inform him."

"No. This must come from you."

"But it's not my decision." Yoel jabbed the table with a finger.

"It was your decision to ask him to speak."

"And you approved it."

"Do you want it to look like we overruled you, or do you want it to look like you are the leader of the synagogue?"

Yoel blew out a breath. Which would be worse? He rose. "They are sharing the evening meal with someone else. He will be told tomorrow."

Micah stood to face him. "Excellent."

Paulos would never again speak in their synagogue.

Wasn't that what Yoel wanted? He didn't want Paulos spewing his lies any more than the elders. So why did Micah's request bother him so much?

Perhaps because he hadn't had the courage to do it himself before being ordered to.

KASSI GLANCED at the darkening sky as she hurried toward home. Pappa had warned her not to be late again. How angry would he be? He was already frustrated with her—leaving the house too often, buying the bakery, helping "those women" ...

Lida waited outside the front door. "Oh, kyria, you're late again. Your pater is not happy." Arm outstretched, she held the door as Kassi rushed inside.

"I know, I know. Here, take my cloak. I'm only moments late, so maybe I can keep him from becoming too angry."

She shoved the garment at Lida and headed down the hall, but the slave grabbed her hand and pulled her back.

"No, kyria, you must clean up first. Look at yourself." She grasped a handful of Kassi's chiton and lifted it.

The fabric carried stains of olive oil and goat cheese, and the hem was filthy.

"And ..." Lida winced and moved her finger toward Kassi's neck.

Kassi ran her fingers over her skin, touching dried specks of dough. "Oh, Lida, eucharisto." She hurried into her chamber.

Lida moved to the chest at the foot of the bed and selected a deep blue chiton. "Here. I'll take the soiled one." She left the room with the dirty chiton and cloak.

Kassi pulled the clean one over her head, and Lida returned a moment later with a bowl and a cloth. She set the bowl on the floor. "Why don't you wash your face while I wash your feet?"

Kassi glanced at the mirror. Her hair looked like she'd been in a windstorm. By the time she finished brushing it, Lida had removed Kassi's sandals, cleaned her feet, and set out a clean pair.

Kassi rose and hugged Lida. "Thank you so much." She looked in the direction of the triclinium. "Now to face my pater."

"Be confident. He respects that."

Kassi hurried to the dining area and took a seat beside Larissa.

Pappa set his goblet down. "You're late." He spoke without looking at her.

She reached for a piece of fish. "I know, Pappa. I'm sorry—"

"I told you not to let it happen again."

"I know, but I couldn't help it. Another woman came to the bakery today. She had no place to live, no money—"

"Then obviously she's a beggar." Argos scowled.

"Or a prostitute," Kadmos added.

Kassi clenched her fists under the table and paused a moment to calm her frustration. "She isn't a beggar or a prostitute. She needs a little help—"

"And how long do you think you can support these people?" asked Secundus.

She brightened. Maybe she could finally make them understand. "That's just it, Pappa. I'm *not* supporting them. All I did was buy the bakery and an oven. They are now earning money." She looked around the table. Why was no one as excited as she was? "They work, they make bread, we sell it, and they get paid. They're close to supporting themselves now, and soon they won't need me."

More blank stares.

"Then why did they need you in the first place?"

"There's no way they could have started this on their own. None of them had money, let alone the position that would allow them to buy the building—"

"Kassandra!"

She had never seen Pappa's face so dark.

He sat up. "This is too much. It must stop."

She played with a piece of bread. "I can't stop helping people. We have so much, and they have so little."

"Because we earned it." Kadmos threw one hand in the air.

"*You* didn't. You inherited it." Kassi spat her words.

His eyes shot arrows at her. "So did you."

"Yes, and I am using my inheritance to help others, not myself."

Overlapping voices mingled with Kassi's as she tried to defend herself against her brothers.

"Enough!"

All heads turned toward Pappa. Had he ever shouted like that?

"My daughter, you have to stop doing this."

"Doing what?"

His face twisted into an ugly version of the pappa she knew and loved. "Mingling with those ... those people."

"Poor people? Hurt people?" How could he hold them responsible for being poor?

"They are not our problem. And you're embarrassing us," Argos said.

Pappa glared at him, and her brother turned his attention to his food.

"How am I embarrassing you?" she asked.

"Today in the agora, one of the councilors asked me if I knew what you've been doing. Buying that building and doing I don't know what in there, with a group of people that wouldn't be allowed on this side of the Via. They are *not our people*, Kassi."

"Well, *our* people don't need my help."

"The bakery is up and running, so let the women have it, and behave."

She shrugged. "I'm sorry. I can't ignore them when there is so much more I can do."

"Kassi, if you persist in acting this way, I'm afraid I cannot let you continue to teach Penelope." Kadmos threw a questioning glance at Pappa, but he wasn't rebuked.

"I must agree." Argos added.

"What?" Her breathing came faster. "What have I ever taught them that's so bad?"

"Nothing. Yet."

"Argos, hold on a moment." Larissa put her hand over her husband's, but he pulled it away. "Kassi has been wonderful to the girls. All three of them. She's taught them history, numbers, reading ... no one else will do it."

"I've let her teach them because it wasn't hurting them. But now, neither we nor the girls can afford to be connected to her."

"So, because you're angry at Kassi, the girls are prohibited from learning?" Larissa asked.

"Why do they need to know how to read or write? They're *girls*." Kadmos chuckled.

"That's how these women end up in the situations they are in." Kassi scoffed. "They have no skills to help themselves." It was so simple. How could they not understand this?

"This conversation is over." Pappa rose. "Kassandra, you will act like the daughter of the politarch should act."

"And how is that? Exactly?"

"Sell the bakery. Get your money back. Marry Damianos." He headed for the door.

His words sliced though her heart like a Roman dagger. Could she do that—go back to life as an idle, pampered, ignored woman? "Pappa, I don't think I can do that."

He stopped mid-step, then turned to face her. "What did you say?"

"I can't do that," she whispered.

"Are you defying me in my own home?" He stalked toward her. "Think carefully before you answer."

She did think. Was she ready to deal with the consequences? Whatever they were, she wasn't ready to give up the new life she'd come to treasure. "I'm so sorry, Pappa. I wish I could ... I can't."

His face hardened for only an instant. "I wish you could too," he whispered. He turned and left the room.

Kadmos shook his head, and Argos smirked.

What had she done?

16

Some of the Jews were persuaded and joined Paul and Silas, as did a large number of God-fearing Greeks and quite a few prominent women.

— ACTS 17.4

Slumped on a couch in the triclinium, Yoel wrapped both hands around a tall cup of pomegranate juice.

How had he gotten to this point? He felt like a stone tossed in the ocean, waves coming at him from all sides. Was anyone happy with him at present? Jason and Micah weren't. Paulos and Leah would be displeased with him before sunset.

Leah took a seat beside him. "You're not drinking."

He raised his face to her. "What?"

She pointed to his full glass. "Your juice. It's your favorite, but you haven't taken one sip."

He told her what the elders had decided.

She remained silent for several long moments. "What will you tell him?"

Yoel shrugged. "What I've been instructed to, I suppose."

"Does he have to leave the house as well?" Her voice held a sharpness he rarely heard.

"Micah didn't say, but I don't think he'll be welcome to continue staying here."

"Where will he stay?"

"I don't know. He'll find somewhere, I'm sure. He has many followers already." He finished his juice and joined Paulos outside, munching on a pear.

Yoel sat beside him. How did he deliver such news? Warning him the other night was hard enough, but this ... telling a Pharisee he was not welcome in the synagogue?

"I assume you have bad news for me."

Yoel nodded. "I do. You cannot be surprised."

"I'm not. In fact, I'm used to it." He took another bite, as if he didn't know—or didn't care—he was about to be evicted from home and synagogue.

"I'm supposed to tell you that ..." He paused, summoning his courage. "That you are no longer welcome in the synagogue."

Paulos nodded. "And why is that?"

"You know why." Why would he ask such a foolish question? "I warned you not to talk about Yeshua again, and not only did you mention him, you said Yeshua offers salvation to everyone, even the Gentiles."

Paulos swallowed. "Because it's true."

How could he say such things? "It cannot be true. It goes against everything the sacred texts tell us."

"On the contrary, it fulfills every promise of Adonai."

"You quoted a few prophesies. You obviously misinterpreted them."

"I quoted more than a few. And there are many, many more."

Yoel sat back. "Such as?"

"From the beginning, Adonai has never changed His plan. He told Abraham, 'All the families on earth will be blessed by you.' David himself said, 'The whole earth will acknowledge Adonai and return to him.' And through the prophet Malachi He tells us, 'My name is honored by people of other nations from morning till night. All around the world they offer sweet incense and pure offerings in honor of my name. For my name is great among the nations.' That doesn't include Isaiah, who promises salvation is for *all the world* numerous times."

"But *the law* is the foundation of all. The covenant depends on the law. How can there be salvation where there is no obedience? Our very existence depends on adhering to the law of Moses."

"The law was merely a placeholder, a substitute until the Redeemer came. The law teaches us how to live, but it *cannot* grant salvation."

"So, a Roman can receive Adonai's forgiveness without following a single commandment?"

"Yes. If it's not for everyone—"

"No!" Yoel pounded his fist on his thigh. "It is for us *alone*! It must be. He Himself said, 'The Lord your God has chosen you out of all the peoples on the face of the earth to be His people, His treasured possession.'"

Yoel had been feeling sorry for Paulos, expecting that the man would have at least some remorse for the chaos he had caused. How could a Pharisee hold such dangerous beliefs, let alone tell others to accept them?

All the world, indeed. How could the Jews be the chosen people of Adonai if He offered all His gifts to everyone, including their conquerors? His sympathy vanished like smoke. He stood. "You will have to go. All of you." It was all he could do not to point toward the door.

"I'll collect my things and tell the others." Paulos calmly rose and headed for his chamber.

Yoel grabbed his arm. "Stay tonight. Make arrangements to stay elsewhere tomorrow."

"Are you sure? We'll go now if you like."

Yoel nodded. "You'll never find a place to sleep at this hour." Not to mention Leah would kill him if he sent guests away hungry.

Paulos chuckled. "You wouldn't believe where I've slept. Sleeping on the road wouldn't be the worst."

"I'm not surprised."

"Then todah. We'll be gone at dawn." The Pharisee headed inside.

Yoel released a sigh. That could have gone so much worse. At least Paulos had the dignity not to cause a fight here in the garden with Micah and the others watching from the safety of their houses.

But why did Paulos have to force such a conflict at all? Why keep pushing his ridiculous views until he was forced to leave?

It didn't make sense.

But the man had pushed. And pushed. And now he had only himself to blame.

THE AFTERNOON SUN cast long shadows as Kassi headed home. It had been a long, grueling day. All she wanted was a long, hot soak in the family's bathing pool before dinner. She grabbed some clean clothes before heading to the back corner of the house, passing Pappa's office on the way.

"Kassandra! I need to speak with you."

She paused and took a step backward. Pappa hunched over his desk, reed pen in one hand, a parchment in the other, eyes on her.

"Could we talk later? I was hoping to bathe before the evening meal."

He looked up. "We will talk now."

Was he angrier than she realized about last night? She hadn't thought so, but then he'd always been hard to read. "All right." She approached his desk.

He tapped his pen on the table. "I've thought about what you had to say last night."

"I know. I'm deeply sorry. I was disrespectful and arrogant, and I apologize."

"You're right. You were."

"It will never happen again."

"I'm sure. But your disrespect is not what I wanted to discuss."

She frowned. "What then?"

"Your marriage to Damianos."

She closed her eyes. "Oh." *Please don't make me do this.*

He stood, tapping the pen against his palm. "Let's set aside the fact that you refused to obey me in front of my family."

"Again, Pappa. I'm sorry for disrespecting you."

"And not for your words?"

"I regret how and when I said it, but I meant what I said."

"I appreciate that, but I cannot accept your refusal."

"What do you mean? It's my decision. You don't need to *accept* it."

He carefully set down the pen. "I'm not making myself clear. You *have* no choice."

"Are you going to drag me to his domus?" She huffed. "Force me to sign the decree?"

He sighed. "Nothing so vulgar."

"Then what?"

"If you don't agree—this very moment—to cease your activities, all of them, and marry him, you may no longer live here."

Pappa's words hit like a kick to her gut. Her stomach tumbled and her knees began to give way. "You would kick me out of my own home?"

"It's not *your* home. It's *mine*." Pappa circled his desk to stand before her. "Now, what is your choice?"

"Pappa, you cannot mean this..." Her voice cracked, and she

closed her mouth to stifle the sobs that threatened to burst from her.

He placed a hand on her shoulder. "Just as you did, I meant what I said. Marry him or leave my home."

How could he do such a thing to his only daughter?

"I am doing this for your good. You need to take your proper place in Thessalonike."

"This seems like it's more for your good than mine." She clamped her trembling hand over her mouth. When would she learn to think before she spoke?

Pappa remained silent, but his displeasure was evident.

"If-" She paused to calm her racing heart. "If I agree, how soon would the marriage take place?"

"This week."

"Wha...?" Kassi struggled to take in air, let alone speak. "Th-this week?"

"As soon as it can be arranged with Damianos and his family."

She fought for breath, sucking in great gasps.

"You can marry him and live as you do now, with fine food and clothes, slaves to attend to your every need, and the respect of all Thessalonike. Or you can continue to act like a petulant child and lose it all."

"When do you want an answer?"

"Now."

"Now? I can't have time to think?"

"If you tell me time would help you to change your mind, you may have all the time you need. But I suspect you've been thinking of nothing else for days."

He was right. Ever since she had opened the bakery, she'd felt purpose. A reason to get out of bed each morning. She loved watching the women blossom into people who respected themselves and each other, who relished the simple act of caring for themselves and their children after society had discarded them.

The very society Pappa now urged her to be part of.

Tears burned her throat, but she had no choice. "I'm sorry, Pappa. I love you more than anything, but I can't."

"Very well. You may gather your things and go."

She struggled to move her feet, but they felt nailed to the floor.

"You make take Lida if you wish. She was a gift to you."

"I don't know where I'll sleep tonight. How can I care for another? ... May I come for her later? When I'm settled?"

"As you wish." He shrugged and returned to his seat.

She stared at him, but he focused on the scrolls in front of him. She staggered to her chamber and collapsed onto the chest at the foot of her bed.

Lida pushed the door ajar and peered in. "May I enter?"

Kassi nodded.

Lida sat and enveloped her in a hug. "I am so sorry, kyria. Is there anything I can do?"

Kassi turned into Lida, wrapping her arms around the older woman's waist. "I'll miss you more than anyone." With her face buried in Lida's shoulder, her words were muffled, but Lida would understand.

Lida rubbed a hand down Kassi's hair. "I'll miss you too. You are as close to a daughter as I'll ever have."

Kassi released her and sat up, tears covering her face.

Lida swiped them away, her work-roughened fingertips soft against Kassi's skin.

Kassi sniffled. "I don't know where to begin. What do I take? What do I leave?"

Lida rose and held up a pair of cloth sacks she'd brought with her. "You'll need some clothes."

Kassi stood to allow Lida to open the chest.

"Any favorites?"

She shrugged.

Lida held up a deep red silk chiton.

"Not silk. I'll have no need for it."

Lida selected several linen chitons and placed them neatly at the bottom of the bag. She added her undergarments and a pair of sandals, then moved to the table in the corner and added the hairbrush. "Any of this?" She pointed to the cosmetics.

Kassi neared her, laughing dryly. "No. I never needed them before. I won't need them now."

"I'll get you some food." Lida handed her the half-full bag before exiting the chamber with the empty one.

Kassi surveyed the myriad of bottles and boxes and jars on the small table, most unopened, until the blue bottle caught her attention.

Mamma's perfume.

Perfume was for the wealthy, the patrician, and that was the world Kassi was turning her back on. Still, it was the only possession of her meter that remained. All else had been swept away by either Pappa or the passing of time. She picked it up and held it to her chest, hot tears blurring her vision. Should she take it now, when she didn't know where she would be staying tonight? But if she left it, would it be here if she returned?

Maybe Lida would keep it safe for her.

She returned it to the table, but it landed awkwardly. The container toppled on the edge of the small table. She lunged to catch it—too late. The tall-necked vessel smashed to the floor and shattered. The crash of delicate glass exploding against hard tile was expected, but the piercing ache that skewered her heart caught her off guard.

Kassi dropped to her knees among the scattered pieces. The scent of lavender saturated the air and memories consumed her heart, unleashing a flood of tears.

How could she have been so careless? That precious bottle had been her only tangible reminder of Mamma.

Now it was gone.

JASON LEANED the blowpipe against the wall. "The light's gone, Gai. Let's go home." He stepped outside and they headed for the gate.

"Jase!"

Ari's face was an unexpected blessing. He hadn't seen his friend for the last two weeks or more. He'd known the newest politarch would be busy digesting the written and unwritten laws, meeting other officials, and learning council procedures, but since Jason had been so busy himself, he'd hardly noticed. "What are you doing here?"

"I wanted to talk to you. I waited so I wouldn't interrupt your work. How's it going?"

"We went over today's goal by two. But we're still over twenty short. It will be tough to finish on time."

"This your new apprentice?" Ari pointed to Gaius.

"Yes, this is Gaius. And he's the only reason I have even half a chance at meeting that deadline."

Ari fell into step with them. "I went to a meeting that visitor of yours had."

Jason sighed. Why could he not get away from Paulos? "First, he's not *my* visitor. I only took him to the synagogue. Second, what meeting? What did he say?"

"He said that the God of Israel, your God, offers salvation to everyone."

Not again. "I know. I heard, and I talked to him about it."

"Did you know this?"

"Of course not." Jason huffed. "It's total nonsense."

Ari's face fell. "You think that?"

They turned onto the cardo. "Yes, I think that. It goes against everything I've ever been taught."

"I have to tell you something." Ari stopped and faced him. "I believe everything he said."

Jason rubbed his temples. Where had his calm, rational friend gone? It was too late in the day for news this incomprehensible. His body ached, sweat poured off his forehead despite the chilled winter air, and he hadn't eaten today. "Start from the beginning."

They resumed walking.

"A couple weeks ago, Secundus decided the shade sails over the forum needed to be repaired. His daughter had mentioned a skenopoios she'd met who'd moved to Thessalonike. I was sent to him to make the arrangements. The next day, I went with a couple of the city slaves to deliver the first of the sails. He was repairing a belt, and three people were sitting with him as he taught from your Scriptures. I ended up staying there for several hours."

Jason glanced to his side to be sure Gaius was with them. "And what did you hear?"

Ari turned to walk backward, facing Jason. "He was talking about your God, the Jewish God." He wore a smile wider than Jason had ever seen.

Jason was far too tired for this kind of conversation, but Ari was excited, and Jason couldn't bring himself to contradict him. "I know you've not been a worshipper of the Greek gods for years, but what about my God suddenly has your attention? You've never been interested before."

"Because he was saying that this God loves everyone, even the Greeks. He loves us and forgives us when we do wrong. No more sacrifices and elaborate rituals." Ari waved his hands wildly as he spoke. "No more petty, warring gods who care more for themselves than each other. And no more doing whatever you like, seeking after only your own pleasure and wealth, hurting others around you as long as you show up to the temple once in a while and perform what's required. This God—*your* God—loves people enough to help them become better people."

Jason dragged a hand through his hair. "Ari, I don't know what to say. You've always been so reasonable, so logical. This doesn't make any sense."

"But it does, Jase. It makes perfect sense. I've always thought the gods of Greece didn't make sense. There are too many, and they aren't any better than we are—they're just more powerful. Or at least that's what the priests tell us. I've never seen them do *anything*."

"That much I agree with. Idols, statues, are not gods. Wait here a second. Gaius lives on this street." He stopped. "Good night, Gai."

"Good night, kyrie. Tomorrow?"

"Of course." He watched as Gaius ran to the fourth building and bounded up the steps.

"Don't you think you need to know a bit more before you decide to abandon your people's gods?"

"You know my meter has been attending the synagogue, yes?"

"I know."

"She's been telling me what she's learned for years now. I only half listened. But after what Paulos said, it all fell into place. I've talked to him every day this week."

This time Jason halted. "You have?"

Ari faced him. "Yes, in his workshop at the harbor."

"Ari, are you sure you want to do this?" Jason shook his head. "You know my God demands total, undivided devotion. What about when it comes time to make a sacrifice in public? Like to Poseidon in a couple weeks? What will Secundus say if you don't participate?"

"I don't know." He shrugged as he started walking again. "I've talked to Paulos about that. In fact, I've spent the last three days thinking about it." He pressed a clenched hand to his chest. "But I believe with every bone in my body that Adonai is the only God, that Yeshua is the Christos, and that I can do nothing else but worship Him and do as He asks. Whatever happens, happens."

"You could lose your position. You know that, don't you?"

"Of course, but what else can I do? Yeshua gave His life for me. I owe Him mine."

Ari had never been concerned about anything beyond the next day or two. His pater's wealth meant he'd never had to worry about material things. His parents adored him, and he'd always been given the best of everything—food, clothing, education.

But this was a totally changed man.

Perhaps Jason should consider doing as Ari did, or at least learn a bit more before he dismissed what Paulos had to say.

But his dodh, not to mention the rest of the community, already barely considered him one of their own, and he would never be Greek no matter what he did. He would have no one.

The price was too high.

17

Do not withhold good from those to whom it is due,
when it is in your power to act.

— PROVERBS 3.17

CRIMSON AND GOLD SNEAKED THROUGH THE LOW BANK OF WISPY clouds as Kassi hurried down the Via Olympos. The ano poli was becoming darker by the moment, with only a waning moon and faint firelight escaping through small windows.

At the cardo, she came to an abrupt halt. Where was she headed in such a hurry? What would happen to her? Panic clawed at her throat, and she struggled to take deep breaths.

God will never leave you.

Paulos's words invaded her mind like rushing water.

Adonai will never fail. He is always faithful. He always keeps His promises. And as He promised the Israelites, He will never leave us.

Paulos said the promises were for the Greeks as well. It seemed impossible, but it was the only thing she could cling to.

Adonai is with me.

Her breathing calmed, and her fists unclenched. Peace flooded her mind.

So, what were her options?

She could return home, tell Pappa she'd marry Damianos, and give up the bakery.

Impossible. Not only would she be miserable, the women would be on the street within days, if not hours.

She didn't have to know everything this moment, but only the next step. Right now, she needed to find someplace safe to sleep. People often slept in the temples. Isa admitted she'd done that before. It was dangerous and a last resort, but it was possible.

Adonai, if You really love me, please help me.

She continued walking, praying an idea would come to her. *Show me where to go.*

It wasn't safe outside after dark. She needed to get inside, quickly, but where?

The bakery. She could stay there, at least for tonight.

She doubled her pace, then turned left at the Via Regia. Pausing at the entrance, she fumbled for the key she'd tossed in the bag, then worked the lock. Inside, she leaned back against the door. Her breathing slowed.

It was darker than she'd imagined. With one hand out to guide her past the walls, she made her way to the back. The cold oven's mouth was open wide, mocking her.

After dropping her bag on the floor, she lay a bag of flour on its side. She removed her cloak and lay down, sucking in air through clenched teeth. She shivered as her arm, hip, and thigh touched the cold tile floor. Her flimsy linen chiton provided little warmth and less comfort, and she pulled her cloak over her trembling body. Her stomach growled, but she was too tired to get up again and grab a leftover loaf.

She wrapped her arms around her body and closed her eyes.

God of Israel, keep me safe.

Kassi bolted awake at the sound of her name.

"Kassi! What are you doing here?" Isa stood over her, hands on hips.

She'd meant to be out of the pistrinum before the women arrived. Now everyone would know.

"My pappa kicked me out of the house." She sat up and rubbed the sleep from her eyes. "I didn't know where else to go."

"Why would you come here? This is not a safe place. You didn't even lock the door behind you."

She must have been too flustered to remember to set the bar across the doors.

Isa offered a hand. "Did you get any sleep at all?"

"Not much." Kassi yawned and accepted the help, her body aching from the hard floor.

The door slammed and laughing voices reached her.

Thalia.

If only she could disappear.

Pheres appeared first. "*Theia* Kassi!" His face brightened, and he wrapped his arms around her legs in a hug.

His simple act of unabashed love filled her with joy. She wasn't sure when he'd started calling her Aunt Kassi, but she loved it.

Isa retrieved the bag of Kassi's possessions. "Thalia, I'm taking her to our place. Can you get the fire started? I won't be long."

Kassi rubbed her hip. "No, Isa, you can't. I won't pull you into my troubles."

"Nonsense. I pulled you into mine." She flashed a momentary grin. "Come on."

Kassi followed, and it took only a moment to reach the small apartment.

Isa pointed to a stool then crossed to the corner of the main room where a round table held a small brazier, the fire out. She ladled a scoop of liquid into a glass cup and brought it to Kassi. "Still warm."

Any kind of fire inside was forbidden as the rickety structures could burn up in a heartbeat. But there were few other options, including buying cooked food from disreputable vendors or spending money they didn't have for a good meal from someone like Publius.

Kassi lowered herself onto the stool and wrapped her hands around the warm glass. She raised it to her lips and blew on the hot liquid. The scents of honey and cinnamon filled the air. She sipped, and the wine warmed her face. The heat flowed down her throat to her chest, and her lungs could fully expand once again without the sting of cold sea air.

No wonder they risked the fire to counter the frigid air sneaking in under the doors.

Isa sat facing her. "You could have come here." Her voice was soft.

"I didn't want you involved. If my pater came looking... In fact, I should go now."

"Please stay." Isa reached for Kassi's hand. "I had no idea things like this happened to people such as you."

"What do you mean?"

"I thought only women like us were mistreated, abandoned ... tossed away."

Kassi scoffed. "Families like mine have all the same problems as everyone else. We're just better at hiding it. Most of them would do anything to avoid being embarrassed, to keep our 'friends' from talking behind our backs."

"Sounds like Thalia's family."

"But I thought Thalia's husband died," Kassi said.

She nodded. "He did."

"She wasn't really abandoned, then. He didn't intend to die, I assume."

Isa took the glass from Kassi and returned to the table. "Of course not. But he died visiting a place he was not supposed to be. There were others in her family—and in his—who could have helped. They chose not to." Pain mixed with anger clouded her face. "It's not uncommon."

"I'm so sorry."

"Me, too. But we found you, and the bakery. And new friends." She sat and held out the newly filled cup.

Kassi ran her finger down the lines on Isa's arm. "I don't think I ever knew what this meant to you."

Isa sat. "I'm Thracian. It's a sign of my family's rank. We were nobility, at least before we were taken by the Romans." She rose. "You're staying here, so let's get you settled. You need some rest."

Kassi looked around the tiny two-room apartment already housing five people. "You have no room."

"There is always room for someone we love." Isa smiled. "You should know. You taught us that."

She hadn't meant to teach them that. It was just the way Kassi thought. And though it was against her nature, maybe now it was time to receive instead of give.

YOEL STROLLED along the lower agora, searching the market stalls for something to eat. He disliked coming here and had been to the market maybe five times, all of them when Leah was ill. Micah, though, had insisted on meeting outside the community.

Micah was late, and Yoel was hungry. The aroma of cooking meat made his mouth water, but all he wanted was a sesame honey bar. He found the proper vendor and scanned the line of people waiting. How long would it take to be served?

Micah strolled toward him. "I'm sorry to keep you waiting. My wife insisted I eat before I left the house."

And yet Yoel had left before Leah had a chance to cook anything because Micah wanted to meet at sunrise. "Well, I need to eat."

Micah gasped. "You would trust something cooked by Greeks? How do you know if the food has been cooked according to the law?"

Did Micah believe he hadn't thought of that? "I am waiting for pastelli." He pointed to the shop.

"I don't like them. The seeds get stuck between my teeth," Micah mumbled.

Yoel stepped up to the merchant, holding up two fingers. "Pastelli, please."

"I'm out," the vendor barked.

Yoel groaned. He'd been looking forward to the sweet treat.

"There's a new pistrinum across the road in that yellow building." The vendor pointed. "I've heard excellent things about it. They sell pastelli."

Yoel stepped away. "Do you mind going with me?"

"Very well."

The pair crossed the cardo. With its bright paint, the building could not be missed. Yoel peered inside at the table covered with bread in many shapes and sizes. Several people waited before them, and they took their places at the end of the line.

"You did tell him, yes?" Micah asked.

So that was the reason he wanted to meet in the market. He didn't trust Yoel to do what he was ordered to do.

"Yes, I told him yesterday." *As you commanded.*

"How did he react?" Micah asked. "Did he argue?"

"Surprisingly, no. It was a bit strange. He accepted it quite well."

"Because he knows he's spewing lies. He has no defense." Micah spat the words. "And he's left your home as well?"

They moved closer to the table.

"He was gone when I awakened this morning."

"Where did he go?"

Yoel stepped up to the table. "Two pastelli, please." He shrugged. "I don't know. He didn't seem worried about finding somewhere. Said he'd slept on the road before."

Micah huffed. "Even more reason to keep the Pharisee out of our synagogue and away from our people."

The young woman frowned but handed him the sesame bars. Yoel handed her a coin, and they moved toward the exit.

"If you have nothing else to tell me, I'm going back. The others may want to talk to you as well." Micah left, heading toward the community.

Yoel bit into the first of his bars and headed back toward home. The sweet honey and the crunch of the seeds almost took away the stress of the last few weeks.

A woman hovered at the edge of the market, her painted eyes beckoning.

Yoel shuddered. Such blatant disregard for the laws of God.

A large group of people, men and women, had gathered in the corner nearest the ocean. Crowds were common throughout the city —at least the parts he'd seen—but this one seemed different. He slowed as he neared it.

Anger rose as he recognized the voice.

Paulos.

Yoel stepped to the edge of the crowd, standing on his toes, straining to catch the face of that man.

His voice reverberated as he spoke to the pagans gathered around him. "The Jewish scriptures tell us no one is righteous, not even one of us. The law tells us what we should do, but it cannot make us righteous. It can only hold us accountable to God. Through the law, we become conscious of our sin."

"Then what can we do? Can we ever stand righteous before a holy God?" asked an old man.

"Yes. Because now, *apart* from the law, God's righteousness can be obtained by anyone, through faith in Yeshua of Nazareth."

Yoel pushed his way forward.

"Even us Greeks?" asked a young man near the front.

"Yes."

Yoel peered through the narrow crack between two men.

Paulos stood there proudly, beaming as he twisted the Scriptures.

"There is no difference between Jew and Greek because we've all sinned. We've all fallen short of the glory of God. But just as all have sinned, all can be made right with God by His grace. We are redeemed through the sacrifice of Yeshua, who died as our atonement. The Jewish texts say there is no forgiveness without the shedding of blood. Yeshua was sinless, so when he spilled His blood, it paid for the sins of all the world."

Yoel's blood boiled. He had never been in favor of allowing the Greeks to attend synagogue, but at least those worshippers knew they could only find Adonai there.

Now though, Paulos had gone far beyond what the synagogue leaders offered to the God-fearers.

Yoel tossed the pastelli to the ground and stalked from the agora. He needed to catch up with Micah, convene the elders, and inform them of this heresy, let them know that Paulos had offered the word of Adonai to pagans who had no intention of becoming God-fearers. Keeping him from the synagogue had only thrust him among the Greeks, and Paulos had tossed the holy words of God along the streets and byways of Thessalonike like they were so much trash.

Salvation came only through the law. Moses had made that abundantly clear. God cherished His people so dearly that He gave them the law, and only by following it could one be saved from the penalty of sin. It could not be obtained through *anyone* else, or by believing it to be so.

This could not stand.

The elders were right. Paulos had to be stopped.

MOVEMENT at the door caught the corner of Jason's eye as the potter waved at him.

He blew hard into the pipe before answering. "Yes?"

"There's someone waiting to see you at the entrance to the village."

What was the problem? "Send him in."

"It's a woman ..."

A woman? Perhaps an order. He could use the work, but he couldn't begin until the seventh of Poseidon. Hopefully, she wasn't in too much of a hurry. "Thank you. Give me a moment."

Jason handed the pipe to Gaius. "I'll be back." At the door, he turned. "You can start the next one."

Gaius winced. "Alone?"

Jason grinned. "You can do it." He began down the path, the air cooling his face after the wretched heat of the furnace.

A familiar figure waited for him near the gate, bent at the waist, hands on knees, breathing heavily.

His breath caught, and he rushed to her. "Kassi? Are you all right? Are you hurt?" He scanned her body, looking for blood, bruises, or other injuries.

She straightened, her hand on her belly. "No, just winded. I ran all the way here. But I didn't know which one was yours."

Proper Greek women did not run. Her face was lined with worry, her eyes lacking their usual fire.

"Come have some wine." He beckoned for her to follow him to his shop, where he filled a cup and handed it to her. "What are you doing here? And why did you run? Is something wrong?"

She took a few long breaths before she drank the wine. "I heard your uncle banned Paulos from the synagogue. He came to the bakery with another man, and they were talking about it. Paulos had to leave the house as well."

He wasn't surprised Paulos had incurred the wrath of the elders, not after what he said. But he never would have imagined Yoel would put him out on the street.

Dodah must have been furious.

He shook his head. "My uncle already blames me for introducing Paulos to the synagogue. I am sorry, but I don't think there's anything I can do to help."

She grasped his arm. "But you can. He'll need a place to teach, a place to stay. And you have that big house—"

Was she kidding? "*My* house? What about your house? Yours is bigger than mine."

Her face clouded. "It's not my home anymore."

Her words hit him with the force of a punch. "What? How—"

"Yesterday, my pater said if I didn't agree to marry Damianos this week, I-I couldn't live there anymore."

How could any man do this to his daughter? To a young woman? Had Secundus no idea what could happen to her? "Wait—yesterday? Where did you sleep last night?" He shoved away visions of her on the street, in an alley, huddled in a corner of a temple...

"I stayed at the bakery last night. Isa found me and took me to her place, but I can't stay there long. They don't have enough room as it is."

"Where are you going to live?"

"I don't know." Her eyes misted.

His heart ached for her. Was what he'd taken as fatigue really sorrow over her pater's rejection?

"Shouldn't you worry about where *you're* going to sleep instead of trying to find a place for Paulos?"

She waved a hand. "I'll find something. But Paulos ... I don't know who else he knows who can help him."

He studied her face, always so full of concern for others. What a strange and wonderful woman. With enough troubles of her own, she spent her time trying to help those who had less than she did.

"They can stay with me, I guess." If it made her happy, he'd do almost anything.

"He'll need a place to teach, as well."

Allowing them to sleep at his house would be bad enough. Allowing him to spread his outrageous theories, though, might cost him more than he was willing to give. "Ari said he was teaching in his workshop the other day. Can't he keep doing that?"

She shook her head. "He can only teach a few at a time there."

"I don't know... Yoel ... he won't be happy."

"You just said he's already not happy with you." She set her empty cup on a shelf and studied the myriad glass vessels.

He chuckled wearily. "That's true." What could Yoel do to him, anyway? "All right. What do I need to do?"

"Nothing. All he needs is some space."

"And a place to sleep. For all three of them, I suppose?"

She nodded. "Is that too much?" Her fingers skimmed the bottles, trays, and cups of all colors and shapes.

"No. But I don't have time to get anything ready. I need to get this order done."

She turned back to face him. "I can take them to your house and help them settle in."

"All right. I don't have any food in the house." He reached into his belt. "Here's some money. Can you buy them something?"

She waved off the money. "Don't worry. We'll figure it out."

"Take it. Please. And the key."

She hesitated but finally accepted the proffered coins. He jerked his thumb over his shoulder. "I have to get back to work."

"All right. Thank you." She hurried toward the gate.

Jason returned to the shop, but Kassi's news weighed heavy. First Ari decided the preacher told the truth. Now Kassi had persuaded Jason to allow the man to live with him. He wanted to distance himself from Paulos, but it was becoming increasingly difficult.

18

"Fellow children of Abraham and you God-fearing Gentiles, it is to us that this message of salvation has been sent."

— *ACTS* 13.26

"THANK, YOU, AHUVATI." YOEL REACHED FOR THE HONEYED WINE LEAH had set on the table. He downed it in one gulp.

Leah lay a finger on the box strapped to his arm. "Why do you have these on already? You've not yet eaten."

"I'm going to the synagogue early. I need to pray."

She put her hands on her hips. "The man is gone. You got what you wanted. What is there to pray about now?"

He searched her face, trying to decide if her tone was accusatory or not. It was plain she'd not been in favor of his actions, though she'd said not one word.

"I plan to ask for His blessing." He turned and headed for the door.

"Maybe you should pray for His forgiveness instead."

Her voice was so low he wasn't sure he'd heard her properly, but there was no time to ponder that now.

He reviewed the last three Shabbats on his short walk across the courtyard to the synagogue. What would today hold? Would Paulos and his accomplices be there? Yoel had made it clear Paulos was not to return, but would he listen?

He trembled with holy rage at the memory of the Pharisee's blasphemy.

Pulling on the door to the left, he opened it wide then inserted a hook on the door into a circle of wire on the wall. He repeated the process with the other door.

His footsteps echoed off the stone walls as he stepped over the threshold and scanned the dark, cold room.

No Paulos. No Silas or Timotheos.

There would be no vile talk of the Galilean. No mention of forgiveness without blood sacrifice, and most importantly, no offer of salvation to the Gentiles.

Yoel relaxed. Closing his eyes, he drew in a long breath through his nose, relishing the sweet, lingering fragrance of myrrh and cassia. A simple scent compared to that of the temple in Jerusalem, which had seven ingredients. He'd smelled that incense only once, when Abba had taken him to Jerusalem for *Pesach*, but the memory of its beautiful aroma remained.

The steward entered the room. He touched the wick of the oil lamp he carried to another, then continued to each lamp along the walls. Soft light warmed the corners of the room.

From a large niche in the wall, Yoel selected the scrolls that contained the readings for today and carried them to the table. He unrolled the scroll containing the law to its proper place and did the same with the one filled with the writings of the prophets.

Families filed into the synagogue, taking their usual seats. Children squirmed, and mothers shushed. Fathers quietly recited prayers while babies slept on their shoulders.

The building quickly filled. A few of the Greeks were missing, but that was fine. Micah would miss their offerings, but for Yoel, it was worth the loss. Had there been no Greeks in the building to begin with, last week's debacle might never have happened.

Jason did not appear.

Yoel took his seat, his conversations with Paulos swirling in his head. Maybe the Pharisee was right. Perhaps Yoel needed to allow Jason to mourn his abba and imma a bit longer. Maybe he *should* show his nephew he mourned Simon's loss as well.

Or maybe Yoel himself reminded Jason of his abba, and it was too painful for Jason to be here, to see his abba in Yoel's gestures, to hear his voice as Yoel spoke, to look into the eyes the brothers shared.

Yes, that had to be it. He only needed to wait, and all would be right again, the way it had always been and always would be.

Adonai would make it so.

It FELT strange not to be in the synagogue on the seventh day. But Kassi couldn't see why she should go. Paulos and his friends wouldn't be there, and it seemed clear that anyone connected with him was not welcome.

The morning's bread had gone quickly. Kassi arranged more on the center table. An empty table didn't look good, and so far, they'd had no problem selling the previous day's bread at a lower price.

"This is quite a little business you've got here."

Kassi's friend Zelia stood in the doorway, her arrow-straight dark hair fluttering in the slight breeze. Why couldn't Kassi ever look as beautiful as Zelia? With her cheeks pinked and skin lightened by makeup, she looked like a Greek goddess. Kohl-ringed eyes and light green eyelids announced to all she was a woman of status, with money for cosmetics of the highest quality and slaves to properly apply them.

Once, Kassi had also had the money and the servants, but the few times she had allowed Lida to do her best, Kassi had never looked like Zelia.

Kassi rushed to the door and drew her into a warm hug. "Come in and see."

She grabbed Zelia by the hand, but her friend planted her feet. "I can see from here, thank you."

"Ummm ... all right. Well, that's the oven I had built." She pointed to the back of the pistrinum.

"It's enormous."

"It has to be large enough to bake many loaves of bread at once. I have twelve workstations. Or eleven since we use one for storage— flour, oil, nuts, whatever else we put in bread." *And Jason's glasses.* "Oh, you have to try this." Kassi hurried to the table and grabbed one of the braided loaves she'd made.

Zelia held her hand up, palm facing out. "I'm not hungry."

"Just one bite." Kassi ripped off a small piece and held it up.

Zelia took it reluctantly and placed it on her tongue. Her face softened. "That's delicious, actually. One of these women made it?" She gestured toward the workspaces.

"No, I made that one." Kassi laughed.

"*You* made it?"

Kassi smiled until she saw Zelia's grimace.

"You're making bread *and* selling it? You're an artisan *and* a merchant?"

Artisans and merchants were not highly thought of, though Kassi had never been sure why. They had skills others didn't have.

"No, I'm only the owner. I make some now and then because I enjoy it. I find it relaxing, adding new things to the dough and braiding six, eight, even nine strands, making it beautiful. And I know I'm helping so many other women at the same time. And their children."

"Can't you just give them money? Do you have to be *here*"—she scowled—"every day? With *them?*"

Kassi resisted showing her irritation. She was getting tired of hearing these strong women, who had endured so much, referred to as *them*, or *those* people, usually by those who had never earned any of what they had.

She grasped Zelia's arm and led her outside where the women wouldn't hear her judgments. "What's wrong with what I'm doing? How is helping people ever bad?"

Over Zelia's shoulder, a man watched them, one hand on a dagger strapped to his waist. Zelia's slave, no doubt.

Zelia nodded to him but pulled Kassi away. "Listen, I came here to tell you people are talking about you."

"Who?" Kassi bristled. "What people?"

"Everyone."

She pointed her thumb over her shoulder. "These people aren't, so who is everyone?"

"The people in the ano poli, who else? Your pater, your brothers, the council ..."

"My family has been making their thoughts abundantly clear for a very long time, and as for the others ... they mean nothing to me. I don't care what they say."

"Perhaps you should."

Though she'd like to end the conversation and send Zelia back to the north part of town, curiosity got the better of her. "What are they saying?"

"They're talking about all this. And the synagogue and—"

That wasn't fair. "You're the one who invited me to synagogue. Now you're telling me that's a bad thing?"

"Synagogue is fine. Not everyone likes that you're worshipping the Jewish god instead of the approved Greek gods, but it's acceptable. You know how many of us there are. Or *were*. But you've taken it too far, as you always do."

Kassi let the insult pass.

"Now you're listening to that wandering preacher, and you've left the synagogue, meeting in the agora, or workshops, or wherever you are now." She adjusted the sash of her white linen chiton. "And then there's Damianos."

"Damianos?" Kassi huffed and crossed her arms over her middle. "Have you ever met him? I mean had a real conversation with the man?"

"No."

"Of course not, because it's impossible. He came by here, insulted me and my bakery and the women. Told me he would sell it as soon as we married, though it's mine, legally. Said I needed to be 'fixed.'"

Zelia lifted one shoulder. "I don't know about *fixed,* but you do need to be controlled."

"Controlled?" A bitter taster flooded her mouth.

Zelia shrugged. "That might have been too strong a word. Maybe 'guided' would be better."

"I don't need to be guided or controlled." Kassi's voice was louder than she intended.

Zelia's guardian took a step closer.

"Damianos is a well-respected leader of the city. He's handsome, wealthy, powerful—"

"*You* marry him then."

"Kassi, what more could you want in a husband? What do you think you'll find?"

"Someone who doesn't treat me like a possession ... something to be 'controlled.'"

Zelia laughed. "And where do you think you'll find someone like that?"

Jason is like that. "Settle for wealthy and powerful if you want. I'd rather be alone."

Zelia studied her for a long moment. "I don't know what happened to you."

"I found there is more to life than status and money."

"Perhaps. But I don't want a life without either." She turned on her heel and left Kassi in the street.

Kassi had always considered Zelia the most beautiful woman she had ever known. But at this moment, that beauty was nowhere to be found.

———————

As the last scraps of weak sunlight filtered through heavy clouds, Jason made sure Gaius was safely inside his insula before turning for home. His shoulder was worse, and he couldn't lift his arm without excruciating pain. All he wanted was a bite to eat and his bed. He pushed open the door and stepped inside.

His guests sat in the garden along with two strangers. One was tall and well-built, wearing the deep red cloak of a Roman soldier, although he wore no other military gear. His companion was a bit shorter and much younger.

Very little Paulos did surprised Jason anymore, so he slipped into the culina and found some bread, then retrieved an apple from the cold room before greeting them.

Paulos beckoned. "Jason, sit with us."

Jason groaned silently but joined them.

"I'd like you to meet Quintus and Epaphras. They are two of the leaders of the church in Philippi. They brought a generous offering for our work." Paulos patted a bag at his side.

"I'm pleased to meet you both. I apologize for not being here to greet you."

"Paulos told us of your dilemma," the younger one said. "We prayed for you."

Jason's eyes widened. "You prayed for me?"

"Of course. We pray about everything," Quintus said. "We just finished praying for Paulos and his complete healing."

"Healing?" Why did he need healing?

"I thought you told him," Silas said. "He should know."

Jason's heartbeat doubled. What was going on?

Paulos's face clouded for the briefest moment.

Too tired to remain patient, Jason snapped. "What happened?"

Paulos sighed. "There was a young slave woman in Philippi who was controlled by a spirit of prophecy. I ordered the spirit to leave in the name of Yeshua, and it did. The problem was that her owners now couldn't make money from her talent. They beat her mercilessly, and she ran away. They became angry and had Silas and me arrested on false charges."

"And beaten," added Timos.

"And thrown into the deepest part of the prison," said Quintus.

Prison? "But you were released, so you must have been found not guilty of the charges, yes?"

Paulos shook his head. "There was no trial."

Jason huffed. "Roman justice has no mercy for those who are not Roman."

"True," Silas said. "They only released us when they found out we were citizens."

"You're Roman citizens?" Jason whistled through his teeth. How did he not know that? "Why didn't you say so at the beginning? Before you were beaten?"

"I try not to use my citizenship unless absolutely necessary. Those I bring to Yeshua will rarely be citizens. How can I justify using my status to get out of dangerous situations when they cannot do the same? We will *all* face persecution. They need to know they can bear up under it, and I need to be an example."

"That's quite a sacrifice," Jason said.

Paulos smiled. "It's not a sacrifice. It's love."

"Love?" Jason raised an eyebrow. "For those you don't know?"

"Love is the most powerful force in the world. Love will not allow me to do anything that would be offensive to unbelievers. I put everything in this life—beyond the gospel—under the control of love so I may bring all to the Mashiach."

"How do you do that?" Jason bit into his apple.

"If a man cannot hear, he can't believe. So, I try to remove all barriers between myself and my hearers. I can't change my appearance, but I can change my habits, my preferences, my entire way of daily life. I do not wish anything I do or say to cause someone to be offended and thus hindered from faith in Yeshua."

Jason swallowed. "Couldn't they still be offended at your words?"

"Of course. And many are. If someone is offended by the holy words of Adonai, that is his problem. But if that same person is offended by *me*, then it's my problem."

Jason stood. "I need to get some sleep, but please feel free to stay as long as you like."

"We'll be leaving tomorrow," Quintus said. "We're anxious to get back to our families."

"There's an empty chamber next to mine."

"Thank you," Quin said.

He took a step away but turned back. "What happened to the girl? The one who was beaten so badly?"

Quintus beamed. "She's my wife."

Jason smiled and padded toward his chamber.

Paulos caught up with him. "May I have a moment of your time before you retire?"

"Of course." Jason halted, although he struggled to hold his eyes open.

"I'd like to invite some people to share a meal with me tomorrow evening while I teach."

"A meal? Was he asking Jason to host a dinner? "Paulos, I'm sorry, you're welcome to stay here, but I have neither the time nor the money right now to host a dinner."

"I would never ask that of you. We will arrange and pay for everything. The gift from Philippi arrived at precisely the right time." He grinned. "As Yeshua Himself said, 'Our Father knows what we need before we ask Him.'"

"If you say so."

"I just want your permission to use your home."

"I already told Kassi you can use my home to teach."

"There may be a few more than you were expecting."

Jason. "Sure. Use whatever you need." As long as they required nothing from him, he didn't care.

"Perhaps you'll join us?"

"I'll see. If I finish the day's work in time, I'll be here."

At the moment it was difficult to decide which would be less appealing—keeping his aching and weary body at the shop as long as possible or coming home to a house full of strangers listening to Paulos's stories of the man he claimed was the Redeemer of Israel.

19

The righteous choose their friends carefully,
  but the way of the wicked leads them astray.

— PROVERBS 12.16

YOEL PRAYED AS HE MADE HIS WAY DOWN THE COLUMNED, COVERED
stoa that lined the south side of the upper agora. *Adonai, God of Abraham, Isaac, and Jacob, guide my steps and my words. Help me as I seek to guard the faith of my fathers from this man who seeks to destroy it.*

He read the sign outside each door as he passed.

Platon, Computantis. He had no need for a bookkeeper.

Linus the Iatros. Or a doctor.

Auspex. No name. Perhaps his customers, like him, were supposed to divine it.

Finally, at the end of the stoa, of course. *Hesiod the Advocatus.*

He hovered outside the door murmuring one last prayer before he entered.

A man sat at a desk, bald head bent over parchment, hand scribbling furiously with a reed pen.

"I was hoping—"

He silenced Yoel with one raised finger.

Yoel scanned the office while he waited. The tiled floor was dotted with dirty footprints. The room was lined with shelves, each one stacked with scrolls. Some were sprinkled in dust, while others appeared to have been recently unrolled. A pile of coins sat on the corner of the desk next to three pens and an open container of ink.

After a long moment, the man looked up. His chiton was frayed at the neck, and at least two of the pins that held his sleeve closed had been lost. He was younger than Yoel had expected. Younger could be good or bad. He could have a better memory, but would he be experienced enough for a case like this? "May I help you?"

Should he turn around and leave? The man had been referred to him by several of the synagogue members, though they had no idea what Yoel wanted a lawyer for. Perhaps he should trust them.

He sat on the couch in front of the desk. "My name is Yoel ben Samuel. I am the leader of the synagogue. I need your help."

"The synagogue?" He furrowed his brows. "What could I do to help you? You have your own law."

"There is a man, new to town, who is causing us trouble. He is defiling our faith, offering to Greeks what belongs to us. He twists the Scriptures to fit his own ideas—"

Hesiod waved his hand. "I'm sorry. I'm not understanding. Is he breaking any laws? *Roman* laws?"

Yoel shrugged. "I don't know. That's why I've come to you."

"Who is this man?"

"He is Paulos of Tarsus."

"Is he a teacher? Is he not allowed to teach others your religion?"

Yoel squirmed in his seat. "He actually studied in Jerusalem under one of our greatest leaders."

"Then I don't see the problem."

"It's what he's saying ... and who he's saying it to."

Hesiod blew out a sharp breath. "Tell me precisely what he's said, and I'll see if there is anything that can be done."

"He is proclaiming our Mashiach has come."

Hesiod shook his head. "I don't know what that means."

"Our God, Adonai, promised in the beginning that He would send a Redeemer who would save us from our sins. Paulos claims that a criminal in Judea, who was crucified by the Romans, is this Redeemer."

The lawyer sighed loudly. "Your faith is a protected religion under Roman law—the only one. Rome will not get involved in who is saying what. You can preach whatever you want, as long as you don't proselytize."

"What if he is proclaiming this man is not only our Redeemer, but the redeemer of all people?"

"Do you understand how Roman law works?"

Yoel shook his head.

"Roman law is meticulously codified." He rose from his seat and strolled to the shelves. He pointed to three shelves of scrolls. "This list deals with the offenses committed by the leaders of society and by governing personnel. The required penalties are listed for each crime. But the list does not deal with offenses against religion or crimes committed by plebeians. Crimes like those are not specified and are outside the list."

"Then what happens?"

"An accuser alleges a crime has been committed by someone. The judge and his counselors—in Thessalonike that would be the politarchs—listen to the case and decide if there is any guilt that requires punishment."

Yoel thought. What could Paulos have said that could be considered a crime?

"What if he proclaims this man as king? That must be illegal."

"That's true. But that would be treason." He returned to his desk.

"Then I want to accuse him of treason."

He raised his brows. "Against the emperor?"

"Yes."

Hesiod was silent for a long moment. "The very suggestion of treason almost always results in death for the accused. Even if he is not executed, his life will be ruined. Are you prepared to accept the responsibility of that because someone is saying something you disagree with?"

Yoel pressed a finger on the desk, its tip turning white. "I don't just disagree with it. It is a *lie*."

Hesiod leaned nearer. "And I ask again, are you prepared to accept responsibility for this man's death?"

Was he? What would the elders say? Could Yoel stand by and watch as Paulos was executed?

Hesiod picked up his pen. "You think about that while I check the law and make some inquiries. Come back tomorrow."

EVERY BENCH in Jason's peristyle was filled, with people sitting on the walkways or hard tile. Voices overlapped with laughter and the giggles of children. He'd not expected so many would come. Then again, considering what Paulos had to say, it was no wonder they were anxious to at least hear him.

The only things on Jason's mind, however, were his throbbing shoulder and his looming deadline. If it weren't already dark, he'd be at the shop now, even as tired as he was.

Kassi breezed by him, two platters of bread in hand. "Quite a crowd, yes?" She continued to the garden and passed out bread.

Paulos joined him. "Kassi is an excellent baker, don't you think?" Paulos asked.

"Yes, she is. Did she bring all this?"

"She brought it, but I paid her for it. The women she has working for her should be paid for their labor."

He gestured to the crowd. "It must be quite expensive to feed them all."

"I only feed them in the beginning. It doesn't take long before they all begin to share. And I've learned if I am to reach the Greeks, I must teach at night after the workday has ended, since Greeks and Romans don't observe any kind of Shabbat rest—and criticize us for doing so." He chuckled.

"You don't think you should meet on Shabbat to teach them about the Jewish God?"

"I always try to reach my brethren first, so I am with them on Shabbat. Besides, from the beginning, starting with the first believers in Jerusalem, the custom has been to gather on the evening of the first day of the week and share a meal."

"Why the first day?"

"Yeshua rose on that day."

That was a not a topic Jason wanted to discuss. "Can't you ask people to bring their own food?"

"Look around." Paulos nodded toward those gathering in the garden.

Stained and damaged chitons revealed most of those present were craftsmen and people who lived south of the Via Regia. Dirty, tattered sandals adorned the feet of those who either worked for others or labored every moment of daylight to feed their families. Most of the children were barefoot. Only a few had baskets with cloth-wrapped bundles Jason assumed contained food.

"The news of Yeshua is always more appealing to those who have little. They know what is truly missing in their lives and realize what Adonai can give them. Those with much, those who have never wanted for anything material, have a harder time recognizing the needs of heart and soul."

Ari joined them, putting a hand on the teacher's shoulder. "Paulos, Shalom."

"Peace to you as well. It's wonderful to see you here. And your imma?"

"She's helping Kassi."

Paulos laughed. "Of course she is. I'll greet her later. It's time for the lesson." He picked his way around those seated to the center of the garden. "I'm so glad you've all come to hear the good news of Yeshua. First, I want you to know who I am, and why I must preach about the risen Christos."

Jason leaned toward Ari. "I've got to get some sleep," he whispered.

"Like Yeshua, I am a Jew. I was a Pharisee. I grew up studying the sacred texts." Paulos held up a codex. "When I first heard of Yeshua, I was incensed. Like the synagogue leaders, I believed He was a blasphemer and a traitor to our faith. As a Pharisee, I couldn't allow His message to continue. So, I persecuted my fellow Jews."

Only steps away, Jason halted and turned. Paulos sounded remarkably like Yoel.

"Persecuted how?" asked a young man.

Paulos took a deep breath. "Men and women were imprisoned because of me. I watched a man battered with stones until he died … and I was happy about it."

Paulos was freely admitting he imprisoned Jews for following Yeshua?

As angry as Jason's dodh was, it was easy to understand Paulos feeling the same way. So what changed his mind?

"Then one day I was traveling to Damascus," Paulos said. "I'd asked for, and received, permission to hunt down Yeshua's followers wherever they were and bring them to Jerusalem to be imprisoned. On the road, He Himself appeared to me and asked me why I was persecuting Him. I'll skip the next few weeks for now and say I spent three years learning from Him. I tell you this to show you that the gospel I preach was given to me by Yeshua the Christos."

Jason crossed his arms. Paulos heard from the Mashiach?

"Why should this matter to you? Because it should prove to you, unmistakably, that forgiveness is available for all. If Adonai can forgive me, who abused His children, who persecuted Him, He can forgive everyone. His death is the ultimate sacrifice, and His shed blood paid the price for all sin. There is nothing you can do to make

Him love you more or to make Him love you less. He loves you because He created you. All you need do is come to Him."

"Even us? Who have worshipped other gods?"

He knew that voice. Jason searched the crowd, and his mouth dropped. Belos? When had he come in?

"Everyone. If you abandon all other gods, and worship Him alone, you are His."

A young man Jason didn't recognize stood. "What about the Romans?"

Silence hovered over the crowd like a black storm cloud. Tension rose.

"Even a Roman, *if* he repents and worships Yeshua." Paulos spread his arms. "After all, a Roman is no worse than I am."

The young man turned and stalked from the room. The Romans had only a nominal presence in Thessalonike, but who knew what he or his family had experienced elsewhere?

"Adonai told Abraham, the father of the Jews, 'All nations will be blessed through you.' So now, anyone who believes becomes a child of Abraham and is blessed along with him."

"Must we follow all the laws of the Jews?" Another voice he recognized. Publius. "There are so many. I don't even know them all."

"Not if you are not a Jew. Our scriptures say, 'Cursed is everyone who does not continue to do *everything* written in the book of the law.' But no one can perfectly obey the law. If you want to be counted righteous, you must live by faith in the Christos who redeemed us from the curse of the law."

The law—a curse? A strong word, but Jason knew its tyranny. As a child, he could earn his dodh's anger with the slightest infraction. But now he wondered, was that anger born of fear? Fear of the wrath of God?

Abba had always tried to keep the law, but he hadn't been afraid of a misstep. He seemed to innately know what was necessary to please God and what only pleased the synagogue leaders.

Jason longed for that kind of peace, the assurance that God was pleased with him.

Could he have it just by believing this Yeshua had already paid the price?

And even if he could, would it be worth cutting himself off from his only family?

HE'D SAID IT AGAIN.

As the others gathered their belongings and slipped from the garden, Kassi circled the room. She picked up empty baskets and stacked them, Paulos's words echoing in her mind.

God's forgiveness is for everyone.

Could it be true? Did Yeshua die for *her*?

"Kassandra, thank you again for arranging this space for us. It's perfect." Paulos's gentle voice startled her.

"It is, isn't it?"

"And Julia would like you to stay with her."

"That's wonderful. Isa's place is so small. I'm hoping the bakery will soon allow them to afford a better apartment."

"I'll be praying about that. But I didn't have a chance to answer your question last week."

"My question?"

"I told you Yeshua had said, 'If anyone hears My words, and does not obey, I don't judge him, because I didn't come to judge the world, I came to *save* the world.' You asked me how that could be."

"That thought got a bit buried under everything else that happened this week." She picked up several cups and stacked them on the plates.

"It has been eventful, hasn't it? And thank you so much for arranging our stay here with Jason." He handed her a stray glass.

"I was only a messenger."

"As am I."

"I think you're more than that."

He sat on a crooked bench. "Do you know what the last words Yeshua ever spoke on earth were?"

Kassi shook her head as Julia came and took the stack of dishes from her.

"He told His followers to go and make disciples of *all nations*. He said they should baptize them and teach them to obey everything He had taught them."

Kassi sat on a nearby stool. "But I still don't understand. Why should the God of the Jews care about the rest of the world? They all have their own gods, if you believe they are gods."

"Do you believe that?"

"No. I believe your God is the only true God, but I don't see why He would care about me."

Paulos's eyes gleamed. "Oh, but He does! Deeply, intimately, unfailingly, because He created you, as He created me, and Ari, and Jason. He created you to be exactly as you are, and He lives to give you hope and peace and joy." Paulos leaned forward and grasped her hand. "Kassandra, do you believe that Yeshua is the Christos, God's Son, who offers forgiveness of sins?"

"For the Jews, yes."

"No, no! Without any qualifications, any limitations. Do you believe this?"

"I want to."

"If He is the only True God, the Living God, then do you believe He created the whole world and everything in it?"

"Of course."

"Then why can't you believe that since He created you, He loves you as He loves me, and offers that same forgiveness to you as to me?"

"I guess that makes sense. But are the Jews still God's chosen people?"

"They are. He set His favor on them and set them apart from all the peoples of the earth. It was to them God gave the covenants and the law and the promises. Yeshua was a Jew, and His ministry on earth was to them. So, in that way, salvation must come from the Jews."

Her hope deflated. "Oh. I see."

He squeezed her hand. "It *comes* from Israel, but is *given* to all, because He abounds in riches for all who call on Him. Both Greeks and Jews can be saved by faith in the Christos because God is the One who has mercy. No one can earn salvation. It is a gift to anyone who accepts it, whether Jew or Greek."

How she longed to believe that.

"Kassandra, let me show you something." He reached for the codex and opened it, then flipped through the pages until he found what he searched for. 'Do not fear, for I have redeemed you; I have summoned you by name; you are Mine.' Kassandra, do you hear that? *You are His.* He delights in pouring out His love for you until you are drowning in it."

Pouring out His love for me. For me? Why? Why should such a powerful God care about one woman in Makedonia? The thought of being loved by God in such measure was beyond her comprehension.

It was also the most joyous feeling she had ever experienced.

"He loves me?"

"He loves you."

"He loves me." She laughed softly. "He loves me."

"Do you wish to receive His forgiveness to save you from your sins and guilt, death and judgment? Do you wish to live with Him forever?"

"I definitely do!"

He laughed. "Since I met you, I've thanked God every time I've thought of you, because I know He began a good work in you, and He will finish it."

A good work ... in her? Begun by Yeshua? She'd never thought of anything she did as being the work of God. What a marvelous thought.

"May I pray for you?" Paulos asked.

She bobbed her head, her heart too filled with wonder to find words.

"I pray that your love may abound more and more in knowledge and depth of insight, so that you may be able to discern what is best, and that you may be pure and blameless. May the God of hope fill you with all joy and peace as you trust in Him, so that you may overflow with hope by the power of the Holy Spirit.

"I ask that our glorious Father give you the Spirit of wisdom and revelation, so that you may know Him better. I pray also that the eyes of your heart may be enlightened in order that you may know the hope to which He has called you, the riches of his glorious inheritance in the saints, and His incomparably great power for us who believe."

There was a lot in there she didn't understand. But all the uncertainty, all the shame, all the fears she'd experienced since the day she'd met Isa and decided to concentrate on others instead of herself faded away.

There wasn't a doubt in her mind now.

Yeshua was the Redeemer.

She was doing holy work, the work of Adonai.

And she was loved, unconditionally.

20

The LORD is close to the brokenhearted
and saves those who are crushed in spirit.

— PSALM 34.18

SWEAT SLID FROM JASON'S FOREHEAD AND DOWN HIS CHEEKS, AND salty drops hung on his lips.

Gaius set the cup on the cooling shelf. "Last one." He yawned and dragged his arm across his forehead.

The last rays of light snaked hot fingers through the open roof. Jason stretched his arms above his head, pain shooting from his right shoulder down to his hand and across his chest. He groaned and massaged the joint with his left hand, but it didn't help much. He'd never felt such pain or fatigue.

"Kyrie, are you all right?"

"Just a bit sore." Jason forced a smile. "Thank you for asking."

The boy had dark circles under eyes that struggled to stay open. "Why don't you go home? You look exhausted."

He raised a brow. "It's my turn to watch the fires."

"Don't worry about that."

"But kyrie, you can't do it. You're tired, too. I want to do my job."

"I'll get someone else. The others know the order we're trying to fill, and they'll be glad to help." He draped his cloak over his shoulders and fastened it with an iron fibula.

Gaius stared at the stack of boxes. "Then can I help you take the glasses to the pistrinum? We have three days' worth here."

Jason had been too weary to take them the last couple nights, and Gaius's offer was a blessing. "Of course. Thank you, Gai."

Gaius picked up two of the crates and moved to the door. He turned to Jason. "Shall I wait for you?"

"No, go ahead. I need to get someone to watch the fires, and then I'll be right behind you." He pointed at Gaius. "And tomorrow, come in a little later. You need some sleep."

He grinned. "Yes, kyrie. I'll see you there."

Jason lugged the remaining four crates outside. The sun had just set, and he hoped at least one person remained in the village. He peeked in the potter's shop.

"Belos, do you think you or Glaukos could take our turn watching the fires? I sent Gaius home. If you can't stay, I could come back after I deliver this load."

Belos looked up from his clay. "What happened?"

"Nothing why?"

"You're rubbing your shoulder."

He hadn't realized. "Just a little pain. Can't wait to finish this order."

Belos rose and came to the door, rotating his hand in a circle. "I understand. Potters get pain in their hands and wrists. Too much time caressing clay." He laughed. "Of course we can watch the fire. We must help each other. Deliver your load and get some sleep. And here." He disappeared into his shop and returned with a handful of shelled almonds. "Eat these. For energy."

"I'll eat at home."

"No, you won't." His wife appeared beside him. "You've said that before, and you don't eat enough."

Jason sighed and popped several in his mouth. They were tastier than he expected.

"Eat them, whether you like it or not," she said.

"Yes, imma." He laughed, ignoring the agony in his heart more than the ache in his shoulder.

"Oh, I'm sorry, Jason." Her face paled. "I didn't mean—"

"Don't worry. I appreciate it, and it's nice to be cared for. Thank you." He leaned toward her to place his left arm around her, the nuts held with his other hand.

She patted his chest. "You are cared for. Don't forget it. And get some sleep."

Belos laughed. "Leave him alone."

The pair retreated into their shop, and Jason stooped to collect his glasses.

He dropped the rest of the almonds into one of the glasses. A shard of pain skewered his right shoulder as he grabbed the top slat of the bottom crate and lifted all four. The stack was too tall to carry on his shoulder, and the weight pulled on his upper arms and wrists as he held it waist high. He clenched his jaw, freezing for a moment until the ache lessened.

The load grew heavier as he trudged along the Via Olympos. Maybe he should have left some for tomorrow, but that thinking was the reason they had six to take tonight.

He stopped and lifted one knee to rest the crates on his thigh. Bringing his hand to his shoulder, moved his elbow in a circle. The throbbing subsided a bit, and he resumed the task, quickening his gait to try to reach the bakery as soon as possible.

He'd taken only a few more steps when unbearable pain seized him. It screamed down his arm and into his hand. His fingers splayed and the crates slipped from his grasp.

The boxes strained against his left hand, but the weight became too much. He watched helplessly as the glasses slid to one side. He tried to recapture the boxes, but his fingers refused to obey.

The crates crashed to the ground. Cups flew in all directions and collided against stone, shattering into hundreds of pieces. Straw fluttered down and covered the mess. Pale almonds dotted the piles of shimmering fragments of glass.

Jason dropped to his knees and surveyed the disaster. Two days' work gone—two days he didn't have. He covered his face with his good hand. It was over.

He fell back onto his seat. He draped his left arm across his knees and rested his head. He could never catch up now. Damianos had made it clear if he was one glass short, he would institute the penalty. Even if he could sell every piece he'd completed, he wouldn't have enough to pay it, and it was doubtful he could sell two thousand individual glasses. Who needed that many, other than someone who owned a bathhouse?

He'd failed his father. Gaius would have no job. He'd have to try to sell his house, and if he couldn't, Damianos would take it.

Why had Abba agreed to such a condition?

He'd counted on Jason.

And that had been his fatal mistake.

He jumped as a hand landed on his back and looked up to see Gaius standing over him.

"Kyrie?" The concern in Gaius's voice only increased Jason's despair, but he could only shake his head. He had no words.

Gaius bolted. Jason couldn't blame him. He was a clever boy, and he could see what lay in store for him.

Jason slipped off his sandal and used it to scrape the shards toward the edge with his left hand, his right arm useless. Pieces piled up on each other, reflecting moonlight like so many jewels. A beautiful picture hiding a devastating truth. He'd need to scatter straw over it all to keep anyone from stepping on it until he could return to do a better job.

Footsteps pounded up the cardo. Who else would be out at this time of night? He sat back on his heels and stared into the darkness.

"Jason!"

Kassi? What was she doing here? He pulled his cloak over his right arm.

She hurried up the street with a torch in one hand and a broom in the other. He couldn't decide if embarrassment or relief won out.

"Oh, Jason, I'm so sorry." She knelt, holding the torch over the mess. "Oh, no... did you lose them all?"

"Yes. I don't..." He shook his head. "I won't make the order now. I've lost everything."

Holding the torch high, she moved some of the straw aside. "There are several left in here." She counted under her breath. "There are at least twenty undamaged."

"So what? Twenty doesn't help! I've still lost almost 160." He tossed the sandal to the ground.

She gasped and grabbed his left hand. "You're bleeding." She turned it palm up, revealing tiny crimson cuts crisscrossing his bloody fingertips. He hadn't even felt them.

Gaius rushed up, Thalia behind him with two more brooms.

Jason's cheeks flamed. He felt like a small child who'd been caught in some mischief.

Gaius and his imma silently swept up shattered cups.

Kassi handed the torch to Thalia. "Jason, why don't you come with me, and let me take care of your hand?"

Why not? He couldn't be any more embarrassed, and he was in too much pain to be much help.

At the bakery, Kassi put the torch in a holder on the wall and pointed to a table in a workspace. "I'll get some honey for that hand."

He clambered onto a tall stool while she went to the far wall to retrieve a small pot from the shelves and returned.

"Here you go." She lifted the lid.

He laid his left hand, palm up, on the table. He tried to stick two fingers of his right hand into the pot, but he still could not force his hand to do his bidding, and the throbbing was only growing worse.

She froze briefly but said nothing, then dipped her fingers into the honey and smeared it on the bloody fingers of his outstretched hand.

"You may have to get someone to help you for a couple days. You need to let that shoulder rest."

"I'll have plenty of time to let it rest. I'm done."

She brightened. "You finished the order? That's wonderful."

"No, I haven't finished!" Shame filled him as she recoiled. He hadn't meant to shout. It wasn't her fault. "I'm so sorry. I didn't mean to raise my voice at you. I'm sore, I'm tired, I'm hungry, and now I've lost my shop and my home. But I shouldn't take it out on you."

She moved closer and dipped her fingers into the honey again. "What do you mean you've lost everything? You have five more days."

"There's no way I can make up what I've lost. I was behind already—not by much, but this ... this is insurmountable."

"No, it can't be. We can figure something out."

"I can barely lift my arm." He moved his cloak aside, exposing the angry rash that now ran from his knuckles to above his elbow.

Her hand covered her mouth for a long moment. "I think I have some almond lotion." She rose, but he stopped her.

"Don't bother. I'm going home to sleep for three or four days."

Her eyes pleaded with him. "Jason, no. You mustn't let Damianos win."

"Why not?" He stood. "He always does. He always will."

ARE you prepared to accept responsibility for this man's death?

The advocate's words echoed in Yoel's ears as he made his way up the cardo.

Death was perhaps a little extreme. Wasn't there was a way to just make him leave Thessalonike? And never return?

He turned onto the stoa of the upper agora, passing office after office until he reached the end. The carved marble plaque beside the door boasting *Hesiod the Advocatus* gleamed as if it had been polished that very morning.

Yoel breathed a prayer from one of David's psalms before he stepped into Hesiod's office.

Blessed are You, Holy One, who are enthroned upon the praises of Israel. In You our fathers trusted; they trusted and were saved. They cried to You and were rescued.

I cry out to you now, Holy One. Save us from this wretched man who distorts Your words.

At the sound of the door, the lawyer looked up from his parchments. His face turned crimson, and he bolted from his seat. "You did not tell me all the facts." He rounded his desk, his breathing quick and shallow, one finger jabbing at the air between them.

Yoel took a step backward and spread his hands. "What facts? I told you everything I knew."

"The man is a citizen."

Was that all? Yoel relaxed. "We are all citizens."

"Not of this city. Of *Rome*." Hesiod's face would explode if it turned any redder.

Yoel's chest seized. A Roman citizen? How did a Jew—a Pharisee, no less—become a citizen? "I don't ... I don't understand. Are you sure?" Perhaps Hesiod was mistaken, had him mixed with another Paulos. It was an extremely common name.

"He's from Tarsus."

Yoel searched his memory, but Hesiod's words still meant nothing. "And..."

Hesiod leaned back against his desk. "Pompey made that whole area a Roman province over one hundred years ago. His father or grandfather likely rendered some service to Pompey. I don't know what. I quit listening because *It. Doesn't. Matter.*" He banged a hand against the side of the desk with each of the last three words.

He folded his hands together at his waist. Then he closed his eyes for a long moment.

Was he praying? Meditating? Reconsidering, by any chance?

He stepped behind his desk once again. "He's a citizen." His voice was once again controlled and low. "I will *not* press charges of treason against him. I would advise you to drop this matter now. No reputable advocate will pursue this for you." Hesiod dropped to his seat, picked up his pen, and turned his full attention to his parchments and tablets.

There would be no convincing him to help.

Yoel trudged from the office. The brightness of the morning belied the dark mood that had crashed down on his shoulders. He'd failed.

What would the elders say?

Think this through.

Yes, this attempt had failed, but there had to be other ways to bring Paulos to justice. He couldn't let that man continue to spread his malicious lies. He had to do something. But what?

There was one possibility. It was risky, a last resort. It could make things worse, but he had no choice.

YOEL STOOD before the wooden double doors of the domus of Secundus, right foot tapping furiously.

Why was he afraid? The politarch was a mere man, and Yoel was doing nothing wrong. The Jews of Thessalonike were well thought of. He had every right to ask for help from the chief politarch.

Still, his foot would not rest.

He raised a fist and delivered three sharp raps on the entrance.

Silence greeted him. But it was a large house, and it must take time for a slave to reach the door.

What should he say when he was admitted? Thoughts and words and fears jumbled together in his mind. If he was unable to make sense of them, he wouldn't make it past the door.

The doors swung open. A slave woman about Yoel's age stood before him. "May I help you?"

She had likely served in this household since she was a child, knew everything and everyone. Yoel's first job was to get past her.

He bowed. "I am Yoel, the archisynagogos and an elder in the Jewish community. I have come to seek the help of the politarch in a matter most vital."

A brow rose. "He is expecting you?"

"No. But I do need to see him."

"He knows you?"

"He does. We have broken bread together." Only in Yoel's home, of course, with the elders. He'd not been to the domus and would never eat there.

She studied him a moment, then nodded curtly and stepped to one side. "Enter."

Yoel stepped onto the mosaic-tiled floor, and she closed the doors behind them.

"Wait here." She disappeared.

He had passed the first obstacle.

The house was not as ornately decorated as he would have supposed, but it was elegant in its simplicity.

Secundus strode down the hall toward him. "Yoel. Welcome to my home. Lida, bring us"—he spun to face Yoel—"no wait, you cannot, can you?"

"I cannot." Yoel smiled.

"I apologize. A habit whenever I host guests. I meant no offense."

He dipped his head. "None was taken. Indeed, it was kind of you to remember."

Secundus headed across the atrium to the far corner. "Let's talk in my tablinum. It's quiet, and we won't be bothered." He stepped into the small room and gestured to a chair as he took his seat behind an ornate desk. "Now, how can I help you today?"

"We have a recent visitor to our city. Perhaps you've heard of him. Paulos of Tarsus."

The politarch leaned an elbow on one arm of his curule chair. "Yes, I've heard. Nothing concerning, as far as I understand it."

Secundus understood nothing. "Not concerning? He is defiling our faith, offering to Greeks what Adonai—what our God has reserved for us alone. He bends the Scriptures to fit his own ideas, claiming our promised Redeemer has come."

The politarch sat straighter. "I'm familiar with most of your religion, but I wasn't aware of any teaching about a redeemer."

"From the beginning, our God promised He would send a Redeemer who would save us from our sins. Sacrifices would no longer be necessary as this Redeemer would somehow forgive all our sins."

"No sacrifices? What's wrong with that? That sounds like a good thing."

"He claims a man crucified in Judea as a criminal is this Redeemer."

Secundus chuckled. "A criminal. Really? Not a good way to start a religion but not illegal. You can preach whatever you want as long as you don't proselytize."

This was turning into a repeat of his conversation with the advocate.

"What if he is proclaiming this man is not only our Redeemer, but the redeemer of all people?"

Secundus shook his head as he leaned again to one side. "Still not illegal."

What did Yoel have to do to make him understand? "Something must be done about this. He's destroying my community." He struggled to keep his voice under control as he scooted to the edge of his chair. He was not above begging, if that's what it took.

"I'm sorry, but he's done nothing that breaks *our* laws." He offered a soft smile designed, Yoel was sure, to calm him.

It had little effect.

The politarch spread his hands. "These men are still Jews and have the protection of the empire, even if their beliefs differ slightly from yours."

"Differ slightly? He is ripping apart the very fabric of our faith. Adonai is the God of Israel alone. Nothing he says can change that." Yoel rose and leaned his palms on the desk.

Secundus rose to face him. "They're meeting peacefully, and unless they become violent, there is nothing I can do."

The ground beneath Yoel's feet threatened to give way. "Please."

Secundus rounded his desk and placed a hand on his arm. "You know I respect you and your people. I always have. You make excellent citizens of our city. Your people cause no trouble. You work hard and pay your taxes. I would help if I could."

You could if you wanted to.

"Have you checked with the lawyers?" Secundus asked.

"I did."

"Who?"

"Hesiod. He refuses to prosecute because Paulos and Silas are Roman citizens," Yoel said.

"That, I did not know. It complicates matters enormously."

"So I'm told."

"Even if he is found guilty, the harshest punishment I can give a citizen is banishment."

A weight lifted. Not having a man's death on his hands was far preferable. "As long as he is stopped from spreading his poison, that's fine with me."

"But first, you have to get him to the council house."

The relief evaporated. "How do I do that?"

"There are other advocates." Secundus's voice was low, conspiratorial.

"Those in the agora?"

He nodded. "Their methods are ... questionable, but if there is a way, they can find it. If you can get him before the politarchs, I'll make sure he's banished." He returned to his intricately carved chair.

"Who should I—"

Secundus held out a hand, palm out. "Stop. I can neither hear nor say more."

"As you wish."

"You're an excellent leader, Yoel."

"Thank you." Yoel bowed and left the house. His feet barely touched the stones of the Via.

Praise from Secundus and Paulos banished. What more could he want?

21

A friend loves at all times,
and a brother is born for a time of adversity.

— PROVERBS 17.17

KASSI STARED AT THE CRACKED CEILING. SHE HADN'T SLEPT MUCH. The joy of two nights ago, of learning how much the God of Israel loved her, had been lost in the murkiness of worry about Jason. His slumped shoulders and weak voice haunted her, not to mention his wounded body.

She rose and slipped out the door of Julia's villa. She shivered and pulled her cloak tighter around her chest. The morning sun gave enough light to see where she walked, but not enough to warm her.

There had to be some way to fix this. Something someone could do. But what?

She unlocked the bakery door and closed it behind her. She shoved wood into the oven, coaxing the embers to life.

If only there were someone who could help. Jason had mentioned once his pater had trained the glassblower in Amphipolis. But that was two days away and two days back, and the deadline was four days away.

A bright orange flame leaped to life, spreading light and heat. She paced, the words of the prophet which Paulos had shared swirling in her mind. He'd said the Jews were God's chosen people, and Jason was Jewish.

God, will You help me to help him? Give me an idea. Don't let him lose everything.

Isa entered, Thalia and the boys following. "You're here early."

Kassi shrugged. "I couldn't sleep."

"Why not?" Isa grinned as she grabbed a stack of bowls. "Does this have anything to do with the glassblower?"

Kassi frowned. "Why would you think that?"

"He seems to be the subject of many of your thoughts lately."

Gaius trudged in, rubbing his eyes.

"I thought you were supposed to sleep late." Isa placed a bowl on five of the tables.

He leaned against a half-wall, his shoulders hunched. "Guess I'm used to getting up before dawn. But now I don't know what to do. I have nowhere to go."

Kassi patted his shoulder. "You're always welcome here. Maybe you can help me figure out a way to help Jason. I wish I knew how to do what he does. Then I could help. With two blowers, he could cut the time needed in half. He'd meet his deadline then."

"I know how." Gai's habitual bright smile returned. "Making glasses with a mold isn't that hard. It's the free blowing he does that requires skill."

"You can do it?" Thalia said. "I thought you were his apprentice."

He nodded. "We've been taking turns, trading off when we get tired. I've been doing as much as he does the last few days because his shoulder is so sore."

"Who holds the mold when you blow them?"

"He does. Anyone can do that. A child could do it."

Her gloom melted away as an idea began to form. "Come with me." She bolted out the door.

"Where are we going?" He scrambled to keep up.

"To see a friend." She hoped. It was still quite early, so there was a reasonable chance he hadn't left his home for the day. "Follow me."

She'd been to Ari's house before. When his pater served as politarch beside hers, they often shared dinner with the other councilors and their families. She remembered them as long and excruciatingly boring.

She passed Pappa's domus and moved to the last one on the Via, on the other side of the street. She knocked on the door and told the slave she needed to see Ari.

"And you are?"

"Kassi."

"Kassi?" It wasn't until he peered down his nose at her that she realized her appearance wasn't that of a resident of the ano poli. She straightened her back and jutted out her chin. "Kassandra, daughter of Secundus."

The slave raised a brow. "Wait here." He closed the door.

"What was that about?" Gai asked.

"I don't look like someone who belongs here anymore. People in the ano poli are ... not very welcoming to others."

The door opened, and they were allowed into the atrium. The slave returned with Ari. "Kyrie, is this woman who she claims to be?"

Ari grinned. "She is indeed."

The slave all but sneered at her.

"You can leave us. And we'd love some fruit and bread." He beckoned to them. "Let's go to the garden."

Kassi and Gai followed him to the back of the house.

"You have no idea how much you're talked about, do you?" asked Ari.

"I do, actually. And I don't care."

Ari chuckled as he dropped onto a bench under a flowering tree. "What do you think of the preacher, Paulos?"

"A great many things, but we have no time for that right now." Kassi paused as a different servant set a tray of cheese and steaming bread before them. "Do you know what happened to Jason last night?"

"No, why? Is he all right?"

"Not really, no." She relayed what had happened.

"How much did he lose?"

"He dropped two days' worth of cups," said Gai.

"Two days." Ari winced. "How is he?"

"Terrible. He's given up," she said. "And his shoulder and arm—he looks like he's been in a fight. Well, one arm does."

"I could try to talk to Damianos, but he delights in making others miserable." Ari shook his head. "But that contract leaves no options."

"I have a better idea, I think," Kassi said. "But we'll need a lot of help."

"Tell me what to do."

HARSH LIGHT CLIMBED through the window and into bed with Jason. He groaned and draped his left arm over his eyes, but such a tiny bit of darkness was not strong enough to banish the unwelcome light.

Despair and guilt smothered him.

Abba would be so disappointed if he were there.

No, if Abba were here, this would not have happened. This was Jason's fault, and his alone. Everything Abba had built—and his abba before him—had been lost in one weak moment. Centuries of success, gone in an instant.

All Jason's memories revolved around the shop. Those that

didn't, took place in the house. Both would be gone in a matter of days.

Loud banging on the front door interrupted his thoughts.

He rolled to face the wall, ignoring the pain.

More banging, like several fists pounding.

Groaning, he rose and slipped on a dirty tunic. He padded to the door and opened it a hand's width.

Gaius, Kassi, and Aristarchos waited outside. If they'd come to comfort him, they could turn and go home.

"What do you want?"

"We've come to help you," Ari said.

"Help me what?"

"Finish the order. Come on. Let's go."

"You can't help me. It's too late." He just wanted to go back to bed. His head felt like it was full of straw, and every muscle in his body ached. He started to close the door, but Ari placed his foot against the frame before he could.

"We've talked to the potter. We can do this, and we can get more help if we need. Please let us do this for you."

"It's no use. I'm too far behind. We'll never catch up."

Ari pushed the door open and stepped inside. "Do you want to lose it all without trying to save it? You still have four days—five if you count Shabbat."

Jason had always valued Ari's brutal honesty, until now. "No, I can't." He opened the door wide and faced the group. "I hadn't taken the glasses to the pistrinum for the last couple days. We finished so late, and I was exhausted ... Anyway, last night I was carrying two days' worth. I lost 140 cups. That, plus 320 for the next four days, and what we were already short ... that's about 500 in four days. We weren't even making eighty a day. It can't be done."

"It can't be done by *one blower*," Gaius spoke confidently.

"We only *have* one blower," Jason said. "Not even that. Right now, I can't lift the pipe. The molten glass is too heavy."

"Haven't you been training Gai?" Kassi moved to stand behind the boy, her hands on his shoulders.

He had been. But Gaius couldn't move as fast as Jason. "That's still only one."

"Train me. Gaius said he learned in a few hours," Ari said.

There was no way this could work. He refused to be distracted by hoping for what could never be. "We have only one furnace. Two blowers can't work at the same furnace."

"The potter said we could use his for as long as we need."

"Belos?"

Ari nodded.

"You've already talked to him?"

"He's more than happy to help." Ari grinned triumphantly.

Jason ran his hand through his hair. Why would Belos do that? Give up his furnace? How would he make any money for the week?

Jason gestured to Kassi. "How are you going help?"

"Gai says you need one person to blow and one to hold the mold. If he can do it, so can I."

"Gai and I blow, you and Kassi hold the molds. And at night, I can carry the full crates to the bakery," said Ari.

He aimed his gaze at Kassi. "What about the pistrinum? You can't close it for five days."

"Isa can handle it. She's delighted to. And Melas will come after he's finished at the mill."

Jason shook his head. It was too much to take in. He'd finally accepted it was all gone and all his fault. To think it could still be accomplished, and that so many people would be eager to help him...

"Can't you at least try?" Kassi's voice was soft, but her words were powerful.

As much as he wanted to, Jason couldn't say no to her. He shrugged. It would be over in five days either way, so why not? "All right."

"Change your chiton first. You smell." Ari laughed.

Jason changed, and Belos was waiting outside his shop when the group arrived.

"Belos, how can you give up your furnace for five days? We—I can't do that to you."

Belos grinned. "Don't worry about it. Unlike you, I can do a great deal without the fire. I can form as many vessels as I want, and they can dry until I have the furnace back. And the other potters"—he looked over his shoulder at a group now approaching—"have offered any extra space in their furnaces if I have something that needs to be done now." He put his hands on his hips. "I told you. We look out for each other. And Damianos has cheated almost all of us. Trust me. We're happy to help."

Jason's heart dropped. "He has?" How many people had that man alienated in the city?

"Some of us managed to get paid eventually, *if* we had a contract, and *if* we went to the agoranomos. Or threatened to. In fact, I'm the one who convinced your abba to start using contracts. He hated it, but I'm glad now he did."

So am I. "What did he do to you?"

"He wanted a matching pair of amphorae for a gift to the governor. He had extremely specific instructions, and they took me over two weeks to craft. Then he refused to take them or pay for them. Said he found a better gift."

Jason's jaw tightened. "How much did you lose?"

"Twenty drachmae. I did sell them, but not for what they were worth. No one else could afford them. You can see why I'm happy to help you. We need to show him we won't be taken advantage of by him anymore." The fifteen or so men and boys standing behind him all nodded their assent. "We'll all help in any way we can."

The relief Belos's words brought was tempered by great responsibility. He had a chance to reclaim everything he thought he'd lost, but now, if he didn't finish, he would let the other artisans down as well.

Can't you at least try?

"Let's get started then. Gai, take a container, and let's transfer some of the melted glass into Belos's furnace."

Maybe it would work. Maybe not. But at least now he had a chance.

WHEN TIMOS SHOWED up at the village at dawn to take her place, she didn't argue. The glass shop was hot, stuffy, and rank with the stench of sweat.

She'd lasted only a day, but the others still had three or four more to endure. This was her idea, and she couldn't just disappear. If she couldn't help with the actual production of the glasses, maybe she could help those who were doing the work.

What did she want most yesterday?

Rest. Cool wine. Food.

She couldn't give them rest, but she could feed them. She hurried to the agora, heading straight for Publius's popina.

"Kassi! Chairé."

"I need your help."

"Of course, anything for you. What do you need?"

"I need some food that can be eaten with one hand. I love your meat and bread but the juice ... I need something not so messy."

"Messy?" Publius put a hand to his chest.

Her face warmed. "Publius, I'm sorr—"

"You've not offended me." He laughed. "I know what you mean. You've thought of bread, I assume?"

"I'm heading to the pistrinum next."

"What's this for, anyway?"

"Aristarchos and I are trying to help Jason with his order for Damianos."

Publius spat. "What did that overbearing ... what did he do now?"

Kassi explained. "I need something they can eat while they're working. Something to keep them going, to give them energy. They have four more days."

"All right." The vendor nodded and drummed his fingers on the table. "You go to the bakery and gather some bread. Tear it so they can pop it in their mouths. I'll gather dried fruit and nuts. Maybe some hard cheese."

Kassi crossed the cardo to the bakery. "Isa, I need your help."

"Of course."

"We need to get whatever we have left from yesterday, rip it into bite-sized pieces, and put it in a basket."

Isa nodded and grabbed a basket. "Can I ask what you're doing?"

Kassi ripped bread as she told Isa her plan. "They're so exhausted. I wish I could think of something to do for them besides food."

"Take some sleeping mats. Perhaps they can take turns and rest a bit."

"I think they'd need at least one more person for them to be able to do that. We need two glassblowers and two helpers working all day."

"My boys can help." A young woman emerged from the stall beside Isa.

Kassi blinked. "I ... who ...?"

Isa pulled her away. "I apologize, Kassi. Phaedra came here yesterday, with her three children. I told her she could work here. I know I should have checked with you, but ..."

"No, Isa, that's wonderful. I trust you implicitly, and I don't ever want to turn anyone away." She glanced at Phaedra. "How old are your boys?"

"They're nine and ten," Isa said. "She also has a girl, seven, and she's been helping around the bakery. They're hard workers."

"Perfect. Where are they?"

"In the market," Phaedra said. "I sent them to get something to eat with the last of my coins. They'll be back soon."

Kassi turned to Isa. "I don't have any mats. Does anyone sell them?"

It was doubtful. Only the poorest slept on reed mats, and since they rarely had money to buy them, they crafted them.

"The boys can bring ours. Four mats and two helpers," Phaedra said.

"You don't even know Jason. Or what he's doing. You don't know me!"

"I know what kind of person you are," Phaedra said. "You've helped Isa, and I want to help you. And your friend."

Kassi wrapped her arms around the woman. "Eucharisto," she whispered.

Isa snickered. "We all like Jason. Not as much as you, but ..."

Heat climbed up her neck. "You hush."

While she waited for Phaedra's sons, she returned to Publius to collect what he'd gathered. Phaedra met her with the mats, and when the boys appeared, Kassi led them to the village, an amphora of honeyed wine in each hand. The boys each carried a basket of food and a mat under each arm.

Kassi peaked inside the shop. Jason hovered in the corner counting glasses. He reached for a tablet and marked on it, then shook his head and set the tablet aside.

Lines marked his face. The rash on his arm was an angry red, and his left hand was dotted with cuts from the broken glasses. He looked up and closed his eyes for a long moment, then rubbed his hand down his face.

He was exhausted.

She left the baskets outside and stepped through the doorway, slipping past Ari and Timos. "Jason."

"Kassi. I thought you went home."

"Come outside. I want to show you something."

He let out a weary sigh. "We—"

"I know. You're busy. This will help, I promise."

He followed her out.

"These are Hector and Orion. Their mamma is new to my shop, and they've volunteered to help. If I can help, I figure so can they."

"We still have only two blowers. Even if I taught Timos, there's no room."

"I know, but you need to rest. You teach Timos, and then you can take a break. I brought food, wine, and sleeping mats. You could even take a quick trip to the baths."

Jason shook his head. "I don't know ..."

"I know you slept here last night."

"How...?" He shook his head. "Gai has a big mouth."

"He cares about you."

"I know." He allowed a slight smile.

"Isn't one of the reasons for your Shabbat to let your mind and body rest? Even the Greeks recognize the wisdom in that, though they don't admit it in public. Take a break, and you'll be much more productive, I promise. You're asleep standing up."

His shoulders slumped. "All right. Gai can go first."

"I think you should. Gaius can teach Timos." She fixed him with a stare she hoped would convince him of her determination.

He nodded.

"You can lie down under that tree." She sent the boys across the path with the mats.

She turned back to Jason. "Eat first."

"Yes, kyria."

"Very funny." She picked up a basket and pulled back the top. "Publius arranged this for me. Let's see. We have nuts, dried figs and cherries, raisins, and cut apples. Some cheese, and of course, lots of bread. Oh, look! He included some pieces of meat. We tried to make it all so you could grab some while working."

"I'm not hungry."

"Just a few bites, then."

Jason narrowed his eyes as he popped a dried cherry in his mouth. Then another, and then a handful of small chunks of cheese. "Guess I'm hungrier than I thought." He grinned.

"Thought so." But she needed to get the food off the ground. Not only would animals get to it, if the men couldn't grab something quickly as they passed by, they wouldn't bother. She handed the basket to Orion, then stepped next door to Belos's and rapped on the door frame.

The pottery shop was bigger than Jason's. In the far corner, Gaius and Glaukos were busy producing cups. Several sat on a shelf that had been pulled close to the furnace, slowly cooling. In a corner in the front half of the room, Belos sat before a wheel forming a tall jug.

"Belos?"

He looked up. "Yes? I'm sorry, I forgot your name."

"Kassandra."

"Can I help you?"

"I know you're already doing so much, and I hate to ask. But do you know where we could find a small table? I brought some food."

He grinned as he stood. "Excellent. Jason didn't eat well as it was, but these last days ... I've tried to get him to eat."

"Thank you. I appreciate that."

Belos removed a basket of clay from a table tucked in a corner, then carried it outside and set it up against the wall next to the door.

"We try to help each other out here. The people of the upper city like our wares, but they don't want to know us."

"I'm sorry." She'd been like that once. Perhaps not intentionally snubbing them but making no effort to think about them, either.

Together they arranged the baskets of food, and she set the amphorae and some cups beside them.

"There. I hope that helps." She looked around for Jason. "Where did he go?"

Orion pointed toward the tree.

Jason lay on a mat, arm over his eyes, already asleep.

22

The integrity of the upright guides them,
but the unfaithful are destroyed by their duplicity.

— PROVERBS 11.3

THE DEEP BLUE GLASS SPARKLED IN THE LAST RAYS OF SUNLIGHT LIKE A precious jewel as Jason held up the final cup.

Gaius raised his arms over his head. "Two thousand!"

The room burst into applause, and Jason breathed an enormous sigh of relief. They'd had to work into the evening of Shabbat, but they'd finished in four days. The last cup had been crafted just after sundown, and they'd slowly cooled for most of today. The terms of the contract had been met.

"Are we sure we have two thousand?" Jason counted the last two crates, touching each glass. He checked his tablet.

Kassi took the tablet from him. "Jason, we all counted every single cup in every single crate this week, several times. You have the whole amount."

"You have twenty extra, in case one breaks." Ari pointed to a basket sitting near the door, blue glass peeking out from golden straw.

"Sorry." He winced. "It's ... You know what I stand to lose."

"We know," she said. "But you won't lose anything. I promise."

His cheeks heated as she gave him a quick hug.

Ari approached. "All right, Gai, get one of those crates. I'll get the other, and the extras, and let's head to the pistrinum."

"Why do that? That's the wrong direction." Jason pointed to the baths.

"We have to get the other crates," Ari said.

"But you should still take those two straight to the bathhouse. We'll have to make several trips as it is."

"Gai already left for the bakery, so we may as well all go there." Ari left before Jason could object.

"But ..." Jason gave up. He was far too weary to argue. He stepped outside and waited for Kassi.

He had so many questions, so much that needed to be said. But his exhausted brain couldn't sort out the overload, so he just walked silently next to her.

When they arrived at the bakery, the doors stood wide open.

Inside, a crowd awaited him. Thalia and her other two sons, along with Paulos, Timos, and Silas. The boys who brought the mats stood beside a woman who must be their imma, and a little girl. More of Kassi's bakers gathered in small groups chatting. At the sound of footsteps behind him, he turned to see Belos, Glaukos, and a few other artisans.

Ari put two fingers in his mouth and whistled. The room silenced. "All right. The crates are in the back workspace to the right of the oven. Everyone take one, or more if you can, and there should be enough of us to carry them all in one trip. Wait outside the door, and Jason will lead us."

As each received their load, Ari moved to Jason's side. "That should shut Damianos up for a while.".

Jason struggled to keep his jaw closed as he watched over twenty people, some total strangers, gather to help him when they should be at home eating their evening meals.

Why?

Ari slapped his shoulder. "Last four are waiting for you and me."

Jason followed his friend to the corner where Paulos waited. After Jason and Ari each grabbed a box, Paulos set a second on top of Ari's. He kept the last for himself.

"Are you sure you want to do that, Paulos? On Shabbat?"

He grinned. "If we can pull a donkey out of a hole, surely I can help a friend in need, yes?"

"If you're sure."

Ari chuckled. "I have no idea what that means, but let's get going. We're all waiting for you to lead the way."

Outside the bakery, a line had formed that stretched along the Via Regia to the cardo. He strode to the front and led them to the upper city.

The bathhouse loomed above them, perching on the hills abutting the northern wall. It was visible from everywhere in the city. If Damianos wanted a monument to his wealth and status, he had achieved it.

They reached the massive building, and Jason banged on the wooden double doors with his foot.

He was about to do it again when the door opened enough for a head to poke out. A young man surveyed the line of people and slammed the door without speaking.

Jason turned and made a face at Ari, who grinned as if he couldn't be having more fun.

After a long moment, the door opened again just wide enough for Damianos to step outside. He spread his feet, crossed his arms, and glared at Jason. "You said you'd be here yesterday. You're late."

"The document specifies this date."

"I'm not accepting this delivery. And you will owe the penalty."

"Do you want to do that in front of so many witnesses?"

"And Secundus's daughter?" Kassi took a step nearer.

"Secundus is the one who chose me to marry you. You refused, so who do you think he will believe when I tell him you were late?"

"We have witnesses."

Damianos scanned the people in line. "I see slaves. And women." He laughed.

"No one here is a slave."

"Perhaps, but still, they are women and"—he focused on Gaius and his brothers—"children."

"And a politarch." Ari moved into view.

"Secundus will believe me," Jason said. "We may be *women and children*, but there are quite a lot of us. If you don't let us in, we'll set them here on the ground. I doubt they'll last past sunrise. Then, when we examine the contract, and the agoranomos rules against you, you'll have neither the cups nor the money you will still owe me." He set his box on the ground. "What is your decision?"

Damianos huffed and turned on his heel, whispering to the slave before disappearing.

Trying to hide a smirk, the slave opened the door wide. The group filed inside one by one and gathered in the atrium.

The young man led them down a hall, dark but for the light of a waning moon shining through the enormous windows that lined every wall except the northernmost one. He opened a door into a large, empty room. "You can put them here."

Jason set down his crate against the wall. His chest slowly relaxed, and each breath came more easily than the last as the others laid down their cargo one by one.

Kassi approached, smiling at him. Two steps from the growing piles, her sandal caught on a rough edge of stone, and she lurched forward.

A chill flooded his body, soaking every muscle. They may have twenty extra, but each crate held forty. He lunged to save the box, putting one hand on the bottom and one across the top, grasping the far edge.

Kassi held tightly to the box, helplessly trying to keep it from falling, but if she didn't let go and let him have it, all the glasses in it would be destroyed.

Ari leaped forward and grabbed her around the waist. "Let go! Jason has it."

She opened her hands, and Jason pulled the box safely away. Kassi fell forward, but Ari kept her from slamming against the floor.

Jason added the box to the lower stack, then counted the boxes.

Forty-eight, forty-nine, fifty.

Was it finally over?

It was.

He'd filled the order, saved the business, and kept his home. The group surrounding him was almost as happy as he was.

He couldn't have done it without them.

THE AROMA of fresh bread billowed from the oven, filling the bakery. It was Kassi's favorite time of day—just after sunrise, when loaves began popping out of the oven one after another like Roman soldiers marching into battle. Warmth from the fire led the bakers to shed their cloaks, and bare arms moved rapidly, nimble fingers kneading, forming, and placing hot loaves under cloth to keep the bread hot and soft.

Kassi sorted the loaves on the center table—braided breads on one end, loaves full of nuts and fruits on the other, and plain loaves in the center.

Isa joined her. "You look awfully happy." She winked.

"I'm looking forward to hearing Paulos tonight. And it's good to be back here. I missed it."

"Those the only reasons?"

She ignored the comment. "Oh, Jason has invited everyone to his home tomorrow night for a celebration."

"I'm sure they'll all be excited to go."

"But you must come too."

Isa frowned. "I did nothing to help. Those boxes were too heavy."

"Nothing? You kept the bakery going for almost a week. I couldn't have helped him without you. You're the only one I trust to take care of this place."

She smiled. "All right then. I'd love to go."

As Kassi stepped back to admire the display, heavy footfalls called her attention to the door. She bristled when Damianos sauntered into the bakery. She moved halfway to the door.

Damianos stayed near the entrance, waiting for her to come to him, no doubt.

Kassi kept her feet planted.

The muscles in his jaw flexed.

A cloth dangling from her fist, she pointed to her right. "We have a lot of plain bread if you would like to purchase some. Otherwise, I'm quite busy." She didn't have time for him.

"I didn't come for bread." He stomped closer, fists clenched at his sides.

"Then is this about last night? You need to talk—"

"How dare you tell the entire city I am not worth marrying." His nostrils flared.

Annoyance burst into anger. "I did no such thing!"

She scanned the building, searching for a reaction to her raised voice. Heads jerked back down to the dough in hand.

He glared. "I've heard it from more than one person."

"I told no one. I've spoken to no one in the ano poli except Aristarchos. Not my family, not my friends, not Pappa's slaves. I don't know who said that, but it wasn't me."

"But it's what you *think*." He leaned toward, eyes shooting daggers.

"Actually, it's not." Her voice softened.

He stood straighter, his eyes still fixed on her.

She returned his gaze. He really was quite handsome. Dark,

short hair framed deep brown eyes and a strong jaw. Broad shoulders and uncommon height gave an impression of strength he likely didn't have, considering his lifestyle of leisure. When he smiled, his face lit up. Too bad it didn't happen more often.

"Damianos, I'm probably the only woman in Thessalonike who wouldn't love to be known as your wife." She shrugged. "But this is my life now. And it may mean I never marry, that I'll live in a tiny apartment on the top floor of a decaying building, and become known as a merchant, a pariah of the upper city. But it fills my heart with a joy I sincerely pray you know one day."

Warmth filled her chest as she thought of Isa and Thalia and the others, who now looked forward to waking up each day instead of dreading it, living in fear. "I can't give it up, not for anyone."

"I think that's a very bad decision."

"Perhaps, but it's mine, and mine alone."

"I hope it doesn't end up making your life much worse." He turned and stormed away.

Was that a threat?

YOEL STOOD outside the door of Jason's house. Leah had sent him to make things right, as she put it. She'd sent a dish of lentil stew—Jason's favorite.

He failed to see what *he* had done wrong, but he did want to give Jason a chance to deal with Paulos before engaging one of the unofficial advocates. He took a deep breath and rapped on the door.

Jason answered.

Yoel stepped over the threshold, holding the dish covered by a bright yellow cloth that held fresh bread. "Leah sent you some food. You must miss your imma's cooking. She always could make a delicious lentil stew." He set it on a shelf and removed the cover. "May I dish you some?"

"Of course."

"Do you have a bowl?"

Jason led him to the culina and gestured toward a shelf of dishes. "Pick one."

Yoel chose one and ladled some of the steaming stew from the small pot. He handed it to Jason with a round of bread.

Jason dipped his bread into the stew and blew on it as Yoel dished himself some. "It's good. Tell Dodah thank you."

"We missed you yesterday."

"I had to finish the order. You'll be glad to know I won't lose the house or the shop."

Yoel cleared his throat. "There's a rumor in the community that Paulos is staying in your home. I told the elders, and your dodah, that couldn't be true.

"Ah. So that's why you've come. I knew you couldn't have come just to see me."

Yoel's face heated. How to get out of this without lying? "I admit, it was Leah's suggestion. But I am happy to see you."

"As far as your question, he is. All three of the visitors are staying with me now." Jason took another bite.

"Why?" Yoel's breath came fast and hard as his brows furrowed. "Explain this to me."

"I gave shelter to someone who needed it. Why is that so hard to understand? It's commanded by Yahweh in the law: 'When a foreigner resides among you in your land, do not mistreat them.'"

"Adonai also praised Mattathias when he was overcome with zeal for the law and killed the king's officer who was forcing them to sacrifice to Greek gods. Paulos is desecrating the law."

"How is he doing that?"

Yoel set his bowl on the worktable. "He is offering salvation in return for nothing. No obedience, no sacrifice. The holy things of Adonai were given to us alone—if He had wanted the pagans to be saved, He would have given these gifts to them. But He didn't."

"I'm not going to debate scripture with you. I offered food and a place to stay." He shrugged and moved toward the triclinium.

"That's it. I've done nothing wrong, and I don't know why you're treating me like I have."

Yoel followed and sat facing his nephew. "Ben ach, Jason, I'm concerned about you. Your abba is not here, and I'm compelled to make sure you stay on the right path. You've not kept the Shabbat holy, and now you give shelter to one who seeks to destroy the law and the Jewish nation. I don't think it's good for you to spend so much time with him."

"I disagree." Jason continued eating.

Yoel leaned in and laid his hand on Jason's shoulder. "Ben ach, I'm asking you to stop this. Paulos does not belong in Thessalonike. Send them on their way."

"You know I can't do that, Yoel."

Yoel folded his hands in his lap. "I have connections with synagogues across the diaspora. We share information. Do you know what happened to these three in Asia?"

"No."

"Paulos once traveled with two men named Barnabas and Markos, but Markos deserted them. Or was sent home. No one knows quite why, but you will admit a man is judged by his companions."

Jason nodded.

"Paulos and Barnabas continued to the city of Lystra, where they claimed to be Zeus and Hermes, messengers of the gods. The priests of the temple of Zeus joined the people and offered sacrifices to them."

Jason's brow furrowed. "They allowed this?"

"Apparently. I've heard nothing otherwise. At this point, the synagogue leaders acted and taught the truth to the crowds. Paulos and Barnabas were expelled from the city. There is talk that he was stoned, but that obviously can't be true." Yoel leaned near and waited until he'd caught Jason's eye. "Are these the kind of people you want to be with? To learn from?"

Jason remained silent but set his bowl on the table beside him.

"Will you now do as I ask?" Yoel silently begged Jason to obey.

"I need to talk to Paulos first."

"You don't believe me?"

"I believe I must give them a chance to tell their side of the story. If this is true, as you say, *if* they have claimed to be gods and accepted sacrifices, then yes, I will make them leave my house."

"How do you know they won't lie?"

"They might. But if you trust your sources, then you shouldn't have a problem with it. The truth will come out, one way or another."

After an awkward goodbye, Yoel left.

The truth will come out, one way or another.

Normally, Yoel would agree. But from what he'd seen the last weeks, lies could always outrun truth.

He'd given Jason a chance to do the right thing, and he'd refused. Yoel had no choice but to find a lawyer.

23

You make known to me the path of life;
> you will fill me with joy in your presence,
> with eternal pleasures at your right hand.

— PSALM 16.11

STANDING AT THE EDGE OF THE LOWER AGORA, YOEL DRAGGED HIS hand down his beard. If only Jason had agreed to send the men away yesterday, he wouldn't be in this position.

Was he really going to do this? Could he hire an advocate to help him get rid of Paulos and his campaign of lies?

Doing business with a forum advocate would be bad enough, but the *agoraioi* who hung out in the market, although proficient in the law, searching for business were considered unethical, dishonest, and generally disreputable. It was an extreme solution to an extreme problem. If Yoel was going to protect the purity of the Jewish faith, he was going to have to do some unpleasant things.

After the failure of Hesiod to find a way to prosecute Paulos, Yoel had made some inquiries, discreetly he hoped, as to the best of the agora lawyers. He'd consistently heard two names.

Titos was generally regarded as the better of the two, but he'd been told Solon was the one who would take the most risks, argue the toughest cases, and skirt the edge of the law.

Exactly the kind of man Yoel needed.

He approached the vendors nearest him and inquired about Solon.

One of the men eyed him as if he were asking about a criminal but remained silent.

Another pointed to the other end of the agora. "*Those* men keep their own company over there."

Yoel furrowed his brows but moved on. Why such disdain? Was it that these agoraioi were far worse than he'd been led to believe?

But which one was he? At the far corner, men in fine tunics stood in small groups of two or three. Any one of them could be Solon.

He approached a pair of men talking and cleared his throat. "I'm looking for Solon, the *agoraios*."

The shorter one scurried away.

The remaining man was younger than Yoel expected. A long nose that appeared to have been broken more than once dominated his face. Deep set eyes peered out from above flushed, fat cheeks.

"I am." A smile spread like oil over his face. His eyes shone brightly, but somehow the expression still felt disingenuous. "How may I be of service to you, my honored friend?"

Yoel rolled his shoulders, trying to shake off the discomfort. "I need help with a problem."

"And what problem is that?"

Yoel scanned the agora, looking for what, he didn't know. No good Jew would ever see him here. Still, he felt like an errant child expecting chastisement at any moment. "There is a man who is spreading misinformation about our faith. I need him stopped."

"And how do you wish for that to happen?"

Irritation pricked his skin. "I don't know. That's why I came to you."

"And why did you come to me instead of one of the many others here?" He waved a hand, taking in the whole of the agora.

"I heard you were ... successful."

"If you won't tell me the truth, then I can't help you." He turned to go.

When he'd stalked a few steps away, Yoel hurried after him. "I was told you put results above ..." He looked around again, lowering his voice. "...above following the minutiae of the law."

Solon studied him a moment. "As a Jew, I would think you valued even the tiniest part of the law."

"I do—the law of Moses. For the laws of Rome, I have not as much regard."

Solon laughed. "Then we know where we stand. A very good start."

"Shall we go discuss this in your office?"

He laughed louder as he gestured to the whole of the agora. "This is my office. I see no reason to pay to hide away in a room. The city is out here. The people are out here. I need to be fully aware of all that goes on to properly represent my clients."

That sounded more like an excuse to keep all the coin he received than a thirst for knowledge, but no matter.

"Let us walk." Solon strolled slowly along the walkways, and Yoel fell into step beside him. "Tell me about this man."

Yoel repeated what he had told Hesiod. "The forum advocate I saw said there was nothing to be done, that Paulos had broken no laws."

"And who was that, if I may ask?"

"Hesiod."

Solon scoffed. "He knows the law backward and forward, but he has no imagination. He can only go after a problem straight on."

"Whereas you..."

"I go at it sideways, from behind, above, around—there is always a way. For the right price."

Yoel halted. "But I understood advocates were not allowed to charge for their services."

Solon turned and faced Yoel. "That's because they are sons of wealth and privilege. They can afford to study the law because they don't have to work to eat. They consider making the law available to those less educated their way of contributing to society. But those of us who are born less fortunate ..."

Judging by the silver fibulae on his chiton and new leather sandals, Solon had more than caught up to men like Hesiod, and his protestations of poverty rang hollow.

"Still, he's right. The law says we cannot charge for our service. There are always expenses, however."

The man was living up to his reputation already.

"And how much would those expenses be?"

"One hundred denarii."

Over three months' salary? His hopes of stopping Paulos vanished like mist. "I'm sorry. I shouldn't have come here. I have nowhere near that amount, and if I did, I couldn't risk it. I am accountable to the elders." He pivoted on his foot.

"Wait." Solon hurried to face Yoel. "How about this? Fifty denarii, and you pay only if I'm successful."

Yoel winced. "Fifty is still too much by far."

"Twenty-five."

Hope came back into view. Better. Much better. He nodded. "I think that could work. But you should meet all the elders first. I'll need their input."

"We could meet over a meal." Solon's ample stomach showed his love of food. "I'd be honored to host you at my home. How many would be coming?"

A bit of heat pricked Yoel's cheeks. Had Solon forgotten Jews couldn't dine at the house of a Greek? Or was he unaware? Or perhaps he was testing Yoel. Now was not the time to alienate the man, just after gaining him as an ally. "My wife is the best cook in the community. We'd be honored to host you."

Solon's face brightened. "Excellent. And when would this meeting take place?"

"Two days from now?"

Solon sucked air in through his teeth. "The sooner we make a plan, the sooner this man is out of your lives."

Perhaps he wasn't as bad as Yoel had thought. "Tomorrow night, then. Come to the synagogue, and I'll take you to my home."

"I'll be there." He flashed another oily smile and left.

As the man waddled away, Yoel's stomach soured. He'd thought he'd feel better after getting some help, not worse.

Had he made the right decision?

At a sharp knock, Jason hurried to the front of his home. Four men waited there, each loaded with boxes or sacks.

"Come in." Jason allowed them to pass. "In the culina."

The men lugged their deliveries to the kitchen and placed them on the long tables, taking away the wooden boxes they'd carried them in. "The wine will be delivered momentarily," said one. "Publius said he would collect the serving dishes after."

"Thank you."

"Yes, kyrie." The man bowed his head and exited with the other three.

Jason examined the delivery. Three cloth bags occupied one end of the worktable. He opened the first, holding wrinkly shelled walnuts. Another was filled with pale shelled almonds, and a third with green pistachios peeking out from their casings.

He removed another cloth to reveal a silver platter covered with sliced pears and apples, their red and green skins a burst of color. Another was heaped with dried fruit—dark raisins, deep purple plums, crimson cherries, and figs the color of a setting sun.

He lifted the lid of a pottery bowl, and the earthy aroma of garlic and leeks filled his nostrils. Three roasted fish topped with cheese rested on a bed of cooked cabbage and onions. An enormous bowl of thick lentil stew completed his order. Publius had more than lived up to Kassi's praise.

"Something smells delicious." Paulos entered the culina and surveyed the food. "This looks like much more than a simple dinner."

"It's supposed to be simple, but I do expect a lot of people. I asked Ari to invite everyone who helped in any way to get Damianos's order finished."

Timos joined them and snagged a dried cherry. "Who prepared all this food? It must have taken most of the day."

"I have no idea. I asked Publius to take care of everything. He was surprised and said he doesn't often deal with entire meals, but I told him to engage whomever he needed. I knew he would deal with me fairly."

Kassi entered the culina. "I knocked, but you didn't answer. I thought you might need some help."

He grinned. "I do. How did you know?"

"Publius told me you had asked for everything needed for a large dinner, and I figured you weren't familiar with hosting such a gathering."

"Imma always did that." He shrugged. "But it's not dinner, really."

Timos chuckled as he studied the food on the table.

"All right, it's dinner." Jason laughed. "I wanted to thank everyone for making sure I didn't lose everything. It's the least I can do."

"This wasn't necessary," Paulos said. "We were happy to do it."

Kassi neared the table and surveyed the offerings. "How many are you expecting?"

"I invited everyone who helped me. Twenty? Thirty? I'm not sure."

He followed her as she stepped away and peered into the dining area. "That many won't fit in the triclinium."

His chest tightened. "I know, but what do I do? I can't send half of them away." He wanted to show his appreciation. Would he end up insulting them instead?

"We could eat in the garden, like when Paulos teaches. It might be fun. You could talk to everyone, not just the person next to you."

"I'm happy to try."

"You're going to need serving spoons. Can you find them?" She breezed back into the kitchen and around the room gathering plates and cups, finding everything although she'd never been there before, then loaded it all onto a platter and carried it to the peristyle.

Julia joined them, carrying a platter overflowing with pastelli.

"Ari told me about your dinner. I've been praying for you ever since I heard about the contract. And I made these, but Ari forgot them."

"Julia, you didn't have to do this. But thank you!"

She set the sweets on a bench. "Ari will remember in a few moments. When he arrives, make sure he knows they're here."

"You're staying, aren't you?"

She shook her head. "I wasn't part of this."

"You said you've been praying. I'd say that's a big part," said Paulos.

Ari entered the garden, leading a parade of people— all the bakers, Belos and Glaukos, and a few of the other potters.

Ari wrapped his arms around Jason and slapped his back. "It's done. And as I'd hoped, the look on Damianos's face made it all worth it."

Jason chuckled. "Almost." He would still happily trade seeing Damianos's expression for not having to endure the whole affair, but Ari was right in one thing—it was over. "And thank you for getting everyone here. I knew you were the right one to spread the word."

"You're very welcome." Ari looked at the food, now placed on several low tables in the garden. "When do we eat?"

Jason clambered onto a stone bench and cleared his throat. The crowd quieted. "I know this is unusual, but I brought you all here to say thank you. Without you, I wouldn't be here in my own home. Whether you prayed, helped make glass, brought food, kept the bakery going, carried the glasses to Damianos's house in a parade ..." He couldn't stop a grin. "That was fun."

Ari chuckled. "It was."

He sobered again. "But without you all, I would have ... I don't know what I would have done. I don't even know most of you, but I'd like to. We have fresh bread from Kassi's bakery, nuts, fruit, wine, fish, stew, and I'm not sure what else. Eat, talk, get to know one another. And enjoy the food, which Publius has brought to us."

One by one, the guests grabbed a bowl, filled it with food and found someone to talk to.

Ari joined him. "She's quite something, isn't she?"

Jason nodded. "Without her, this evening would have been a disaster."

"I think more than this dinner would have been a mess." He clapped Jason on the shoulder. "Most of these people are here because of her. We wouldn't have had enough help, and we would have gone hungry while we were there."

Ari was right. Kassi was the only reason he'd succeeded.

How could he show his appreciation?

Kassi stacked the last of the clean plates on the worktable. Publius had taken all his serving dishes away, so they'd been left with only plates, cups, and a few large bowls.

Jason moved to her side. "Kassi, you didn't have to do this."

"And who would do it then? You?"

He nodded and grinned.

She scanned the culina. "Your house is beautiful."

"Abba liked giving my imma the best."

"Then why did you build south of the Via? You could have so much more in the ano poli. Locating south lumps you in with the other artisans."

His jaw tightened. "I am an artisan. And I'm proud of it."

Her face heated. "I didn't mean it like that. You and all the craftsmen do something most of us can't. I've never understood why working with your hands—creating something which didn't exist before—is looked down on. Why is producing beautiful *and* useful things less respected than writing or painting? Everyone loves the result, but most like to pretend it appeared out of thin air." She placed a hand on her chest. "I'm not one of those people."

He smiled softly. "I'm sorry. I overreacted."

"No. I should have chosen my words more carefully."

"Abba built here because this spot is halfway between the synagogue and the shop. Besides, we're the only glassblowers in town, and Abba knew his skill would become known, and it wouldn't matter where he lived."

"Why does it need to be halfway?" She placed the plates back on the shelf.

"We can only walk a certain distance on Shabbat." He shrugged. "I know. There are lots of rules. Most of them don't make sense to me, but Abba taught me to follow them."

"May I ask what happened to your parents?" She returned, leaning back against the table, her hands on either side.

Pain clouded his face as he shifted his weight, one hip against the table.

That was a bad idea. "I'm sorry. I shouldn't have asked. You don't have to answer."

"It's all right." He stared past her as he recited what must have been a horrible memory. "I didn't even tell them goodbye that morning. They left as soon as the sun rose, and I was still asleep. I ..." His voice trailed off.

"Tell me about them."

"What? Why?"

"They're a part of you, so I want to know about them."

His face relaxed. "Imma was a lot like you."

"How so?"

"She didn't always follow the rules. She kept track of all the orders, the money, the deadlines. Most men would think her incapable because she was a woman, but Abba trusted her completely. They stopped telling people what she did because it made them doubt the business. But she knew, and Abba knew, and that was enough for her."

"They must have loved each other very much."

"They did. There were quite a few jealous young men in the community when they married, I'm told. She was beautiful. Dark hair, dark eyes, dimple in her right cheek."

"Like you."

He nodded. "She had *no* trouble attracting suitors, and Abba wasn't considered the best catch."

"Why not?"

"I'm not an expert on this by any means, but Imma said he was considered rather plain and very shy. But he was gentle and humble, and that appealed to her over the men who boasted to her about their success."

"He sounds a lot like you."

"Abba was ... Abba always saw the best in everyone. Even when confronted with evidence, he believed there was a reason for any bad behavior, any angry words. All that was needed was more patience, more forgiveness. I think that's why it appeared he hovered between Greek and Jew."

"But he didn't?"

"No. It only looked like that. He dressed like a Greek, shaved his beard, gave me a Greek name. But no matter what Yoel says, he *never* denied his faith. He never missed synagogue. He taught me the Scriptures, prayed with me daily."

"And he taught you to blow glass?"

"He did. Growing up, I spent more time in that shop than I did here. And when I made mistakes, which of course I did, often, he never got angry with me."

"He sounds like a wonderful father." Not like hers.

"When I first started, I wanted to make something other than the plain cups and plates that anyone can afford—the things he'd built his business on. I thought we could do better, make special items we could sell for a lot more. I tried to make some fancy perfume bottles." He chuckled. "The first ones were awful. The color wasn't mixed properly, and they came out all blotchy. I got better, though, and figured out how to make one color kind of spin out from the other. I made some quite beautiful ones."

Her breath caught. "What did they look like?"

"They were round on the bottom." He held his hands in the shape of a ball. "They had long necks and a glass stopper."

"What color?"

"I did some in several colors. Little bits we had left from other orders. Blue, purple—I don't remember what other colors. I think we sold a few, and there are some still in the shop somewhere. But Abba wanted to concentrate on the everyday items."

Her stomach tightened. "I might know someone who bought at least one."

"You do?"

She pulled in a shuddering breath. "My most treasured possession was a perfume bottle my pappa gave Mamma. It was a beautiful dark blue with white spiraled around it. She kept lavender oil in it. I used to smell it when I wanted to remember her."

"It *was* a treasured possession? What happened to it?"

"I broke it when I left the house. Now all I have left are memories."

"Sometimes that's enough. I have *things* of theirs. I have the business. This culina is full of glass objects we made together. But my memories are what I cherish. That may be the closest I get to having my own family."

"Why would you say that?"

"My dodh told the community my abba abandoned the faith. He and Imma and I were not held in high regard. No good Jewish girl would ever marry me. And neither would a respectable Greek girl. So, I've saved my shop and my house, but I'll likely be alone for the rest of my life."

"Jason, that's not true." She scoffed. "Look at all the friends you have, all of these people here tonight who were more than happy to help you."

"You're right. And I thank Adonai for them. But friends don't give you children."

She chuckled. "Too bad we can't marry. It would solve both our problems."

He tilted his head. "It would, wouldn't it?" One corner of his mouth turned up, revealing his dimple.

Her face heated, and her fingers curled around the edge of the table. "But we can't."

"Why not?" He moved to stand in front of her. "Your abba sent you from his house. He has no say now."

She studied his face. He was almost everything Pappa would want for her in a husband. He was successful, honest, hard-working ... but not Greek.

He closed the distance between them. His fingers hovered over her cheek as his eyes held hers. "Seriously, why not?" he whispered. "You're strong, caring, and smart enough to avoid spending your life locked in a house so no other man can see how beautiful you are."

She blinked. "You think I'm beautiful?"

His smiled widened. "Of course. Why wouldn't I?"

His unwavering gaze unnerved her, and she gripped the table more tightly. All her life, she'd lived in Mamma's shadow. Pappa had never complimented her, only compared her—unfavorably—to her. But Jason had something good to say every time they met.

"You're so different from the men I've met before."

"Is that good or bad?" His hand moved toward the back of her neck, and his thumb grazed her cheek.

His touch warmed her. "Good. Very good."

He bent to kiss her, his lips meeting hers. How could so gentle a touch send a powerful yet delightful shock down to her toes?

Ari's voice startled them, and Jason pulled away.

She peered around him at the doorway, and then relaxed when no one was there. Half a moment later, Ari appeared in the doorway. "There you are, Kassi. Mamma and I are ready to go. Do you want to walk with us?"

She nodded, her voice gone.

Jason slipped by Ari and left the culina.

Standing in the doorway, Ari looked from her to Jason in the peristyle, and then returned his gaze to her. "Umm, we'll wait outside." He disappeared before she could respond.

She found herself alone in the kitchen. Why had Jason left? Did he regret his actions?

She hoped not, because she certainly didn't.

24

The wicked plot against the righteous, and gnash their teeth at them
.

— PSALM 37.12

JASON PACED FROM ONE SIDE OF ARI'S ANDRON TO THE OTHER, HIS finger and thumb rubbing his temples. "I don't know what to do."

"How many days has it been?" Ari leaned against a column, one ankle crossed over the other, his usual stance.

"Four. Four days, and still Damianos has not yet shown up to pay me for all those glasses. At first, I thought perhaps the delay was because he was so busy with the festival, but the festival's well under way, the baths are in full operation, and I still have no money."

"Maybe it's time for you to go to him."

"I don't want to do that." Just the thought of confronting Damianos made his breath come faster.

Damianos had status, money, and connections to the governor

and the politarchs. Jason had none of those things. But it was becoming clearer by the day that Damianos wasn't planning to pay.

"I think you're right, though. I guess I'll head to the Great Baths of Damianos."

Ari laughed. "I'm sure that's what he calls them. Or maybe the Baths of the Great Damianos."

It would be funnier if it weren't so accurate.

"I don't know how much time he spends there," Ari said. "I think he just collects the money and leaves managing it to others. If he's not there, he'll be at home."

Jason paused at the door. "I don't know where he lives."

"He lives on the Via on the other side of the cardo. Third villa. There's a statue of a lion beside the door."

How appropriate.

The baths weren't far from Ari's villa. Jason told the slave at the door he needed to see Damianos.

"He is not here." The young man, wearing a short woolen chiton and bare feet, couldn't be much older than Gaius.

"Is he at home?"

"I cannot answer that."

Jason wasn't getting any information here. "All right, I'll check there."

He marched back down to the Via, turned right, and counted three houses. A roaring lion, his open mouth at the level of Jason's head, guarded the door. Jason halted, wiping his palms on his tunic.

When a slave answered Jason's knock, Jason told him needed to see Damianos. "I know he's here."

He didn't, but he knew he'd be turned away if he couldn't convince the slave he was sure.

The young man disappeared but returned almost immediately. "I'm sorry. He is terribly busy, and he asks that you return tomorrow."

"I've already waited four days for him."

"You'll have to come back."

Jason folded his arms. "If I leave here today, I'll go to the agoranomos. Tell him that."

The slave raised a brow. "Wait one moment."

Jason paced while he waited.

Finally, the door opened a third time, and the slave beckoned. "Please follow me."

Jason scanned the atrium. Enormous tapestries hung on several walls. Brightly painted sculptures, including a bust of Damianos, stood on pedestals. A silver tray full of fruit and almonds, along with two amphorae, sat on a table on the right side of the atrium, surrounded by couches, undoubtedly where his pater met his clients each morning. Further back in the house, he saw a fountain and several more slaves rushing about.

The man led Jason to a small room on the far side of the atrium. He knocked on the open door. "He is here, kyrie."

"You may go." Damianos spoke without looking up.

The slave gestured for Jason to enter then backed away, leaving the door open. Damianos continued reading a parchment, ignoring his guest.

This was a game, a way for Damianos to assert his control. Jason wouldn't let it destroy the calm he'd worked hard to hold onto all morning.

The tablinum was as richly decorated as the rest of the house. A niche with tiny silver gods and burning incense adorned the left wall. The earthy scent of costly frankincense filled the room.

Finally, Damianos scratched a reed pen across the bottom of his parchment and turned his gaze to Jason. "My slave says you asked to see me. Why is that?"

You know very well why. "I'm here because you owe me a great deal of money."

Damianos waved his hand as if shooing away an insect. "It's not that much."

"Then you should have no trouble paying it."

Damianos released a long sigh. "I spent most of my cash getting the baths open. I have money coming in now, but I've not collected it all."

"I've waited four days. The baths are open, and you've been collecting fees for the same four days. I've seen how busy they are. You should have the coins by now."

He furrowed his brows. "I'll give you half."

Jason considered the offer. Considering all the times Damianos had reminded Jason of the penalty, was it possible he had planned on never paying all along? That he ordered more than he thought could be produced, so in the end he would end up with enough glasses and pay nothing?

That was not going to happen. Jason had paid for the raw glass. His friends had given of their own time, and Jason himself had paid with pain, sweat, and blood.

"No. I earned it all, and I want it all." He kept his voice calm and low. "I've been more than patient. I will give you until sundown tomorrow to bring me my money. If you don't bring it by then, I'll see the agoranomos the next the morning."

He left without another word.

Jason stomped into his peristyle, thoughts of Damianos churning in his head and his stomach growling. He wandered into the culina to find Timos unpacking a bag full of dried fruit. Guilt pricked his chest. "You know, you don't have to do that. You're my guests."

"We like to contribute. There are three of us, after all."

"You do more than contribute. But where are the others?"

"Paulos went to meet one of the city slaves at the warehouse to hand over the last of the sails."

"He's finished with them all?"

"He works hard. And quickly. But he left this for you." He handed him a codex, much like the ones Imma had kept. This one was thicker, though.

Jason flipped through it. "What is it?"

"It's a copy of the books of Moses and the prophets. He said you should start in Isaiah." Timos surveyed the food and tilted his head toward the cardo. "I forgot the honey. I'll have to go back to the market. Join me?"

The pair walked in silence for a while, until Jason remembered Yoel's accusations. "May I ask you about something? Something I heard about you?"

"Of course. You can ask me anything."

"My dodh came to visit me, and he told me what had happened in Lystra. Or at least, a version of it."

"Ah." Timos raised his brows. "And what was this version?"

"He said you spoke to the people there and claimed to be Zeus and Hermes, messengers of the gods. The Greek priests approved and offered sacrifices to you." As he spoke the words aloud, their foolishness struck him.

Paulos had given him no sign whatsoever that he would allow this to happen. In fact, he consistently proclaimed Yeshua as the Son of the Only Living God.

Timos grinned. "I wasn't with them yet, but they did visit Lystra, and they did preach—"

Jason grabbed Timos's arm and pulled him to a stop. "I apologize. I know that isn't true. I promised Yoel I would ask, but now I'm sorry I did. Every word any of you has spoken since you arrived has been to glorify the One True God. You needn't explain any further."

"I appreciate your faith, but I think Paulos would want you to know the whole story before you decide. Would you rather ask him about it?"

Jason opened his mouth to protest but changed his mind. "No. Go ahead." He'd rather not allow Paulos to see his doubt.

Timos resumed walking. "Paul and Barnabas spoke to the people about Yeshua. And many were responding. Both Jews and Greeks were deciding to follow The Way, receiving forgiveness of sins. One morning, a man came forward. He couldn't walk—had never walked. One of the priests of Zeus brought him to us and said if Adonai was indeed the only God, that He should heal this man right then."

"Heal him. Just like that?"

Timos nodded. "We don't believe we should put God to the test like that, but the whole city was holding its breath, watching. Yeshua did say we should ask for whatever we need, so they did." He chuckled, his eyes radiating his excitement and his hands gesturing wildly. "And God responded with mercy."

"I wish I had seen it. Paulos said the man jumped up. They saw his legs grow strong and straight, and he took the first steps of his life."

"Sounds like something from the texts of Elisha."

"I don't know who first called them by the names of Zeus and Hermes. It wasn't Paulos or Barnabas, I assure you," Timos continued. "One of the priests brought bulls, garlands of brilliant flowers around their necks and heads, to the city gates to sacrifice. They tried to convince them otherwise, but it was no use. The people shouted praises to the false gods ... They couldn't stop them no matter what Paulos said."

Jason frowned. "Then how did the Jewish leaders get involved?"

"They'd had much the same reaction in some other cities, without the bulls." Timos spread his hands. "Some of the Jews from Pisidian Antioch and Iconium had followed them—"

"They followed them from *Antioch*? That's what—four or five days' travel? Why would they do that?"

"The story actually starts many years ago, in Syrian Antioch, before I knew them. The *ekklesia* there—that's what Paulos has come to call the groups that are part of The Way—commissioned Paulos and two other men to share the news of Yeshua with Jews in Asia. They started in Cyprus, sailed to Perga, and then traveled inland to Antioch in Pisidia. Their first Shabbat there, Paulos was invited to speak to the synagogue," Timos said. "He taught them much as he did here—how righteousness is available to all by faith in Yeshua. As they left the synagogue, the people invited him to speak again the following Shabbat and share more about Yeshua. Word must have spread, because the following week, nearly the whole city showed up to hear his message."

"And the leaders didn't like that, I'm guessing."

Timos sighed. "They *abhorred* it. They began spreading lies and refused them entrance to the synagogue. So Paulos took his message to the Greeks. The leaders hated that even more and chased them out of town."

"This is when they went to Iconium?"

He nodded. "They spent several months there and had quite a vibrant ekklesia started. More and more came to hear about the Christos every week, with many believing and choosing to follow The Way. But again, the synagogue leaders didn't like it and considered it blasphemy."

"Like my dodh."

"Yes. They began plotting a way to harm Paulos, so they escaped and came to Lystra. That's when I met them." He shook his head. "The leaders followed. Again. They began to talk to the Jews in Lystra, accusing them of abandoning the only true faith, and won many of them back to their side." Timos swallowed and was silent for a long moment. "Paulos was stoned."

Jason pictured the very alive Paulos. "Stoned?"

"Yes. They dragged him outside the city walls and left him for dead," Timos said. "We gathered as many as we could who still purposed to follow Yeshua, and we prayed. We prayed for a miracle —and, amazingly, he got up and walked back into the city."

Jason raised a brow. "After being stoned?" Timos had to be exaggerating.

The grin returned to Timos's face. "After being stoned. They'd been staying with my imma and me, so we took him back there. Imma tried mightily to convince them to stay a while, and she almost prevailed. But in the end, they didn't want to endanger us any further, so they left the next day."

"And you went with them?"

"Not that time. They returned a little over a year later, and that's when I went with them. My poor imma—she didn't know whether to be thrilled I would be sharing news of The Way or sad because I was leaving her."

That story was nothing like what Yoel had told Jason. He didn't believe Yoel had intentionally lied to him. He'd only repeated what he'd been told. But it fit his purposes, and Jason knew Yoel would never accept Timos's version as the truth.

Every day, Jason came closer to believing what Paulos said was true.

His life was complicated enough already. Could he handle the changes such a decision would bring?

YOEL FORCED himself to stop pacing in the vestibule of the synagogue. Solon needed to see him as confident, righteous, bold, and not as a man drowning, grasping at any hand offered him.

Heavy footsteps echoed through the empty stone building.

"Yoel." The advocate strode toward him, hand held out.

Hidden under the sleeves of his cloak, Yoel grasped his wrists and bowed slightly. "Solon. Welcome."

The advocate pulled his hand back without a trace of insult. Did he understand Yoel's refusal as a religious command, or was he used to being disrespected?

Yoel gestured toward the courtyard. "Shall we? My wife has a stack of hot bread waiting for us."

Solon rubbed his hands together. "Excellent. I love fresh bread. The hotter the better."

Yoel ignored the stares as he led the Greek across the courtyard to his home. Young children gawked openly while women and older girls threw glances their way from under lowered lashes, and men looked past them.

The aroma of baking bread reached them before Yoel and Solon entered the dining area. The elders clustered on the other side of the table, as if the solid wood would protect them from whatever unrighteousness followed Solon like an ominous cloud.

Yoel cleared his throat. "Micah, elders, I'd like to introduce Solon to you. He is the agaraios I told you about."

Solon bowed.

Micah stepped forward, unabashedly eyeing the Greek, drumming the fingertips of one hand against the other. Finally, he turned his gaze to Yoel. "You think he can help us?"

"He knows the Roman laws. We do not."

Micah thought a moment and nodded. "That much is true."

As the silence threatened to smother them, Leah breezed into the room, a platter overflowing with bread in one hand and a pitcher in the other, as if she'd been waiting for a cue.

Thank Adonai for such a wise woman.

She set the bread on the table, filled each cup with juice, then silently left.

Yoel gestured to Micah. "Please, sit."

Micah took a position on the center couch along with Lior.

"Solon?" Yoel reclined on the couch nearest him and gestured for Solon to join him. Two more elders took the remaining couch as Leah entered again.

The Greek lowered his ample body and reached for a round of bread. He ripped off a large bite with his teeth, chewed it roughly, and swallowed. "Excellent! Well done, woman."

Leah smiled as she set down a platter of roasted fish and root vegetables.

Micah glared at Solon as he rose. "Let us give thanks to Adonai."

The others folded their hands and waited for Micah to lead them.

"Blessed are You, Lord our God, King of the universe, who brings forth bread from the earth." Micah sat and reached for some, placing it on the small plate set before him. "Now, So—I'm sorry, what was your name again?" He tapped his temple with two fingers. "The mind, it grows weak as we age, no?"

Yoel gritted his teeth. Nothing could be further from the truth when it came to Micah.

Solon only laughed. "Solon, if you please."

"Yes, Solon. What is it you think you can do for us?"

Solon wiped his hands on the cloth before him. "You know, I'm certain that your religion, unlike others, is protected by the emperor."

"As it should be."

He fixed his eyes on Micah, making no move to put another morsel in his mouth. Perhaps he was as good as people claimed.

"We pose no threat to the empire," Lior added. "We bring only good. We work hard, pay taxes, and we are model citizens."

"Which is why this Paulos is such a threat." Micah tapped a finger on the table. "He must be stopped before he ruins the reputation of all of us. But he's a citizen. What can be done?"

"Ah ha! But this, which may appear his greatest protection, is also his greatest weakness." Solon grinned as if he had a delicious secret.

"How so?" Yoel asked.

"Citizens are expected to protect the empire. To follow the rules, to worship the emperor as god, and above all, to not proclaim another." He placed a bite of fish on his tongue.

"But I understand you can barely imprison a citizen, let alone execute him," Lior said.

Solon choked on his food. "Execute him? Who said anything about his being executed?"

"No one." Micah glared at his son. "We just want him stopped."

Solon wiped his face. "Your son is right. Citizens can't be imprisoned until found guilty. What we need is for him to be *banished*."

"You can do that?" Yoel asked.

"Most magistrates don't want to deal with prosecuting a citizen. They'd rather send him down the road. Let the next city deal with him. And for most citizens, banishment is truly a fate worse than death. Maybe not so much for your man, though. He seems to travel a lot." Solon cackled. "And we can easily see why, no?" His shoulder shook as his laugh turned into a wheeze.

"What do you suggest we do?" asked Micah.

"We show proof that he has been proclaiming another god, another king."

"I doubt any of his new followers would admit to such a thing," Yoel said. "They're all enthralled with him."

"Will our word be enough?" Lior said.

"You leave that to me." Solon took another large piece of fish. "I have plenty of people who will say whatever you want them to."

"You would ask them to lie? On our behalf?" asked Micah.

Solon sighed. "Do you want to win or not?"

"Yes, but ... lying?" Micah winced.

"Did he say these things or not?"

"Of course," said Yoel.

"Then what does it matter if my people heard him directly or heard it from you—if it is the truth?"

Micah pondered the question for a long moment. "It *is* the truth. Do what you must."

The fish in Yoel's stomach soured.

He glanced up as Leah entered with a bowl of fresh fruit. He tried to catch her eyes, but she either did not see or refused to look at him.

As she left the dining area, the weight that had settled on Yoel's shoulders two days ago pressed heavier.

25

He says, "Be still, and know that I am God;
  I will be exalted among the nations,
  I will be exalted in the earth."

— PSALM 46.10

JASON OPENED THE DOOR.

Ari pushed by him as soon as there was enough room.

It was unlike Ari to be even slightly rude. Jason followed him to the peristyle. "What's wrong?"

Ari paced. "I just came from the council house."

"I didn't realize you had a meeting this morning."

"It wasn't a meeting. He called me to his home."

"Secundus?"

Ari nodded.

That couldn't be good. "Why?" Jason sat across from him.

"Two things. First, he's getting a lot of pressure from the Jewish community."

"About what?"

"What else? Paulos."

Jason threw his arms in the air. "They already kicked him out of the synagogue. What more do they want?"

"They want him gone."

Jason frowned. "Gone?"

"Out of Thessalonike altogether."

"Seriously?" Yoel had apparently obtained the support he needed from the council. Or at least Secundus.

Ari nodded. "The leaders don't like it that he's still preaching forgiveness for Greeks. Not to mention that a number of Greeks have left the synagogue—and have taken their offerings with them. They believe Paulos has, in effect, stolen those offerings from them."

"But that's not true! He spends every day working. He won't even take food from me. He's paying for his food and shelter."

"He is?"

"Yes." He pounded a fist into his other palm. "For reasons like this. He doesn't want people saying he's taken advantage of anyone."

"Well, that money is still not going to the synagogue, so I don't know that that will calm them much."

"I don't suppose you have any influence with Secundus."

Ari blew out a long breath. "That's the other thing."

"What is?"

"He wants me to marry his daughter."

Jason struggled to take in air, as if his chest was being squeezed in a vise. "Kassandra?" Unless Kassi had a sister he didn't know about. The blood drained from his face, leaving him cold. "I'll ... I'll get some wine." He stepped into the culina, more to compose himself than get the drink.

It was customary for fathers to find husbands for their daughters. Ari was successful and respected. He had status. He was handsome, intelligent, and wealthy. Why should it surprise Jason that someone wanted him for their daughter? The surprise was that it hadn't happened before. Jason forced himself to ignore his own feelings. If marrying Ari could reconcile Kassi to her father, then no matter how much it hurt, he wanted that for her.

He grabbed an amphora and two cups, then returned to the peristyle. "It sounds like you should take it as a compliment. He sees you as a good husband for her."

Ari groaned. "I don't want to."

Jason offered Ari a glass. How could he not want to? Kassandra was everything any man could desire in a wife. Was it her independent personality? Her habit of blurting out whatever she thought? Jason found it endearing, but most men would resent it. "Do you have a choice?"

Ari released a deep sigh. "It doesn't look like it. He made it very clear, without ever saying it, that his support depends on my marrying her."

"And without that support, what happens?"

"He'll criticize every suggestion I make. That's if he ever lets me speak at all. Whatever happens, I can be sure this will be the only year I will serve as politarch. And I think he'll banish Paulos, no matter what I say."

"Do you think it'll be that bad?"

Ari blew out a sharp breath. "I do."

"Then why not marry her? I wouldn't mind being married. Someone to come home to every night? Someone to care about? To care about you?" He drained the last of his wine and reached for the amphora to refill his cup. "Is there someone else you would rather marry?"

"No." Ari huffed. "That's just it. I don't want to marry *anyone*. And I especially don't want to marry someone my best friend is in love with."

Jason nearly spat out his wine. "I am not in love with her."

A fleeting grin crossed Ari's face. "I'm not going to discuss that with you right now." He rose and paced. "You forget I have six siblings. My grandparents live with us. A couple of daughters-in-law. Five children. I love them all, but the house is always brimming with people, and that doesn't count the slaves. It's crowded, noisy..."

He halted and faced Jason. "Why do you think I spend so much time here? It's not only for your brilliant conversation and honeyed wine."

Jason took another drink. "What are you going to do?"

"I don't know." He raised his cup. "Maybe you should marry her."

"Why would she want me? Compared to you?" Not to mention he hadn't seen her since that night, and he had no idea what she thought about it.

"You sell yourself short, my friend. You're not as handsome as I am, of course, but you're kind, generous, and successful. I know many young women who would marry you tomorrow." He grinned.

"*Jewish* women?"

"If you make that a requirement, you reduce your chances drastically."

"I don't make it a requirement, but my uncle would."

Ari shook his head. "You have no right to tell me to defy Secundus when you won't tell your uncle you can make your own choices."

"That's different."

"How? Your uncle has no more hold over you than Secundus has over me. Yet we both feel constrained to obey."

"So, what do we do now?"

"The only thing we can do. Pray."

KASSI KNOCKED on the door of what used to be her own home. It felt strange, and she missed Pappa and Lida, but she hadn't the slightest desire to live there again.

Lida opened the door.

An overwhelming urge to hug her enveloped Kassi. But she was merely a guest now, not family, so she folded her hands at her waist. Her eyes misted and her throat burned. "I've missed you so."

Her face softened. "I've missed you too, kyria." Lida looked over her shoulder. Servants rushed about, completing their many tasks. She cleared her throat and stood straighter.

"I received a message my pater wants to see me."

"Please, follow me." Lida stepped aside to allow Kassi to pass, then moved to walk before her.

"Do you know what it's about?"

The slave shook her head. "I couldn't say, kyria."

Couldn't or wouldn't?

They quickly reached the tablinum. "Your guest has arrived, kyrie."

Your guest?

He gestured to a couch. "Come in."

Kassi took a seat, and he sat on a couch facing her.

"I invited you here because I want to offer you a compromise."

Compromise? Pappa never compromised. A glimmer of hope sparked in her chest. "And what would that be?"

"If you have such a problem with Damianos, I offer you another option. Aristarchos."

All the air left her lungs. "Ari?" When did that happen?

"Yes. You've known him since you were children."

"That's true, but..." She shook her head.

"Do you have a problem with him as well?"

"Of course not. It's not him that is the issue, it—"

"Good then. I've already spoken to him."

"And he agreed?" That didn't sound like him.

"He will."

Which meant he hadn't yet actually agreed. And possibly that Pappa was manipulating or threatening him as well.

He stood and paced before her, head high, as if he were addressing a crowd. "If you agree to marry one or the other before spring, you may return home. You will have all the same privileges you had before and will continue to enjoy once you marry."

Only the timing had changed. She should have known the "compromise" offered her nothing. "Pappa, nothing has changed."

"Meaning?"

"I don't want that kind of life. Those privileges mean nothing to me now. I have no desire to be wealthy but miserable."

He halted an arm's length away. "Why would you be miserable? You would lack for nothing. Indeed, you lacked nothing when you lived here, but you threw it away. And for what?"

"For the bakery. I employ women in need of help, women who have no other recourse."

"Those people are not your responsibility!"

She rose to face him. "You taught me that those who are successful are obligated to reach out to those who need help, that we must view our wealth as a trust for the benefit of the community. You yourself have given vast amounts to renovate the baths."

"Yes, to benefit the *community*. Not vagrants who wander our streets."

"They are not vagrants." She took a breath to calm herself. "Who was it who said, 'It is indeed worthy of great praise, when man treats man with kindness'?"

He waved a hand in dismissal. "Yes, yes, the honorable Seneca."

"And he said to show *man* kindness, not the community." She huffed, her heart pounding.

"That is enough." He moved to his desk and sat.

"Where are you living?" His voice was a bit softer. "How are you surviving?"

"I'm staying with Julia, meter of Aristarchos."

His mouth fell. "Julia? Why would she allow you to do that?"

"She didn't *allow* me. She invited me. She's a caring and thoughtful woman."

"Then if you are already living with him, in his house, you should have no problem marrying Aristarchos."

"I'm living with her, not Ari. And it's her house, not his."

"My decision has been made. People are beginning to think I cannot control my own family." He shook his head. "I'm sorry, but I can't allow this foolishness to continue. For the first time in over ten years, I did not earn the most votes in the last election."

She blew out a harsh breath. "Because you are no longer the most popular man in Thessalonike, I must marry—"

"My daughter," he half-raised his hands and let them drop, "why are you doing this to me?"

"To *you*? What am I doing to you?"

"Embarrassing me. And your brothers." He shook a finger at her. "All of ano poli is talking about you."

"I'm sure that's an exaggeration."

"Perhaps. A bit."

She stood. "I'll tell you what I told Damianos when he came to see me, and what I told Zelia. I have a new life now. And I may never marry or live in a luxurious villa. I may never be admired by the city's elite, but my heart will be filled with joy and purpose. I would love to be known as your beloved daughter, but if I have to choose that or everything else, the choice is easy." She neared him and placed a kiss on his cheek. "Goodbye, Pappa."

How late was it? In the dark culina, Jason poured a goblet of wine and ripped off a piece of that morning's bread.

The codex Timos had left with him lay on the worktable. All the words of the prophets in one place. He ran his fingers over the parchments, each tiny word painstakingly copied. Small stacks of parchment carefully sewn together and then glued into a cover— the work of a skilled skenopoios.

If he believed the prophets spoke the words of Adonai, the answer had to be here. He turned to the section Paulos had shown him a few days ago.

People despised and avoided him,
a man of pains, well acquainted with illness.
Like someone from whom people turn their faces,
he was despised; we did not value him.
In fact, it was our diseases he bore,
our pains from which he suffered;
yet we regarded him as punished,
stricken and afflicted by God.
But he was wounded because of our crimes,
crushed because of our sins;
the disciplining that makes us whole fell on him,
and by his bruises we are healed.

Who else could Isaiah have referred to except this Yeshua? Despised, rejected, pierced, crushed—not words that described a champion. But words he'd heard used to describe Yeshua.

The prophet also promised the Mashiach would bring peace and healing. Since childhood, Jason had been told that peace would come when the Romans were vanquished. But what if this was different from a military peace? *More than* a political peace? What if it was a personal peace? A peace with Adonai?

"*Without the shedding of blood, there is no forgiveness of sins.*" Another precept he'd learned at Imma's side. Yeshua definitely shed blood. Could that truly bring forgiveness?

Jason thought about all the other prophecies Paulos had shown him—that He would be born of a virgin, of the house of David, die on a tree, and be buried in a rich man's grave.

That He would live again to conquer death.

Death had tried to destroy Jason's world, taking not only his parents but his identity, his purpose, and his passion. Yet Paulos talked about death as if it were as powerless as a blade of grass against an iron sword.

He flipped a few pages back to a passage he'd heard before but never thought about.

Do not fear, for I have redeemed you; I have summoned you by name;

you are Mine. When you pass through the waters, I will be with you; and when you pass through the rivers, they will not sweep over you. When you walk through the fire, you will not be burned; the flames will not set you ablaze.

You are mine.

Such incredible promises.

"I will be with you ... when you pass through the waters ... when you walk through the fires ..." Not if, but when. He would still have to face the floods and fires, but Adonai, King of the Universe, would be with him.

Was it worth it?

He chewed on stale bread and thought through it all again. All the prophesies, all the expectations of a mashiach, everything he knew about Yeshua.

In the end, it came to this—Yeshua was either a traitor to the Jews who had been rightly crucified as a blasphemer, or he was the Mashiach every Jew had been expecting since Moses led them from Egypt.

Yoel had made it clear he believed Yeshua was a criminal who could offer nothing. He hadn't freed Israel from the Romans, so he couldn't be the Mashiach. And yet Yoel was angry, afraid, and constantly worried he might lose his position.

Paulos, on the other hand, exhibited peace, joy, and delight in his Redeemer, even after all he'd endured. Such certainty, such absolute ... faith.

The choice seemed clear, but what would Jason suffer if he decided to follow The Way? What would he lose? His family? His community? His reputation? Paulos had been beaten, imprisoned, stoned, and left for dead.

A lot to endure. A lot to lose. But what would he gain?

He had to give Yeshua a chance to show Jason the truth.

He set down his bread and wine and knelt on the cold tile of Imma's culina.

"Blessed are You, Lord our God, King of the universe. I call out to you, God of my fathers, of Abraham, Isaac, and Jacob. If Yeshua ben Yosef is your Son, if He is our Redeemer, our Savior, I want to know Him. Reveal Him to me."

He waited.

And waited.

I gave my life as a ransom for many—for you. My blood was poured out for the forgiveness of your sins.

His eyes shot open. Was someone here?

Or was Yeshua speaking to him, as he'd asked?

Come taste and see that I am good.

The voice was in his heart, not in the room.

A verse Abba had taught Jason as a small boy jumped to mind. "You have made known to me the path of life; You will fill me with joy in Your presence, with eternal pleasures at Your right hand."

Yeshua had made known to him the right choice, the only path to life. The promise was equally clear—eternal life.

I accept the sacrifice You made for me. I want to follow You, follow The Way. I want to serve you, to live for you like Paulos does. Show me what to do next.

Peace like Jason had never known filled his mind, his body. The fear and guilt he had lived with for weeks evaporated like dew. The Mashiach had indeed come to earth, and he had set Jason free.

He sat on the floor, soaking in newfound joy and peace until he was overcome by exhaustion. Too tired to move, he lay on the floor in front of the fire and slept in the presence of his Redeemer.

26

THE FIRST LOAVES EMERGED FROM THE BRICK OVEN, GLOSSY SLICES OF black olive peeking out from under the crust like rocks on an unpaved road. Kassi loaded the bread onto a wide basket and carried it to the long table in the aisle. She'd set the first one down when a man in a short woolen tunic appeared in the doorway, hands clasped behind his back.

A slave? What rich woman would send her slave to purchase bread from this bakery?

"May I help you?"

"Kassandra, daughter of Secundus?"

She nodded. "Yes. I am Kassandra."

He extended one arm, a scroll in his hand.

She neared him and accepted the scroll. "What's this?"

"I only deliver, kyria." He turned and marched away.

She untied the leather thread and unrolled the parchment.

The transaction involving the building you currently occupy did not finalize due to non-payment of transfer taxes, and it has subsequently been purchased by another. If you have any evidence to the contrary, you are ordered to appear today at the office of the agoranomos at the third hour. If not, you must vacate the building by the twelfth hour of tomorrow.

Her knees buckled, and she grabbed the table to keep from collapsing.

"Kassi, what's wrong?" Isa rushed toward her and led her to a stool in an empty stall. "Your face has lost all color."

She couldn't let Isa know they might lose the building—and along with it, the only means of support for these vulnerable women.

"I haven't eaten yet. I'll be fine."

"I'll get you some bread." Isa turned to go.

"No, I'll go to the popina and get an obeliskos. Maybe some wine. Don't worry." She hurried out the door, the scroll clutched to her chest.

She had paid the tax, that she knew for certain. But the proof was in her chamber in the ano poli.

Who could have done this to her?

Pappa? Surely not. He would be much more direct.

Damianos?

Perhaps. Maybe Pappa knew something about this. She had to retrieve the receipt of the taxes from his villa, so she could ask him then.

If he would talk to her.

But she had every bit as much right to go to the politarch with a problem as any other citizen of Thessalonike.

Didn't she?

JASON STIRRED as sunlight pouring through the window kissed his face. He hadn't slept so soundly since ... since that awful day when he'd been told...

How late had he slept? Memories of last night came into focus, and joy awakened his soul.

He recited the prayer he'd said every morning since he could talk.

I give thanks before You, King living and eternal, for You have returned within me my soul with compassion; abundant is Your faithfulness!

This time, the thanks flowed from not just his mouth or his head, but from deep within his heart. Abundant couldn't begin to describe Adonai's faithfulness. It was overwhelming, like a river bursting from its banks.

His heart was light, but his body wasn't. The tile floor had not been kind to him, and his right shoulder now screamed in unrelenting pain. He rolled to his hands and knees, then managed to stand on stiff and aching legs. He glanced at the empty table. He'd eaten the only loaf of bread last night and now there was nothing left.

The pistrinum. Thoughts of Kassi's beautiful face prompted a smile.

He hobbled through the empty house and stepped outside.

Columns cast shadows across the Via Regia. Cats wandered in and around the small shops of the artisans. The youngest children squealed and chased each other while their older siblings worked alongside their parents.

Everything seemed the same, and yet nothing was the same.

His joints loosened as he walked, and the painted yellow walls of the bakery soon came into view. Before he reached them, however, Timos sauntered out, alone, a large bag of fresh bread in hand.

"Jason, shalom." He walked to meet him. "You were deep in sleep, so we decided to buy some food."

"Thank you. I'm starving." Jason turned and headed back to the house with Timos. "So you saw me?" What must they think of him?

"I did. Paulos and Silas did not come in the culina." Timos pulled a loaf from the bag, ripped it in two, and handed Jason half.

They quickly reached the house. Paulos and Silas sat with Gaius in the peristyle. He must have missed them on his way out.

"Look who I found wandering around the agora." Paulos laid a hand on Gaius's shoulder.

Jason caught the boy's eye. "Why were you at the market?"

Gaius shrugged. "The shop's closed, and the bakery is boring."

He chuckled. "Don't let Kassi hear you say that. Does your imma know where you are?"

"Timos told her," Silas said.

"And I bought bread." He grinned at Gaius, holding up the bag. "And pastelli."

"Help with the food and you can have *one*." Jason nudged him to follow Timos and Silas into the culina.

Gaius returned with a honey sesame bar in one hand and a large platter of still-warm bread in the other. He placed it on a low table and sat next to Jason.

Jason picked at the crust of his half. Had his decision last night opened him to the same kind of life as Paulos? "Do you ever wish your life was different than it is now?"

"Do I wish I never was beaten, hungry, cold, threatened? Of course. Any reasonable man would. But would I give up Yeshua for that? Never. Everything else I consider no more than dung next to the incomparable worth of knowing Yeshua the Mashaich."

Jason continued to study the bread in his hand. "You don't have any concerns about continuing to preach this message? What if one of these times you really die?"

"There's a good chance I will."

He jerked his gaze to Paulos. How could he be so calm? "And

you don't worry about this, every day, every time you open your mouth?"

"If I let worry steal my time, my strength, and my joy, what good will I be? Besides, man can do nothing to me unless Adonai allows it. If I live, I live *for* Him. And if I die, I go to live *with* Him. How can I lose? Yeshua has already won any battle I must fight." There was not a trace of fear on his face or in his voice.

Timos appeared with a pitcher of wine and cups, followed by Silas holding sliced apples. They took their places on an empty couch and allowed Jason to contemplate Paulos's words. "Is that true for everyone who decides to follow Him?"

Paulos fixed his deep brown eyes on Jason. "Is that what you decided last night?"

The same smile Jason had when he'd awakened covered his face once more. "It is."

"Following The Way may not be easy, but you will not be alone. He will always be beside you, fighting for you. You will never be truly defeated."

From most people, the words would ring hollow. But from one who had repeatedly laid down his life for his Redeemer, they were full of promise, hope, and strength.

Jason wouldn't likely face the trials Paulos had endured, but facing Yoel with the news would be almost as hard as facing a whip.

Adonai, help me. Not for my sake, but for Isa, Thalia, Maera, and all the other women.

Kassi tucked the scroll in her sash as she hurried down the cardo toward Pappa's house. The life she'd enjoyed while she lived there was no longer hers and never would be again, but in losing it, she'd gained so much more.

But to keep it, she needed to find that piece of parchment.

She also wanted to see if Lida would join her—as a free woman —once she had a permanent place to live.

She knocked on the door.

Lida grasped Kassi by the arm the moment she opened the door. She pulled her inside, then dragged into Kassi's chamber and shut the door.

This was completely unlike her. "Lida, what's wrong?"

"Your pater has another visitor."

"Who? Who's here?" asked Kassi.

Lida shushed her with a finger over her lips. "The archisynagogos."

Jason's uncle? "Why would he be here?" she whispered.

"It has something to do with the visitors that are causing so much trouble."

They're not the ones causing trouble. "Where are they?"

She gestured down the hall. "The tablinum."

"All right. Thank you." Kassi moved, but Lida grabbed her hand.

"Are you sure you wish to approach him now?"

"I won't let him see me."

"Then best to remove your sandals." Lida bent to retrieve the sandals and straightened, handing them to her kyria. "And Kassi?"

"Yes?" She accepted the shoes.

Lida's dark eyes begged for understanding. "Please do not betray me."

"I would never do that." With her free hand, Kassi patted the wrinkled hand grasping hers. "Don't worry. He won't know you even saw me." She kissed the old woman's cheek and crept across the atrium. With sandals dangling from one finger, she neared the door of the office and paused. She tipped her head, straining to hear through the closed door.

"You're sure you can banish them?" *Yoel's voice.* "They'll be gone for good?"

"Just get them to the council house. I'll take care of it."

"You'll be hearing cases today?"

"Yes."

"For how long?"

"It depends on how many there are. We start at the third hour, and we should be there until late afternoon."

Yoel shook his head. "It must be concluded today. Shabbat begins at—"

"If you don't make it today, we'll hear cases again next week."

"I am not waiting that long."

Secundus paused for a long moment. "Get him there before the sixth hour and I'll make sure your case is concluded in time."

Yoel rose and bowed his head. "Thank you, Secundus. We appreciate this more than I can say."

Pappa's heavy curule chair scraped along tile. Footsteps moved toward the door. "I'm happy to help however I can. I'm sorry I cannot do more. You know the politarchs value your community."

The door opened a fraction.

Kassi's heart raced. If she were seen ... the results were too horrible to think about. Chest heaving, she pulled up her chiton and flew down the hall, then pressed herself as flat against the peristyle wall as possible.

"As we value your leadership. I'll see you soon."

"We'll be waiting."

The pair reached the front door.

After Pappa sent him off, would he return to his tablinum or head for the garden—directly toward her?

Beyond the peristyle lay the passageway that led to the servants' rooms. Kassi raced across the garden and down the narrow way. One door stood open, and she ducked inside, stopping short of slamming the door closed. She placed her ear against the wood, listening for any sound that told her Pappa might have seen and followed her.

Now what? How would she know when it was safe to leave?

She willed her heartbeat to slow. A sigh of relief, louder than she'd intended, escaped her lips, and she froze. Had anyone heard?

How long should she wait before bolting for the front door?

She counted to one hundred, then reached for the handle.

It moved.

Kassi's heart stopped. Her lungs refused to take in air. Was it Pappa? No, he would never enter a slave's chamber.

But what if he'd seen her slip inside? What would he do if he found her here?

He didn't necessarily know she'd heard anything. She could be here looking for something to take with her. He'd said she could take whatever was hers.

Would he believe that?

As much as she hated to admit it, he would. She was a mere woman, after all. Head not suited for business, let alone intrigue.

The handle moved again, and the door opened.

She held her breath.

"Kyria?" A harsh whisper sounded on the other side.

Lida!

Kassi jerked the door opened to find the old woman waiting. "Oh, Lida. I'm so glad it's you." She threw her arms around the old woman's neck. "I was so afraid ..." Her throat burned.

Lida patted her back. "I was watching. I would never have let him find you. I would have dropped something or ... he wouldn't have found you."

"I'm sorry I came back here. I don't know whose chamber I entered."

"Mine." Lida smiled for only a moment. "But now you must go. You must warn Paulos."

"I know." She tossed her sandals to the floor and slid in one foot. "Wait ... what did you say? Why do *you* want me to warn him?"

"The new servant? He came from Antioch. He learned from Paulos himself. He told us about the Christos who has come to save the whole world."

Joy poured over her like sweet oil after a bath. "He did?"

"Every week we gather to learn from him. Even Mannus has joined us lately."

Overwhelming delight consumed her fear. Lida and Mannus following The Way? She could never have even hoped for such a gift.

"But go now." Lida pulled Kassi toward the garden and then the atrium. "Just make sure they leave."

Kassi turned. "Pappa will banish him anyway. Why not wait? He can spend a few more days with us before he has to go—and you all could come. Maybe Pappa—"

"Kassi."

Lida's sharp voice interrupted her imagining.

"That man, the Jewish leader, was here a few days ago, and your pater sent him to one of the agoraioi."

Kassi nodded. "They're just bad lawyers, right? That might even be a good thing."

Lida shook her head. "I heard them talking about treason. Do you know what the punishment for that is? You need to get Paulos out of Thessalonike. *Now.*"

The delight of just a moment earlier faded.

What now? She needed to know what Yoel and the lawyer had planned. They had to be stopped. At the very least, Paulos and his friends needed to be taken somewhere Yoel could never find them.

Their lives depended on it.

"Go out the back entrance." Lida led her to the door used by the slaves.

She bolted from Pappa's house down an alley that led to the cardo just in time to see the Jewish leader heading toward her. She slowed and sneaked down the wide, pillared street, trying to keep up with Yoel while at the same time remaining unseen. It was unlikely he'd recognize her as anyone other than one of the Greek worshippers, but she couldn't take any chances.

She followed him, ducking behind columns when necessary, avoiding his gaze. Disapproving stares were aimed her way, but she had little reputation left in the upper city, and Paulos was in serious danger. She would happily sacrifice what little good standing she had left to protect him.

YOEL STROLLED ALONG THE CARDO, feeling more hope than he had in weeks.

He fixed his eyes on the southern gate, ignoring shop owners and customers on either side. Nothing must distract him from his purpose. He'd promised Solon he would meet him in the lower agora to give him a final answer before midmorning, and the sun was climbing. Finishing before sunset was imperative.

As he crossed the Via Regia, he wrapped his hand around the back of his neck, trying to rub away the tingling that persisted there. He rolled his shoulders, but his discomfort only increased.

Could someone be following him? He paused and turned around, scanning the wide street. A young woman, maybe a girl, slipped behind a pillar. She dressed like a resident of the upper city, but she wasn't acting like one. Running and hiding like a child, hair mussed and falling in her face, her cloak sliding from her shoulders. A Jewish girl would never behave in such an embarrassing manner, out on the streets alone.

He waited, but when she didn't reappear, he resumed his journey, trying to appear as unconcerned as possible, then spun back again.

No one was there.

Must have been his imagination, fueled by nerves ... or fear.

When he reached the agora, he hovered at the market's entrance a moment. The scent of roasting meat at the popina made his mouth water. Too bad he would never eat meat prepared by Greeks. He aimed for the food and spice vendors on the far side.

At the edge of a group of men, Solon caught his eye. He marched toward Yoel. "What did your elders decide?"

"They've approved of your plan. And the politarchs will be expecting you within the hour."

"And the payment?" He held out a hand. "I believe we agreed on one hundred denarii."

Had the man forgotten their conversation of two days ago? Or was he just trying to get whatever he could? "The agreement was for twenty-five denarii, and only if you are successful."

Solon grinned. "Very well. And where do you think this man is?"

"He's usually at the warehouse on the harbor, but if he's not there, he's probably at ... at the house of his host." No need to let Solon know Jason was his ben ach. Yoel gave him directions to Jason's house.

"I have men waiting for my instructions. We shall leave immediately." He glanced over his shoulder as he strode away. "I'll see you there."

Yoel watched Solon as he gathered a crowd of ragged men Yoel wouldn't speak to on the street. Had he done the right thing? The elders assured him it was necessary. Secundus assured him it was legal.

But Yoel wasn't so sure.

The last thing he wanted was to bring undue scrutiny to the community. As it was, the Jews enjoyed a singular privilege—as long as they didn't proselytize, they were allowed to worship as they saw fit. They were exempt from required military service, from making the expected sacrifices, and from attending the feasts. A public trial would remind everyone how much freedom they had to worship as Adonai required.

Freedom no one else had.

And yet, if Paulos wasn't stopped, the empire might see his speech as trying to bring Greeks and Romans to Judaism, and then they could lose it all.

If it were only a matter of balancing risks and rewards, the elders would be right. But was that all there was to it? Was it necessary to destroy a man's reputation in the process?

Yoel sighed. No matter how distasteful this was, he could see no other option. Because the bottom line was not what the politarchs or Caesar had to say, or even what the people thought. The only thing that mattered was what Adonai said. And He'd made it clear that the Jews were His chosen people, that salvation belonged to the Jews, and that He'd entrusted the blessings of David to Israel.

Not to the Greeks.

Not to the Romans.

To Israel alone.

27

But other Jews were jealous; so they rounded up some bad characters from the marketplace...

— ACTS 17.5

KASSI HOVERED AT THE MARKET'S ENTRANCE. THE FRESH SEA AIR AND the scents of cinnamon and cardamon competed with the odor of fish, not always successfully.

Yoel had approached a group of men who gathered at a corner. She'd been taught since she was in her mamma's arms to avoid such men—men who had no real job, no money, no purpose in life. Men who showed up at sunrise hoping for a job that would last a day or two, waiting for the end of the day when they could buy leftover food for a copper coin, and usually causing—or at least enjoying—trouble in between.

She heard her name and spied Publius waving her over. She hurried to his stall.

"Publius, can you tell me which are the agoraioi over there?" She gestured to the group.

He nodded. "The ones dressed much more nicely than the others. They hang out here and will argue any case, as long as you pay them."

"If they require payment, why go to them instead of the forum lawyers?"

"If the approved advocates don't think they can win, or if a matter is too small for them, they won't take a case. Or if they decide there is no case to begin with."

"Like a case of a teacher who said what some didn't want to be heard?"

"As I said, these are men who will argue anything. They're often very good, sometimes better than the forum advocates. They can bend and twist the law like a rope."

Kassi groaned as everything she'd heard at the house made sense.

She desperately needed to hear what Yoel was planning, but she wouldn't be welcome anywhere near them. If she dared to get close enough to hear, she might be assumed to be a prostitute. Yoel had said "today." But when? How much time did she have?

"Publius, I need a huge favor."

He smiled wide, placing his hand over his heart. "For you, Kassi, anything. I owe you my life. And Maera's."

She positioned herself between the vendor and Yoel. "Do you see that man over there, behind me? The Jewish leader?"

Publius squinted, searching the crowds over her shoulder, then nodded. "Sure. Why?"

"That is Yoel, the archisynagogos. He means to take Paulos to the politarchs. None of the forum lawyers will help him, so he came to the agoraioi." She swallowed.

Publius frowned. "I see one man there I've hired a time or two before. He's not like the others. He's a decent man who needs work.

I'll find out everything I can." He shoved an obeliskos at her. "Sit and eat this. You'll look less suspicious."

He ambled toward Yoel, greeting various vendors as he passed them until he drew near Yoel—not too close, then fished a coin from his belt while he beckoned to a man who stood alone. They spoke a few moments, then Publius hurried back, his face clouded.

"It's bad, Kassi."

She rose to meet him. "What?"

"That advocate, Solon? He's the worst of all of them. As soon as the Jewish leader leaves, he plans to gather a group of men, march them to the warehouse, and take Paulos and his friends to the politarchs." He shook his head. "And if they're not here, Yoel told them to go to Jason's house."

Her blood ran cold. "I have to warn them." She shoved the uneaten food at his chest and raced from the agora.

"Wait! I'll come with you!"

She dared not stop. If she had any chance of saving Paulos, Publius would have to catch up.

Jason jumped up as the front door burst open, and Kassi flew through it.

"Kassi? What are you doing here?" He tossed his bread on the table and raced to her. "What's wrong? What happened?"

"Pappa…" She panted, bending over to catch her breath. "He, he…"

Paulos approached and laid a gentle hand on her shoulder. "Take a moment. Breathe slowly, deeply." He looked to Jason. "Some wine, maybe?"

"I'll get it." Timos hurried away.

"Come, sit." Jason placed a hand on her back and guided her toward the peristyle while Paulos closed the door.

Silas pulled another couch into the circle, and Kassi took a seat.

Her breath had slowed almost to normal when the door slammed open again.

Jason peered over his shoulder into the atrium. "Publius? What —?" Why was everyone rushing into his house?

The vendor rushed toward them. "She came to the agora, and when I told her what I'd found out, I had to follow to see if I can help."

"Help with *what*?" Jason spoke through clenched teeth. What could have alarmed them both so much?

Timos offered Kassi a cup of wine. "Here."

She drank most of it in one gulp.

Jason sat next to her. "Now what are you two talking about?"

Publius sat across from Kassi. "You start."

"I went to Pappa's house to find a document. When I arrived, your uncle was there."

As Kassi related what she'd overheard and what Publius told her, an invisible hand squeezed Jason's chest. He poured himself a glass of wine and drained it. How could his dodh do such a thing? He'd been upset at what Paulos preached but this ... this was unbelievable.

"I don't understand." He looked to Paulos. "Why? Is he afraid he'll lose his synagogue to you? Or his people?"

Paulos shook his head. "My experience is that usually, these men are not bad or even overly ambitious. They believe they are being zealous for Adonai. They think I am blaspheming, claiming a man to be a god. They expect a militant Mashiach, someone who will ride from heaven with a great army, swords flashing, to save us from the Romans. They're not looking for a silent lamb to be slaughtered to save us from our sin." He smiled. "Your uncle is not a bad man. I lived with him for almost three weeks. He's doing what he truly believes will be best for his people."

"We have to get you safe." Kassi jumped up. "You need to hide from the lawyer and those ..."—she shook a finger toward the agora

—"those men. They have the authority to do whatever is necessary to get you to the politarchs."

"Then we go to the politarchs. We'll not allow any of you to put yourselves in danger," Paulos stood, his face as iron.

Jason shook his head vigorously. "No. Paulos, we need you alive and well to take your message to all the world. Isn't that what you said?"

"I'm prepared to give my own life. I am *not* prepared to sacrifice anyone else's."

"I don't see how anyone else is in danger. They're seeking only you."

"You allowed the believers in Damascus to help you escape." Silas's voice was soft.

Paulos remained silent, his thoughts battling one another. Finally, he nodded.

"But where should they go?" asked Jason. "The bakery?"

"No." Silas rose. "We've all been seen there. They'll go straight there if they don't find us here."

"Ari's house? Julia would welcome you." Kassi suggested.

"No." Paulos's eyes flashed, and his voice was harsher than Jason had ever heard. "If things get rough, we don't want her involved. We need some place they would never think of."

"You can come to my house," Publius offered.

"Your house?" asked Jason.

"Do you know how dangerous it could be if they should somehow find us there?" Paulos asked.

"Kassi hired my niece at the bakery and saved her life. I'd do anything to help her. And," he turned to Paulos, "once I heard you near the temple. I was very intrigued. What you had to say makes more sense than everything else I've been taught my whole life. I want to know more."

Paulos smiled. "I'd be happy to tell you more any time."

"Let's get you safe first," Publius said.

Jason shrugged. "All right. If you're sure. I can think of nothing better."

Publius jerked his head toward the door. "Follow me."

"No," Kassi said. "I'll take them. No need to give anyone who may be watching a hint of where we're going. You stay here with Jason and Gaius." She beckoned to the three. "Better get your things. You may not be coming back here."

They disappeared and returned almost immediately.

"We don't carry a lot." Silas chuckled.

"You've done this before?" Publius asked.

Timos flashed a sad smile. "You have no idea."

Kassi led Silas and Timos out the door.

Paulos stopped as he passed Jason. "Todah rabah for all you've done for us. I rejoice more than you can know that you've decided to follow The Way." His eyes moistened. "My heart aches unceasingly for my kinsmen. It's good to know my visit here has borne fruit among my people."

"Your visit isn't over."

"Perhaps not. But remember what I said. I have no idea when these words of Isaiah may be needed, but I feel Adonai would have me share them with you again. Never forget—*You are His.* When you pass through the waters, He will be with you. And when you walk through the fire, you will not be burned."

"I'll remember." Jason steered them toward the door. Paulos had given him good words to tuck away for the future. But for now, he wasn't the one in danger.

KASSI HURRIED, leading the men to what she fervently hoped was safety. Paulos caught up quickly.

"So how did you save his niece's life?" Timos asked.

"She was married. They lived on a farm outside the walls. One of their slaves became pregnant with her husband's child, and when she complained, he beat her." She frowned, the multi-colored bruises on Maera's body coming to memory. "Quite badly. Then he sent her away. She came to Publius for help."

"Such behavior is abhorrent," growled Silas. "A man who has been blessed with a wife should treasure her."

"We should all treasure each other. We are Yahweh's beloved, His most precious creations. He is willing to die for us, and yet we so often treat each other like we are worth less than the ground we walk on," said Paulos.

The group walked in silence for a moment, but Kassi felt compelled to fill the air with words. Any words. "Publius has taken her in like she's his own daughter. I don't know wha—"

Paulos took her hand and squeezed it. "It's going to be all right, Kassandra."

"What-what do you mean?" Surely, he couldn't know the turmoil she was in.

"Silence is all right." Paulos grinned. "And you don't have to worry about us."

"This isn't the first time this has happened," Timos added.

"You mentioned that. How do you deal with it if it keeps happening?"

"We know Adonai is in control of our lives, not the politarchs or the archisynagogos or agoraioi," Paulos said. "We aren't in a battle against mere men, but against spiritual forces of evil. The battle is not here on earth but takes place in the heavenly realms. Adonai is our champion. He fights for us. And He never loses."

"So, if He is fighting, what do we do? Just accept whatever comes?"

"Moses once told the Israelites, 'Adonai will fight for you; you need only to be still.' We do what we can, and then we stand firm in faith. Rest in the knowledge that Yahweh holds our lives in the palms of His hands, and nothing is allowed to touch us unless it is first filtered through His fingers."

She halted as fear tightened its cold grip around her neck. "You mean he might let you die?"

Paulos slipped an arm through hers and nudged her forward. "For me, life is nothing unless it is for the Christos. And death is not a loss but a gain. For it is only in death we receive the eternal life bought for us by the blood of Yeshua."

It made so much sense, yet it seemed an impossible task.

They'd just reached the popina when their attention was drawn to a mob of unruly men marching toward them from the city gate—led by the agoraios Kassi had seen with Yoel.

Kassi grabbed Paulos by the wrist. "Follow me. Hurry!" She raced down the alley and turned left at the end. The others caught up, running at her side. The speed at which the old men moved astonished her. "This is it." She opened a door and ducked inside. "Come in."

They tumbled inside, and she slammed the door shut. She stood with her palms on the door, eyes closed, catching her breath.

The men had apparently not found Paulos at the warehouse by the sea. That meant they were headed to Jason's.

She opened her eyes to see Paulos standing beside her. Silas and Timos were in the atrium, faces and hands raised to heaven, lips moving in silent prayer.

Paulos gestured toward the street. "Go now. Go to Jason, and make sure he is safe."

"But—"

"We'll be fine. You fight here on earth, and we'll fight in the heavenly realms." He joined the other two, hands lifted. "Abba, Father, we pray that these, Your children, may be delivered from wicked and evil men. For You, Adonai, are faithful and will strengthen and protect them from the evil one. Your Word promises that whoever dwells in the shelter of the Most High will rest in Your shadow. We say with the psalmist, 'You are my refuge and my fortress.'"

As the prayers of the men continued, Kassi slipped out and rushed to Jason's.

God, protect me, for I am Yours.

THE FRONT DOOR slammed open a third time. Before Jason could cross the peristyle, a heavyset man in a bleached chiton and deep blue cloak marched in as if the house were his. He stood feet apart, hands on hips. "I am Solon. I seek the owner of this house."

Gai froze. Jason touched his shoulder as he stood. "I'm Jason. This is my house." He glared at the man. "Why are you in it?"

"I am here to take Paulos of Tarsus to stand before the politarchs."

"He's not here."

"Where is he?" the man barked.

"I don't know." That wasn't a complete lie, yet it wasn't the truth either. But the looks on the faces of the angry men crowding his doorway, aching to burst into his home like hungry wolves, told Jason he couldn't take the chance of sending them anywhere near his friends.

And Kassi.

"You won't mind then, if we check to see if you're telling the truth." Solon crooked a finger at the crowd behind him. "Search every room in this house. Any place big enough to hide a man." He neared the group and helped himself to a loaf of bread.

Before Jason could object, men poured into the atrium. They spread out to every area—bed chambers, the toilet, everywhere. From the culina came the sounds of pots and jars falling, crashing to the floor. Anger mixed with grief as glassware made by Abba shattered.

Jason ran to the tablinum where a man jerked tablets and codices from the shelves and tossed them over his shoulder. Who did he expect to find hiding on a shelf? In his chamber, someone was pulling clothes from the chest at the foot of his bed and tossing them across the room. The chest was nowhere big enough to hold a man.

There was nothing Jason could do to stop what was happening, so he returned to the peristyle. Publius sat with his arm around Gai's shoulder, who hunched on a bench as if he could make himself invisible.

Jason sat on Gai's other side. "As soon as they realize Paulos isn't here, they'll leave. We'll be all right, yes?"

Gaius nodded weakly.

Within moments, the men regrouped. "Nothing, kyrie," they reported one by one.

Heavy footfalls echoed as Solon stomped toward Jason, mouth full. "Where did you take him?"

"I took him nowhere." This time he told the truth.

"That's true. I've been here with him," Gaius added.

Solon smirked as he tossed the bread on the floor. "Then I guess you'll have to do." He stepped back and looked to his men, then gestured to Jason. "Take him."

Take him? Jason's heart pounded.

Men rushed him. Two grabbed his arms, and he jerked from side to side to shake them off, sending searing pain down his arm with every movement. It didn't work. "I've done nothing wrong. What do you want with me?"

"You housed him."

Jason clenched his fists. "I offered hospitality, as is the ancient custom of Greeks, Romans, and Jews." He struggled again, to no avail. "And my responsibility for their actions stops at my door. You know this." His protests fell on unhearing ears.

Solon brought his face close. "This is different. Your 'guest' is proclaiming a god and king other than our emperor. You *will* answer for your actions."

Men on either side of him pulled him to the door while he struggled to stay upright. Two more men fell in behind him, pushing and shoving. A hard punch landed on the side of his lower back and still more pain pounded throughout his body. He arched his back, and one of the men kicked him behind the knee. Unable to break his fall, his chest collided with the floor, his arms nearly wrenched from their sockets. He managed to keep his head from smashing into the tile as well, but a knee in his back kept him pinned.

"Stop! Let him up!" A voice rang out from the front door.

Jason twisted his head toward it.

Kassi stood with a hand over her mouth, tears streaming down her face.

How much had she seen?

Solon made a face. "Get him up. Bring the other two."

He was yanked by his arms and once again shoved toward the door. He looked back at the other two.

Poor Gaius shivered with fright, silent eyes imploring Jason to make it all stop. Publius sputtered and fumed but complied. Each was held by at least three men. One would have been able to control Gaius. Two was unnecessary, and three was just cruel.

For the boy's sake, Jason needed to stay calm. He gave in to the hold on him, all fight draining away.

"Gaius." He tried to catch Gaius's attention. "Gai!"

Gaius turned his gaze to Jason, his lip quivering, his face devoid of color.

"We'll be all right. This isn't your house, and you're not the host. They can't hold you responsible."

Of course, he'd thought they couldn't hold him accountable either, but the fingernails digging into his biceps screamed otherwise. He smiled as best he could, and his apprentice seemed to relax. A bit.

Gaius and Publius were led out first.

Kassi reached for Jason as he passed, but the men pulled him away. He looked for her through arms and bodies, but the guards jerked him, hurrying to catch up to Gaius, Publius, and Solon.

Paulos's last words to him seemed now strangely prophetic.

When you pass through the waters, He will be with you. When you walk through the fire, you will not be burned.

You are Mine.

28

So do not fear, for I am with you;
do not be dismayed, for I am your God.
I will strengthen you and help you;
I will uphold you with my righteous right hand.

— ISAIAH 41.10

KASSI COULD BARELY BREATHE AS JASON, GAIUS, AND PUBLIUS WERE dragged from the house like so many bags of grain. She hurried to keep up.

How could Pappa do this? Had he known they'd bring Jason if they couldn't find Paulos, or had the agoraios gone further than was allowed? From what she'd heard, both at her home and in Jason's atrium, there was no complaint whatsoever against Jason.

The group reached the cardo and turned toward the council house, the guards tugging the men along so forcefully they were barely able to keep up.

Jason fell again. The crack as his knees hit the stone road, along with his groan of pain, made her stomach ache. The men yanked him by his arms to his feet. He had to be in excruciating pain.

There must be something she could do.

If Pappa had helped start this, could he end it? She grabbed her chiton, pulling it up above her shins. She ran north, past the group which now was picking up onlookers like a magnet attracted iron filings.

Her lungs burning, she raced toward the forum, weaving in and out of Thessalonike's elite and ignoring their vile glares.

Pappa looked up from his conversation with the other politarchs when she burst into the building. "Kassandra!" His surprise gave way to annoyance. Standing before a knee-high riser with five curule chairs arranged in a stick-straight line, he avoided the bemused stares of his fellow rulers.

She marched down the wide center aisle, stopping an arm's length away from him.

He moved nearer. "You gave me your decision, and unless you have—"

"What did you do?" She struggled to keep her voice down. She didn't need the politarchs and all their guards and assistants watching their exchange.

He grabbed her upper arm and dragged her away from the dais. "Never speak to me in this manner again."

The other politarchs stared, and Ari herded them away. Did he know what was happening?

"I apologize, Pappa." Being disrespectful wasn't going to get her any answers. "But I came by this morning, and I heard you and the archisynagogos. I know you conspired with him to bring Paulos in 'by any means necessary.'"

He stuck his chin out as he crossed his arms. "I did no such thing. I knew Yoel planned to bring in this man, but I didn't know any specifics."

"Really?" *Remain calm, Kassi.* "You knew the forum lawyers wouldn't take his case. I've heard you say since I was a child that if they won't represent you, you have no case. Yet this time you *sent* Yoel to one of those men that stops at nothing to win their case."

"Nothing I did is illegal." His voice was less hard, but his face remained stolid.

"Then you will be shocked to learn that, at this moment, they are bringing in the glassblower. And two others."

He paused, but his face remained emotionless. "Whatever for?"

She clenched her fists. "Paulos was staying at his house. When they couldn't find the teacher, they grabbed him, a vendor, and Jason's apprentice. A *boy!* He can't even grow a beard yet, and they are dragging him to the politarchs."

"Oh, no." The inflexibility melted from his face, and he rubbed his temples.

"*Nai.* And they've hurt Jason."

"Jason?"

"The glassblower."

He looked up. "Badly?"

She shoved aside the memory of a sandaled foot connecting with the back of Jason's knee, and his groans of pain. "They struck him. They kicked him. He fell on the way here. I don't know what shape he's in now because I wanted to beat them here. I'd hoped I could talk you out of this wicked plan."

His resolve regained, he scoffed. "It wasn't wicked, and I didn't plan it. The synagogue leader has let it get out of control."

"But treason? You can't sentence them to death."

Pappa paced, rubbing his smooth chin. "We may not decide there is enough evidence to hold a trial, so no need to worry quite yet."

"But the charges are ridiculous. Can't you dismiss the case?"

"There is nothing I can do at this point. Once a charge is made, we're obligated to hear it."

She straightened, her courage growing. "These people are very important to me."

Years of practice as a magistrate had taught Pappa to hide his personal feelings. But a slight twitch in his eye told her the news had caught him off guard. "Why? Why are they so important to you?"

"You worship the gods only because you are expected to, not because you believe any of it. They've done nothing for you. Yet you spend more money on incense than on people. And you care only for yourself and others who speak and dress like you." She suddenly felt countless pairs of eyes staring. She dropped her head and studied her sandals, her cheeks flaming.

"Tell me,"—his voice softened—"is it the preacher or this glass-blower who is so important to you?"

Her cheeks heated as she raised her gaze to meet his. "Both."

"And yet I assume it is not the preacher you are willing to risk this humiliation for?"

She shifted her weight but kept her eyes on him. "No."

"I see." He looked toward the front entrance, and her gaze followed his. The mob must be nearing. People crowded in, each trying to gain a better vantage point than the next before the defendants were brought in.

He waited to catch her eye again. "And why is that?"

"Jason asked me to marry him." It was more of spontaneous thought than a genuine question, but still...

Another twitch. "And you agreed?"

She hadn't made up her mind until this moment. If he'd decided to follow The Way, she'd have told him yes already. "I haven't yet. But I love him."

He returned to his seat on the dais without another word.

Fighting her way through the rowdy onlookers and judgmental glares, she claimed a seat on the first row.

———

YOEL HURRIED from the agora toward the council house of the city rulers. Solon had told him to meet them there.

He stepped under the arched doorway. As Secundus had promised, all five politarchs waited at the far end of the room atop their x-legged chairs, arranged on a riser that allowed them to peer down their noses at the people they were supposed to represent.

Couches lined the wall to his right. Each appeared to contain an advocate and his client. Stone benches filled either side of a center aisle, already full of spectators, while still more onlookers stood in the space to the left. Judging by their dress, the center contained citizens, while a larger number crowded into less than half the space.

A lawyer presenting another case stood in the area between the citizens and the rulers, though whether he was trying to impress the politarchs or the people wasn't quite clear. Whenever he wanted to make a point, he turned to the spectators. His arms flailed wildly. He tossed out praise for his client and insults at his opponents with abandon.

Yoel scanned the rows of men waiting for their turn to see the rulers. How long would they have to wait? He'd never appeared in this court, nor had anyone he knew, but he understood hearings generally finished quickly while a trial could take all afternoon.

At the front of the room, a pair of tall, well-muscled men in short chitons—court slaves—hovered on each side of the dais, each with a dagger on his hip. Their eyes darted left to right and back again, never stopping. A third man stood in front of the rulers, a thick iron staff gripped in his right hand.

A commotion started behind him, and Yoel stepped out of the way as Solon marched into the room, chest out and chin high.

The agoraios made his way to a pair of empty benches and watched as his entourage followed.

Had they found Paulos at the warehouse? Or had they gone to his nephew's home? It was difficult to see past the brutish men that surrounded the accused.

As the men filed past, Yoel searched for Paulos, but the man was conspicuously absent. He saw neither Silas nor Timos, either. Who were they bringing then?

A pair of Solon's hired men dragged in a terrified young boy and shoved him to a seat.

Another pair brought a man Yoel recognized as one of the vendors from the agora.

Horror clutched Yoel's heart as yet a third pair entered the room with Jason in their meaty paws. The benches full, they shoved him toward the wall, his shoulders and head slamming against hard stone.

Yoel's chest felt like stone. Leah would kill him if anything happened to her only nephew.

Yoel flew to Solon and grabbed his arm. "What is this?" He gestured toward Jason. "Why is my ben ach here? He has nothing to do with this." His head felt as it would explode.

"Your nephew? You should have told me. That's excellent!" Solon laughed.

"Excellent? How is this *excellent?*"

He grinned wickedly. "It will make our case appear all the stronger. Your charges can't be attributed to revenge, or jealousy, or any other petty emotion. They must be true, or you wouldn't make the charge against flesh and blood."

"But I *didn't* make a charge against him." How could Solon have twisted his instructions so? "I forbid you to do this. You cannot put my nephew in danger." Yoel glanced at the row of stolid faces on the platform. "Who knows what they'll do to him?"

Solon shrugged. "It's too late now. We have a time scheduled with the magistrates, and we have to bring someone. If I don't show up with a case, I will never be trusted by them again." He pointed to Jason. "*He* is harboring the ones you wish to bring a charge against, and in the eyes of the law, he is as guilty as they."

The guard slammed the end of his staff on the tiled floor. The sound echoed off the marble walls, but Yoel's heart pounding in his ears was louder still. He sank to his seat and waited.

And prayed.

Case after case was heard and dismissed, ruled on, or set aside for later. Finally, Secundus beckoned to Solon, who sauntered to the front and faced the rulers. His men shoved Jason and the others forward and placed them to his right.

"I come before this wise and learned council to right a grievous wrong. I know that only the wisdom of this court can save this city from utter ruin."

Secundus waved a hand in a circle, urging Solon to skip the blatant flattery.

He nodded. "A dangerous man has lately been spewing lies and untruths, encouraging our citizens to abandon their worship of our gods, and worse, setting before them a new god and king!"

The politarchs sat up straighter. Such a serious threat required serious attention.

"This can only lead to total chaos." Solon continued. "Indeed, I am told these men have been fomenting rebellion throughout the Empire, and this is not their first appearance before a magistrate. Only weeks ago, they were whipped by the magistrate in Philippi."

Secundus sighed. "The charge, Solon."

"I appear before this august court to bring a charge of treason against *this* man." He spun dramatically and pointed to Jason.

JASON'S JAW DROPPED.

Treason? How did they get to *treason*?

The empire's penalty for a non-citizen convicted of such a crime was death, as prolonged, excruciating, and demeaning as possible.

His breath came faster. His legs shook, his head spun, and for the first time, he was glad he was being held up.

"This man?" Secundus frowned and pointed to Jason.

"No!" Yoel's voice rang out behind him.

Yoel? Jason strained to see him, but with a man standing on either side, he couldn't turn enough to see his dodh's face.

Secundus looked to Ari. "Isn't this your friend, the glassblower?"

Ari nodded, his face dark. "He is."

Then say something! Help me!

Yoel strode to face the rulers. "This is my nephew. He has done none of the things he is accused of."

Secundus ignored Yoel and leaned forward, one forearm on his knee, his other hand grasping the arm of the chair. "Why is he here, Solon? How is he guilty of treason?"

"He is supplying the criminals with shelter."

"All are innocent, Secundus," Yoel said.

The politarch narrowed his eyes at Yoel then fixed his gaze on Solon. "Who is the man with him?"

"He's a vendor and was seen supplying the visitors with food and drink."

"And the other? By Zeus! He's just a boy!"

Jason leaned forward to catch Gai's eyes. Jason's heart ached at the sight of him, eyes wide and legs wobbling.

Solon shrugged. "He was in Jason's home. We brought everyone we found in the house."

"Let the boy go." Secundus spoke between gritted teeth.

"But, kyrie. He—"

"You have but a moment of my patience left."

Solon grimaced but nodded to the men holding Gaius, who released him.

Kassi rushed to him and pulled him to sit beside her. He collapsed into her, his head on her chest and his arms around her waist. She wrapped her arms around him, one hand on his back and the other stroking his head.

At least Gaius will be safe. Jason returned his attention to the dais.

"And where are the men who are saying these things?" Secundus said.

"We unfortunately could not find them. But *this* man"—he pointed a chubby finger at Jason—"has welcomed them into his house. They meet almost daily and worship a new god, defying Caesar's decrees by saying that there is another king."

"And who is this other king?" asked Secundus.

"He is called Yeshua ben Yosef," answered Yoel. "He—"

"Not *you*." Secundus pointed a finger at Yoel, then turned to Jason. "You. Is this true?"

Jason drew a long breath. "Yeshua is the Son of the true God, the only Living God, the God of the Jews, the Redeemer promised to Israel since the foundation of the world."

"I care not about your religion. Does he claim to be king?"

Yeshua wasn't a king and had never claimed to be. "Yeshua does not rule over any earthly kingdom. He is no threat to Caesar or the Empire."

Solon laughed and faced the crowd. "Then where is his kingdom? In the mind of his followers? Or only in his own mind?"

The people laughed with him.

Jason sighed. How did he explain something he didn't really understand himself?

KASSI'S HEART SWELLED. Jason was a follower of The Way.

"I can answer." Kassi rose, keeping one hand on Gaius's shoulder.

Pappa's eyes grew wide as they fixed on her. "You can?"

"It's a spiritual kingdom. Yeshua rules as king over the hearts and minds of those who willingly submit to His authority."

"What kind of authority?" Pappa asked.

Solon scoffed before Kassi could answer. "If he controls these people, how is he not a threat? Couldn't he order his followers to march on Rome, as Julius Caesar did?" Again, he played to the crowd, and again he was rewarded.

The guard pounded his staff three times.

No one quieted.

Three more times, slower, harder.

The room still buzzed.

Solon raised his chubby hands. The crowd calmed at his command, but a scowl lined Pappa's face.

Kassi cleared her throat. "Yeshua's followers are those who acknowledge and joyfully surrender to His leadership in their lives. The kingdom of God is spiritual, not physical. He Himself told the Judean procurator His kingdom was not of this world. Repentance, not revolt, is necessary to be a part of His kingdom." She stared down her father and the others. "We are no military or political threat to the Empire."

"We?"

"I also worship Yeshua."

Pappa's eyes locked on hers, but he gave no response to her revelation. He stood and cast a long glance at Jason. "We shall return shortly with our decision." He stepped down, followed by the other four, and disappeared into a room behind the dais.

Kassi looked for Jason, but he was already being hustled to benches along with Yoel and the agoraios.

Pappa would see Jason wasn't guilty of treason.

Wouldn't he?

She dropped to her seat and flashed a smile at Gaius that she hoped communicated confidence she did not feel. Why would Yeshua allow this to happen now, when Jason had decided to follow Him?

Nothing is allowed to touch us unless it is first filtered through Yeshua's fingers.

Wise words from Paulos. He had faced death often yet was completely at peace. Shouldn't she be as well?

Adonai, give me Your peace. Help me to remember Jason is Yours, and that You love him more than I ever could.

Her heart calmed. Still, she had to admit she wanted him safe.

She wanted him found innocent.

She wanted him with her.

29

JASON CAUGHT ARI'S GLANCE AS THE POLITARCHS ENTERED THE ROOM and climbed to their seats.

Was there a hint of a smile, or was it just wishful thinking?

Jason was afraid to hope. Jews were well respected in Thessalonike, and Abba had been more so, but they still had no legal rights. If found guilty of treason, or even harboring others guilty of the same, he would be executed. An invisible weight kept his lungs from expanding and a sour taste filled his mouth.

Secundus faced the crowd, his face emotionless. The councilors had to vote, but it was known Secundus nearly always got his way. If he thought Jason guilty and wanted him away from his daughter, what punishment would he pronounce?

Jason frantically searched the room. Was there any chance he could flee?

The hand around his arm squeezed tighter, as if the thug holding him could hear his thoughts.

The other politarchs sat as Secundus straightened his shoulders and took one long step forward. His eyes scanned the crowd, waiting for absolute silence. He nodded to the armed slaves standing on either side of the politarchs.

Hands on daggers, the men moved to stand before the rulers. "Silence." Their voices, deep and strong, rang out over the room, and conversations evaporated.

"We have heard the arguments and made our decision. This is a religious disagreement. This is not a matter for the civil authorities."

What did he say?

"There will no punishment for those brought before us this afternoon."

Jason blew out a long breath, then filled his lungs for what felt like the first time since the men burst into his house. *Thank you, Adonai.* If he weren't being held up, he would drop to his bruised and aching knees in worship.

The crowd erupted. Solon rushed toward the dais. "This is unacceptable! How can you think this is fair?"

Fair? Nothing had been fair since the day the men from Amphipolis arrived with news of his parents' death.

One of the guards crossed to stand before Solon, towering over him.

Solon snorted, then his eyes moved to the dagger strapped to the slave's hip. He silenced and backed away.

"As I said." Secundus fixed his eyes on Jason. "We find no evidence to support the charge that these men have any interest in turning this dead man—Yeshua?"—he raised a brow at Jason, and he nodded—"in turning him into a king. He is no threat whatsoever to our only king, the emperor Tiberius Claudius Caesar Augustus. *Vivat imperator!*"

"*Vivat imperator!*" The crowd responded with one voice. "Long live the emperor!" reverberated throughout the building, echoing off walls and floors. Fists punched air, and each tried to outshout the other.

Jason studied the people gleefully cheering for the king who ruled from afar, who represented the empire that had conquered this very city two hundred years ago. Even some of his fellow Jews had joined in.

Secundus raised his hands, and the noise subsided. "Therefore, I find neither the man Paulos nor those who have offered their hospitality guilty of any crime. However—"

The crowd erupted once again.

Secundus tried to calm the people and regain their attention. Instead, he ended up waiting—again—for quiet. "However, although I shall not rule on what this man preaches, I must take into consideration the peace and safety of Thessalonike. From the size of this crowd, which includes many of the Jewish residents of our city, it is painfully obvious to me this disagreement will only widen the rift already created. For that reason alone, we have decided that Paulos of Tarsus and his companion Silas are to leave our city immediately."

Jason's elation disappeared. Immediately? How could Paulos prepare the believers to stand strong without him?

"How do we guarantee that he leaves? They could simply move him to another house." Solon spoke without his usual bluster.

Ari rose. "What about a bond? If they aren't gone by morning, they lose their money."

Secundus nodded. "Thank you, Aristarchos."

"It must be an amount they are not willing to risk losing," added Solon.

"Your part of this hearing is concluded, Solon. Please let us discuss any judgment. If you can't do that, we can escort you from the area."

"I apologize, kyrie." Solon slunk to his seat next to Yoel.

Secundus beckoned to the other rulers, and they huddled atop the dais.

Thanks to Damianos, Jason didn't have much coin. If they demanded too much, he'd still be forced to sell his house. Thank Adonai, Ari was there to argue in his favor.

After what seemed an hour, Secundus faced the room again. "Our decision is this: the defendants will forfeit the amount of one thousand drachmae. A bond—"

"Excellent." Solon shouted over the crowd.

What little hope Jason had left evaporated. A thousand silver coins? That was over three years' salary for a laborer. There was no way he could come up with such a sum.

"*If* I may finish." Secundus's voice showed his exasperation with the constant interruptions. "A bond of property, along with ten drachmae, may be given in lieu of cash. The men—Paulos and Silas —must leave by morning, and if they return within five years, all will be forfeited."

Jason couldn't believe his ears. Only ten drachmae?

Solon jumped to his feet, his round face bright red. "Ten drachmae? This is outrageous. I will appeal to the governor." He shook a fat fist in the air.

"No, you won't." Secundus turned to go.

"Of course I will." He stormed toward the front.

Was it not over after all? How long would such an appeal take?

Secundus slowly stepped to the edge of the dais and leaned toward Solon. "You didn't bring this charge on your own behalf, did you?"

Solon squirmed under the ruler's harsh stare. "Well, no ..."

"You are here to represent the synagogue leader, are you not?"

"Yes."

"He's not a citizen, so he can't appeal to Caesar. And you can't do it for him. This is over. Release them. Now." Secundus straightened and turned his back on Solon.

Solon huffed but signaled to the men holding Jason and Publius. Crushing fists dropped from his upper arms, and Solon's hired mob slithered away.

Jason fought his way against the crowd of people. Where was Kassi? He tried to rub his upper arms but flinched. His skin was already red, and purple finger marks were now beginning to appear.

He reached the bench where she'd waited with Gaius, but it was empty.

Where had she gone?

"Let's go home." Publius slapped him on the back. "I'm hungry."

Might as well. If Kassi wanted to see him, she knew where to find him.

KASSI HURRIED ACROSS THE ROOM, one hand grasping Gai's, shoving through onlookers, lawyers, and defendants. She reached the benches along the wall where Jason had been standing, but he was gone. She stood on her toes and scanned the room. There, over by the entrance. She raced to catch him.

"Jason?"

His hug wrapped her in warmth, but it ended too soon.

"Kassi. I can't believe you said that. What will your father do?"

"I aim to please my heavenly Father, not my earthly father. What were the words of Yeshua that Paulos told us? 'Whoever denies Him before men, He will also deny before His Father in heaven.'"

"Still, it's risky."

Her gaze held his. "I didn't hear you denying Him."

He grinned. "But I'm Jewish. My religion is protected. For now."

She hovered her fingers over the amethyst-colored spots on his bicep. "Does it hurt?"

"Not unless I touch it."

"We'll put some marshmallow root on it." She glanced at his other arm and then his bruised and bloody knee. "And some honey on that." Her heart ached. "I'm so sorry this happened."

"It's not your fault." His voice was soft. "Thank you for coming. You didn't have to."

"Yes, I did. I would never have let you go through this alone."

His face paled and he took several paces back.

What had she done? Had she offended him somehow? Again?

"Kassandra." Pappa's voice sent chills down her spine, and she turned to face him.

"Pappa."

He accepted a scroll from one of the guards hovering nearby and held it out to her. "Lida found this and gave it to me."

Her hand went to her belt, but the scroll was not there. It must have slipped out in the domus. Fingers of fear wrapped around her heart.

Despair supplanted the feelings of warmth. "Oh, no." She'd forgotten about the tax, and the third hour had passed. Had she lost the pistrinum?

"I sent Mannus to take care of this for you."

Hope flickered. "You did?"

He nodded. "This was Damianos's doing. I knew you would have completed the sale correctly. You are my daughter, after all." He allowed a slight smile. "But Damianos bribed—or threatened—one of the slaves in the agoranomos's office to write this."

His last visit to the bakery came to her memory. "He threatened to hurt me somehow. I wonder what he'll try next."

"Nothing. I've made sure of that. He'll pay your glassblower, too. By tonight."

"I don't have to marry him?" She was almost afraid to hope. Keeping her out of legal—and public—trouble did not mean he'd forgiven her indiscretions.

"Not him. Not Ari."

Joy exploded in her soul. She longed to throw her arms around him, but he would be appalled at such a public display. "Eucharisto, Pappa. I- I don't know what to say. I'm sorry for all that has—"

"Did you mean what you said? That you now follow the Jewish God?" Pain and confusion left shadows in his eyes. He'd never been so easy to read.

How to explain this? She'd always backed off whenever he questioned her. *Yeshua, give me the words.* "He is the only True God. He is the only God who searches for us instead of the other way around. Yeshua *loves* us enough to die for us. He is always with us, guiding us, protecting us, teaching us, instead of sitting on Mount Olympos demanding sacrifice."

"Perhaps I should learn more about him."

Pappa, interested in Yeshua? "I'd be delighted to teach you."

"I'd love that."

An astonishing thought—Kassi, a mere woman, teaching the chief politarch. "Thank you for what you did. For not calling for a trial, for not sending him to prison."

"It was the right thing to do. The charge was clearly exaggerated and frankly, untrue. This should never have been brought before us." He sighed. "I apologize for allowing myself to be misled, and I'm sorry for the pain your friend suffered."

"Thank you," she said.

"I'm also sorry I had to send them away, but I do have to consider the safety of the city. We can't allow such violence."

She nodded. Though it wasn't Paulos's fault, she did understand Pappa's reasoning. She glanced over her shoulder as Jason and the others made their way toward the door.

"You should go with them."

She jerked her head back toward Pappa. Was that permission? "You approve?"

He stiffened his back. "Approve of what?"

"Of my going with them?" Perhaps she'd only heard what she wanted to hear. Did she want to know? She may as well know it all now, though. "Of my being one of them? Of the pistrinum? Of my marrying Jason?" She searched his face for a hint of where he stood. "Or are we saying goodbye?"

He clenched his jaw and studied the tiles beneath his feet.

"Goodbye, Pappa." She turned, but he called her back.

"I don't want to say goodbye, *meli*," he whispered, head still down.

Her breath caught. *Sweetheart*. He hadn't called her that in years.

"You are my daughter. S'agapo. And"—his gaze met hers—"I'm proud of you."

Had he ever told her he loved her before? "Pappa." She threw her arms around his neck, and he held her close.

He held her a few moments more before he pulled back and smoothed his chiton, glancing around to see who might have noticed. "I know I was not a loving pater to you. After your mamma ... I was so afraid of the pain ... I vowed I would never let that happen again. Not even with you. I focused only on my position, where I could be emotionless. Now I see what I've missed." He kissed her forehead.

"S'agapo, Pappa."

"I love you, too. Now go, meli. To him. Go where you belong."

She stretched to kiss his cheek, then hurried after Jason.

JASON TURNED as a hand grasped his bicep.

"Wait." Yoel stepped in front of him. "Please?"

Jason yanked free of his grasp and gently rubbed his arm.

"I'm so sorry, ben ach. This is not what I planned." Tears lined Yoel's lower lashes.

"Really? What did you have planned? For this to be done to Paulos and his friends? How is that any better?"

Yoel did not respond.

Jason huffed and left Yoel at the entrance, then caught up to the others. Gai laughed and chattered, arms flailing, running a few steps ahead and then back to Publius, who seemed mainly concerned with eating.

Jason's mind held darker thoughts.

What did Secundus want? Would he order his daughter to return home and marry Damianos? Or perhaps Ari? That would be better for her but agonizing for him. Secundus had sent her away from the house. How did he have any authority over her? Still, he was the chief politarch, so he likely could do anything he wanted.

Jason had to let such thoughts go.

Soft, hurried footsteps behind him drew his attention. He turned to see Kassi, half running, half walking, trying to catch up. He turned and walked backward, his steps lighter, waiting for her to catch up.

She laughed. "You're going to trip if you don't watch where you're going."

He spun back around, and she fell into step beside him.

"What are you going to do?" she asked.

"What do you mean?"

"About the deposit."

He shrugged. "I have no choice. I have to pay it."

"Do you have one thousand drachmae?"

"I only have to give them ten and sign a document acknowledging that if Paulos returns to Thessalonike in the next five years, they can take my house, my business, whatever they need to equal one thousand."

"Oh. That's not too bad, I guess."

"What's worse is he has to leave tonight."

"We still have most of the day left." She glanced at the sun at its apex.

Jason smiled. "You're right. We can all learn a lot before then."

"Looks like Publius and Gaius went straight to his popina." She gestured to the odd pair.

Food sounded good, but they needed to find Paulos first and let him know what had happened. "Isn't this the street?" he asked.

She nodded and turned into the alley. They arrived at Publius's house, and Kassi pushed the door open slowly. "Paulos?"

No answer.

Could they have gone after him even after their loss in court? Could Paulos have been found? Solon seemed perfectly happy to have Jason instead, but others may not have been so happy let it go.

Kassi started to enter, but Jason blocked the door with his arm. "Let me go in. Wait out here."

Kassi crossed her arms. "Why?"

The last thing he wanted was for her to get hurt. "Please? Let me make sure it's safe first."

Annoyance colored her face, but she stepped back.

He crossed the threshold and scanned the atrium. "Paulos? It's Jason." The bedchamber doors on either side were open, and he poked his head into each one.

Empty.

He crept down the hall. In the peristyle, two benches had been pulled to the center. Two bald heads and one covered with dark, curly hair were bent in prayer.

"Paulos?"

The old man stood to face him, his smile bright. "Jason."

Jason breathed easier, and his shoulders relaxed.

Paulos drew near and placed a hand on each of Jason's shoulders. "Are you all right?" He glanced up and down Jason's weary body, concerned eyes landing on his knees and bruised biceps. "Oh, Jason... I'm so sorry. You should have let them take me."

"Nonsense. Who knows what would have happened to you? You have cities to visit and people to tell about Yeshua."

"You should have heard him," said Kassi. "He boldly proclaimed his faith in Yeshua."

"No, I didn't. You had to explain for me."

"I may have put your thoughts into words, but you still stood up to Pappa."

Paulos stepped back. "Jason, you've been a follower of The Way for less than a day. You can't expect to understand it all yet, let alone explain it. I learn more about the depth and strength of Yeshua's love every day."

"You do?"

"What did the politarchs say?" Silas joined them.

"I have to post a bond."

"How much?"

"The bond is ten thousand, but he only has to pay ten." Kassi smiled. "My pappa was very generous with the terms."

"We'll give you that from our funds," Timos said.

Jason shook his head. "No, you won't. I'm expecting a large payment from Damianos."

Paulos frowned. "And the rest?"

Jason drew in a deep breath thought his nose. "My house and shop will be collateral."

Paulos closed his eyes. "Oh, Jason, I'm so sorry."

Silas stepped closer. "Wait. Collateral against what?"

"You have to leave. That," Kassi said, "Pappa could not change."

"When?" asked Paulos.

"Tonight."

Paulos's jaw dropped. "Tonight? Oh, that's so soon. Even in Philippi they let us stay a while. Of course, we needed to heal." He paused. "How long do we have?"

"They said you must be gone today, but I think we should wait until dark. No need to draw any attention to yourself. And..." He grimaced. "There's more."

"What?" asked Paulos.

"What could be worse than leaving tonight?" Timos asked.

"You cannot return for five years."

"That long?" Pain filled his eyes. "Then my children, we have not a moment to waste. Timos, buy some food. We'll have one last meeting of the ekklesia."

"I'll help Publius spread the word." Silas followed them out.

"I must prepare," Paulos said. "There is much I need to teach you if you are to lead the ekklesia here in Thessalonike before we move on."

"Lead Thessalonike?" Jason laid a hand on his chest. "Me?"

"Of course. Who else?"

"But as you said, I've been a follower of the Way for less than a day."

"You will have Kassandra and Aristarchos to help you." He marched toward the door.

It was good Paulos had some confidence in Jason, as he had none in himself.

JASON SIGHED. "How am I supposed to lead the ekklesia? I know nothing." He closed the door behind them.

"You know the Scriptures. That's more than most."

"Perhaps."

"I'll help as much as I can."

Good, because I can't do this alone. Adonai, help me.

They walked quietly for a while, until Jason broke the silence. "We have a few moments while everyone comes to the house. I want to give you something, but it's at my shop. Will you come with me?"

She nodded.

"And be patient until we get there?"

She smiled. "I promise."

He veered away from the Via Regia and turned toward the shop. Once there, he reached to the back of the top shelf for a wrapped object. "As soon as you told me about this bottle, I recognized it. I helped Abba make this. They were a pair, meant to be a gift for some official's wife. I forget who." He shrugged.

"Anyway, he never picked them up. We later learned Rome had sent him to another city. Abba sold one, but they were so expensive then, not like now."

He held it out to her. "I want you to have it. I even filled it for you."

She pulled the cloth from the object and gasped. *Mamma's bottle.* She drew her fingers along the white swirls. It was generous of him to give her not only the bottle but to fill it with lavender oil. How would she tell him she would never wear it?

"Oh, Jason. It's unbelievably kind of you. But ... I'm not that sort of woman anymore. I don't wear perfume. It reminds me of the Upper City and their selfishness—"

He pulled off the stopper. "Smell it."

"What?"

He grinned. "Smell it."

She brought it to her nose. "Olive oil?"

He stepped closer. "I know who you are. I know you live to show compassion and help others. I know you love Adonai and will faithfully follow The Way all your life. I know you value love, not status. And most of all, I know you're a baker, not a woman of leisure. But you can still remember your imma every time you pick up this bottle to pour oil over flour."

"Oh, Jason." Her eyes misted. "This is a wonderfully thoughtful gift."

"You're a thoughtful woman."

"You'll lead the ekklesia well."

He rubbed the back of his neck. "I'm still not sure."

"I don't think Paulos would give you a task he believed you cannot complete. And I don't think Adonai would either."

"You believe I can do this?"

"I do."

He was silent for a long moment. If only he could see himself as she saw him. "There's a wisdom book by Solomon."

"The king? David's son?"

He nodded. "There's a proverb in it that says, "'Two are better than one, because they have a good return for their labor. If either of them falls down, one can help the other up. But pity anyone who falls and has no one to help them up.'" He swallowed. "I'll need you to help me."

"I already told you I'd help."

He swallowed. "I don't mean ... Not just with the ekklesia."

"Then..." Realization covered her face. "Oh ... you mean..."

"Marry me? Be my partner, like Imma was Abba's. I can't do it alone."

"You won't have to."

A smile covered his face as he pulled her close, touching his lips to hers.

Her arms slid around his waist and up his back, and for the moment, the rest of the world was silenced.

He pulled away. "S'agapo."

"I love you, too."

He kissed her once more, then placed his hand on her cheek. "Are you ready for this, then?"

She nodded. "I think so."

"I was remembering something Paulos told me that morning before any of us knew what was coming. He said, 'Following The Way may not be easy, but you will not be alone. He will always be beside you, fighting for you. You will never be truly defeated.'"

"That sounds like him."

"As long as we remember that, I figure we'll be fine."

"You're right. Let's get started. We still have a long day ahead of us."

30

Taste and see that the LORD is good;
blessed is the one who takes refuge in him.

— PSALM 34.8

KASSI ENTERED THE CULINA WHERE JASON PULLED OUT CUPS AND dishes.

"How many people do you think will come?" Jason asked. "In the middle of the day?"

Kassi sighed. "I know. I can close the bakery, but most can't afford to do that."

A rap on the front door interrupted them.

"I'll answer it." Jason returned a moment later laden with baskets and bags. "Publius sent food. Silas and Timos are behind me with more."

"How wonderful!" Kassi set everything on the table. The aroma of cooked fish and fresh bread filled the air as she unwrapped and uncorked and spread it all on the wide surface. Thank Yahweh,

Jason's imma had loved to cook, or there would never have been enough room for it all.

"Can I help?" Jason moved to stand beside her.

"You can pour the wine." She handed him an amphora of honeyed wine.

He accepted it but wrapped his hand around hers and didn't let go. "I hear Paulos's words, and I still have no idea how we're going to do this. Even together, I wonder if we can do it."

A thought struck her, one that could change everything. "You know, they didn't include Timos in the edict. Maybe he can remain for a while, help us get the ekklesia stronger."

"Like a few decades?" He grinned as he let go of her hand and filled the cups.

Publius marched in with his nephew, Maera, and Isa, along with others she didn't recognize.

"Isa. You're here." She rushed to wrap her arms around the older woman.

"I am. Thalia and the boys are on their way. Did Gaius bring the bread?"

"The bread?"

"After he came to tell me about the meeting, I sent all the bread we had. For some reason, we sold less than usual today."

"Maybe this is why." Kassi chuckled. "Go in the culina and get something to eat. Oh, there she is." She hurried to meet Thalia, her boys behind her. "I'm so glad you came."

"Publius didn't give us much choice," she said.

"Oh, I'm so sorry. You don't have to st—"

"Actually, he was so excited, we had to come see what he was talking about. To tell the truth, Gai would never have let us miss this. And I wanted to hear the man who got my son dragged to the politarchs." She laughed.

Kassi winced. "I'm so sorry. That was awful. But he handled it beautifully."

Thalia grinned. "Then let's see what this man has to say for himself." She took the basket of bread from Gai. "I'll take this in."

People filed into the culina and returned with food, then searched for a patch of garden to sit in. More people came than she could have imagined. She approached Paulos and Jason.

"Do you think everyone has eaten? Shall we begin?" Paulos asked.

"Have *you* eaten?" Kassi asked.

He nodded. "Yes, I have. Todah for looking out for me."

"We had a thought—what if you left Timos behind? For a while?" said Jason.

Paulos raised a brow. "I suppose that could be helpful." He turned and beckoned to his companion.

Timos hurried over. "Yes?"

"Jason has an idea."

Paulos explained, and Timos agreed. "I'm not sure how much help I can be, but I'm happy to try."

Paulos chuckled. "You know the Scriptures as well as I do. You'll be a great deal of help."

"And at any rate, you know far more than *we* do," Jason added.

Paulos moved to the far wall and faced the crowd. "Welcome. I'm delighted so many of you have come to hear the good news of Yeshua the Christos."

"Most of you have heard about the God of the Jews. He is the God who brought them out of Egypt and settled them in the land that had been promised to them. He is the God who made a covenant with them, where He claimed them as His own people. He is the God who gave them the law, and in return for their obedience, He protected and blessed them. They didn't keep the law, because no man can. But Yeshua fulfilled the covenant with the final sacrifice. And that sacrifice is for all people, of all nations."

"Why would he give his life for us who don't even know of Him?" A young man called out from the crowd.

"The Jewish prophet Jeremiah tells us, 'I will put my law in their minds and write it on their hearts. I will be their God, and they will be my people. They will *all* know me, from the least of them to the greatest. For I will forgive their wickedness and will remember their sins no more.'"

Jason pulled two stools from the culina and placed them against the wall. He and Kassi sat as Paulos continued.

The old man's face beamed. "Think of that—you are the fulfillment of the plan of Adonai. From the beginning of creation, He has had you in His heart and longed for you to come to Him. He moved heaven and earth to bring you here. You who were once strangers and aliens, far from God, have now drawn near through the spilled blood of Yeshua. You are fellow heirs of God's promises."

As he taught, some in the crowd left, whether because they needed to attend to other responsibilities or because they weren't interested in following The Way was unclear.

But no matter how few his listeners became, Paulos taught until the moon made its appearance.

JASON LOOKED at the empty stool beside him. Where had Kassi gone? He entered the culina to find her stuffing two bags with food.

"That's a good idea."

"They can't leave hungry. They have a long journey ahead of them."

"There should be a lot of dried fruit in here." He opened the door that led to the closet in the wall.

She poked her head in. "It's so cool in here."

"No sunlight. Ever. Imma always stuffs it full of dried fruit after harvest. Or she used to."

Kassi rubbed her hand on his back as he gathered pottery containers of various sizes. "I'm sorry."

"Jase."

Jason spun at the sound of Ari's voice.

"I need to talk to you." He closed the distance between them.

Jason had only seen that look on Ari's face two times. The first was when his abba died. The other was the first time he'd lost the election. "What's wrong?"

"I want to go with them." Ari's voice was soft.

"We all are." Jason stepped from the room, arms full of jars and small amphorae.

"No, not just to the city walls. I wanted to travel with them, wherever they go."

"You're leaving?" He let the jars drop to the table.

Ari shook his head. "He said no."

Kassi spun to face them. "Why?"

"He said I was needed here."

"And he's right. You've been a follower longer than I have. We'll need as many teachers as we can get," Jason said.

"I know."

Jason put a hand on his shoulder. "I'm sorry. I know you're disappointed."

"I'll take them as far as Berea to make sure they get there safely. He did say he was certain I would join them someday, so I guess I'll have to be patient." He chuckled. "Not my strength."

Jason laughed. "No, it's not. But I guess you'll learn."

KASSI NUDGED JASON. "They need to go."

"I know."

She peeked out of the culina and caught Paulos's eye, then pointed skyward.

Paulos nodded. "I believe my time here has ended."

Groans filled the air.

Paulos laughed. "Todah rabah. It's nice to be wanted."

Groans turned to chuckles.

"This incident will surely be the first of many here. You will be persecuted for your faith in Yeshua. You'll need to rely on each other. Pray for one another. Study the Scriptures together. I've not had time to teach you nearly enough, so Timotheos has agreed to spend a few weeks here with you, and he will join us again in Athens."

Timos stepped forward. "My Jewish brothers and sisters will turn against you, as they believe you have forsaken the true faith and embraced a false god."

"Then we will fight back. They cannot defeat us." Publius jumped to his feet and searched the crowd for support. He was not disappointed.

Paulos raised his hands for silence. "If you fight back, they will not only conquer you, they will destroy you. Yeshua said, 'Do not resist him who is evil. If someone slaps you on one cheek, turn to him the other also. If anyone wants to sue you and take your shirt, let him have your coat also. Whoever forces you to go one mile, go with him two.'"

Murmurs rippled through the people.

"I don't understand." Many voiced the same thought.

"Yeshua Himself said we are to *love* our enemies," Timos said. "The traditional wisdom of 'love your neighbor and hate your enemy' is not what we are to live by. Instead, we should love our enemies and pray for those who persecute us."

"Why should we do that? Won't they keep attacking us if we don't fight back?" Publius asked.

"If we love only those who love us, what reward do we earn? Roman soldiers do as much," said Paulos.

"And they rule the world." The first young man shouted from near the door.

"Yes. Won't that reveal to them how weak we are?" another added.

Paulos stepped into the crowd. "How much power does it take to hurt someone who has hurt you? To make them hurt more than you? Children do this. The animals of the field can do as much. But how much more strength does it take to shower them with love? To forgive them as we have been forgiven? Love, and let the Father fight for you. Moses told the people, 'Adonai will fight for you, you need only to be still.' And look what Adonai did for them."

The few Jews among them nodded heads. But Kassi had no idea what he was talking about.

"I don't have the time to explain the story to those who do not know it. But that sounds like an excellent first lesson for Timos, yes?"

The crowd agreed.

"A few last words. When the persecution comes, remember this: We don't belong to the world but to Adonai, who has chosen us to come apart. That's why the world hates us. Yeshua said, before he faced the cross, 'If they persecuted me, they'll persecute you too.'"

Jason stood. "Paulos, I'm sorry, but we must be leaving now."

"Yes, yes. I'm sorry. We'll collect our things." He turned to Silas and tipped his head toward their chamber. His remaining listeners quietly left the house.

Their few belongings in hand, the pair met the others at the door.

"Are you ready?" Ari took their bags. "You must be very tired. It's been a long and exciting day."

"Teaching energizes me." Paulos hiked his bag to his shoulder. "And this isn't the first time we've left in the darkness."

Silas laughed. "We're getting used to it."

"Damascus. Jerusalem. Antioch of Pisidia. My own town of Lystra." Timos grinned.

"Timos, aren't you staying with us?" Jason asked.

"I am, but I thought I'd walk with you all to the city gate."

WITH SILENCE WEIGHING HEAVILY over them, the group strolled to the gate that led to the Via Egnatia.

Paulos fell into step between Jason and Kassi. Ari, Silas, and Timos walked ahead of them.

"Paulos, how do you do this?" Jason asked. "How do you endure all that you have suffered and remain so joyful? So full of hope?"

"For me, there is nothing else other than sharing the good news of His death and resurrection. Nothing."

"But you've been so close to death, more than once," Kassi said.

"This is true. And some of those times, believe me, I prayed for Adonai to take me." He paused for a long moment. "But He's chosen to keep me here, and as long as He does, I shall shout the good news of Yeshua as loudly as I can."

THE GROUP GATHERED beneath the eastern gate's towering arches. Thank Adonai for moonlight. Silas embraced Jason, and Paulos turned to Kassi.

"Goodbye, my daughter. You have been a true delight."

She didn't feel like a delight. More like a frightened toddler. "Paulos, I don't feel strong enough to do this. How will we survive without you?"

"When Yeshua returned to heaven, I promise you the disciples felt just as you do. But you know more than you think. You've not only been under my teaching, but you heard the scriptures at the synagogue, for how long?"

"Three years."

"That's long enough to have heard the entirety of the sacred texts read."

He placed his pack on the ground and knelt to open it. "I gave one of these to Jason, and I want to give you one as well. I believe this ekklesia will grow dramatically, and you'll need more than one copy of the texts." He pulled out a codex the size of a tall stack of parchment and stood. "And you now have your own copy. Remember, Adonai will bring to your mind whatever you need, when you need it."

She held out her hands, and he gently placed the book in them. She drew her fingers over the wooden cover. She examined the first sheets inside. "Oh, Paulos, this must have taken forever. It's exquisite."

"Silas and Timos do the hard work. Whenever we are in one place for a while, they copy the scriptures onto the parchments, and we leave them behind. My eyes have grown too weak. If these were in my hand, it would be six times bigger." He laughed. "I just stitch them together."

"I saw you working on this once. I had no idea what it was then." She held it to her chest. "I'll treasure it."

"Treasure the words within." He wagged a finger at her. "Not the container."

"Of course." She gave him one last embrace. What would they do without this amazing, humble man?

"We need to go." Ari's strong voice garnered everyone's attention. "We should get as far as we can tonight so it will be harder for anyone to follow us. How about Berea first? It's a small town, a bit sleepy perhaps, but it does have a synagogue."

"Lead the way." Paulos turned to Jason. "I won't be back. Not for at least five years. You needn't worry about your bond."

Jason smiled. "I know."

Paulos put one hand on Jason's shoulder and the other on Kassi's, and she reached across her chest to lay her hand over his.

"Until then, may Yeshua the Mashiach Himself, and Adonai our Father, who loves us and gives us eternal comfort and hope through grace, comfort your hearts and establish them in every good work and word."

They stepped onto the Via Egnatia, waving before they turned and marched on.

Would she ever see them again?

JASON PADDED to the front door, still sleepy. The last few days had been exhausting, and he ached all over.

He opened the door to face his uncle. "Dodh. What are you doing here?" He struggled to keep bitterness from flavoring his words.

"I came to apologize."

Jason stood, hand on door, trying to understand the words. Yoel had never apologized for anything, ever. "For what?"

"For how things turned out. This was never my intention."

"You said that already. But you never did explain what your plan was."

He gestured inside. "May I come in? Please?"

"Into my home that is too Greek?" Jason regretted his words almost before they left his mouth.

"Please?"

Jason couldn't refuse the pleading in Niyah's eyes. He stepped aside as Niyah moved to the peristyle and sat on one of the benches in the center.

Jason sat facing him. "I'm sorry for my disrespect. I shouldn't have said that."

If Niyah was shocked at Jason's apology, his face didn't show it. "Jason, I only wanted to stop Paulos from spreading his lies and confusing our people."

"But they're not lies, Dodh. Yeshua is the fulfillment of every word the prophets ever spoke."

Yoel gasped. "I heard what you said before the politarchs, but I didn't believe you meant it." He shook his head hard. "You cannot believe this."

"I can. I do. I have studied the texts, and I can come to no other conclusion."

"I'm sorry you feel that way."

"It's not a feeling."

"Nevertheless, you know this is not over."

What was that supposed to mean? It didn't matter. Paulos would be gone tonight, safe from Yoel and the elders.

"Goodbye, Yoel."

———

THE DAY'S LIGHT FADED, and. Kassi carried out platters of bread and set them on a bench.

A knock sounded at the door. Who would knock? The meeting of those coming to learn about The Way wouldn't start until dark. She crossed the atrium and opened the door.

"Pappa! What are you doing here?" Ari and Julia flanked him.

"I went to Julia's. She said your meeting is tonight, so they brought me with them." He looked over her shoulder at Jason, Timos, and the others in the garden. She breathed a prayer of thanks it was clear she wasn't alone with Jason in his house.

"May I come in?"

She stepped back and allowed them to pass her, then led Pappa to the garden where the others waited.

"Pappa, you remember Publius. He is a vendor in the agora."

The vendor stood. "Chairé."

Pappa tipped his head. "It's nice to meet you properly."

She gestured toward the apprentice. "You may remember Gaius?"

He smiled. "I do."

"Gaius is Jason's apprentice," said Kassi.

"Ah, that's why you were there as well that day."

Gai nodded.

"Would you like to sit down? Can I get you some wine?"

"That would be lovely, thank you."

"I'll get it." Gai's face said he was happy to have a reason to leave the room.

"I came by here to apologize again. None of that should ever have happened."

"I thought advocates could bring a case for a non-citizen."

"They can, in certain cases. The problem was that the original case was a religious disagreement, which we cannot rule on unless there is a threat to the city or the empire. This is what Solon—and your uncle, Jason—led me to believe and what he tried to claim, but there is no evidence." He glanced at Jason's upper arms. "I'm so sorry you were injured. And in light of the lack of evidence, I was surprised at your behavior the other day."

"My behavior?" Jason placed a hand on his chest. What could he have done to offend the politarch?

"It was not what I would expect from someone accused of treason, or someone assisting a traitor. Normally we expect shouting, indignation, threats, even if someone is innocent. Especially when someone is innocent, and when the opposing advocate hurls such blatantly false accusations."

"Paulos is not a traitor. He never claimed Yeshua had any plans to rule the empire, or Makedonia, or even Thessalonike."

"That's what Ari said."

"If you are meeting tonight, I'd like to stay. I want to know more about this god of yours. A god who discourages revenge and encourages forgiveness — that could change the world."

"It could, indeed."

EPILOGUE

For now we really live, since you are standing firm in the Lord. How can we thank God enough for you in return for all the joy we have in the presence of our God because of you?

— 1 THESSALONIANS 3.8-9

Paul spent "three Sabbaths" preaching in the synagogue, but probably remained several more weeks with the new believers before he left. He was likely haunted by the fact that he'd left Jason with a financial burden. He'd had to leave the city so quickly, he felt he'd not been able to ground them in the faith as he would have liked, so he left Timothy behind. He wrote to them twice several months later from Corinth, and also sent Timothy back to Thessalonike to check on their progress at least once (1 Thessalonians 3.1).

He next stopped in Berea, where those in the synagogue listened to Paul's teachings, studied the Scriptures for themselves, and decided to follow The Way. But the Jewish leaders in Thessalonike heard this, traveled to Berea and caused trouble for him there as well. Once again, he was forced to leave, and again Timothy and Silas remained for a while to encourage the new church there.

Despite its challenging beginnings, the church in Thessalonike grew to be strong and fearless. They not only spread the news of Yeshua throughout all of Macedonia, but they financially supported Paul in his work.

Paul longed to return to the ekklesia of Thessalonike, and it seems he was able to visit them several years later (Acts 20.1-3). In the face of continuing persecution, they stood firm, depending only on Yeshua. They were a source of joy to Paul, and an example we would do well to follow.

AUTHOR'S NOTES

Jason is mentioned only twice in Scripture.

He appears in Acts 17 as Paul's host in Thessalonike. No explanation is offered as to his identity, indicating he was well known to the community of believers. He also appears to have had some amount of money, since he posted bond for himself and "the others" who had been hauled before the court along with him.

The only other time we read of Jason isLike in Romans 16:21, where Paul refers to a Jason and others as "my kinsmen (or fellow Jews)."

Kassandra is fictional, but she portrays one of the "leading" or "prominent" women, much like Lydia in Philippi. Macedonian women generally experienced more freedom than Roman women, especially in a Greek city like Thessalonike. Unlike women of lesser means, these women had their own money, prestige, connections, and power, leaving them free to explore the many cults and varying religions that abounded. They could buck the traditional expectations to marry, bear children, be quiet, and confine themselves to home.

Many of them attended the synagogue and were what Luke calls "God-fearers"—men and women who worshipped Yahweh but had not converted to Judaism—but somewhere along the way, they found the Truth in what Paul was teaching. Because they had more time and money than most, many of them likely became leaders in the ekklesia. The church would have had a remarkably different and probably much more difficult time without them.

Secundus, the chief city ruler, is fictional. In Acts 17, Jason is hauled before the "politarchs," a rare title used only in free Macedonian cities, and not found elsewhere in Greek literature. Skeptics claimed Luke not only made up this word, but most of Acts as well.

However, in 1835 a Roman arch was discovered at Thessalonike, and on it were inscribed the names of six of that city's politarchs, including men named **Sopater,** Secundus, and **Gaius.** Since then nearly 20 other inscriptions have been found, proving that Luke was (once again) correct. Most of these came from Thessalonike and many contained the name **Aristarchos.** I've chosen to make one of them Ari's grandfather.

The church actively joined with Paul in his work. Luke writes that Paul was at one time accompanied by Aristarchos and Secundus from Thessalonike, as well as Sopater from Berea. Aristarchos and a man named Gaius were with Paul in Ephesus and were caught up in a riot started by an angry silversmith. Aristarchos then traveled with Paul from Greece to Asia and was on Paul's final journey to Rome. He was with Paul to the end and is described as Paul's "fellow prisoner" and "fellow laborer."

Thessalonike is proof that in the midst of persecution and suffering, our faith can be strong and vibrant.

You became imitators of us and of the Lord, for you welcomed the message in the midst of severe suffering with the joy given by the Holy Spirit. And so you became a model to all the believers in Macedonia and Achaia. The Lord's message rang out from you not only in Macedonia and Achaia— your faith in God has become known everywhere.

1 THESSALONIANS 1.6-8

MY THANKS TO...

Yeshua the Mashiach, my Redeemer and Deliverer.

My family, for your encouragement, your patience, and for making your own dinners.

David Hill of The Glassmakers, for answering endless questions about Roman-era glassmaking and glassblowing, pointing me to resources, and proofing the glassmaking excerpts.

The Archaeological Museum of Thessaloniki, for providing me with copy of The Glass Cosmos, the catalog of their exhibition of the same name with more than 400 glass artifacts of exceptional art and technique from northern Greece.

My beta readers—Rita, D'anah, Carroll, and Monica. Your support means so much to me.

My editors—Erynn Newman and Pegg Thomas.

And **you**—Thank you for reading. May my words bring you closer to Him.

ABOUT THE AUTHOR

 Carole is a Californian living on the East Coast. When she isn't writing, researching, or editing her latest book, you can find her (and her cat) watching British television, googling obscure facts, or talking to one of her four kids.

For more information and to sign up for my newsletter:
caroletowriss.com
carole.to/newsletter
carole@caroletowriss.com

facebook.com/NovelistCaroleTowriss

amazon.com/Carole-Towriss/e/B009ZVHM8I

bookbub.com/authors/carole-towriss

ALSO BY CAROLE TOWRISS

By the Shadow of Sinai

By the Waters of Kadesh

The Walls of Arad

Prize of War

Deep Calling Deep

Sold into Freedom

GUIDEPOSTS NOVELS

Ordinary Women of the Bible

A Other's Sacrifice: Jochebed's Story

No Stone Cast: Eliyanah's Story

The Dearly Beloved: Apphia's Story

Extraordinary Women of the Bible

The Ones Jesus Loved: Mary and Martha's Story

Milton Keynes UK
Ingram Content Group UK Ltd.
UKHW032046180324
439698UK00004B/368